ACCLAIM FOR
THE DEAD OF WINTER

"A cleverly conceived plot about the strange and terrifying power of love."
Globe and Mail

"A

"A classic tale   'll read in
its genre...a   ...u rare creation."
Ottawa Citizen

"A gripping murder mystery...thoroughly engrossing...
Appignanesi's piercing probe into the psychology of the
deranged fanatic is in itself worth the price of the book"
National Post

"At once a murder mystery, a psychological study of
obsessive jealousy, and a meditation on gender relations
and political ideals, this book aims high and hits its targets
with deadly accuracy. This is a novel of real depth, and, I
suspect, lasting impact."
Montreal Review of Books

"Appignanesi's fifth novel explores love and jealousy, image
and reality, and confirms her reputation as a compelling writer.
The Times

"An intriguing novel...richer and stranger than a mere thriller."
Guardian

SANCTUARY

Lisa Appignanesi

McArthur & Company
Toronto

SANCTUARY
McARTHUR & COMPANY

PRINTING HISTORY
First Canadian paperback edition, McArthur & Company, 2001

FIRST PUBLISHED IN CANADA BY
McARTHUR & COMPANY
322 KING STREET WEST
SUITE 402
TORONTO, ONTARIO M5V 1J2

National Library of Canada Cataloguing in Publication Data

Appignanesi, Lisa
  Sanctuary

ISBN 1-55278-134-8 (bound) ISBN 1-55278-187-9 (pbk.)

I. Title.

PS8551.P656S26 2001   C813'.54   COO-930298-0
PR9199.3.A66S26 2001

The publisher would like to acknowledge the financial support of
the Government of Canada through the Book Publishing Industry
Development Program (BPIDP) for our publishing activities.
The publisher further wishes to acknowledge the financial support
of the Ontario Arts Council for our publishing program.

10 9 8 7 6 5 4 3 2 1

Printed and Bound in Canada by Transcontinental Printing

Truth is rarely pure and never simple

Oscar Wilde

PROLOGUE

The madness buzzed round and through her with all the vehemence of flies fighting over a fat corpse. She wanted to kill him. She had never wanted anything with quite such force. For three days and three nights the desire had swarmed through her, obliterating everything else. Yet she named it madness, which meant that she couldn't be – not altogether, not yet – despite the repeated dose of poisons.

Beneath her, the sea beat against the base of the cliff in a torrent of white foam. She could picture him there, his head a white football bobbing amidst the waves until they picked him up with indignant force and crashed him into the boulders. Over and over again. It would have to be over and over, so that she could wave to him from the cliff and smile sweetly as he shouted 'Help' into the void.

She wanted his dying to be slow, an eternity of fierce deaths, one for each of the months in which he had been dead to her. One for each of the early days of muteness and inexpressible pain. A revenge killing, that's what it was, with herself as the avenging angel, a bright creature emerging with the evening star from the gathering indigo clouds to orchestrate an un-hurried end. His small, preening smile would go first. The cheeks would wobble and sag. Horror at his own fate would spread across that smug face. She wanted him aware, begging for mercy.

Last night she had imagined him in a huge bubbling cauldron. They had all danced round him, proud cannibals, glowing in the heat and light of the fire, plucking off bits of him and throwing them to the dogs while he was forced to look on at his own dismemberment. She had kept the penis for herself, had stamped its shrivelled skin and sinew into the dust. A morsel not fit even for the dogs.

Could it have been only six days ago that she had confronted him? Not so very far from where she now stood. She had chosen the point beneath the crooked windswept tree, where the grounds of the house merged with the steep footpath. The surveillance cameras of this mind-bending establishment didn't reach beyond that, she presumed, though there was no evading their baleful gaze at either end of the headland. He walked here every day just before sunset. She had watched him, certain of his movements, the junctures at which he would slow or stop.

When she had told him, he had patted her on the shoulder and chided her, as if she were a patient in the midst of a delusion. He had fobbed her off with some waffle about them all being his sons and daughters. Yet something had shifted in his eyes. Both of them knew the truth.

She had been prepared for anything except out-right denial and the hairy ringed hand moving round her shoulder to her breast, caressing, as if he were unaware of it, as if that were all women ever wanted, a palliative for any wrong. For a moment she had been so surprised by the nature of the touch that she hadn't moved away. In the time that it took for her to recognize his growing heat, the contempt she had kept at bay all week had catapulted into loathing. With it came that overarching desire for vengeance.

That very evening, in the stillness of her room, she had written the letter and stolen away to post it. She wanted to see what he would say to her now.

The setting sun spangled the sea in silver. She imagined blood tipping the waves. 'A wine-dark sea', Homer had said. Darkened by light or sludge, or perhaps by the blood of heroes. No heroes here. Just him. Him and the moaning wind.

He was right on time. He walked slowly towards her along the path, an ugly man, puffed into bigness by his own lying self-importance. He wasn't expecting her, and his brow creased into his glistening pate as he spied her.

She raised an arm in greeting and wished the Furies to her side so that together they could do their worst.

PART ONE

1

Manhattan was all rain. Not the usual grey drizzle polite to umbrellas, but rain that pounded against roofs with the vehemence of a thousand demented drummers, made whirlpools of potholes, rivers of gutter streams, a swamp of Central Park. Rain impervious to the windscreen wipers of both chequered cabs and sleek limos, let alone macs and hats and the fashionable hairdos beneath. Rain that seemed not so much to want to wash the city clean as to wash it away.

The woman who stood with her forehead pressed to the penthouse window of an Upper West Side apartment thought of portholes in torrential seas and Noah's Ark beneath an obliterated sky. She thought of impenetrable fog and of her daughter when she was still a child and safely at home, singing, 'Rain, rain, go away,' in a high-pitched voice that mingled desire and anger.

Now it was Becca who was away, and the rain looked as if it had come to stay.

She was a small woman, no more than five foot three in her flat shoes, though she went by the imperious name of Leo and sometimes lived up to it. Today, a baggy, white, ink-stained shirt floated round her jeans and her slenderness, giving her a street urchin's air. Her face, naturally pensive with its downward cast of lips and shadowed eyes, openly displayed the marks of her thirty-eight years. When she bothered to pay attention, she rather liked the tinge of melancholy newly prominent bones and lines added to an earlier bland prettiness. It made her face more familiar to her, gave it a semblance of the internal image she had of herself, which was of a practical, matter-of-fact woman, one who was nonetheless occasionally prey to the force of intuition.

'Rain, rain, go away,' she sang, so loudly that she surprised herself, then remembered that last night she had dreamt rain. Odd rain, brown rain, because she was underground and it was coming from the roof of some vast sort of cavern which encompassed a labyrinthine city, though its buildings and paths were all deserted.

She pushed the unsettling image away and glanced at the clock perched high on the white wall. She paused to decipher the time; she had to pause because the clock's hands and numbers moved backwards. Anticlockwise. 'For your dream time,' Jeff had joked when he had given the clock to her all those years back. 'Just imagine time moving into the past. It'll minimize your pronounced sense of deadline.'

Like some prop out of the Hitchcock films he adored, this overblown obscenity of a clock had tickled her one-time husband's fancy. Not hers. She had grown to hate it. Yet it was still here, well over two years after he had slipped into the past. In fact, the only object she had managed to shed from what she liked to call the second period of her life was the marital bed. For a reason she could no longer comprehend, she had replaced it with a purple

16

divan, a scream of colour in an otherwise white and minimal bedroom.

Bristling with the energy of leftover irritation, Leo strode back to her desk. She straddled the stool, picked up one of several pens and bent to her drawing. Swift, certain strokes produced the long, frizzled hair and capacious girth of a scowling figure seated at a café table. Across from her, a slimmer shape took form, an elegant woman in a good suit, a copy of Tolstoy's *Anna Karenina* in her well-manicured hands.

A bubble blossomed from the head of the first figure. 'Ya say "family" these days and what d'ya think of? Eh? Eh?'

A second bubble. 'Ya think politicians, ya think problems. Yes, ma'am, big problems. Ya think joint credit cards, abuse, beating, mental cruelty, bullying, adultery, delinquency, divorce, revenge!'

A third bubble bloomed as the sizeable figure reached for the book and opened it. 'I say it's time to bring Tolstoy up to date for modern Manhattan. I'm gonna begin my next opus with the timely sentence . . .'

A big, satisfied close-up smile. 'All unhappy families are alike, but a happy family is happy after its own fashion.'

'Leonora H'. The signature grew with a flourish at the end of the strip.

Leo stretched and arched her back. She permitted herself the quasi-secret indulgence of a cigarette and puffed deeply as she re-read the strip. She was pleased with her Wife of Wrath today, pleased with all her Merry Wives of Manhattan, their moans and groans about former husbands and really existing

17

mothers and lazy children energetically vying with each other for subtlety or grossness. She was even more pleased that four strips were nearly ready and she had bought herself four weeks of time. There would be no happy or unhappy families for her over the coming weeks. She and her friend Isabel Morgan were about to play out their very own road movie.

A heroic road movie it would be, too, given that Isabel was in the driver's seat. When they had talked about it before Christmas, Isabel had evoked mythic expanses – ribbons of road disappearing into sky and weather, small-town cafés with screen doors and suspicious men, desolate motels, lonely desert and jagged mountains. In her last e-mail she had specified a white convertible, adding, 'Make it big. Savannah, Georgia, here we come.'

Never mind the deluge. Isabel would relish its danger, and the rain was bound to clear as they headed south, then slowly west; ultimate destination, California, where they would see Becca, newly at Stanford University – though not her father, Jeff, and his partner.

His all too youthful partner, Leo added to herself. So youthful that, in the first weeks of their separation, she had thought of sending him the anti-clock with a little acerbic note to underline his banal desire to make time move backwards. But the gesture had seemed to lack dignity, and the dirty ring the clock left behind on the wall evoked other grimy absences. It hadn't been the moment for a whitewash. So the clock had stayed.

Leo glanced at it again. Isabel should have been here by now. Her flight from London was due at four and it was almost seven. The rain to blame. She stared out the window. Manhattan's famous skyline had vanished into a blur of looming shapes, punctuated only by out-of-focus lights. Closer to, her wooden tubs and terracotta pots, with their array of fluttering pansies and stiff daffodil shoots, looked as if they might float away.

On impulse, Leo pushed open the sliding window and stepped out onto the roof. She walked to the iron rail and peered down at the street. A single bobbing mushroom of an umbrella moved down the canyon between the buildings and turned the corner. A car splashed along the street, but failed to stop at the entrance of her building. She stepped back from the edge and, raising her face to rain and sky, let herself be drenched through. It made her feel like a child, unafraid, open to the weather, defying the elements. It felt wonderful, the rain dripping over her eyelids.

The noise began somewhere behind her. A muffled droning, coming closer and louder until it blotted out the pounding of the rain. A hideous mechanical whirr which, for some reason, reminded her of a sound in her dream. She opened her eyes to see the black predatory shape of a 'copter moving directly above her, so low she could make out the pilot's silhouette, so low she could feel herself being sucked into its rotor power.

Her breath came with sudden inappropriate quickness. The fear again. She could taste it in the dryness of her mouth. For a moment she stood frozen in position. Then, with an effort, she fled into the safety of her apartment. The menacing drone was still there, echoed now by the screech of street-level sirens.

A shudder went through her, a bodily intuition of disaster.

Hair streaming, she accessed the two-week-old

e-mail from Isabel which noted her arrival time. Simultaneously she dialled Kennedy Airport.

The flight had landed with only a fifteen-minute delay.

Leo took a deep breath, hesitated, then punched in her former husband's number. Becca should have arrived at Jeff's house in the Berkley hills last night. She had chosen to spend her brief Easter break there, rather than fly back to New York, and now she was there again. If Leo was in luck, the daily would pick up the phone. She crossed her fingers behind her back.

It didn't help. Jeff picked up the phone, his tone changing from breezy charm to stilted politeness as he heard her voice.

'Yes, she's here. Out in the garden with Tip. Want me to get her?'

'No, don't bother. I was just checking that . . .'

'We won't eat her or beat her, you know.'

'I wasn't—'

'Good. I'll tell her you called. '

'OK.'

'By the way, Cora's pregnant.'

'Oh? That was quick.' The edge crept into her voice, despite herself.

'I've always been a fast worker. In that department, at least. You remember that.'

The line went dead.

'Bastard,' Leo muttered into the receiver. She sat very still for a moment and then wiped the conversation from her mind. She wouldn't think about that. Not now. Becca was fine and Isabel would be here any minute.

Isabel wasn't, not even after Leo had showered and

dried her hair. Nor after she had donned black trousers, a satin-lined black jacket and a crisp white shirt free of ink stains – suitable attire for a visit to the deco chic of the Rainbow Room, where Isabel had said she wanted to stop off on the first of her two evenings in New York.

Waiting was not one of Leo's more pronounced skills. She poured herself a finger of whisky, swallowed some nuts, skimmed an article in the *New York Times* on cloning, skipped through several others on the juridical, presidential and everyday meanings of the term 'sexual relations', plumped the cushions on the striped blue and white sofa for the tenth time, put on a Steely Dan track she had loved since she was fifteen, danced across the wide parquet floor, pulled some yellowing leaves from the giant fern which adorned the far corner of the room-long stretch of window and pressed her forehead to the glass pane once more.

By nine o'clock the trickle of anxiety had flowed into full tide. She imagined pile-ups on the freeway, cars toppling over the Triborough Bridge, lunatic drivers pulling knives which ever-heroic Isabel refused to acknowledge as a threat, bodies . . .

She picked up the phone again and, as she waited for a response from the airport, she told herself she should have gone to meet her friend. But they had a policy about that, had done ever since that year in London when their friendship was seeded: neither was ever to bother meeting the other. Now each had a key to the other's apartment, so they needn't even make a point of being in when they landed in each other's city. Life had little enough time in it as it was.

'No, ma'am, we can't check on individual passengers.'

'But—'

'Rules, ma'am. Can't do it.'

'But my step-daughter . . .' Leo heard herself lying. 'I'm so worried.' A sob came inadvertently into her voice.

'Sorry, ma'am.'

'But what do I do? How do I . . .' The sob was there again. 'Who can I call?'

'Your step-daughter? Just a minute, ma'am.'

There was silence for a moment, and then the man came back. 'What's your name, ma'am?'

'Morgan,' Leo lied. 'My step-daughter is Isabel Morgan.'

She listened to the clacking of keys.

'There's no passenger by that name on the flight you mentioned.'

'No passenger by that name,' Leo repeated dumbly.

'Maybe she caught herself a later flight.'

Leo imagined Isabel stuck in a traffic jam on the way to Heathrow. 'Can you check?'

'No, ma'am. Have yourself a good evening, ya hear.'

He hung up with too much alacrity, as if he was afraid she might ask his name or make more trouble.

Leo paced – past the blue and white sofa, the curving velvet chaise longue and the glass dining table with its six distempered chairs, through to her work space and, by ingrained habit, into Becca's room, as if her daughter might still be there, curled in her bed, her lips puckered in the snuffles of sleep. Instead, there were only Becca's old posters and photographs crowding the walls, a host of stuffed animals parading across the bed and lolling in a cushioned wicker chair. Becca's childhood was waiting for her should she ever want to return to it, now that she herself had left it far behind. Stifling a wave of nostalgia, Leo closed the door softly and went to check on the spare room, once Jeff's study, and now neatly arranged to receive Isabel.

Back at her desk, she examined her unnecessary anxiety. She found causes for it in the deluge, in Becca's visit to her father and his newly pregnant partner, in the monster helicopter. Isabel had simply missed her flight and would appear a little later. There was no lack of flights between London and New York.

She shed her jacket and bent to her drawings once more. The strip had been born some four years earlier, with four central characters whose everyday lives it chronicled with a wry glance at changing fads and fashions. There was burly Bella, an ageing activist and one-time schoolteacher, who ran a workshop on parenting at the 92nd Street Y. There was svelte socialite Clio, whose divorce had gone on almost as long as her marriage and at far greater expense. As her latest attorney, matter-of-fact Judith, kept pointing out to her, every month cost her a facelift. Finally there was Bella's niece, budding retro rock star Jenny – aka Seraphita – and her energetic entourage, chic or louche, depending on the month.

Leo added cross-hatching and shading, inked in a menu of over-the-top coffees with skimmed, semi-skimmed or killing milk. When the phone rang, her leap for the receiver underlined what had really been on her mind.

'Isabel,' she boomed.

'No, Leonora, it's me. So she hasn't arrived yet. I was just checking.'

23

Leo struggled to keep the instant reproach out of her voice. 'She'll be here soon, Mom.'

'You know how I worry.'

'Yes. I can't talk now. I'm waiting for a call.'

'I was just wondering . . . Given this weather . . . it might be more sensible to postpone your travels. It—'

'I'll ring you tomorrow, Mom. Bye.' Leo cut her off.

Since her split with Jeff, Leo felt her mother's attentions had grown to unmanageable proportions. Jeff, it had retrospectively occurred to her, had acted as a barricade against her mother's latter-day wish to ensnare her in a closeness which had never really existed between them. Not in childhood, when her mother had been too busy with her own life, and certainly not in adolescence. Her father had died when Leo was fourteen, and her mother's rapid remarriage to a psychiatrist had enraged Leo.

'But you were once a patient of his. It's unethical,' she remembered shrieking.

'That was years and years ago, and only for three months, darling,' her mother had replied with an air of placid self-contentment. 'You'll see. It'll be nice for you.'

It hadn't been. Uprooted from her English boarding-school, which had become the closest thing she'd had to home while her father and mother travelled South-East Asia for various aid organizations, Leo, at the age of seventeen, was an utter stranger to the Manhattan that was her birthplace. The Park Avenue apartment, with its antiques, plush carpets, unopenable windows and muffled silence, had all the attractions of a prison after the rambling grounds and noisy girls of her Cambridge school. Leo had left the newly-in-love couple as soon as she could, gone off to Harvard to study art history and never looked back.

It was there that she had met Jeff. They were married two weeks before Becca was born. Leo hadn't yet reached her twenty-first birthday. Jeff had been twenty-six and was just completing his Ph.D. She had dropped out of her course in order to look after the baby. A woman out of step with her time, perhaps, but they had been happy then. Very happy. And gradually she had taken up drawing, which had been her earliest love. She was good at it. The commissions for children's books had come first of all. It was work that allowed her to follow Jeff, first to Amherst, then to New York, not to mention that wonderful sabbatical year in London, when she had first encountered Isabel.

Leo found her hand reaching for the telephone. Without thinking, she punched in Isabel's London number. She let it ring and ring. No answer. Not even a machine to leave messages on, which could only mean that Isabel was certainly on her way. Leo peered out the window, as if she could generate her friend from the murky darkness of a sodden Manhattan. The drone was back, a low vibration in the distance. With it came the shiver.

Food. That was what she needed. She raced into the kitchen and pulled a slab of mozzarella, some plum tomatoes and a focaccia from the fridge. She warmed the bread and made herself a sandwich, adding a garnish of fresh basil and pimiento for colour as much as taste. As she did so, a cockroach squeezed through the tiny crack at the far edge of the scrubbed counter and scuttled towards a crumb. She hit it hard with her shoe and cleared it away with controlled disgust.

When they had first moved into the apartment, which had still contained bits of the prior occupants' furniture, cockroaches had swarmed at them from beneath an old mattress like an army of slippery shielded warriors. Despite fumigators, they had done battle with the redoubtable creatures for years, until Leo had begun to think of them as elemental companions, as constant and inevitable as the dreams unleashed by night.

She capped the arrangement on the tray with a glass of Chardonnay and took it over to the sofa. Eating was something she had to remind herself to do these days. With Becca gone, there seemed little point in cooking unless friends were coming over, and of late that had become rarer and rarer. Once she had loved the whole lavish business, had thought of her kitchen as an alchemical chamber. Chicken remains would become slowly simmering stock, bubbling with carrots, a stick of parsley, fragrant herbs, a dash of paprika. Eggs would be transformed into towering soufflés, tangy with lemon or pungent with Gruyère and a whiff of coriander. Fish would be filleted and moulded into strange blossoms with grape and cucumber centres.

Now the hours slipped by with no need for the punctuation of food. Her mother kept telling her she had grown too thin. But then, she had never been very big.

Reaching for the zapper, Leo flopped down on the sofa and channel hopped. Somewhere there must be news. Instead she found an old Paul Newman movie and let it play while she ate. When she had finished, she lay back into the cushions and watched the screen. Gradually its images blended with those of her own creation. Though she was certain she was

26

awake, she saw Isabel coming into the room. Isabel, at last. But Isabel as she had been when they first met all those years ago.

It was Thanksgiving, a blustery November night, and despite the thick curtains in the Notting Hill house where she and Jeff had been invited to a party, they could hear the wind wailing through the windows. There were some thirty guests, maybe more, seated at an assortment of tables in the candlelit room. Above an ornate fireplace hung a bleached canvas, from which the shadowy outlines of a woman's face emerged. It was a mysterious face, haughty and etched with sadness, and Leo's eyes kept returning to it as if the woman on the canvas wanted her gaze to be met. From the distance of her table, she couldn't quite make out how the artist had achieved this particular effect, at once hard-edged and ghostly.

When the tables had been moved away and their host had enjoined them all to dance, Leo had approached the canvas, drawn to it far more than to the events in the room. A voice from behind had startled her. 'Gorgeous, isn't she? Intriguing, too. I wonder what she does in everyday life.'

Leo had turned to see a long-legged woman sheathed in a glistening emerald dress. Above the pronounced dip of décolletage rose a marble-white neck and a face which mingled curves and angles to striking effect. Curling, deep-set eyes looked into hers. Leo had found herself taking a step backwards, in awe perhaps, as a forthright hand plunged towards her.

'Hello there. I'm Isabel Morgan and I'm not a Brit.' The grin was disarming.

'Neither am I.'

27

'I know. I know all about you. Well, some, in any case. I've been talking to your bloke. That's why I came over to meet you.' The woman called Isabel Morgan had winked, whether in complicity or something else Leo hadn't been certain.

But it had led Leo to say, 'And what do you do in everyday life?'

Isabel's laugh had been throaty. 'Not a proper question when in England, and certainly not so soon, but I'll tell you in any case. I work at the Consumers' Association, on the research side. Though maybe not for much longer.' And then, before she could elaborate, she had been whisked away by a plump, beaming man in garishly blue spectacles over whom she towered by a proud head.

Later Leo had seen her dancing with Jeff, who was so obviously smitten that, for a moment, she had suffered an unmistakable pang of jealousy, though she was also lost in admiration of the woman's unsettling beauty. She had rarely seen beauty carried with such ease and innocence.

As they were making ready to leave, Isabel was suddenly at her side, placing an intimate hand on her arm.

'Let's have lunch. I'll ring you. And by the way, I've found out about the woman on the canvas. An American ambassador's wife. Dead now. Beirut, I think. Oh dear.'

Above the whimsical smile, Isabel's eyes were suddenly wide with visible grief. Her arms stretched towards Leo, but she was tugged backwards, drawn by an invisible force and propelled through a gaping door which cracked shut with a bang.

Leo started awake. She was perspiring, her mind a

jumble. Isabel. The noise. A noise unlike the blare of the television. She leapt up. Outside, on the roof terrace, the tub containing her azalea had blown over. Shards of pottery lay strewn amidst wet earth. Struggling to right it, Leo had a sudden, swift certainty that something was terribly wrong. Wrong with Isabel. She had only had that kind of searing intuition once before in her life.

2

Four days later Leo was bound for London aboard a morning flight. Her grey wool suit was businesslike and impeccably neat, her auburn hair brushed to a soft sheen. Only the blue shadows beneath her eyes betrayed her state of mind. She leant back into her seat and tried to relax. Beneath a bank of white-grey cloud, the sea she loved was invisible. The crew and passengers might as well have been, too. They bore as little semblance to reality as cardboard cut-outs in a children's picture book. In front of her lay the volume she had blindly picked out at the airport shop, but she could make no sense of what her eyes skimmed.

She had spent the last days in an anxiety which bordered on panic and sometimes toppled over into it. Isabel had neither appeared nor made any sign. Leo had made a frenzied series of phone calls trying to track her down. Conversations with London friends they had in common and a flurry of acquaintances had yielded nothing. No-one seemed to have spoken to Isabel in some weeks or had any but the vaguest notion that she was travelling to New York. Since Isabel no longer had an office job, there was no office to ring to see if she had been checking in and out regularly.

Leo tried to remember the name of Isabel's current

editor and failed. Perhaps she had never known it. Isabel was always secretive about work-in-progress. Indeed Leo had no clear idea what her friend had been working on over the past months. When they had met in London for a brief few days just before Christmas, Becca had been with her and, between shopping and excursions to galleries and theatres, there had been little time for intimate talk. It was one of the things Leo had been looking forward to about their planned journey south. Now, instead of the warmth of that conversation, there was only the arctic chill of absence and the realization of how easy it was to disappear when one lived alone.

The New York police Leo had finally resorted to calling had been of little help. She could still hear the contempt in the voice of the officer she had spoken to.

'Look, lady, we've got enough on our hands without having to go in search of someone who isn't even an American citizen. Someone who's changed her mind about a visit here.'

When she had delivered her strips, Leo had gone to talk to the news editor at her paper. Letting her concern show, she had asked him whether he could possibly at least find out for her whether Isabel Morgan had arrived in the US. Her last round of calls to the airlines who flew the London–New York route had met with a blanket refusal to check passenger lists. Even the mother or step-mother card hadn't worked.

'Leave it with me,' the news editor had said. 'I'll put someone on it.'

She had been about to ask him how and when, but his phone was ringing and he was already ushering her out of his paper-strewn office with a wave of his stubby-fingered hand, mouthing 'This afternoon' as a voice barked down the other end of the line.

Leo waited by her phone, forcing herself not to check her e-mail every ten minutes and keep the line engaged. At three o'clock, the promised information had come. To the best of any computer's knowledge, no-one by the name of Isabel Morgan had landed at Kennedy Airport. Or Newark, for that matter.

Within the next hour, Leo had spoken to Becca to tell her she was going to London and, because of course he had once more answered the phone, to Jeff.

'I see,' he had said with a note of disapproval. 'But you know Isabel's never been very reliable.'

'What do you mean?' Leo had been unable to keep the leap of anger out of her voice.

'Oh, nothing. It's none of my business.'

'She's always been reliable with me.'

'That's fine, then,' he had added maddeningly. 'But don't worry too much. Here's Becca.'

Leo leant back into her seat and sipped the mineral water that had made its way onto a table she didn't recall opening. On the tiny screen in front of her, a map emerged out of a background bluer than any sea. An arrow charted their route, a clean arc, defined by a broken line, which grew solid with the passing miles. Numbers appeared, specifying altitude and temperature and the ever-diminishing distance between her and Isabel. She closed her eyes and made herself believe that. Strangely enough, the memory of Jeff's casual cynicism about her friend helped. If only Isabel's absence could be explained by a simple change of mind.

Her thoughts strayed to Jeff. It was funny how all the things she had once overlooked in his character, found funny or even endearing, now irritated her to the point of barely controlled frenzy. For example, his way of telling her not to worry, to relax, to let time make its own shapes. Initially this had seemed to be a way of caring for her, but it had become an entrenched form of bullying, so that she felt hounded by his injunction not to worry.

It was the same with her work. She had always appreciated his comments – his compliments as well as his criticism. But particularly since the strip had brought her a certain fame, the tone of his criticism seemed so sharp that it subverted everything else. He would laugh, say something was wonderful, that a certain line or insight was particularly apt and then destroy it all with a barb about how middle class it all was.

But then, a wife's rising star, as the cliché went, was rarely calculated to make a husband dance for joy.

Worse was Jeff's habit of seemingly approving her friends and then finding something just a little bitchy or malicious to say about them. It was always this last trait which stayed in her mind, niggling away when she next saw them, so that she had to make a concerted effort to overcome his judgement. His comment about Isabel had been true to form. Yet Isabel had been his friend, too. In fact, in that first year in London she had quite squarely been a friend to the two of them.

'Lasagne or chicken, ma'am?' A cheerful voice broke into her reverie.

'Chicken, I guess, please.' Leo returned the wide, fixed smile and reached for the proffered tray. She edged the silver flap off the small plastic dish. A moist aroma of artificially spiced gravy attacked her nostrils. She fought back an attack of queasiness, quickly replaced the lid and crumbled a roll instead, placing crumbs in her mouth one by one, as if chewing were an insurmountable obstacle.

A break appeared in the cloud. Through it she could almost see, and certainly imagine, the indigo ocean with its foam-crested waves. Her mood lifted slightly. She bit into a wedge of cheese.

That was what love was about, she reflected. Imagining Superman where there was merely Clarke Kent. Seeing only the good, exaggerating it and ignoring the rest. And she had been in love with Jeff, from that very first moment when he had helped her pick up the pile of books she had clumsily dropped in the library queue. He had been so handsome, with that crop of dark curly hair and liquid eyes, like one of Caravaggio's boys, so that when he had fixed them on her and asked, 'You're from England?' and listened intently to her faltering, 'Not quite,' she had been altogether smitten.

It was important to remember that. To remember, too, how blissfully happy they had been in the years after Becca's birth, Jeff even gentler with the baby than she was, in awe of her. And the loving had been good then, too. She mustn't allow the certainty of those memories to evaporate, or to be eroded by the events of recent years. If she did, she would turn into one of those embittered old women whose life story was a never-ending plaint. Like one of her frizzled characters, with a vengeful slash for a mouth, embittered and alone.

'Not quite Wolfgang Puck cuisine, is it?' the man in the aisle seat said to her, misinterpreting her expression as she put down her coffee cup.

'No, not quite,' Leo echoed. 'But then, that would

34

just about cost us the price of the flight.'

He laughed engagingly. 'Too true.'

She looked at him. He had a broad, slightly pock-marked face, with friendly, polished button eyes and a short bristle of brown hair above a furrowed brow. His accent was old-fashioned, older than him, though he was certainly younger than her. Oxbridge probably.

'Are you flying on business? Pleasure?'

She shrugged. It wasn't a question she could answer. 'And you?' she returned the courtesy half-heartedly.

'Just coming back. Business, though it was pleasurable.'

'Lucky you,' she said with too much longing.

'Yes. I guess. It was a conference stint. Only problem is conferences have the unfortunate side effect of making you voluble.' He grinned apologetically.

'What was it on?'

'Oh, this and that. Memory, trauma.'

Leo stiffened. 'You're a therapist?'

'No. An addict, though. I'd love a cigarette. The forbidding increases the longing.'

She gave him an uneasy smile and turned towards the window. After a moment, she lifted her laptop onto the table.

'Just to put your mind at rest, I'm a historian. Second World War and all that. The terminology floats.'

'Too much,' she found herself muttering under her breath, and then, to put an end to the conversation, she switched on her computer.

'OK then. Snap.' He drew out a similar machine and focused determinedly on the screen.

The stiff embarrassment of his posture brought

home to Leo just how incapable she had become of ordinary encounters over these last years. She was too prickly by half. Suspicious, too. It was as if she couldn't take anyone on trust and elicited rejection even when she didn't know if she wanted it. It was because she spent too much time alone. Yes, because she wanted to spend too much time alone.

It suddenly occurred to her, as she floated at a height of 33,000 feet, that one by one her New York women friends had all fallen away from intimacy. She wasn't altogether sure why. Maybe she just said no to invitations too often and ceased to make any of her own. Maybe she didn't want to see people who were part of a past she would rather bury, people who reflected her failure to make her marriage work. Or maybe she had simply become too boring. Yes, certainly that. She gazed into the trough of self-pity and refused the temptation of diving in, all four trotters at the ready.

There was Isabel. Only Isabel had stayed close, indeed grown closer since her separation. Yes. That was when the bond between them had really been cemented.

After Jeff had left, Isabel had flown over from London and, like a sister in need, had seen her and Becca through. Sensitive to the pain beneath Leo's stiff mask of wryness, Isabel had allowed her to remain silent, or talk and moan, none of which seemed possible with her New York friends, who inevitably let pity or covert glee slip. Or simply manifested too much rage on her behalf. Isabel, instead, had been matter of fact, treating the split as one more step on life's erratic journey. Leo had felt that, in front of Isabel, she could say anything and meet with neither disapproval nor a prurient curiosity. Isabel had made her laugh, too, as she welcomed her on board the ship of single women, where it was an aberration even to consider having a man in one's life and mind every day and night of the year. Her buoyant presence had helped put Leo on an even keel.

It was during those weeks that their knowledge of each other had reached new depths. For the first time they had really talked about their childhoods. They had discovered that, despite their evident differences, there was an odd symmetry between them. They were both only daughters who had spent much of their girlhoods in schools far away from what were roving homes. Neither was fond of her mother. Isabel's father had died when she was barely four, and they had speculated on whether the paternal death had been a greater loss to Leo, who could remember her father, or to Isabel, who had no vivid memories at all. 'Harder for you,' Isabel had said. 'I've never seen any need to replace mine. No loss. No new boss.'

Ever since those weeks and their free flow of intimate conversation, Leo felt she had become a little like a junkie with a peculiar addiction. She needed a regular dose of Isabel to keep her spirits high. She needed the catching up. The narrative of life only seemed to take on weight and meaning when recounted in Isabel's presence. Her friend's radically different outlook, the inevitable unexpectedness of her responses, the inflection her words and laughter put on things, the sheer pleasure of being with someone whose energy and love of life were boundless had become as regular a necessity to her as her work. And she felt that Isabel's need matched hers.

They had dreamt up this spring trip together across the United States in the depths of those short winter days Leo had spent in London just before Christmas. It was a dream of sun and open skies borne out of cold and darkness, and Leo hadn't known just how much she was looking forward to it until it seemed it wasn't to happen. She couldn't stay in an apartment full of only absences and the fear that mounted with each moment of passive waiting.

With an effort, Leo examined the panic which had taken her over since Isabel had failed to appear. It was undeniable that her motives for being here, on this plane bound for London, had an edge of selfishness. Yet she knew that Isabel would not have stood her up casually or abandoned her without a word of apology. And if Isabel was in some kind of trouble, then Leo, her sister of choice, as she had once called her, had to help.

She forced herself out of her reverie and, searching for tangible clues for Isabel's failure to arrive, scrolled through the e-mail folder that bore her name. Her friend's letters were all there, stored in reverse order, starting with the most recent. Leo opened the first, already well over two weeks old, and read the flight arrival time and hurried words.

'Just greetings, beautiful. Busy, busy now. See you v. soon. Going off to do research.'

What research had Isabel gone off to do? She had always been intrepid, Leo reflected. In the early days of their friendship, when Isabel had still worked for the Consumers' Association, she had gone off to investigate everything from soap powders to cars to the pricing policy of supermarkets. Once she had started to write her 'A day in the life of . . .' column, the research took on a different turn. She would somehow convince corporate and media executives, bankers and financiers, social workers and hospital consultants, oil-rig workers and long-haul lorry drivers to allow her to shadow them for a few days, after which she would produce columns which walked a taut line between reportage, hilarity and exposé.

Had some scorned subject decided to take his revenge on her? Had she got herself involved in an investigation which had taken a dangerous turn?

A scene plummeted into Leo's mind. She saw a dank shed on some remote Hebridean island trapped in rain. Isabel, her hands and feet bound, hopped towards a locked door, pounded at it and scratched splintered wood . . .

Dread tightened Leo's throat as tangibly as a garrotte. She coughed. She couldn't stop coughing.

'Here.' The man at her side turned concerned eyes on her and poured some of his wine into her glass. 'Have some of this.'

Leo drank, nodded what she hoped was a grateful thank-you and turned an embarrassed face back to her screen.

Earlier messages from Isabel gave no particular clues. Her date and time of arrival in New York were twice reiterated, together with her enthusiasm for their projected journey. The brevity of these messages, now that Leo looked at them in this new exploratory light, surprised her. In her mind her conversations with Isabel were endless. Indeed, when she checked her 'sent items' file, her own letters rambled at far greater length than her friend's.

Uncomfortable at this realization, Leo quickly scrolled down to the bottom of the file, to 4 January 1996 – the starting point of their e-mail correspondence. She had just gone on-line then, as if it had taken Jeff's departure to vault her into the modern world. Isabel's first message was a New Year's resolution list.

I will:

1. Seduce my latest shrink, one Daniel Lukas, as soon as he gets a proper haircut.
2. Axe the current beau, who has grown far too needy.
3. Drink only the very best wine.
4. Lose ten and a half pounds, the half straight away.
5. Refuse all invitations to book launches and celeb parties – unless I gain a stone and grow vast enough that no puffed-up media executive can cast furtive eyes over my shoulder in search of a more powerful puffed-up executive or starry bimbo.
6. Ring my mad mother at least once a month, whatever the emotional cost.
7. Make a serious attempt to move into a new flat before the chaotic clutter of this one overwhelms what little remains of my brain.
8. Be patient with my neighbours, despite their overflowing washing machines and disgusting habits.
9. Give up the flap of the weekly column and concentrate on my book.
10. See my friend Leo more often, now that she has had the good sense to scrap her vagrant husband.

Leo smiled, despite herself, as she read and reread the list. Whatever the fate of Isabel's other resolutions, the last had taken hold. Their transatlantic flights had developed a kind of regularity and they had seen each other either in London or New York, once even in Paris, at intervals of no more than four months, packing long accounts of their lives into short bursts of togetherness.

Another of Isabel's resolutions had also come good. Towards the middle of 1997, her book on childhood had appeared. It was an odd choice of subject for Isabel, who had no children and apparently wanted none. The book itself was nothing if not provocative. Childhood was an idea, Isabel contended, an imaginary terrain drawn by adult hopes, fears and memories distorted by nostalgia or blame. Colonized by novelists, psychotherapists, sloganeering politicians and social workers, it had little to do with the real lives of children.

As background for the book, Isabel had spent some months working in two very different families as a nanny, another few in a children's home and then some in a school, and finally a period as an observer in the juvenile courts. The book that emerged was a compendium of interviews counterpointed by analysis and historical background. A flurry of controversy had attended its appearance. When Leo had seen Isabel a month or so after its publication, they had discussed her ideas for the length of an evening, and then Isabel would talk about it no more. It was as if the book no longer existed for her. 'I'm on to the next one,' she had said with an enigmatic smile.

Quickly, Leo moved to the letters which followed that meeting. Something must be in them to signal what Isabel had decided to take on next, no matter how secretive she was about work-in-progress. She read through entertaining babble about boyfriends, cats, London life and what Isabel named her 'headlines from the couch'. She paused at one of these.

'Now his rebarbative voice has got under my skin. It comes with me everywhere, like an allergy I can't shed. And he still hasn't cut his hair.'

'Quit,' Leo had said to her over the summer. 'I can't imagine why you bother.'

'Nor can I,' Isabel had groaned, shaking her head in self-derision. 'It's hell.'

Then, in the autumn, had come the news that Isabel had, indeed, quit. Leo clicked to the relevant e-mail.

'That's it. I'm through. I hate him. I'm leaving. He's a monster of pride and manipulation. Tell you all about it when we meet. I'm going to expose their ruthless mind games. See if I don't.'

Leo gazed at the word 'expose'. Was this it – the subject of Isabel's research? A little thrill whose origins she couldn't quite place went through her. Yet when she and Isabel had met at Christmas, Isabel had said nothing more about her therapist. Perhaps Becca's presence prohibited it: Becca was fond of her shrink grandfather who regularly plied her with exorbitant gifts.

Leo skimmed the next few letters and then paused to read a longer one more carefully. It was one of Isabel's diatribes, this time concerning the clandestine infiltration of genetically engineered or modified products into run-of-the-mill supermarket foods, the stranglehold of the multinational producers, the megabucks involved, the difficulties of the small organic farmer, the duping of Third World growers, the probability of dire effects on the food chain, not to mention the environment. 'I have a good mind to do some infiltration myself. Monsanto are

42

about as saintly as my arse!' she finished roundly.

The cough came to Leo's throat again, a constriction she couldn't control. She sipped the remains of her wine.

'You all right? I'll get you some water.' Her broad-faced neighbour slipped out of his seat and came back a moment later carrying a small paper cup.

Leo sipped. 'I think I must have caught a cold. All that rain. And then the temperature shifts, freezing one minute, beach weather the next.'

'Weird isn't it? Almost makes you believe in the power of that Al Niño who's getting all the hate mail in California.' He chuckled.

'You heard about him in England?'

'Oh yes. And we have our share of millennial anxieties – global warming, environmental destruction, rampant cloning, epidemic depression, rising suicide rates. Makes you want to curse the decimal system.'

Leo felt a smile tugging at her lips. 'You mean the zeros are at fault.'

He shrugged. 'Seem to be, from a historian's perspective. The last millennium produced a spate of apocalyptic anxieties, and every turn of the century seems to bring its own. This time round we've even built them into our computers. Global collapse is nigh.' The grin contradicted his words. 'I'm Tim Hoffman, by the way.'

'Leo Holland. You don't, by any chance, know a woman in London called Isabel Morgan?'

'Isabel Morgan. Let's see.' His forehead crinkled. 'Journalist, isn't she? She's the woman who writes a column in . . . which is it . . . the *Independent*? Acerbic and exuberant by turn. Come to think of it, I haven't read anything of hers in a while.'

'That's her. Yes.'

43

'Can't say I know her, though I saw something about her in the press just recently. Media section of the *Guardian*, I think it was. The photograph caught my eye.' He flushed a little and hurried on with a self-deprecating laugh. 'Professional deformation of the historian. You remember trivia. It was in one of those gossip or small-item columns. It said she was being mooted as a presenter for some television series. Channel Four.'

'Oh?'

'Is she a friend of yours?'

Leo nodded, but she was no longer really listening. Her mind was racing. Could the explanation for Isabel's failure to turn up in New York be as simple as a sudden television shoot which had usurped all her attention? So much so that she had forgotten even to alert Leo as the tapes rolled in some distant location? It didn't seem likely, but it was just possible.

With the sense that she was clutching at the thinnest of straws, Leo clung to the possibility. Any hope was better than her nameless, brooding apprehension.

The road into London glimmered with the last rays of pale spring sunshine. By the time the taxi had come to a virtual standstill in the congestion of King's Cross, night had fallen. And there were still miles to go, Leo reckoned as she watched the meter tick its way to astronomic heights.

Some eight months back, Isabel had left the stuccoed comforts of Notting Hill for a part of London Leo hardly knew, so well had it kept its secrets from foreign eyes. It was tucked away beyond Clerkenwell, to the back of the financial district. The

Barbican was the only place of note close by, together with a gloomy little square of a cemetery where William Blake and John Bunyan lay buried beneath dank stone unencumbered by ivy or flowers. It was an area of old office and factory buildings, punctuated by the occasional four-storey house and a smattering of Sixties tower blocks that were so run-down they seemed to tilt forward, ready to dive into the tawdry parking lots that surrounded them.

On her last visit here, Leo had been converted by Isabel's enthusiasm to a dawning appreciation of the neighbourhood – the bustling flower market at Columbia Road; the jostling crowds at Brick Lane and Spitalfields, where Cockneys vied with Bangladeshis and the fashionable young over the purchase of cheap dresses or bits of furniture and crockery; the new comedy clubs and gyms brashly moulded into the ground floors of nineteenth-century factories; a graceful old Wesleyan church hidden between derelict office blocks; minimalist restaurants in cool colours serving rediscovered English food, such as shanks of underdone lamb, or quail, and school puddings.

Now, as her taxi swerved past the futurist curve of the Old Street roundabout and turned into a desolate road, all of Leo's initial misgivings surfaced. She shivered beneath the solitary street lamp, which cast its murky yellow glow only on a muddy stretch of car park surrounded by grimy disused factories. The one on the right was the site of Isabel's new loft. Hurriedly, Leo paid the taxi driver, who gave her a crooked smile and pointed towards the top of the structure. 'Looks like someone's expecting you.'

Leo veered round, her heart pounding. Isabel was here. She peered up into the distance. On the left of the building, which gave onto the car park, a raised blind showed a rectangle of light. Bending over the ledge was a shadowy figure, arm raised in greeting. Leo hesitated and then returned the wave. As she did so, she realized that Isabel lived not on the top floor, but on the third, and that the close-cropped head of the waver could not be Isabel's unless, in a lightning decision, she had suddenly cut her hair. She heaved her carry-all over her shoulder and walked slowly towards the door, four concrete steps up within a functional porch. On impulse, she rang Isabel's bell and waited, then repeated the action, half expecting to hear her voice over the videophone. But all she heard was the low rumble and squeak of the taxi's departure. In its wake, the street had an ominous quiet.

Taking a long breath, Leo reached in her bag for the keys. She was relieved when the door opened to their complicated action. She switched on the light. To the right of the staircase stood an aluminium-painted table she didn't remember. Atop it was a fern in a large pot and a pile of post. Feeling like an inter-loper, she flicked through the pile. All the letters bore Isabel's name. She stuffed them into her bag.

On her way up, she noted that the stairwell had acquired a collection of silver-framed photographs, surreal colour shots of women posed against tower-ing cityscapes. Only when she reached Isabel's landing did it come to her that the eerie quality of the images came from the fact that the women were dis-play mannequins, and the buildings just distorted reflections in the windows of the storefronts where they stood.

With a furtive sense she couldn't explain, Leo unlocked the door to the apartment and swiftly reached for the light. As she walked through to the large sweep of a lounge, her heels set up a cavernous echo on the polished wooden floor. She looked around nervously. The place was chill and, for Isabel, uncannily neat, almost too empty, as if she had done a thorough clean-out before leaving.

When Isabel had bought the apartment, it had been one large, high-ceilinged, unroomed loft, with a score of windows on three sides. She had had walls put in to create three smallish rooms, a bathroom and an open-plan kitchen, which still left a good-sized living and dining area, backed on one side by floor-to-ceiling bookshelves. At one end, forming a rectangle, stood two bright sofas and easy chairs, at the other was a long, ultra-modern refectory table, topped by a lavish pewter bowl. Gone were Isabel's old assortment of Victorian bric-a-brac, her paper weights and flea-market wooden figurines and walls chock-a-block with animal prints. On the wall here there was only a single large abstract in vibrant yellows, reds and pinks. It was as if Isabel had determined to leave London for LA without crossing any geographic frontiers.

Leo placed her bags out of the way in a far corner of the room, then carried the post into Isabel's study, a functional cubby hole to the back of the bookshelves. The desk was uncannily bare. No papers, books, magazines or forgotten coffee cups littered the available surfaces, only an aluminium tray, stuffed with what looked like an assortment of bills, stood at the far edge of the desk's L-shape. Next to it was the telephone, devoid of a flashing red light to signal messages. All of it was utterly unlike the casual messiness that attended the Isabel she thought she knew.

This sense of unfamiliarity followed her into the living room and kitchen, which were both so pristine that she might have been entering a model home unit. Just to reassure herself that Isabel had not suddenly decided to move out, leaving only minimal items behind to entice potential buyers, Leo flung open one turquoise kitchen cabinet after another. The crockery was there, even an assortment of teas, spices, tins and condiments ... and a jar of instant coffee. She needed that to settle her nerves. She flicked on the kettle. The refrigerator opened on a carton of long-life, a tub of marge and some marmalade. Nothing else. It was all, Leo reflected as she poured water into a mug, acutely unsettling.

Coffee in hand, she continued her inspection. The blinds on the living-room windows were mostly up. It came back to her that, over Christmas, her friend had made something of a ritual of pulling every single one of these down as soon as it was dark and pausing to switch on the room's various lamps. 'I hate the night coming in ... and there's so much more of it here,' Isabel had murmured. Quickly, Leo repeated her friend's gesture, noting that, even if nothing else was certain, she now knew that Isabel must have left home in the daytime.

The bedroom looked as if it had never been slept in. The striped duvet and matching pillows were carefully plumped. No renegade dress or T-shirt, no stray shoe disrupted the order, not even a book to mar the symmetry of a plinth-based night table. The television stood opposite the bed on a discreet stand. Leo slid the wardrobe door open. Isabel's clothes hung there, tightly packed, emitting a slight whiff of cedar. Leo stared, urging the array to offer up some clue. Surely if Isabel had packed for a longish journey, the ranked dresses, suits, trousers and shoes would have shown some gaps. Nothing made any sense.

She slid the door shut with a bang and stepped quickly backwards. Something crunched and crackled underfoot. She looked down. A piece of glass. She bent to it, and only then noticed the shattered vase. It lay in fragments along one side of the room, as if someone had thrown it in a fit of rage from its customary position on the small table, which stood beneath the window. That was where Isabel had placed it when Leo had given it to her as a house-warming present, loving the flowing Lalique lines of it, the embossed strands of ivy on its side.

The broken vase was the single discordant note in the virginal harmony of the apartment. Why this? Her eyes fluttered across the room and paused at the window. The blind here was down, but it quivered slightly. She pulled it open with a jerk and watched it judder upwards. The window it exposed was slightly ajar at its base. She pressed her nose to it and looked out into the yellowy night of the city. The cross street lay below, a narrow, quiet road with only a smattering of parked cars and darkened buildings. As she wondered once more at Isabel's choice of neighbour-hood, she suddenly noticed the weave of an old blackened fire escape clambering up towards the window and beyond.

The scene hit her with the force of a hallucination: Isabel, ready to leave for New York, her bag packed, the apartment completely, if unusually, tidied in preparation for her return. The intruder making his way up the fire escape, slipping in through the window, shattering the vase in the process. Isabel, startled by the sound, running in to find him holding a knife or gun to her.

And then? Leo didn't want to think any further. For whatever reason, Isabel had been abducted. Kidnapped. As she rushed into the study to dial 999, her mind flew back to the diatribe against Monsanto she had read on the plane.

Half an hour later the police arrived, a tall, pink-cheeked young officer with a snub nose, his cap in hand to reveal a thatch of bleached hair, and a stout, no-nonsense woman in identical trousers, but wearing a rough-ribbed navy sweater in place of a jacket. The woman did most of the questioning at first and took the notes. The man, Leo sensed, was suspicious as soon as she said she had just flown in from New York, or maybe it was simply the fashionable affluence of the loft that set him on edge.

Nonetheless, Leo explained with what she thought was extraordinary patience how Isabel Morgan had not turned up in New York on the expected day, how, unable to contact her and worried about her welfare, Leo had come to find out what was wrong. And yes, she had the keys; they were good friends.

'So you want to report a missing person?' the man asked sceptically.

'Yes, that, too. But I told them on the phone; there's been a break-in.'

Leo waved them into the bedroom. She only realized that her voice must have risen to an hysterical pitch when the woman patted her on the shoulder and murmured, 'There, there, dear. It'll be all right.'

'Anything stolen?' the man asked, as he peered around the room.

'I . . . I don't really know. I've just arrived. I don't live here. And that's not the point. Someone came in through that window and must have attacked my

50

friend. Ms Morgan. She's strong, so he must have had a weapon of some sort. There's glass everywhere.'

The officer trod carefully amidst the fragments, looked out and examined the window. After a moment, he gestured to his partner and pointed at something. Leo couldn't make out his mumble.

The woman officer came back towards Leo, who didn't altogether like the solicitous look on her face. She cleared her throat. 'You see, Mrs Holland, that's not altogether likely. Come and have a look.'

She urged Leo towards the window. 'Because of these, see.' She pointed towards two brass bolts at the sides of the window.

His gloves on, the man eased the window upward. It stopped some four inches up. 'No-one could get through that. Well, a cat maybe.'

'The intruder could have put the bolts back afterwards.'

'Not very likely if he was holding a weapon – even more chance of leaving prints.'

The man looked so pleased with himself that Leo wanted to argue. She controlled herself. 'You'll take prints,' she said in her coldest voice.

He shrugged.

'But—'

'Does your friend have a cat, Mrs Holland?' the woman officer asked from behind her. She was holding a piece of the vase up to the light.

Leo had forgotten about Isabel's cat, a huge tabby with prominent whiskers. She nodded once, curtly. 'But there's no sign of him. And there's no food out. Isabel would have left bowls, water . . .'

'It's just that this looks remarkably like a muddy paw print.'

Leo's nails dug into her palm. 'It does,' she conceded.

'Perhaps your friend left in a hurry for some reason and had neither the time to clear up this mess, or to contact you. She just pushed the window down and—'

'That doesn't alter the fact that she's missing.'

'No, no, it doesn't. Of course not. Let's take some more details.' She urged Leo back towards the table. 'How old is your friend, Mrs Holland.'

'Thirty-five.'

The two officers exchanged glances.

'And she holds a British passport?' the man asked.

'I . . . I don't really know. She's from Australia, but she's lived here a long time.'

He scratched his thatch of hair, as if something unpleasant had got into it.

'We can make out a missing person's report, Mrs Holland, but, you know, come a certain age, people are allowed to change their minds, even vanish if they choose, as long as there's no foul play. Disappearance isn't a crime.'

'Isabel didn't just change her mind. I know that.' Leo's voice rose again. She lowered it, reprimanding herself for behaving like a madwoman. 'She isn't like that,' she said more evenly.

'Have you got a picture of her?' the woman asked.

'Yes, yes. I'm sure there must be one. Give me a minute.'

Leo went into the study. She heard them talking in low voices as she pulled open one after another of the drawers in Isabel's study. She should be feeling relieved, she told herself. There had been no horrible intruder, no ghastly struggle. She tried to calm herself and think clearly. She remembered a portfolio from which Isabel had once shown her professional pictures of herself. At last, she located it at the base of one of the shelves built into the desk and hurriedly brought the whole thing back with her. A slew of photographs fell onto the table, one more glamorous than the next. Isabel smiling seductively at some unknown photographer. Isabel, hair flying, astride a bicycle. Isabel showing ample bosom at a party. Isabel looking queenly in candlelight.

This time, she felt rather than caught the glances of the two police officers. 'Yes, she's beautiful,' she said flatly. 'That doesn't mean she's either irresponsible or empty-headed.'

'Of course not,' the man said with a studied air.

'She's a journalist. A writer.' As if to prove it, she passed him a photo of Isabel, pen in hand, gazing meditatively at a notepad. 'Here, have this one.'

They took down details of Isabel's height and weight, asked for a credit-card number which she couldn't provide, and assured her that they would put it all into the system.

'What does that mean?' Leo asked querulously.

'We'll feed her details into the computer, do a cross check on accident records, hospitals, that kind of thing.' The man was suddenly polite now. He put his cap back on his head. 'You'll be all right, won't you?'

She nodded with more assurance than she felt. 'And you'll keep me in touch?'

'Of course, dear.' The woman officer was soothing. With a flash of graphic humour, Leo saw her on a platform as one of the new breed of Labour politicians speaking from a set script. 'She'll turn up soon enough. Don't you worry. Everything will be fine.'

'And don't forget to ring us when you hear from

her. You've got our names and the case number,' the man added.

'Yes, your names,' Leo echoed. 'PC Collins and Sergeant Drew.'

As she shut the door behind them, Leo had the dismal sense that, apart from their better manners, they would prove as useless as the police she had rung in New York. Neither recognized her sense of urgency. Unless there was evidence of a crime, a missing person, it seemed, was a legal anomaly. How much you missed them was evidence of nothing at all.

3

The unexpected ringing shattered the silence of the apartment with all the menace of an ambulance siren. Boiling water splashed over the edge of Leo's mug. A mud-coloured stain spread on the gleaming counter. She shook herself into awareness and raced for the videophone. The small screen showed no face. 'Who is it?' she shouted into the machine.

A muffled voice responded. It wasn't coming from the machine. 'It's me, Mike. From upstairs.'

After a second's hesitation, Leo unlocked the door. A small, intense man with slit dark eyes in a narrow face examined her in consternation. 'I saw the police pulling away.' His tone accused her. 'Thought I'd better check things out. You're . . . ?'

'Leo Holland.' Leo stood her ground. 'And you?'

'Mike. Mike Newson. I live upstairs. Isabel left me in charge.'

'Did she?' She returned his inquisitorial gaze and then relaxed as she remembered Isabel giving her a comical portrait of her new neighbour: 'Slick as his slicked-back hair. Requisite unstructured suit, mind equally unstructured, though the self-certainty is enviable. A man who, by his own assessment, is bound for high places in the media world. Watch out for the bright lights.'

'Come on in.'

'Isabel didn't tell me she was expecting anyone called Leo Holland. You must be the woman I saw coming out of the taxi earlier.' He tapped his jacket pocket from which the rim of his spectacles peeked. 'I'm a bit short-sighted. Thought you were my girlfriend. Her train's late back from Manchester.'

'So you know where Isabel is?'

'Yes.' He folded himself into the sofa as if he were quite at home. 'Off in the States somewhere. She asked me to look after her plants in her absence. Then . . . Wait a minute.' He lurched forward with sudden aggression. 'What were the police doing here? What are you doing here?'

'Isabel and I were meant to be travelling together. She never turned up in New York and never answered her phone. I got worried and flew over. I called the police.'

'Seems a bit hasty.'

'Did she leave you any phone numbers?'

He shook his head. 'She went off sooner than I expected. When I got back from Amsterdam, she was gone. Left me a note under my door, reminding me about the plants. There was a lot of stuff about the cat, too, but she crossed that out and said to forget about it. She'd see to the Beast herself. Good thing, too. I'm not a cat lover and Isabel's is aptly named. No way was I going to take him off to the kennels.'

'Do you still have the note?'

'Shouldn't think so. I tend to chuck things. And there was no reason to. What did the police say?'

Leo told him, then asked, 'Do you have any idea who might know where she went?'

'Not really.' He uncoiled himself from the sofa, suddenly in a hurry. 'I'd better get back upstairs.'

'No-one at all?' Leo insisted. She felt defeat and a long stretch of sleepless night waiting for her in the wings.

'Unless you call that builder of hers. Mine, too, once, but he prefers to be down here. Always seems to be here.' He paused, his face sharp with a leer.

Leo wasn't sure she liked what it implied. 'What's his name?'

'Hamish. Hamish Macgregor. I'll dig out his card for you. I still have it somewhere. Then you can always try that shrink she's forever rushing off to see. I meet her sometimes going out at the crack of dawn, when I'm off to a shoot. She probably tells her everything. Don't know her name, though.'

'Her?'

He stopped at the threshold. 'Guess it could be a him, now that you mention it. But don't go to too much trouble. I'm sure Isabel is fine. She's always running off and coming back. You'll look after the plants then?' He was already halfway up the stairs as she nodded.

'Wait a minute,' she stopped him. 'Do you know anything about Isabel being involved in a TV show?'

'Oh, that.' His face took on a shifty air. 'It's nothing. It fell through. She'll be fine. Nothing to worry about.'

An oppressive silence enfolded her as she went back into the loft. Why did everyone insist that everything was just fine and dandy when she knew differently? It was as if people wanted wilfully to keep blinkers on, to deny anything that ruptured the ordinary flow of their daily lives. Until it was too late.

Not that she herself was any different. She, too, had her selective blinkers, preferring not to see what she felt was there in the hope that it might go away and the world would still be rosy. She had been like that with Jeff, sensing full well that he no longer loved her, let alone fancied her – if that was the right word for it – yet preferring not to confront it in the hope that it would all pass. How many years had she spent in her strategic limbo? Too many. Isabel, who was tough-minded, would never have stood for it.

With a swift shake of her head, Leo put the first disc that came to hand into the CD player. Bessie Smith's plaintive ironies filled the loft. Glancing at her watch, she lowered the volume. It was almost midnight. Only just seven by New York time. She wished she could go out for a stroll and sort out her thoughts, but the empty streets around the apartment felt too threatening. She sifted through the portfolio of Isabel's photographs instead.

Did Isabel have a 'kitchen man' she had failed to tell Leo about? This Hamish Macgregor her upstairs neighbour had taken such a dislike to? Had she gone off with him unexpectedly and failed to come back in time to catch her New York flight? Was that the reason for her disappearance?

Questions. That was all she had.

It was odd how one disruption of the expected threw open the windows on a gale of rank unknown matter that must have been festering just out of sight. Like the evening Jeff hadn't turned up after a conference in California. She had rung everyone then, too – his hotel, airlines, friends – had even rung the police at two o'clock in the morning. She had imagined accidents, rational explanations and, somewhere in the midst of that, she had known, had forced herself to know, that he was betraying her, and had been doing so for a long time. And that was the real reason why he wasn't where he was meant to be. In that moment, the hoarded unhappiness of the past years suddenly rose up to choke her. She had sobbed a storm of salty tears into her pillow, and then she had grown calm. She didn't know where the calm had come from, but it carried an icy certainty with it.

When he had returned the following evening, he carried a large bundle of excuses. He had missed his plane. He had checked in at an airport hotel. He hadn't wanted to wake her. Then he had spent the next day waiting for a flight that had a seat for him. He couldn't get the airport phones to work. He had misplaced his phone card. And so it went on until she had broken into his disjointed narrative and said, 'You're cheating on me.'

There must have been something fierce in her face, because he didn't deny it for very long. He tried instead to make a half-hearted joke of it, had even put his arms around her. She had shrugged him off and said softly, no anger in her tone, 'You've been at it for a long time. And now you can take your bag and go off to another hotel. I don't want any tawdry confessions.'

She realized that she meant it. It wasn't a ploy. She didn't want the fetid heat of the confessional. The prurience. She could imagine his faint air of boasting. The shame that would come with it. Her own. What she suddenly knew she wanted above all was to maintain her dignity. And not to harm Becca. She had managed both. It was he who had railed, so loudly that he had woken the girl. She had given her father a tight hug and obediently gone back to bed. And then Jeff had begun to rail again, a long complicated monologue, not unlike his more colourful lectures on

Tennessee Williams at the movies. She hadn't been able to listen, but she had picked up some of his descriptions of her: stupid, cold, unfeeling, uncaring, a castrating bitch.

This last had toppled her over the edge, as if, until then, she had been walking a tightrope on which she could still turn, albeit with difficulty, and go back. No longer.

'Obviously I didn't cut enough,' she said.

She had taken his bag and dumped it outside the front door.

Of course it wasn't that simple. He hadn't left then. He had slept in the study. She had refused to speak to him, had carried on the war of silence for weeks, except in Becca's presence. Her only words to him were, 'We'll talk once you've moved out.' And she wanted him out. His dramatic features, the heaviness of his eyes, the slight oiliness round his cheeks, his lips moving over food, his habit of chewing too slowly had all begun to disgust her.

Finally, he had indeed packed his bags and left.

Leo gazed at the photos of Isabel which she had unwittingly lined up so that they covered the entire table, like a multi-decked game of solitaire. Why wouldn't these snapped moments of Isabel's life talk to her? The only thing the vibrant face seemed to convey was that, short of being bound and gagged, Isabel, unlike Jeff, would never willingly betray her. And judging from past performance, she would communicate her whereabouts if she could.

Rapidly Leo dialled Manhattan to check her answering machine. Her mother's voice came on, bemoaning the fact that Leo hadn't left her a contact number. Then a message from her editor, telling her

60

the last of the strips was great, and could they have more along the same line. And then nothing. Nothing from Isabel. All these modes of instant global communication and still nothing.

She plugged in her computer and sent a message to Becca, then took her bag into the guest room at the front of the loft. Everything here was neat, too, the double bed made up as if Isabel had been half expecting her visit. She hung her clothes in the small closet. Isabel's cases were stored in here – a large one and a smaller wheeled green one. Was there a middle-sized one missing which Isabel might have packed and taken with her? Leo didn't know. She didn't, she suddenly felt, know anything.

Fighting back tears, she stripped and raced for the shower. The hot, even stream felt good, easing the strains of the day, biting into her back like a proficient masseuse. She rubbed herself down, avoiding the glare of Isabel's floor-to-ceiling mirror. It wasn't the time for confrontation with a body she no longer liked to look at. Instead, she pulled on the white towelling robe that hung there and stretched out on the bed. Sleep, she felt, was a long way away. To shut her eyes meant to release a stream of terrible images, as if her imagination could only focus on the dire events her conscious mind held at bay. After a second, she got up and made sure all the windows in the loft were securely locked. Then she picked up the book on the bedside table: *Buddhism – A Guide to Awakening*. Isabel, as far as she knew, had no religious interests of any kind. Curious. A visitor must have left the volume behind. Inside, there was a slim brochure. She leafed through pages describing an idyllic setting in the countryside which offered retreats, meditation, counselling and a variety of what sounded like psychic therapies. The language reverberated with New Age terminology. Could Isabel have developed a recent interest in all this?

Restlessly, Leo got up again and made her way to Isabel's study.

With a speed that made her realize she had been intending to do this all evening, she rifled through the pile of open post in the silver mesh tray. There were letters from various charities pleading for funds: women's refuges, Ethiopian hospitals, Indian villages, shelters for the homeless. There were bills for gas and electricity and the telephone, all of which seemed to have been paid. There were three invites to art exhibitions, long gone, and several to book launches. Amidst it all, there was a bill from a Harley Street practitioner and one from a Dr D. Lukas at an address in N6. Highgate, Leo remembered, where she and Jeff and Becca had lived during their year in London. She extracted these two from the pile. Both of them were reminders for overdue payments. The second had the word stamped on it in thick, threatening black.

She placed both carefully on the centre of the desk. As she did so, it came to her that, when she was last here, this was where Isabel's computer had sat, a new laptop. Becca had put a happy-face sticker on the bag, so that Isabel could identify it at a glance. And they had all compared notes on the competing virtues of PCs and Macs. Isabel had been vociferous about the superiority of hers, saying she would never support Bill Gates's imperialism again.

Leo looked around the room. Isabel's laptop was nowhere to be seen, which meant she could only have taken it with her and that she was therefore working. On what? That's what everything kept coming back to. If only computers had never been invented, Isabel would have left a stack of papers around, copious notes and interviews.

Interviews. Leo scoured the room for tapes and found a boxful of tiny one-inch cassettes. Where to begin? And where was the relevant tape-recorder? With Isabel no doubt, since there was no sign of it here and the labels on the tapes bore only numbers – probably referring to some filing system that Isabel held within her computer. For a woman who had, in the past at least, been so chaotic in her household habits, it never ceased to amaze Leo how meticulous Isabel was in the organization of her work.

Leo's favourite teacher at her boarding school in Cambridge had been like that. She had told Isabel about her once when they were narrating those past lives which had so little and yet so much in common. The woman, Miss Henderson, was large, with a doughy face that was oblivious to make-up and a blunt potato of a nose beneath faded, lashless eyes and shaggy brows. The basket on her bicycle was always full to overflowing and, inevitably, when she pulled up, her shapeless brown coat and straggly scarf got caught up with her books or groceries, her bag or box of slides, so that one of the girls would have to run up and disentangle objects from her person and carry stray vegetables into the school for her. Miss Henderson seemed to notice none of this clumsiness. There was a blithe insouciance about her; an innocence, too. She treated everyone – girls large and small, other teachers, headmistress or ground staff – in exactly the same way. To Leo, her soft blurry voice was the instrument of kindness itself. And when she lectured, puffing over to the screen to point out details of old master paintings, translating pigments, brush strokes and lives into soaring language, she was magnificent. They all felt as if a benign aunt had transported them to a dazzling party in the Elysian Fields and introduced them to her fast friends, Leonardo and Delacroix, Michelangelo and David.

Once, when Leo had gone to Miss Henderson's rooms for an individual tutorial, she had pulled out three black bound notebooks with a red stripe down their spines. The books opened on columns of tiny calligraphic script which were neatness incarnate. Each entry contained a coded cross-reference to a slide or book on one of Miss Henderson's bulging shelves and, within moments, the paintings Leo most wanted to see appeared magically before her. Leo had thought then that she wanted to grow old like Miss Henderson, certainly not like her mother, who paraded around in jeans and T-shirts or clinging party dresses, pretending to be far younger than her years.

She shook herself back into the present. She would look Miss Henderson up one of these days. She should still be alive. It was only from the vantage point of youth that she had seemed as ancient as her subject matter.

The shelves at the very top of Isabel's study caught her gaze. They held a series of box files, not so unlike some of Miss Henderson's. Tomorrow she would set to work on those. Not now. She was beginning to feel bleary, her eyes smarting after too many disturbed nights, topped by the hours spent on the plane.

As she lay on crisp sheets, she nourished the fantasy that had come to her over these last years, always laced with a tantalizing sense of deep, as yet unobtainable, peace. She and Isabel, old ladies now, but straight-backed and clear-eyed, sharing a house together in some gentle countryside far from the fray. Removed from the welter of passion and the stifling coils of worry. There were paintbrushes and canvases and books and comfortable silences, interspersed by the pleasures of conversation. And beauty – the gleam of sunlight on a dewy slope; a smooth, plump jug stuffed with flowers; Isabel's face, lowered in concentration, the mysteries of her life etched in its fine lines.

Thinking she wouldn't rest at all, she slept un-expectedly well and woke to pale lemon streaks criss-crossing her bed. She wondered at them and gradually worked out where she was. In her initial well-being, she imagined that Isabel, too, was here, just a few steps away in the far bedroom. And then it all came back to her.

She leapt from the bed and pulled up the blinds. A lone man, carrying a newspaper, was making his way into the offices across the road. She glanced at the clock – seven forty-five. She switched on the radio and heard the comforting voices of the *Today* team, one of the few pleasures to attend her arrival, and then busied herself. There was everything to do today. She switched on the kettle to make herself another cup of the vile instant coffee Isabel must have purchased in a moment of deranged efficiency. She twisted open the jar of marmalade and spread two spoonfuls on a slice of crispbread which she'd discovered in a package at the top of the cabinet. Her mouth blazed awake at the bittersweet taste.

With a glance at her watch, she pulled out her address book and began to ring the smattering of Isabel's friends for whom she had numbers. Some she had already contacted from New York, but an update wouldn't hurt. She interrogated the ones she found at home, only to hear once again that Isabel was meant to be in the States. She left messages with others and set up two dates for the weekend, hoping she might garner some clues from face-to-face meetings.

Phone calls done, she carried a stepladder from the doorside closet and perched on it to reach down the first two of the box files from the shelf in Isabel's office.

One of them was labelled 'Cards 95–97'. Leo opened the box to find an assortment of Christmas and picture cards. She whisked through them. Few of the names meant anything to her, and she didn't bother to note the ones with last names, since they would be relative strangers and know little of Isabel's doings. One card was signed, 'Your mother'. She paused at this. Isabel's mother had died earlier that year and Isabel had flown back to Australia to attend her funeral. She hadn't stayed long and her only e-mail comment to Leo had been something like, 'I didn't miss her when she was alive and, though I guess I should miss her now and have some kind of breakdown about our never having come to terms, I just can't find it in myself. Unnatural daughter. She used to call me that. Oh well. Guess I am. Another subject for our travels. G'day.'

Leo turned the word 'breakdown' over in her mind as she looked at the spindly writing on the card. 'Best prospects for the new year,' it read. It was all so formal compared to her own mother, who used to lavish love on paper, if not as often in person.

Isabel had always described her mother as a cold, bloodless woman. A woman who had shuffled her off to her aunt's as soon as Isabel's father had died,

66

and who had then placed her in one boarding school after another because she was too unmanageable to keep at home. Her unruliness was confirmed by the progression of schools. When Isabel talked about these schools, Leo had visions of nineteenth-century establishments which would rival Jane Eyre's in harshness of discipline and puritan purpose.

She stopped over another card because the writing was so familiar. Jeff. For some reason, the recognition made her flush, but she read the message, despite herself. 'Hi, longlegs. How's life treating you? Always yours, whatever the season.'

When had he written this? Was it before or after their separation? It didn't matter; it meant nothing. Jeff was always bantering, fancying himself as Bogey, the irresistible outsider whose existential morality meant he could break all the rules. She slammed the box shut. Enough of that. She was learning nothing useful.

The next box file had an odd label: 'Dreams'. Leo opened it cautiously. It contained sheets of varying sizes, lined and unlined, scraps and Post-its, all in Isabel's writing. Not her best writing, either, but a scrawl that edged into indecipherability, as if the notes had been made in great haste. Isabel picked one at random.

I am lying on a deckchair. The sea is beneath me. A dark, turbulent sea. There is no sun. I don't know why I am naked. I look at my toe. An insect is gnawing at it, a shiny beetle. I can see it clearly. But there is no sensation. I try to move my leg. I can't. For some reason I don't care. I laugh.

Leo shivered. She read through a number of

dreams with growing absorption, feeling an unknown, unimagined Isabel beginning to displace her friend. She was about to stop and replace the sheets when her own name leapt out at her.

Leo and I have arrived at a site of indescribable calm. She is wearing her sweet-serious smile, the one that casts the world in her own composed glow. The air is perfectly still. We are sitting on the deck of a clapboard house. Around us, there are several more, clustered into the bowl of the valley. It must be dawn, because the morning star appears through the dissolving mist on the hills. They are unlike any hills I have seen before; their curves and ledges have a greeny-charcoal tinge. Birds chirrup with a startling clarity. I know we have landed in a sanctuary. A mysterious tranquillity enfolds me.

A white-haired man comes slowly, regally, towards us. Like a Michelangelo deity, stirring life, he raises his hand in an arc and I rise. I walk towards him. I am tempted to call, "Father", but I don't want to rupture the peace.

Leo read the dream twice. Tears clutched at her eyes. The hills above Taos floated into her mind. They would not go there. Not now.

Clumsily, she arranged the sheets back into the box. Her eyes fell on the two bills she had placed at the centre of the desk the previous night. The pile of still-unopened post lay beside them. With an effort, she picked up the top letter and forced herself to tear it open. She was breaking one of her cardinal rules. She had never opened anyone else's letters, not Jeff's, or even Becca's. She had never forgiven her mother's cavalier invasion of her own post. Now she asked Isabel to forgive her.

Dear Miss Morgan,

Thank you for your enquiry of 12 March.

Our laboratories have a policy of not permitting any of our staff to be shadowed. Neither by anthropologists, nor work-experience students, nor, I'm afraid, journalists. The reason is that, in the past, this has always proved disruptive to ongoing work. Should you wish to arrange an interview with Dr Grant, this can certainly be done. I warn you, however, that he is a very busy man and would only be able to fit you in after 20 June.

Yours sincerely,

M. Higgins

The letterhead read Geogen Ltd, Poole, Dorset. Leo felt a small glow of triumph. She had been right about Isabel's Monsanto diatribe. She was certainly up to something to do with the new agricultural technologies.

She ripped open the next envelope with greater assurance. A letterhead she knew instantly came into view. Another bill from Dr D. Lukas. She gazed at it and compared it to the last. Still £360 overdue. Isabel's shrink was pursuing her for payment. What could that mean? With sudden urgency, Leo raced into the guest room and picked up her bag. She extracted her notepad. Nine forty, the clock said. Not too early.

She picked up the telephone, dialled the number the police had given her and asked to speak to Sergeant Drew.

'One moment, please,' a twangy voice replied, then came back a few seconds later to report that Sergeant Drew would not be in until the afternoon. 'Can anyone else help?'

Leo thought quickly. 'No, no. Could you have her ring me as soon as she gets there. It's urgent.' She left her name and number. As she replaced the receiver, she could feel her energy draining away. Before she lost her nerve, she picked up the phone again and dialled Dr Lukas's number.

An answering machine responded. The voice was modulated, low. It elicited messages as if they might really be of significance.

Leo banged the receiver into place. Not yet. The queries would carry more weight if they came from the police.

She ripped open the rest of the letters. There was another from a biochemical firm, repeating almost verbatim what the first had said. There were more charity letters, junk mail offering credit cards and loans, another invoice, this time from a clinic in Marylebone. Leo stared at the bill: £120 pounds were due, it stated. Not overdue. Could Isabel, despite her dislike of private medicine, have been driven by some unknown ailment to a hasty consultation with specialists? Could she be lying ill somewhere, too wary of others' pity to confide? Leo dialled the clinic number. Posing as Isabel's assistant, she asked for clarification on the bill. A harassed woman told her it was for a breast scan and that the results had been forwarded to Dr Holmes. Remembering the name, Leo found the invoice, which bore the Harley Street practitioner's number. This time her query met with a rebuff. The results of Ms Morgan's scan were confidential. They had been forwarded to her.

Leo sifted through the letters in the silver mesh tray once more. There was nothing from Dr Holmes, other than the bill she had already seen. This was now some four weeks old. Surely, if anything had been wrong, Isabel would have returned to see the doctor and another bill would have arrived.

With an irritated gesture, Leo tore open the last envelope. It produced another invitation to a book launch. She was about to toss it away, when she noticed the title of the book: *Scar Tissue*. Could that be linked to an illness Isabel was hiding? Leo positioned the card on the shelf above the desk and looked around her at a loss. She needed to think, she told herself. She also needed air and food, or she wouldn't see the day out. She pulled on trousers and a black T-shirt, dabbed some colour on her lips and, jacket in hand, made for the door.

At its base, she noticed a card and picked it up. Isabel's neighbour, despite his shiftiness, had been as good as his word. Hamish Macgregor, builder and decorator, was now someone with two phone numbers. She retraced her steps and, at a guess, dialled the mobile number first. A woman's computerized voice came on to say that the number was temporarily not in use. The second number produced another woman's voice, this time asking for messages. Leo left one.

Crisp sunlight fell across the narrow street, illuminating the rutted parking lot which now held a smattering of vehicles behind its fence of wire mesh. A biker ripped round the corner. Dust and paper lifted in his wake, a minor tornado of sound and smoke. Leo quickened her steps. She turned into a narrow lane and found herself on a main road clogged with traffic. Scaffolding made a Meccano set of the building opposite. A vast, fluttering banner announced a new luxury development. The city was changing before her eyes. She jaywalked between cars, following a dimly remembered geography which led her into the small square of a cemetery. She raced through it, superstitiously averting her eyes from the lichen-shrouded tombstones. Isabel had told her she adored sitting on one of the benches here, and that she found a kind of peace amidst the silent inhabitants.

At the far end of the square, just where the iron gate opened on to the street, stood a triangular yellow placard, 'Witnesses wanted'. Leo paused to read the full text. A murder had taken place here between midnight and one o'clock on the night of 19 April.

Vertigo attacked her. Buildings reeled towards the gutter. She clung to a rail and forced herself to breathe deeply. Each breath brought a vision – a knife piercing soft flesh, a bullet propelled through frangible bone. She was assailed by a sense of the aching fragility of the human body, a carapace so permeable that it was a wonder it could sustain life at all. She watched gleaming chrome and metal hurtle down the street and wished for its safer skin. For herself. For Isabel. Then, as if she were taking charge of some incompetent child, she ordered herself to reach into her bag, jot down the number advertised on the sign, walk and locate a telephone.

There was a pub opposite. It looked friendly enough, with its hanging boxes of ivy and primula. The door yielded to her push, but a voice from behind the counter brayed out, 'Sorry, not open yet.'

Leo explained that she was in search of a phone, found herself explaining much more than that.

'A knifing, it was,' the bartender announced with a gleam in his eye. 'Knew the bloke. Came here regular, he did. Stinking business. If I'd been here that night, t'wouldn't have happened.' He prodded the air with a beefy fist, his belly quivering with each move. 'Hey, you OK, duck? You gone all white.'

'A bloke?' Leo mouthed.

'Yeah. Lived in the Peabody flats just down Dufferin Street. You need a drink, duck, I can see it.'

'I'm all right. Thanks. Thank you very much.' With an attempt at a smile, Leo let herself out into the cool air. She reprimanded herself. Her leap to wild conclusions was not helping Isabel one jot. She needed to stay calm, to think herself into Isabel's world and skin. What was it like to be in Isabel's skin?

Imperceptibly, as she walked past the stretch of brown-brick Peabody flats the publican had mentioned, she felt her gait changing. Her steps grew longer, her bag swung from her shoulder in more pronounced a fashion. Her chin was high and, every few moments, she flung what felt like a heavy mane back from her face.

The market materialized sooner than she had anticipated. Two rows of stalls selling cheap tapes and kitchenware, Nike tracksuits and children's clothes jostled with the fruit and veg merchants and backed on to an assortment of shops, the likes of which she had assumed London had long left behind. There were tiny tailoring establishments, purveyors of dusty electrical wares, a Hoover repair shop sporting two worn uprights in its window. Brighter premises were dotted amidst these – an organic butcher, his produce laid out in a manner to rival the French; an acupuncturist; a florist whose bouquets were only a little more vibrant than his earthenware pots.

Isabel wouldn't resist, Leo told herself as she made her first purchase. The silky white tulips with their velvet centres would cheer her and force her to think of life rather than death. Never mind the impracticality of carrying them as she did the rest of her shopping.

'Some nice tomatoes for you, love?' A crinkle-faced woman looked up at her with a gap-toothed smile.

Leo nodded and bought a lettuce as well, and apples and bananas, crossed to the other side and found her nostrils attacked by a pungent aroma. She looked behind a stall and saw the fish and chip shop, its gleaming counter already half hidden by a queue of customers. Isabel had dragged Becca and Leo here over Christmas. She had vaunted the establishment: 'This is the real thing,' she had told them. 'No better chips in the whole of London, I promise. And we can eat out or in.' It was so crowded they had eaten in the street, picking their fat chips and cod out of cones of oily paper, the high reek of vinegar mounting in their nostrils. 'Yummy,' Becca had confirmed.

Leo stood in the queue. As she heard the voice of the waiter, she suddenly recognized him. Isabel and he had had a long conversation about the best fish of the day when they were last here. She remembered because of the incongruity of the man's accent. He was Italian. Enrico – the name came to her.

She greeted him when her turn came, ordered sole and chips, and then asked, 'Have you by any chance seen my friend Isabel?' She gestured above her head to convey size, though she didn't need to.

74

'*La bellissima* Signora Isabella. *Non*, not today, not this week, not the last. She tell me she going to the country. She break my heart.' He clutched his chest with a tenor's enthusiasm.

'The country? What country?'

'The countryside, maybe. I don't know. She back soon, I hope.' He gave her a lavish smile with her fish, offered a wink and greeted the next customer.

Juggling provisions with her early lunch, Leo tried to fit this new bit of information into one of the many scenarios she had scripted for Isabel. The country could mean one of those rural addresses on the letterheads of the gene-tech companies.

She was about to turn back into Dufferin Street when she noticed a supermarket tucked under the eaves of an outcrop of the Barbican. Coffee. She had to get some real coffee.

In the event, coffee turned into a trolleyload of groceries, which filled four large shopping bags. She barely managed to heave them out of the store. The sight of a taxi pulling up just in front made her think her luck might be changing. She tried to signal to it but, in the process, one of the plastic bags gave way and oranges, coffee, bread and butter tumbled onto the pavement and rolled off the kerb.

'Here, let me help you.' A man bent down beside her. He had a neat beard, lightly flecked with grey, and smoky eyes which twinkled slightly. A pleasant Indian face. 'I have asked the taxi to wait,' he said formally, and bowed with just an inflection of the torso as he helped her into the cab.

Leo waved her thanks again from the window. Funny, that must be the first time she had instantly liked a man with a beard. It was a rank prejudice and one she recognized. In her strip, all the most odious males sported beards. She loved drawing them. Her stepfather wore a beard – a neat little triangle of an affair, to make him look like Freud, she imagined, though that was where the similarity stopped. It succeeded only in making him look pompous. The shrink he had sent her to as an adolescent in that first year of her return to Manhattan had sported one, too, a vile little goatee which moved with his mouth like a hairy afterthought. The new parental couple had insisted that seeing someone would do her good, because she was so rebellious and uncommunicative. Delayed effects of insufficient mourning, she had overheard her stepfather diagnose on the telephone – to the shrink they were sending her to, she imagined.

She had sat in a vast leather armchair for four times fifty minutes and doodled sullenly as Dr Weiss tried to elicit speech from her. After that, she had refused to return. The price was that she had to smile at dinner. Producing a rictus was marginally less painful than sitting in that overstuffed chair.

The aegis of the new parental couple brought with it a tyranny of meanings. She lived an overexamined life. 'Whys' hovered around her every move like so many vigilantes. If she refused soup and chose to dig into meat, it was because she was angry and wanted to bite at something, perhaps bite off the maternal breast or newly paternal penis. If she didn't feel like dinner or breakfast, she was denying mother love. If she suddenly decided not to go to a party or on a date, was it because she was worried about her femininity or frightened of sex? And when she lost a trifle, an earring or a pen, was she trying to bury her father all over again? The whys spiralled madly at every turn, transforming simple acts or changes of mood into matter of major significance. No wonder she had escaped at the first opportunity.

She could never understand why Isabel had got involved in the whole analytic business. It wasn't that Leo was blind to some of the merits of talking cures – not latterly, and, in any case, not for people who were really in deep trouble. She had read a bit and imbibed more. You couldn't help that in New York, certainly not in the circles in which she moved, let alone at the family dinner table. A good number of her friends had spent years on the couch looking for an impossible cure for the human condition. Chat was fine, but all that fashionable claptrap about link-ing present difficulties to amnesiac moments of infancy, all those good and bad breasts and sexual perversions to do with seeing nanny's knickers, and, even worse these days, all the multiple personalities that grew out of daily rites of suggestion, it really didn't wash. Life dealt you a hand and you played it. Unless you were Woody Allen and could make comedy out of it, there was no point in going to a know-it-all shrink who, after months or even years, would find parents to blame. Just blame them your-self, if you felt so inclined, and get on with it. It was cheaper and wasted less time.

Leo had said all this and more to Isabel when they had talked about it way back, when Isabel had decided psychotherapy was what she needed. 'They're technicians of the normal,' Leo had argued. 'They knock up a little rickety scaffolding of ex-planation, twist a screw of memory here and there, slap on some feel-good whitewash to bolster your self-esteem and, bingo, you have a cosy little suburban house of the sexualized self, with no gables or dusty attics or wonderful detail.'

'You're talking Fifties,' was all Isabel had replied.

'Or maybe just American. I'm learning things. I'm curious. It's a little neutral space, a tiny sanctuary in which to think all the bad thoughts. And knowledge can't be bad. Particularly if you've had a mother as wilfully blind as mine. One who spent a period of her life in and out of institutions.' Isabel had rolled her eyes and laughed and changed the subject. So Leo hadn't probed.

What she had wanted to say was that, whatever her origins, Isabel seemed to her the least likely person to need or benefit from analysis. She had never struck Leo as a brooding, introspective soul. On the contrary, she was a woman of action. No sooner did Isabel express an idea or a plan than it took shape in the real world. She was always on the move, or writing, and she certainly lacked neither lovers nor work. Nor friends to talk to. Leo for one.

It was their differences, she sometimes thought, which had brought them together. Where Leo was quiet, Isabel was a riot of activity. Where Leo, whatever her working success, had somehow stumbled into a traditional path of husband and child, Isabel was a thoroughly modern, independent woman, afraid of nothing. Where Leo had had a grand total of four lovers, and the first three hardly qualified as that, Isabel's came and went with an abundant fluidity which occasionally struck Leo as careless. It was as if Isabel were impervious to the notion of couples. Maybe that was what Leo loved about her. She was a free spirit, immune to the social pressures which posited a coupled or familial happy-ever-after. It wasn't merely that she lived alone – so many women did that now – it was that she didn't even seem to dream that pervasive, leftover dream which was love and marriage.

Over the years, Leo had begun to think that, with men, Isabel must be a person she hardly knew. But then, the intimacies of others were always mysterious. Could a man really be the reason behind Isabel's disappearance? A man like Hamish Macgregor, who had engaged her in some sadistic rite which had gone awry. They were all the rage in Manhattan these days. Or a man like her analyst? Shrinks, lore had it, were always prising patients away from their nearest and dearest.

'It's not that bad, dearie.' The cab driver's voice penetrated her thoughts. 'The sun's shining. You've got all the necessary. Wipe your eyes and I'll help you in with your groceries.'

Leo hadn't realized she was weeping.

'No, Mrs Holland. Nothing.' Sergeant Drew's voice grew formal with irritation, her consonants more pronounced as she mimicked some superior Metropolitan chief. 'Let me repeat it again. Unless we have proof of foul play, we cannot demand that a mental-health practitioner breach patient confidentiality. He says he hasn't seen her for a while. He knows nothing of her whereabouts.'

'He could be lying.'

'He could be. We have no way of knowing. But, for the moment, that's all there is to it. We've found no matches for Miss Morgan in accident records. The doctor you had us ring assured us that nothing was amiss as far as he knew. There's nothing more we can do for the time being. We'll call you if anything comes up. We're very busy here. Goodbye.'

'But—'

The line went dead in Leo's hand.

She put the receiver down with a clatter and paced

the room. The tense ferocity of a caged creature defined her movements. On her third circuit, she paused to rearrange the spiky tulips. They decided her. Whatever he said to the police, Daniel Lukas would know things. Important things. Seeing him would help her know, too. It was also something to do. This helpless waiting had become unbearable.

Yet if she approached him forthrightly, she would hardly succeed where the police had failed. The iron gate of patient confidentiality would come down with a clatter. She had to try a different tack.

At a rough guess, he probably started seeing patients at seven in the morning and, allowing a ten-minute break between sessions, she should be able to reach him at five to the hour. In precisely seven minutes.

Leo poured herself a glass of mineral water and lit one of the exorbitantly expensive cigarettes she had purchased at the supermarket. She doodled. Isabel's face emerged from the tip of her pen, eyes cast down, pensive. Her lips weren't generous enough. Leo scrunched the piece of paper and marched to the phone.

The same mechanized voice answered. She steeled herself, waited for the beep and left a message. 'This is Leonora Gould,' she stumbled as her stepfather's name found its way to her lips. She hadn't known she was going to use it, yet it might help. She rushed on, 'I'd like to make an appointment with you.' She left Isabel's number, hoping he wouldn't recognize it. And if he did, that would have its purposes, too.

She was standing on the top step of the ladder, to reach down another of Isabel's box files, when the phone rang. She scrambled for it. Her estimate of Dr

Lukas's schedule had only been out by some five minutes. She put on her coolest voice.

'Hello.'

'Mom, it's me. Sorry I wasn't here when you phoned yesterday. Are you OK? Has Isabel turned up? What's the weather like?' Becca's voice raced over the distance, warming her. She sounded both incredibly grown-up and the same mile-a-minute chatterbox she had always been.

'I'm fine, darling. And you? Are you managing to study?'

'Not much.'

'But you're having a good time?'

'Terrific. Dad took us to Green's yesterday. And shopping for CDs. I bought a ton. And early to-morrow we're going riding up in the hills . . .'

Leo listened, offered a few reassuring words. When she put the receiver down, she was seized by a sensation of pure longing. She knew with vivid clarity that if Becca were here with her she wouldn't feel so fractured, so close to an edge which gave way only to darkness.

After Jeff's departure, none of her fears about Becca succumbing to misery or launching into full-scale teenage rebellion had materialized. They had handled the separation well, if nothing else. Both had explained to her that these things happened and that neither of them was particularly at fault. People just grew apart.

Leo hadn't let the lawyers talk her into vengeful divorce proceedings, despite Jeff's ostensible guilt. She insisted, above their clamouring voices, that the only agreement she wanted was that Jeff leave them the family apartment and pay for Becca's education. She wanted no alimony for herself. She wanted only to be free of him. She earned enough. And Becca and she had grown closer with his absence, sharing outings, movies, gossip about friends, even clothes. It was as if Becca felt Leo's inevitable loneliness and wanted somehow to make up for it. Not too much, Leo hoped. No, not too much, since she hadn't decided to go to college in New York, but in California. Leo had encouraged her, dreading the possibility of retroactive resentment. Perhaps she also sensed that if she sought her closeness she would be as likely to get a merciful stay of execution from a ravenous tiger as she would from the good young woman who was her daughter.

Leo had been thrust into a freedom she didn't quite know how to use after almost eighteen years of family habit. Like an addiction, she sometimes felt, so hard did it all too often seem to live a life without ties. The time she had once so avidly longed for now cascaded over her with drowning intensity. It was the little things. Sometimes she walked automatically into the supermarket or the laundry, certain that a task demanded performing, only to remember that there was no need. She would fill the fridge with food which rotted away uneaten. Or she would leap up from her desk at four o'clock and start to concoct a milkshake, only to find that it was hers alone to drink.

She had spent more time in galleries and museums and concerts this last year than she had in the entirety of her life. Luckily, she had her work. That sustained her.

Time was one of the matters she had hoped to probe with Isabel. Too much of it, not too little. How did one construct a new internal clock appropriate for a life alone?

She guessed that one of Isabel's blithe answers would have been, 'You don't have to be alone, you gorgeous creature. Make the most of it.'

A lover, Leo sensed, would have been only the beginning.

4

Beneath its glazed dome, Paddington Station was a morning inferno. Drills bored through concrete, sending sparks flying over sheeted scaffolding. Trains screeched and juddered as they pulled in or away. Smoke flew. A gruff male voice droned from the loudspeakers, chanting a litany of strangely incomprehensible destinations. Pigeons scuttled underfoot, pecking at litter. Trolleys clattered amidst the crowd. Backpackers and cyclists jostled with sprucely suited men and women. Helmeted builders in fluorescent yellow tore their way through the crowd. Digital clocks announced different times on each subsequent platform.

Sipping a cappuccino, Leo stood amongst a group who bore the appearance of stargazers. Each and every face was turned expectantly towards the bank of computerized announcements. A number of trains had been delayed, including her own, and the massed ranks of impatient would-be passengers had grown with each passing minute.

At last she was able to board. She sank into the first window seat available, and heaved a sigh of relief as the train lurched into motion. London's suburbs stretched before her, grudgingly giving way to freshly green countryside. Cows looked up with consoling expressions, as if they were all too used to this gigantic worm wriggling through their landscape. Young colts, on legs so spindly new they must have been surprised at their own motion, bolted towards indifferent mothers. Sheep dotted fields magnificent with unfurling trees.

While the train crawled, Leo sketched, her hand racing across her pad to make up for its lack of speed. Years had passed since she had last focused on landscape. She had forgotten how to see, how branches drooped or soared, how they meshed and fluttered in the breeze; had forgotten the intricate fluff of clouds, the gathering shadow at their centre.

Oxford arrived before she was quite ready for it. It wasn't a city she knew, but she didn't pause to take in its beauty. She was now in a hurry. When her turn came in the taxi queue, the driver refused to take her. She had no better luck with the second. The third agreed, with a shrug and a murmur of, 'OK, then, it's a nice day,' but pointed out that, if she was planning to taxi back into town, it would probably be cheaper for her to rent a car.

'I'd never find my way,' Leo replied.

She only realized the full truth of this as they crept through a tangled one-way system, sped along for some twenty miles, and then began a slow trek along winding single-track roads. Nestled round their stone churches, these Cotswold villages had an ancient peace about them, as if they had sprung from the earth without the intervention of man. Yet intervention was precisely the name of the game with the enterprise which was her destination.

She had expected an ultra-modern science park. Instead, when the driver announced, 'We're here,' she could see only a curving stretch of old wall in honey-grey stone, overarched by generous beeches and chestnuts. On the other side of the road, a steep bank gave way to a stream, and then there was nothing but hills and fields.

'Are you sure?'

He nodded, turning into a gap in the wall. A paved drive, flanked by well-tended grounds, gradually led them towards a small parking lot. To its side stood a building which had all the high-windowed grace of a Jacobean manor. An interesting form of camouflage, Leo reflected. She walked slowly towards the front of the building. She had ten minutes to spare, but maybe, just maybe, Isabel, too, would have arrived early. She offered a silent prayer to some goddess of good fortune and looked around. Through a momentary gap in a flank of trees, a ray of sun rebounded from steel and glass. Greenhouses. So she was at the right place. A discreet plaque at the side of the polished double doors confirmed it. 'Origen plc,' it whispered.

She waited. High up, tucked into the centre of the portico, she noticed the roving eye of a security camera. Better to go in; there was no point in attracting suspicion. But getting in was not so easy. The doors didn't give. One had to announce oneself to the videophone.

'I'm here to see Dr Beasley,' Leo said, mustering authority, her voice too loud in what felt like an artificial silence.

The door eased open with the slightest burr of sound.

Leo's eyes flitted around a spacious hall which had been converted into a reception room. She urged Isabel's form to emerge from one of the two leather chesterfields positioned round a glass coffee table.

She wanted to throw her arms around her, hug her close. The fax that had arrived at five o'clock the previous afternoon had convinced her that Isabel would be here. It cancelled an eleven o'clock meeting she had today with Roland Beasley, chief executive of Origen. But Isabel wasn't home to receive the fax, so would turn up at Origen at the appointed time. She would; Leo was sure of it. Exactly a week had passed since she had failed to arrive in New York. The desperate logic of wish and superstition fuelled Leo's certainty.

'How can I help you?' A stern voice beckoned Leo to the far corner of the room.

Leo turned to see a grey-haired woman with the chiselled features of an old-fashioned headmistress. She was poised behind a U of a desk.

'I'm meeting Iris Morgenstern here.' Leo used the name to which the fax had been addressed. It was this which had alerted her to the clandestine nature of the meeting. She understood instantly that if none of the gene-technology companies would see an Isabel who had a reputation as a journalist, then a pseudonym was in order. Isabel had invented one which didn't jar with her e-mail address. What the ploy for the meeting was Leo had no idea.

'We're seeing Dr Beasley. Has she already gone through?'

'No.' The woman fixed her with a diminishing stare.

'I'll wait then, Mrs ... Mrs ... Runcorn,' Leo read the badge pinned to a suit which might have been a uniform.

'Your name?'

Leo gave it and watched her look down a list attached to a clipboard.

'Your name isn't listed here. Nor is anyone called Iris Morgenstern.' She gave it a clipped Germanic pronunciation.

'There must be a mistake,' Leo insisted. 'We definitely had a meeting with Roland Beasley. I've come all the way from London.'

A frown creased the woman's face. She picked up her telephone and dialled a three-digit number. Leo could hear a female voice at the other end.

'Let me speak to her,' Leo demanded in a tone which might have come straight from an assertiveness-training programme.

With a disgruntled air Mrs Runcorn passed her the receiver and turned to her computer, her back stiff in disapproval.

'I'm so sorry, Miss Morgenstern. Dr Beasley was called away last night.' A breezy voice mistakenly addressed her as Isabel. 'I faxed you myself. But don't worry, the publicity post is still open. Dr Beasley will arrange for a new meeting on his return.'

'I see,' Leo murmured, then grew bold. 'Since I've made the trek, perhaps someone can show me round.'

There was a pause. 'I'm afraid that's not possible. Dr Beasley likes to do that himself.'

'Have you got any materials to give me?'

'Materials? You must have received the document-ation pack I sent.'

'I didn't. Nothing arrived. You do have my correct address?'

'I believe so.' She read it out to her. 'And ask Mrs Runcorn for a documentation pack. She should have one to hand. I'll be in touch.'

Nothing, Leo thought as she stepped out into the

88

crisp country air, made any sense. She walked towards her cab, and then, with a quick glance behind her, altered her direction. A bank of snowy spiraea hid her from the front door. She edged towards the ranked trees, through which she had earlier spied the roof of a greenhouse. Another look over her shoulder and she was through the trees. She stopped short. A high perimeter fence blocked her way. It stretched from the back of the main house and as far as she could see in the opposite direction. Within its bounds, there was nothing of the prettiness of the Jacobean house and tended grounds.

Some six large greenhouses dominated the landscape, and beyond them was the barren geometry of rigorously ploughed fields. On a path which led towards the rear of the manor house, she could see two men in floating white lab coats. They were walking away from her. She stepped closer to the fence. A slight hiss alerted her. She moved her hands abruptly to her side. The fence was electrified. Keeping her distance, she peered through lozenge-shaped mesh into the nearest greenhouse. It looked deserted. Row upon row of plantlets she couldn't identify sprouted from well-turned black earth. On impulse, she took her pad out of her bag and sketched their shapes, then added the layout of the greenhouses and grounds for good measure.

On the train back to London, she pondered her drawings, together with the glossy brochure she'd been given. It extolled the marvels of the agriculture of the future, showed photographs of pristine laboratories which could have been involved in any kind of research, gave statistics on earth quality, pest resistance and the potential yields of genetically modified species.

None of it brought her any closer to understanding what had become of Isabel. Why hadn't she cancelled her appointment as Iris Morgenstern herself if she knew she was going to be away? In Savannah, by now. With Leo. And if she hadn't intended to be away, why hadn't she turned up for a meeting which was a gem of a lead for her investigations. Only brute force would have prevented her.

Leo held back the rush of tears. Too many of them these last days. Maybe she had grown new high-speed ducts, as efficient as the lauded new pest-free plants. She forced herself to concentrate. If Isabel had devised a pseudonym for her application to Origen, she could just as easily have used the same name elsewhere. If something had happened to her under that name, the police, after Leo's report to them, would have been looking for the wrong person – an Isabel Morgan instead of an Iris Morgenstern.

Would Isabel ever forgive her if Leo blew her cover just when she might be onto something important? Leo had to consider that, as well as its alternative, which was that Isabel had stumbled onto a secret and been caught. Judging by Origen, stray eyes were hardly welcome in such sites.

A tremor went through her, and with it came dizziness. Jet lag, she told herself. Her mind was fuzzy. Her lids felt heavy.

Rough wool brushed her arm. The seat beside her creaked a little. She looked up abruptly to see a man next to her, a large man with bulging eyes and speckled skin, like an outsize toad.

'Ms Morgenstern, isn't it?' His thin lips curled.

Leo sat up straight.

'No, of course. You don't know me. Gerald Kripps. I saw you at Origen.' He pointed to the document pack which was still on her lap.

'Saw me?' Leo edged closer to the window.

'Yes.' He made a vague gesture. To Leo it suggested a hundred unseen eyes tracking her without her knowledge.

'You made some drawings. I'd love to see them.' There was an edge beneath the casual friendliness of his tone. Leo pretended not to notice.

'Surely you have me confused with someone else. I never draw.'

'Oh? You've applied for the PR post?'

'I have.'

'Funny. You haven't a trace of an Australian accent, yet all your experience seems to have been down under.'

'Oh that,' Leo's voice sounded shrill in her own ears. She modulated it, thinking quickly. 'I spent some of my school years in California. The accent stayed. And my mother's American.'

'How interesting.'

The way he said it made Leo wonder whether she had just contradicted something in the application Isabel must have written. Why was she doing this? More to the point, why was this odious man interrogating her? She was suddenly angry.

'What exactly do you do at Origen, Mr Kripps?'

'I work with Dr Beasley.'

'What kind of work?'

That vague wave again. 'I assist him.'

'In what?'

'This and that.' He turned bulging eyes on her. 'In screening candidates sometimes. We have to be careful, you know. It's a highly competitive industry.'

The last sounded like a distinct threat. Leo felt a laugh rise to her throat. She let it emerge. 'Origen must be losing out to the competition if it can't afford first-class seats for its executives.'

'Don't you worry about my seat, Miss Morgenstern.' He eased his bulk with remarkable alacrity and, as he did so, pushed the brochure from her lap so that it and the drawing pad it contained tumbled to the floor.

'So sorry.' He reached down and extracted the pad. He whisked through it and, with a tug, ripped out the two sketches she had done of the Origen grounds and greenhouse. 'I'll just take these, if you don't mind.' His polite voice bore no relation to his menacing features. 'Take care, now.'

At Paddington, she found herself looking over her shoulder. Where had that dreadful creep got to? The late-afternoon jostle prevented her from seeing anything but the people directly around her. Nor was it possible to stand still amidst the rush of passengers. After a moment's hesitation, Leo made for the underground. If Mr Gerald Kripps were trying to trail her there was no point in making it easy for him by standing in a taxi queue. Nor would she lead him straight back to the loft.

A glance at the placards gave her sudden inspiration. She took the Circle Line to King's Cross, then walked along the dingy platform to the arch which indicated the Northern Line connection. It was here that she saw him, just as the train lurched out of the station. He stood at the door of the second to last carriage. He had the audacity to doff his hat to her.

Had he been following her, Leo wondered. If he had, he would get off at Moorgate and make his way to the apartment. All he would find there was that none of the names on the bells tallied with the one he was looking for. He wouldn't dare to break in. Surely companies like Origen didn't sanction criminal acts. Leo shrugged, almost wishing that now she wasn't there, he would break in so that she'd have something substantial to report to the police. Something that would at last properly engender their help and erase the image of an over-the-top New Yorker she was certain they had of her.

She made her way through endless, dimly lit corridors to wait on the teeming Northern Line platform. When the High Barnet train finally came, she had to elbow her way into the midst of a crowd of rush-hour passengers. Beside her a gaggle of uniformed schoolgirls giggled, their voices pitched high above the judder of the train.

Becca, too, had worn a uniform during their year in London. A brown pleated skirt, white shirt and brown blazer that made her look far more grown up than her eight years. She'd had a little girl's pride in it, and stood up very straight as soon as she put it on. Seeing her pleasure, Leo had felt less ambivalent about sending her to an independent school. They had finally decided on Channing because it was a mere three-minute trot from their flat, whereas the local state school was beyond walking distance, and running a car would have cost the equivalent of school fees. And not permitted her mother the indulgence of contributing to Becca's education.

Highgate Station hadn't changed. As she made her way up the tree-shrouded incline and emerged at Stanhope Road, she almost felt as if she'd come home. Home to a happier time, a time that was all present and future excitement, whereas now. now, she was forced to admit, her predominant emotion was one of loss. Leo prodded the emotion away. She was too young to be old, she told herself. Had told herself often over this last year. Too young to feel her life was behind her. Only the journey with Isabel had provided a future wish.

The white-stuccoed furniture shop still occupied the corner of the street, filling it with an assortment of curving Victorian armchairs and mahogany chests. Opposite stood the neo-Gothic church, its arched interior home to a community arts centre where Becca had attended Saturday morning dance classes, while she and Jeff sipped weak cappuccinos and read papers in its slightly musty café. They had made casual friendships there with other parents. Another life.

Leo resisted the temptation to go in search of happier ghosts and quickened her pace. But they accompanied her. This was the road they had always climbed, up through the narrowing at its crest, all but impassable to cars, past the boys' school, with its tiny triangle of shaded cemetery, and into the high street, where the aura of a village still clung over a hillside of eighteenth-century houses. She paused in front of the newsagent's to get her bearings. She hadn't brought the A–Z she had examined yesterday, but as she remembered it the street shouldn't be too far down the hill.

She passed the old-fashioned hardware store and the bank, a smattering of hairdressers' and estate agents' and, before she knew it, she was in front of Becca's school. In her imagination the distances had stretched and grown. Had she come too far now?

Two brown-clad girls traipsed out of the school door, their chatter as vivid as their laughing faces.

Without thinking, she followed them down the hill. She was there now, at the juncture of Cromwell Avenue. A sharp turn to the left and she would find herself in front of the sprawling house with its generous bay. Would another couple be sitting at the scrubbed pine table with a child poised between them, a daffodil-stuffed vase peeking over the edge of the window? She resisted the tug of nostalgia and forced herself to cross to the other side of the street.

Isabel had come to visit them at the apartment, but only once or twice. During that London year, they had most often met in noisy Soho restaurants or at the National Theatre bar or in front of a Leicester Square cinema. Highgate was too placid and familial a place for the high-voltage Isabel.

Leo continued up the hill. The brick wall on her left hid the rolling fields and shrub-banked lakes of Waterlow Park. She stopped for a moment in front of a wrought-iron gate and looked at the graceful façade of Lauderdale House, site of puppet shows and more coffee mornings, this time at the wobbly tables of the little restaurant perched on the edge of the park. Judging from the posters, children's theatre groups still came here. She thought of little Becca again, her dimpled face beneath a crown of dark curls, so like her father's. She would phone her later and tell her she had been here, but do it in a steady, cheerful voice. She hurried on.

Opposite the bookshop, she saw the street sign she had half forgotten she was looking for: Bisham Gardens. It was a tidy unremarkable street of brick terraced houses. She walked at an even pace, glad of her rubber-soled shoes, slowing only when she reached the memorized number. Apart from its front door, painted in bright Mediterranean blue, and a terracotta window box filled with primroses, the house was identical to its neighbours. Had she expected Gothic arches, peeling paint, an assortment of gables and a wild-haired screaming figure perched on a ledge? Would that have been an appropriate domain for a psychoanalyst? Leo mocked herself.

She tried to see in, but the ground-floor window betrayed no inhabitants, only the shadowy outline of a sofa and a stream of light, possibly indicating another window at the back. At the basement level, just beneath her, the curtains were tightly drawn. For a moment she was tempted to ring one of the three bells at the side of the door. But that wouldn't have served her purpose.

She walked on. The end of the short street came quickly, and before she had met a fellow stroller. A wall marked its end. Beyond it rose the elegant steeple of the parish church. To her left she recognized the precipitous road which wound between the park and Highgate Cemetery. She had walked in both places so often with Becca that the child she then was would ask every day whether they were going to the park of the living or the park of the dead. Funny, given that she knew the streets on either side so well, that she had never in fact trodden the pavements of Bisham Gardens before. Isabel hadn't thought to mention to her that her analyst lived in haunts once familiar to Leo.

Slowly, she retraced her route on the opposite side of the street. Perhaps she would get a better view from there. She felt a need to familiarize herself with the place.

She had only taken a few steps when she saw a woman emerge from a door – that door, she was certain of it. The woman was long-legged and wore trousers. Honey-gold hair fell over her shoulders.

'Isabel,' Leo's shout echoed through the quiet of the street.

The woman didn't turn.

'Isabel,' Leo called again.

A white van came trundling past her, and for a moment blocked her vision. Leo ran. By the time she could see clearly again the woman had disappeared.

She raced to the high-street corner, searching uphill and down, but there was no sign of her.

Had it been Isabel? Leo stood there and rubbed her eyes, wishing them into a clarity she momentarily felt she'd lost. If the woman had gone into a shop, she would come out again in a few minutes. But if she had been Isabel, surely she would have stopped at Leo's call. Perhaps she hadn't heard. Perhaps she was so overwrought, so whipped by inner confusion, that no external sound could penetrate.

Leo waited. She waited for a good quarter of an hour. A score of people passed her. Traffic snaked up the hill, more slowly than the slowest pedestrian. While she waited, Leo made up her mind. She had to know, never mind all her carefully laid plans. She headed back to the analyst's door. As she neared it a man emerged. He was tall and broad-shouldered in a ribbed blue sweater, around which a raincoat flapped as he hopped down the steps with a carefree air. He gave her a nod and a half-smile as their paths crossed. He was so unlike the image she had conjured up that it was only when she pressed the doorbell next to the Dr D Lukas name that it occurred to her he might be the very man she had come to see.

When no answer came, she cursed herself and angrily tried the bell again.

To no avail.

It was still light when she returned to the loft. A soft, early evening glow illuminated the recesses of the spacious room and burnished the floor a deep gold. Leo kicked off her shoes and sat on the crimson sofa. She wished she could kick off the despondency that had overtaken her on her way back as easily.

It had begun in the restaurant, a French-style café she had spotted on her trek up Highgate Hill. She was slowly munching her way through a croque monsieur and sipping a glass of white wine when she felt the depression settling. It was as tangible as a feather quilt, and as oppressive, covering her head, stifling her breath, numbing her feet, so that it was an effort to pay the bill and walk the short distance to the underground. Despite the beauty of the light, it covered her still.

Isabel was gone, sucked up by the earth like some latter-day Persephone. And Leo was alone. Alone and without the necessary resources to trace her. She didn't, she suddenly felt, have the resources for anything. New York and her work had receded into some shadowy distance. Without the bulwarks of habit and duty, she was no-one. Perhaps Isabel had already sensed that and simply abandoned her. Why bother with a dreary friend who had little interest and whose need was as invasive as the smell of rotting flesh. Surely it was her own need that had made her so certain over these last days that Isabel was in trouble and needed her.

Leo struggled to push black thoughts away. It was like pushing a heavy car single-handedly up a steep hill; any lessening of effort and it would slip back and annihilate her.

She forced herself to her feet. A rank of box files

awaited her. Only as she pulled one down did she notice the red light flashing on the telephone. She prodded the messages button. Stupid of her not to have checked the answering machine as soon as she got home.

'Isabel, it's Caroline. Good to hear your voice. You been away? Give me a ring. I still want to convince you to speak in the childhood month at the South Bank. Don't forget. I'll buy you lunch if you've got the time. And I'm going to pester you.'

As she listened, Leo realized that, although she had switched on the answering machine, she had failed to record a new message. Maybe she simply hadn't wanted to lose Isabel's. But the full stupidity of this only dawned on her as she heard the next voice.

'Leonora Gould? This is Daniel Lukas. I've got an opening on Monday at half past two. If you can manage that, don't bother to confirm. That's the fourth of May at two thirty.'

Leo replayed the message several times. She conjured a character from it and gave him the face of the man she had seen in the street. Unlike the face, the voice was formal, each word clearly enunciated, as if anyone who needed to see him must be living in a thick fog. The voice gave little away, yet the message in itself had a casual feel. She noted the slight pause that followed her own queried name. Had Daniel Lukas recognized Isabel's voice? She pressed the greeting-record button to check whether Isabel, in fact, identified herself.

She didn't. Of course, she didn't. She was also Iris Morgenstern, after all. But Leo's relief was only momentary. Daniel Lukas could hardly fail to recognize a voice he had listened to over so many months.

There was nothing for it, she would have to find a way round. For the time being, it was the sound of Isabel speaking that captured her: that warm, slightly husky tone eliciting messages, transforming a mundane act into an event tinged with comedy. 'If you have anything to tell me, do so after the tone. I thank you.'

'Where are you, Isabel?' she whispered into the empty room. 'I miss you.'

For lack of a live answer, she took down the two files labelled 'Letters'. She began to open one, and then, changing her mind, carried them into the bedroom. She needed to put her feet up after the day's exertions and dream herself into Isabel's state of mind. Heavy-limbed, she put on her nightdress and settled herself beneath the lemon-chequered quilt, the two files at her side. She opened both, leafing through to see whether the letters were arranged in any particular order.

The second box contained the most recent correspondence. Again Leo found herself astonished at an orderliness which Isabel seemed to have stretched into her personal life. For these letters, at least the first of them, were indeed personal. The top ones all came from unknown Australian addresses and seemed to be letters of condolence relating to the death of Isabel's mother. Leo skimmed through a variety of spindly scripts which called for decoding rather than mere reading. She had lost the habit of handwriting. She wondered if Isabel, like her, was tempted to skim rather than decipher.

Her lids grew heavy with the repetition of sympathy. She whisked through to the first typed letter. A brief sentence under the banner 'Evolution' indicated that a brochure was now reprinting and would soon be sent to Isabel. Leo imagined more biotech sites. She let her eyes close. Should she communicate Isabel's identity as Iris Morgenstern to the police? She would decide on that tomorrow morning. At least she had managed to give that outsize toad of a man the slip.

She didn't know how long she had slept when a sound woke her, like the turning of a key in a lock. She sat up, her body taut, her eyes as wide as if she had been awake for hours. She didn't dare breathe. She listened. Around her everything was dark. Only the glimmer of a street light threw a jaundiced streak round the corner of the blind. A soft scuffling noise made its way to her, like rats scurrying over a brief stretch of floorboard. It was inside the apartment, she was certain of that. A glow appeared at the bottom of the door. A lamp had been switched on.

Leo thought quickly. Could it be Isabel? No, Isabel would have known where the lights were and would have put them on as soon as she opened the door. Her upstairs neighbour then, Mike Newson, who had the key. But he would have rung the bell first, assuming she might be here. She looked at the clock radio. Twelve forty. She could hear footsteps now, a light padding. They were coming towards her. Swiftly, she picked up one of the box files and positioned herself at the edge of the door. An image of the loathsome man from Origen flashed through her mind.

When the door opened, she launched the box with all her strength towards the burly shape. The sound of the thud was oddly satisfying.

The brutal lunge that landed her on the bed wasn't. Nor was the body which suddenly covered her, fingers pinioning her shoulder, fist poised to strike her face. She put out her hands to stop its progress.

A truculent voice barked at her. 'What the hell do you think you're doing?'

The man stepped back to stand above her. He rubbed his shoulder where the box had hit him. 'You were that far away from having your face smashed in. That far.' His fist made a walloping sound as it hit his palm. 'Well?'

In the half light, Leo focused on a big man with a pugilist's features, all square jaw, cheekbones and squat nose, beneath a glint of blue eyes. Unruly brows arched to meet hair the colour of dark sand.

'It's not a bad face, either.' He gave her a malevolent grin and punched his fist into his palm again. 'So?'

'What are you doing here?'

'Given that I'm the one who's standing and you're, well, let's say prone, I think I get to ask the questions first, wouldn't you say?'

Leo sat up and edged towards the far side of the bed. 'Who are you?'

'Uh uh, you go first. I'll give you ten.'

When she didn't respond, he snorted. 'I have to admit, the great thing about visiting Isabel is that there's never a dull moment. Even when she's not here.'

'You know Isabel?'

'Of course I know Isabel. How the dickens d'you think I got in here? Flew in the window like a fat pigeon? Blew down the door with a big bad wolf puff?' He stopped himself. 'Oh, I see. Isabel forgot to mention I'd be staying here. Typical. But then she didn't mention you to me, either, Miss, Mrs, Ms?'

'Holland. Leo.'

'OK, Holland Leo. Let's shake on it. The name this end is Norfolk, Christopher.' He put out a broad hand.

After an initial hesitation, Leo took it.

'Between us we've got ourselves a damp country and a dank county. What more could one ask? Except that you put a little something on those dainty shoulders and come and sign a truce over a glass of Australia's best. It's right out there in the bag that trailed me here, courtesy of Qantas.'

Her robe securely tied, Leo followed him out of the room. She watched him pull a bottle out of a tan carry-all and rummage through the kitchen drawers for a corkscrew.

'So why'd you try and brain me, Holland Leo?' he asked as he poured the wine.

'I . . . I thought you were someone else.'

'Lucky him. Who?'

She hedged the question. Beneath the charm, she sensed something dangerous about him. She wasn't quite ready for trust. 'Isabel's gone.'

'I can see that.'

'I mean, no-one knows where she is.'

'Sure we do. She's off in the United States of Adventure. Pleasuring herself, no doubt. Or mourning. Maybe a little of both.'

Leo shook her head. 'No, she's not. She never turned up.'

'Are you sure?' He examined her steadily, as if she weren't the most reliable person in the world.

'Altogether sure. She's just vanished. She was supposed to be with me and she isn't. And I can't find any trace of her. Through anyone.'

He fidgeted slightly, then got up from the sofa and

strode across the room and back with the light, easy movements of a man used to the outdoors. His charcoal suit looked as if he'd slept in it for more nights than one.

'People don't just vanish. Not without trace. Or not unless they're very rich. And then the letter in cut-up newsprint arrives. Or the muffled voice over the telephone.' He planted himself in front of her and looked down at her expectantly.

'Well, there've been no letters or muffled demands and Isabel's vanished. People can if they live alone.' There was a plaintive note in her voice which she wished hadn't found its way there.

'You mean in this big bad megalopolis where we're all lonely strays without a place of belonging and a safety net of community, people can just up and disappear and turn up years later in a lot of little pieces in some psychopath's garden.'

Leo couldn't find her voice.

'Isabel's hardly a helpless teeny-tot fleeing the evil carers. She probably met a hunk on the way to the airport and forgot to check in. Either that or—'

Leo leapt up and raced across the room.

'Hey, Holland Leo, I didn't mean to insult.'

She didn't answer him. She was staring at the answering machine. Hamish Macgregor had just come into her mind. He hadn't got back to her, despite the slew of messages she had left on both numbers. And there was no flashing red light now, either. She would try him again first thing in the morning. She went back into the living room. The man was sitting there, stretched out on the crimson sofa as if he'd always sat there, as if this was his home.

He had refilled their glasses and found peanuts. Something in Leo rankled.

'How long have you known Isabel?'

He raised slate-blue eyes to her. 'For ever. Maybe an added day.'

'What exactly does that mean?'

'We met when she was one of your teeny-tots. A veritable Venus fresh from the surf of Bondi and longing to make a mark on the earthly world.'

'What do you do?'

'What is this? The Inquisition?'

'Just an ordinary question. I want to know who I'm flat-sharing with.'

'Your secret sharer is an old hack. Courtesy of the *Sydney Morning Herald*.'

'And what are you doing here?'

'My, my. We started off friendly and now we're getting friendlier and friendlier. At the moment, I'm scoffing nuts. And you?'

'I'm trying to find out what's happened to Isabel. Goodnight.'

Leo stopped herself from slamming her door. She stretched out on the bed. Sleep wouldn't come. The man's sudden arrival, the leap of violence, had all taken on the quality of a nightmare she couldn't shake off. She tried to remember whether Isabel had ever mentioned an old friend called Christopher Norfolk. She listened for sounds, a pattern of movement. When, after some twenty minutes, none came, she decided she could venture out. If nothing else, a shower would relax her.

The living room was dark now, but at its far end light spilled out through the half-open door of Isabel's study. What could he want in there? She tip-toed forward and stopped abruptly.

He was standing over Isabel's in-tray, rifling through letters, half reading. He seemed to know what he was looking for. One of the letters disappeared into his pocket as she watched.

'I'll have that,' Leo heard herself saying. Her voice was as icy as an arctic gust.

He veered round. Something brutal played over his taut, tanned face, then settled into a satisfied smile. He patted his pocket. 'Uh uh. It's mine.'

'What are you doing in here?' As she said it, Leo was abysmally aware that in any open contest of strength she would hardly come out the winner. For the umpteenth time in her life, she rued her slightness. But she repeated her question.

He pointed towards the curve in the desk. A computer was planted on it next to hers. 'We hacks have to communicate with the home front, lady. You've heard about time zones. It's a good one down under.'

Leo looked at his screen which showed an e-mail program.

'And by the way,' he tapped his pocket, 'Isabel and I often share research.'

'Do you now? Is that secret sharing again? Or do you indulge in above-board forms, too?'

He laughed as she turned on her heel, then called after her, 'Hey, Holland Leo, you've worried me. And I don't like the look of the new books our mutual friend has acquired. Tomorrow I'll do some ringing round. Truce, remember?'

Leo's mind was far from a truce. In the morning, she would check to see what materials he had taken. She had a hunch what they would relate to. It occurred to her that he could easily have been sent here by the likes of Origen, or one of its kin, to erase any tracks that might prove contact with Isabel. And

his keys could all too easily have come from her –
against her will.

As her eyes closed, images of terror played over
her lids. She saw a barefoot Isabel striding across a
field, breaking into that easy run of hers, her hair
swinging. And then, suddenly, she crumpled and fell.
She struggled to rise, but an invisible force held her
down, as if she were paralysed, her limbs helpless. A
beetle nibbled at her toes, from which a thin stream
of blood oozed. Like in that dream Leo had come
across in the box file, a dream Isabel might have
recounted to her analyst.

Was it because she felt herself cracking that she
imagined a breakdown for Isabel?

Shivering, Leo pulled the duvet up to her face and
thought of the man behind the name: Daniel Lukas.

PART TWO

NOTES TOWARDS A CASE HISTORY (I)

The beginning was simple enough.

She arrived punctually. Her eyes roved over the objects and prints in the room. Moved so avidly that she seemed to be taking mnemonic snapshots of them for some private collection. Her dress was carmine, tight at the waist and then flouncing into an abundance of skirt. I had the impression that she had imagined me as a Fifties Hollywood host or a casting director on a production of *Carmen*. Her tangle of streaked blond hair was a centre of activity, stroked and prodded by fingers, tossed to show off a profile sometimes delicate, sometimes strong. The gestures didn't feel like nervousness, more a kind of exhilaration. When her chocolate eyes landed on me in slow examination, I realized that perhaps it was I who was intended as the camera.

She didn't wait for me to begin.

'You don't have to explain the rules,' she said, 'I know them.' She smiled the kind of smile that told me she'd break them in any case. 'And I prefer lying down.'

There was a flurry of smooth, unstockinged legs as she stretched out on the couch. High-heeled sandals fell to the floor, ankles arched.

She turned back to glance at me just as I positioned

myself on the chair behind her. I still hadn't done more than nod at her entrance.

'Oh, and by the way,' she said, her face a display of petulant innocence, 'I always end up by seducing my analysts, or therapists, or whatever you all are.'

I had heard the challenge before, but never put quite so forthrightly and quite so soon. The love of the patient for the analyst is, after all, one of the foundation stones of our profession, the very meat of what we set out to work on. Its occurrence has nothing at all to do with our individual charms, as plentiful or few as these may be. The old man of Berggasse commented on it often enough. Transference love, he called it, and wrote a whole paper about how we could go about managing it.

So I was tempted to let her challenge pass until we knew each other a little better, but she was still looking up at me, waiting for a response, and I found myself saying, 'Do you think that's because we don't resist you enough or don't hold you enough?'

It took me a while to realize that, for her, the resistance and the holding were the same.

For now she laughed, with a touch of wickedness rather than humour.

'That's too complicated. It's because you all enjoy it so much.'

In retrospect, I probably should have ended it right there and then, rather than wait for her to end it when it was already too late. But I was intrigued. Patients, after all, can bring their own quota of boredom, the obsessional ones in particular. I know; I've been one. And she – let's call her Anna – promised to be anything but boring. She worked in the development section of a television production company. I judged her to be about thirty-five, an attractive woman who was well acquainted with her own appeal. Well acquainted with the experience of therapy, too, it seemed. For her, the sexually repressed had all already been spoken, as well as acted out, I imagined. Or so she certainly wanted me to imagine. We have travelled a long way in this century from Freud's wonderful hysterics. His geography of our fantasies and needs both fits and no longer quite fits.

'Do you see yourself as a bringer of pleasure?' I asked.

She laughed that laugh again, and turned to stretch back on the couch.

'Pleasure? Let me tell you some stories . . .'

In the first months of our meetings, Anna told me stories. Nothing but stories. A mirrored labyrinth of stories. I listened. I tried to deduce patterns, follow a string which would lead me to her. She sometimes appeared in these stories, but they were principally about others. Nor could I tell whether they were invented or embellished fragments of her own experience. Not that that mattered: fiction and truth on the couch are, after all, often inseparable. The links and ruptures in the speaking provide most of the cues for our work. If analysis is in some measure a confrontation with the life-inhibiting secrets we like, or need, to keep from ourselves, then it is in these links and ruptures that the secrets begin to peek through.

At first Anna's web of story felt seamless. Like a latter-day Scheherazade, she entranced me. It wasn't the useful trance which attends the best therapies, a kind of receptive lulling of the active mind so that one can become the patient. A lulling which is attended by a roving alertness, a readiness to pounce on clues. (The image that always comes to my mind

113

is of a big cat lolling in the sunshine, yet vigilant to the slightest stir in the bush.) No. Anna's magic was such that I was enchanted: I had physically to shake myself to recall that I was at work and meant, at least partly, to be in charge of the evolution of a narrative.

Sometimes, by the end of a session, I would feel that, like some fateful Arachne, she had spun a web in which only I was destined to be trapped.

She had a way with words, and tone and pacing. On occasion, she would choose to sit in the armchair rather than recline. I didn't stop her, as perhaps I should have. I thought that the change of posture might induce her to communicate in the more immediate way of other patients and tell me something of her everyday life, her family. It didn't. It was as if she had assumed Freud's own impatience with polite preambles and little nothings and was telling me that we both already knew that she had a father and a mother and needed to hurry on to get to more substantial puzzles.

From the chair, as she talked, she would watch me. I could feel her weaving her effects in response to the slightest movement of my features.

The word 'pleasure' had sparked her first story and I had thought, given her demeanour and what had come before, that she would tell me something overt about her sexual life. I was wrong.

Instead, she told me about a home she had once worked in. A home for disturbed youngsters. The home stood at the summit of a dirt road at the edge of an unnamed town. Like some ancient monastery, it was constructed out of great blocks of moulded limestone. Sparse twiglets of trees sprouted unevenly from vast urns in its gloomy inner courtyard. Around it, on the ground level, were the common rooms where the young people were bustled into occupational therapies. They shaped wet, clammy clay into freakish forms, splashed paint wildly onto paper, wove rugs out of rags. In the high-ceilinged refectory, they sat on benches at long tables and ate food that was always tinged with grey. There was brown-grey and green-grey and white-grey. The greyness usurped any other definition. But everyone ate and everyone was occupied. Except one boy.

He was about fourteen, a thin stick of a lad with a cap of brown hair and large, empty eyes. He didn't speak. He moved docilely enough, if one took his arm and led him. And if a spoon was brought to his mouth, he would eventually open it. Otherwise he simply sat, as impervious to the life around him as the stone out of which the home was hewn. Everyone had ceased to pay attention to him. No-one greeted him or addressed him. He was simply there, like the walls, a silent fixture amidst the cacophony of the house.

Anna took an interest in him. She greeted him on her arrival and talked to him. She told him about the weather and about the progress of the flowers and vegetables in the small neighbouring garden. She told him about elections and earthquakes in distant places. She behaved as if he could understand every word, though he never responded with sign or language. And every night, before she left, she said, 'Goodbye. Sweet dreams.'

On her final evening at the home, after her goodbye, she added that she wouldn't be coming back. This was the last goodbye.

The boy sat there, as impassive as ever. With a wave, she repeated her goodbye and turned away. It was then that she felt fingers, as soft and light as silk, encircle her wrist.

The length of Anna's pause at this juncture suggested that she had come to the end of something and was waiting for a response from me.

'So perhaps you're telling me that, for you, pleasure lies in caring for others?' I began mildly.

'Certainly not!' she scoffed.

The resistance was good, so I pushed a little further. 'Its opposite then. You take a sadistic pleasure in charming a helpless boy. Your attention woke him into life and then you left him.'

She sat up and gave me an enigmatic smile, then she pulled a watch out of her pocket. Its strap didn't seem to be broken, but she didn't wear it around her wrist. She looked at it. 'Three minutes to go. I like to leave a little early. You can keep the change.' And with that she was off.

At first, though her manner of departure had made me just a little uncomfortable, I thought we had made an excellent start. Only later did it come to me, when I tried to urge her to return to what she had told me about the boy and the home, that this story, like so many of her subsequent tales, had been pre-packaged for my consumption. It was, in its own way, already a case history. Eventually she insisted that she had invented the whole episode.

She was teasing me with the very material of my profession.

It took me a while to begin to see that words, stories, were her form of resistance. For a talking cure to unravel that poses a not-insignificant challenge. I didn't mind. I thought I was equal to the detective work.

But for months I did my sleuthing in the wrong place. It was as if Anna inhabited the perimeters of the coast, while I was searching the heartland. Gradually, I realized that all the real analytic clues lay in the very fact that she told stories. Or they occurred in the frame, the perimeter – the moments before she lay down, or as she was getting up, the arrangement or disarrangement of appointments, the modes of payment. She had a passion for counting out notes in front of me, in the semblance of an afterthought, but so that I could feel dirtied by the transaction. Not for her the usual anonymity of the cheque book.

For too long, though I took all this into account, I let myself be entertained by what happened within the frame.

Analysis, after all, largely attempts to enable a patient to give a fuller, more satisfying account of their life. One they can live with and love with. One which incorporates what we experience as tragedy and loss. It is, at least on the surface, about content. Anna reminded me otherwise.

5

The creak and squeal of taxi brakes alerted Daniel Lukas to the time. He placed his pen into the fold of his notebook, tucked both into the top drawer of his desk and stood up to stretch his legs. Through the window, he could see the woman emerging from the cab. He drew back quickly as she looked up at the house.

From the other end of the long narrow room, the sweep of Waterlow Park was visible. Morning drizzle had emptied the tennis courts. But the plump sticky buds of the chestnuts were busy unfurling into a lime-green too bright for the surrounding greyness. In the distance, the rounded bulk of the South Downs loomed surprisingly close, brought nearer by the needle-sharp towers which now pierced the low London sky.

At the far edge of his garden, amidst the snowy spiraea, he spied the black and white markings of the ball Robbie had lost over the weekend. He had cried hot five-year-old tears over the loss, too many of them. Daniel had hugged and consoled him, but hadn't discouraged the tears. Every little loss brought the big one in its train, and the boy needed to cry. Still, he would be pleased this afternoon to be able to return the ball to him. Not all losses were final.

The bell still hadn't rung. Had his new patient decided not to turn up after all, frightened away at the threshold? He swallowed his irritation and turned back towards the front of the house. Yes, there she was, walking down the street, her russet coat ballooning in the wind. He picked up the book about forensic psychology he was reviewing and immersed himself in its dense pages. When the bell rang again, he wondered for a moment whether he shouldn't bother to answer it, but he knew that would probably only mean delay and more telephone tag, and he had promised himself that he would take on the next new patient who approached him. Too many months had passed in a torpor which teetered dangerously on the brink of despair.

'It's on the third floor,' he said evenly into the intercom.

He heard her running lightly up the carpeted staircase. Running up so as not to run away. She was a little breathless when she reached the open door, her cheeks flushed from the wind and effort.

'Leonora Gould. Hello.' He ushered her in with a neutral smile.

She gave him a forthright stare of assessment, then looked everywhere but at him as she took off her coat. Beneath it she was wearing a well-cut black jacket and trousers. The jacket was buttoned right up to the neck. Its nunlike severity contrasted with the girlish face and the slight tousle of her hair. An attractive woman who didn't altogether want to be.

'I'm so sorry. I couldn't get a taxi, and then I took the Northern Line towards Edgware instead of High Barnet and had to retrace my steps to Camden Town.'

'Oh.' The blatant lie took him aback.

119

He showed her to the sofa, which doubled as a couch.

She looked at it as if it might swallow her up, then poised herself at its very edge, her hands clasped neatly on her knees. She had an air of controlled agitation. He could feel her wanting to move and examine, and restraining herself.

He perched on the chair opposite her. 'Tell me what's brought you here,' he said, after a moment in which it became clear she was now lost for speech.

'I . . . I'm worried about my daughter. You see . . . she's left home now. For college. In California. I live in New York. I'm only visiting here. For work. I'm an illustrator. Doing well, really. Except for this worry.'

Leo tried to remember the mixture of truths, half-truths and lies she had so carefully prepared as an opening gambit, but they no longer quite made sense. The place had confused her. It conformed to none of her expectations. There was no receptionist, no waiting room, no double doors to allow for patient privacy. The carpet on the stairs was threadbare. And up here, the walls were lined with books which spilled over onto the floor and heaved on every available surface. There were none of the carefully placed objects or prints which decorated her stepfather's pristine consulting room, objects to inspire the unleashing of the so-called unconscious. There was no armchair positioned in front of an authoritative desk. Nor was there even a proper couch – sign and symbol of the profession. The room was simply an ordinary sitting room.

Maybe Daniel Lukas wasn't a professional at all. He certainly wasn't the man she had glimpsed on the street and prepared herself to meet. Or was he? The hair could be the same, though there was more grey peeping through its darkness, and the face was more deeply marked, somehow older. If she were to draw him now, his principal features would be his wide brow and the spectacles resting on his aquiline jut of a nose. Above them the eyes were disconcertingly direct, focused in a bedside manner of kindliness. Maybe it was the serious dark-blue suit and the non-descript tie that made the difference. These were slightly shabby, too. The white shirt beneath was badly ironed, the collar frayed. And he looked so stiff sitting there, waiting, none of the casual gallop of the streets.

'Yes?' He made an encouraging sound.

'Where was I?'

'You're only visiting here. And worrying.'

'Yes. I think I'd like to come for a few sessions. Maybe more. I don't know. While I'm here.'

'Do you see someone regularly in New York?'

'Oh no!' The vehement staccato of her voice took her by surprise. She tried to make up for its weight of condemnation, but no formula came to her.

'That's all right then.' He relaxed into the sofa, waited for her to go on.

Her own silence baffled her. Like treacle, it spread through the room, seeped into the cracks in the floor-boards, covered her in its stickiness, then hardened round her as she sought the right words.

He broke through it. He didn't play by the rules. 'I know it can feel a bit strange talking to someone you don't know. It's always difficult. But try and tell me something more about what made you come. Is there a specific problem?'

His voice was so softly engaging that again she couldn't find an answer. She examined her hands for what felt like too long. The knuckles were white. She looked up from them abruptly and met his eyes. They were watchful. She nodded vigorously and then, without knowing why, shook her head in self-contradiction. 'There is and there isn't,' she said at last.

He smiled a small smile that suddenly made him look very young. 'It's not unusual to find oneself in two minds at once.'

'Or three or four,' Leo muttered.

'That, too. Would you like to lie down?' he asked after another protracted pause. 'It sometimes makes things easier. Just tell me anything that comes into your mind.'

Bastard, Leo thought. 'I don't want to lie down.'

'That's fine, too.'

'The thing is, I'm not sure I'm in the right place.'

'What would the right place be?'

She shrugged.

'You can always come two or three times and decide after that if this is a right place. See if this is the kind of conversation that suits you.'

'Conversation?' Leo's voice rose in contestatory zeal. 'Surely that implies that two people are talking?'

'Aren't we?'

She didn't answer.

'You assume that analysts or therapists or what-ever you choose to call us don't talk back?'

'My stepfather . . .' She stumbled. She hadn't intended to say that, but now she felt impelled to finish. 'My stepfather . . . he's an analyst . . . he doesn't talk back.'

He waited for her to go on and, when she didn't, urged her. 'Tell me about him.'

She waved her hand. 'He's irrelevant.'

'Except that he doesn't talk back.'

'Professionally. Otherwise he talks non-stop.'

Daniel watched her avert the grin that had leapt to her face, and saw it settle into a scowl. He couldn't quite locate the source of the discomfort she provoked in him. It wasn't just the opening lie. 'Perhaps we're as different as our patients are,' he ventured.

She studied him mutely.

'Have you ever been in any kind of therapy before?'

Her hair flew with the violence of her denial.

'Well, it's up to you whether we go on. We may not suit each other. You can always shop around.'

'Shop? What would I be shopping for? Mangoes, apples, prickly pears? Is there a job description for the ideal analyst? Something like, "Great listener, perfectly tolerant, highly intuitive. Wise and wonderful. All problems cured."'

Daniel let himself laugh. 'Oh no, and certainly not the last. Not with me.'

'So what do you offer?'

'You'd need to tell me first what you're looking for. Maybe, just maybe, I can help you understand something. Your relationships . . .'

'I hate that word.'

'Find another.'

'It all sounds a bit iffy, this work you do.'

'It can be. But there are other people you can see. Many others. I can give you some names.' He rose abruptly and strode towards the desk at the far end of the room.

'No, no.' Leo's voice was suddenly soft with loss. 'I didn't mean any of that. I don't know what got into me. I . . . I'd like to stay, to give it a try.' She waited for him to turn back towards her and, when he did so, she added, 'You were recommended to me by a

123

friend. A good friend. Isabel Morgan. I trust her.' She studied him carefully. Did she imagine the tension in his face, the slight shiftiness? 'You remember her, of course,' she said firmly, then paused at her choice of words. It came to her that remembering already conjured up a death. She shivered.

'Would it relax you to lie down?'

'You do know Isabel Morgan?'

'I really can't talk to anybody about other patients,' he said gently.

'I'm worried about her.'

Daniel had a sudden sense of the atmosphere around him lightening. Before it had been thick, clotted with suspicion, which cast him into a dubious role. Did she always treat strangers that way, attesting first of all to her own greater knowledge? Maybe that's what the lie had been about. A confirmation of her own greater authority.

He watched her recline, slip her shoes off with a neat, dutiful gesture and tuck her toes against the edge of the sofa. The posture gave her an air of fragility. It was hard to believe that Isabel had indeed sent her to him. If so, the gift could only be a poisoned chalice. Perhaps for both of them.

'I'm very worried about her.' She turned her face to him, resting it on her hand. Wary eyes examined him.

'And you're worried about your daughter.'

'Yes. No.' Flustered by the sudden analogy, Leo protested. 'That's not the same. Not at all the same.' There was no link between Becca and Isabel. Of that she was certain. He was deflecting her. He knew something. She would have to play the game.

She turned away from him and looked up at the ceiling. It needed a coat of paint. On her side the books climbed up too high and hid the moulding, which emerged again above the door in a dusty geometry of stems and leaves.

'What is the worry like?' The voice now seemed to come from some indistinguishable point behind her.

'What is the worry like?' she repeated in a murmur. Her lids felt heavy. She let them droop. 'The worry . . . It's like a dog preying on me. A large-toothed gargoyle attacking my throat so that I can't breathe freely. Or see. It looms there, just at my head, yapping. Blocks my vision.'

'But it's smaller than you?'

'Smaller, yes.' Leo mused. 'But I can't see round it.'

'It blocks your vision.'

'While it's yapping, the plane stays up.'

'The plane stays up?'

'Yes.'

It was her worry that had kept the plane up all the way to England, not the engines. Just the constant vigilant worry that it would plunge, that one of the wings would burst into flame, that it would collide with another plane, that one of the windows would shatter and they would all be siphoned out, like so much dust into the void. Worry acting like homoeopathic magic. She felt that on every flight. Everyone felt like that. The energy of 200 people worrying in unison made jet travel possible.

How odd, this lying here thinking in non sequiturs. Not thinking, it was too stupid for that, but just letting musings float amidst long, watery silences. Yet in the presence of another. A stranger. Where was he?

The voice came in, just on time, as if he could read her thoughts. 'So the worry keeps you up. Keeps you going?'

'Maybe,' she murmured, not quite sure what he meant.

'Your worrying about your daughter keeps you up, keeps you going?'

Leo lurched up to confront him. 'Are you saying I worry for my own benefit?'

He sat there, perfectly still. There were no spectacles now, and his eyes looked very dark, at once piercing and expressionless. It took too long for him to respond, so she repeated her question, which was also an accusation. At last he replied with slow enunciation.

'In this room, Leonora, you say. I don't say. Though sometimes, I repeat.'

She couldn't think of a retort, so she looked at the books behind him. The spine of a Raymond Chandler she recognized leapt out at her. There were more beside it, and next to them a whole long row of detective novels. 'You have a taste for murder,' she said, a hint of menace in her voice.

He let her comment hang. At last he said, 'Following up clues is part of my work, but I'm afraid our time is up.'

'Really? Already.'

'You were late.'

Something in her snapped. 'You're very smug.'

'So you won't be coming back?'

She slipped her feet blindly into her shoes. She hadn't found out anything. Nothing concrete. 'My friend Isabel,' she began.

He cut her off. 'It's time. I'm sorry.'

'I want to come back. Tomorrow.'

He shook his head.

His hair was too long. Isabel had been right.

'Wednesday. At the same time, if you like. And

126

Friday. After that, you can tell me whether you want to go on. You can leave your address on the hall table.'

'For the bill?'

He nodded. 'I charge forty pounds a session.'

He turned towards his desk.

Leo knew she had been dismissed. She grabbed her coat from the chair. She couldn't let him just get away with it like that. 'Isabel has disappeared,' she declared, her tone as incisive as a punishing schoolmistress. 'We have to find her. Do you know where she is?'

He veered towards her. There was a sudden passion in his face. It transformed him, gave him a menacing edge. But his voice was still even. 'I don't. I'm sorry. I told the police. If that's what you're here for, there's nothing I can do for you.'

Leo raced down the first flight of stairs, then paused at the landing. She didn't believe him. No. She walked slowly down the next flight. As she took a pad from her bag and ripped a sheet of paper out, she heard a dialling tone, the beep, beep of a number being punched in. On impulse she opened the front door and slammed it hard. Quietly, she crept back up to the landing and listened.

'Paola, it's Daniel Lukas. Give me a ring. After nine, if you can.'

She heard a click and, after a moment, the resonant tones of a full-bodied soprano filled the house. Leo took a deep breath, tiptoed down the stairs and, with a glance over her shoulder, opened a door at the bottom. It gave on to a room not unlike the one she had left in its shape and assortment of sofas and tables. But here there were pictures on the walls, oils in wild fauve colours, all of them, it seemed at a first glance, by the same artist. At the garden end, beneath the bay window, stood a desk, and next to it an old-fashioned metal filing cabinet. The sight of it set up an irresistible temptation.

One step towards it and the music stopped. From behind her she heard voices. She retraced her steps and, as quietly as she could, opened the external door. A young woman and a child were coming up the short flight of stairs. She nodded at them. The small boy stared at her from eyes so wide they dwarfed his thin face. She tried a smile, which found none in return, and raced towards the high street. A piping voice followed her. 'Who is she? Who is she?'

As she turned the corner, Leo wondered who indeed she was. A woman who lied, who blatantly broke into the privacy of others, whose palms were sweaty despite the chill of the afternoon wind. A woman who couldn't reconstruct much of what she had said, or what had been said to her, in the last hour, as if Alzheimer's had suddenly kicked in with a vengeance. Funny that.

Without noticing she had made a decision, she found herself in the café at the top of the hill. She ordered a cappuccino from a spiky-haired foreign waitress and reached for her pack of cigarettes. She was smoking far too much, more than she would ever dare permit herself in New York. She inhaled deeply and watched the smoke curl into a little cloud just above her head, like one of the bubbles in her strip. 'He knows something,' she wrote into it.

Of that much, if nothing else, she was certain. Daniel Lukas was definitely hiding something about Isabel. It had been evident in the guilty passion of the face he had turned on her. Whatever resources of duplicity it cost, she would find out what it was.

As for the rest, little in the session had gone as she'd anticipated. She had imagined a barrage of psychobabble or near-total silence. There had been neither. Nor was there any talk of sex. Instead, it now came back to her, there had been a condemnation of her worrying. Just like Jeff. She had only used the worry about Becca as a banal opening gambit, and he had used it to hit her in the face. What was the point of paying a shrink if all one got in return was the re-iteration of a former husband's blame? But never mind that. She wasn't there for herself.

Leo sipped her coffee, which was satisfyingly strong, and reached into her bag. She pushed aside the small packet she had bought in Tottenham Court Road that morning, a tiny recorder that would play back Isabel's tapes. She would do that tonight. Now she took out her pad. An unevenly ripped sheet reminded her that she had failed to leave Daniel Lukas her address. Better perhaps. It might have been unwise to give him Isabel's, and the New York one would have raised another kind of suspicion.

For a moment she found herself wondering whether Daniel Lukas dealt with children as well as adults. The small boy with the vast eyes must have been his next patient. Such sadness in that delicate face. She hoped he would treat the child less abrasively than he had dealt with her.

She leafed through to the action list she had made at the weekend, just after she had finally got hold of Hamish Macgregor. The man had been aggressively rude, effing here, there and everywhere, telling her he fucking well didn't know where fucking Isabel had got herself, and who the fuck cared, and that she had better stop leaving fucking messages for him. In this cursing diatribe, she had read all the signs of a jilted lover. But what did jilted lovers who sounded tipsy at three o'clock on a Saturday afternoon do to the women who had jilted them? It was this chilling thought that had decided her. She had rung the police again. This time she got through to PC Collins, who was surprisingly solicitous. Maybe the bristle-haired youth behaved better when he didn't have a superior there in front of whom to play tough guy.

Leo had told him about Hamish Macgregor. She had also told him about Isabel's use of the pseudonym, Iris Morgenstern, and how some man from Origen had followed her back to London from Oxfordshire. For some reason she didn't tell him about Christopher Norfolk, and how he had left the apartment on Friday morning before she had woken up, taking all of Isabel's letters from the gene-tech companies with him. Nor had he yet returned.

PC Collins had listened to her narrative, interspersing only a few questions here and there. At its end, he'd said he and Sergeant Drew would come round and see her again. She was grateful for that.

It was perhaps this minor triumph that had emboldened her to go upstairs and seek out Mike Newson. She wanted to talk to him again about Hamish Macgregor. But her ringing had produced a woman instead, a brunette with a pixyish face and a warm smile, who had ushered her in and instantly offered her coffee.

'Mike's away for a few days,' she'd said. 'We never quite manage to be in the same place at the same time. Probably why we get on so well.'

Leo had answered her grin with one of her own and looked around the loft in amazement. It was a symphony in hi-tech with shiny tables and tubular furniture and a vast black-and-white blow-up of a surreal New York skyline on one wall. A curving aluminium staircase led up to a roof-top floor over-arched by a bubble of glass.

'He's pretty good at decor, too.' Rosie Tanner had introduced herself as she ground beans in a curved aluminium cylinder. 'You're Isabel's friend, aren't you?'

They had chatted and, for the first time, Leo felt that someone shared her concern. 'I tell you what,' Rosie had offered. 'If Isabel's not back by whenever it is she was due to return from the States, that's when we really have to start worrying. She'd never leave that Beast of hers in the kennels for a day longer than promised. She loves that cat. She thinks it understands her when she speaks and knows what she's thinking when she's silent.'

Leo ordered a bottle of mineral water and lit a second cigarette. However sensible Rosie's words had been, they did little to still the apprehension which mounted in her with each passing day. To do nothing but wait, she felt certain, was to invite the worst. When she had asked Rosie about how Isabel had been over the weeks before her disappearance, Rosie had confided that Isabel hadn't been at her best. 'I'm sure it was to do with her mother's death. Two years ago, when my father went, I was right over the edge, not that I realized until later. Maybe Isabel decided to go east, rather than west. To Australia, I mean. To revisit childhood sites and sort herself out.'

Leo had pondered this possibility for the length of the weekend and had tried it out on the two friends of Isabel's she'd met. The first, an anthropologist at London University, had told her he was certain Isabel was fine. When he had last seen her – a month ago it must have been, time moved so fast these days – Isabel had had the look of secretive excitement about her that meant she was hot on the trail of something or other. No, he didn't know what. Isabel wouldn't divulge and they had spent most of the time talking about his own last trip to Papua New Guinea. There had been no mention of her making a visit to Sydney.

The second friend, a fellow journalist, had shown a little more disquiet. She'd confided that she thought Isabel had been at something of a loose end since her book on childhood had come out; really since she had given up her regular column. Books were fine and well, she said, with a touch of acid in her voice, but someone as gifted with people as Isabel shouldn't be forced to be on her own for too long.

'You think she felt lonely?' Leo had asked softly. 'Was there no-one in her life?'

'Oh, I didn't mean that. There's always someone in Isabel's life.'

'Any idea who?'

The woman shook her head. 'No. She was being a little cagey when I last saw her. No-one special, I imagine. And we spent most of our time talking about Buddhism, of all things. Maybe she's gone and holed up in a monastery.'

'Without telling anyone?'

'She probably told someone. That shrink of hers for a start.'

'You don't think she might have gone back to Australia for a second visit?'

'To see her aunt, you mean?'

'Maybe.'

The woman shrugged. 'She wasn't long back when I last saw her. But it's possible. She was certainly fretting about her, I know that. A little angry with her about something, too. But she wouldn't talk.'

Leo had stayed up into the small hours hoping that Christopher Norfolk would return so she could grill him about Isabel's aunt and get her phone number. It surprised her how little she really knew about the life of the woman who was her closest friend. But then, if the situations were reversed, Isabel wouldn't have Leo's everyday points of reference, either – her mother's number, her editor's . . . Life was like that, all parcelled up. And the Atlantic was a big ocean.

When Norfolk didn't turn up, Leo had resorted to Isabel's letters of condolence from Australia. She found one with a telephone number printed on it and dialled it straight away. There had been no reply on any of the occasions she had tried.

Nor was there any word from Isabel on her answering machine in New York.

Leo looked down at her list again and studied the names, together with the brief notes she had made next to them. She added the name Paola beside that of Daniel Lukas. She couldn't place where, but she knew that she had seen or heard the name before. She focused on the name at the top of her list, Hamish Macgregor, and the words 'jilted lover?' she had written next to it. A memory sprang into her mind: Isabel at a party – way back when it must have been, because she could see Jeff clearly at her side. Isabel was laughing, her face radiant. 'The current boyfriend told me to go and get shrunk 'cause I can't sleep with the light off. What he's really enraged by is the fact that I kick him out of bed before dawn. Don't want to wake up with him there, do I!'

As if someone had pushed a fast-forward button, the laughing face underwent a metamorphosis. It was

133

suddenly very white, the eyes protruding in terror.

Leo leapt up to pay her bill and wiped the image away. That's what worry was about, she told herself, producing the worst imaginable picture so as to prevent its realization. Daniel Lukas had refused to understand that. Maybe shrinks were so busy delving into the past that they had no idea how people went about arming themselves for the future.

Though she wasn't altogether certain it was true, the thought gave Leo a moment's pleasure.

Daniel Lukas heaved the small boy onto his shoulders, waited for the 'giddy-up' and cantered towards the net which hung from the back of the house.

'OK. Now. Get it in there. Yes!'

The black-and-white ball looped through the net and bounced onto the grass. The boy squealed and clapped his hands. 'I did it! I did it!'

'You did.' Daniel let him scramble for the ball and then hugged him close. 'You want to try again?'

Robbie nodded, his face too serious. 'I'll see how many I can get out of ten.'

'Three would be good.'

'I got three last time. Six would be better.'

'We'll try for six then.'

They played. When Robbie reached the magical score of six, he beamed. 'Shall I try one more?'

'One more it is.'

The ball teetered round the edge of the basket and edged through.

'Yes!' Robbie raised his fist in football-fan triumph. 'We did it, Pops.'

'Did it brilliantly. And now it's time for some food. I can smell cooking.' Daniel took his son by the hand

and led him through the garden door into the kitchen.

'I wish Mummy could have seen me.'

Daniel held his breath. The boy hadn't mentioned his mother for some weeks now and, though he never wanted to force the talk, he was always pleased when Robbie initiated it. 'So do I. She would have been proud.'

'That lady had hair like Mummy.'

'Which lady?'

Robbie cast him a suspicious look as he clambered into the chair at one end of the long refectory table. 'The one who was coming out of the house when we got home. Didn't she, Martina?' He addressed the young jean-clad woman who was positioning a large bowl between them.

'She did. Almost like your mummy's.'

'I thought she'd gone by the time you arrived,' Daniel murmured. He thanked the au pair with a nod and forked pasta onto three plates.

'No. And it was just like Mummy's,' Robbie insisted. 'Didn't you notice?'

'Now that you mention it . . .'

'You've forgotten Mummy,' the child accused him.

The comment surprised him. He was about to deny his son's statement, but he held back. The boy was telling him something. Telling him with the inevitable attendant guilt that he, himself, occasionally forgot about his mother. He tried to choose his words with care. 'We can't remember all the time, Robbie,' he said slowly. 'We couldn't get on with things if we did. But that doesn't mean we forget. I haven't forgotten. You haven't forgotten.'

'I've forgotten her nose.'

'Nose?' Daniel laughed. 'We can look at some pictures later, if you like.'

'OK.'

After he had tucked his son into bed and they had read two of his favourite picture books together, Daniel went back up to the consulting room that doubled as his study. He was troubled by the fact that his new patient had overlapped with his son's return home. He had thought he'd timed it better. Robbie must have been first out of school today and covered the short distance home in record time.

With Eva's death, he had decided to move his consulting room into the house. It saved travel time and, since he had cut down the number of private patients he saw, it also saved on expenditure. With careful scheduling there was no need for his professional life to intrude on the boy's home life. That was essential, both for his ever-fanciful patients and for his equally impressionable child. But today there had been a blip. Not that the effect it had produced had been altogether bad. Robbie had made use of it in his own way. And after dinner, when they'd gone upstairs to look at photographs, they had both managed to laugh at a picture in which Eva was pulling one of her funny faces.

More than ten months had passed since the cancer had taken her over and away. Ten months during which mourning had driven them over its bumpy course. At first Robbie had been frantic, throwing himself violently into activity, endlessly visiting friends, refusing any conversation which might have anything to do with his mother's death, denying the loss. Then a kind of depression had set in. He was listless, absent-minded, short-tempered, refusing food. Daniel had made him talk then, abstractly at first, about plants and animals dying, and then increasingly about his feelings, about what he missed of his mother, her hugs or grumpiness or piano playing.

Daniel had told his son that sometimes he, himself, felt so angry about being abandoned that he wanted to throw things. It didn't seem fair. And the boy had taken his cue and thrown a toy monster across the room and, whether by accident or intention, had managed to shatter a framed photograph of his mother. There had been tears after that and, little by little, more talk. And now, gradually, he hoped that the boy's precarious sense of power would come into perspective. He knew its wild fluctuations. Badly dented, and he was guilty of not having been able to keep his mother alive; overblown, and he was responsible for killing her. Thankfully, Martina had stayed on with them and provided another point of continuity, a cheerful and robust presence, often more substantial than his own.

Nonetheless, although his son's chance meeting with Leonora Gould had had no adverse effects today, if she did decide to return, he would have to move her hour forward. He studied his desk diary, with its neat diagonal lines through Tuesday and Thursday afternoons, which he spent in family therapy at the Marlborough, and decided that next week he could offer her the morning hour he usually kept free for writing. It was the writing, alongside Robbie, which had kept him going over this last, difficult year. Without them he might have gone off and done a stint in Africa with Médecins Sans Frontières or some similar organization. He smiled at his own fantasy.

It wasn't that Daniel didn't like his work. He was devoted to it. It was simply that, in these months since Eva's death, or perhaps earlier, when her illness was taking its final toll, he had felt he wasn't altogether in control of his own responses. He hadn't done particularly well today, either. She was an interesting woman, this Leonora Gould. All that belligerence erupting in odd places. She obviously hated the fact that she had decided to take the step across his threshold, the little leap of faith into analysis, despite her evident hostility for his profession. He tried to think if the name Gould conjured up any articles. Her stepfather, she had said.

No, at the end things had gone slightly awry. It was when she had pressed him about Isabel Morgan.

He let the name he had kept at bay for hours invade his consciousness. He had mishandled that, too, at the last. Things should never have been allowed to take the course they had. It had all been mixed up with the period of Eva's dying and he wasn't in charge of himself. Then, too, Isabel was such a fascinating patient that the rules didn't seem to apply. Though he had prepared himself, he had never quite believed the end would come before they were both ready for it. Nor had he counted on the manner of her return. And now she was evidently in trouble.

He covered his face with his hands and sat there for a moment, letting the full shame of that last meeting swamp him.

When the phone rang, he reached for the receiver with something like relief. Paola Webster's resonant accented tones fell upon his ear.

'Paola, hello. Thanks for ringing back.'

'It's nothing, stranger. I am happy to hear from you. Very happy. You leave me for too long.'

'We should get together. Have a late supper, or a

drink. Some time this week, if you can make it.'

'OK. You have an opening at the Marlborough, maybe? I've been waiting.'

Daniel swallowed. 'No, it's not that. But let's catch up. I could manage tomorrow evening or Thursday.'

'Wednesday would be better for me.'

'I have a meeting on Wednesday. Sorry.'

'Of course. How could I forget. The Institute.' Paola spat out the site of his professional affiliation as if it were a synonym for shit.

Daniel let it ride. 'What about tomorrow, then?'

'OK. Tomorrow is good. We go to nice restaurant I discover. In Islington.' She pronounced it with an accent on the last syllable, so that it sounded like an exotic location. 'Euphorium. A good name for us, no?'

Couldn't be better, Daniel thought with a sinking feeling.

6

The diaphanous gown restored a radiant Imogen to womanhood. She walked towards her erratic father and placed herself between him and her jealous husband. Together they took their bows. Around them stood the malevolent queen and her spoiled son, the two brothers lost and found again, the treacherous Iachimo, who, hidden in a casket, had stolen his way into Imogen's chamber, and all the lords and ladies and Roman tribunes of Cymbeline's court, not to mention the wordy soothsayer.

Leo, seated at the far end of the third row of the Barbican Theatre, joined in the prolonged applause. It was a strange play, *Cymbeline*, she reflected as the lights went up. The complications of its plot were so contorted that she was uncertain whether she had grasped any more of it than the fact that the pure, ever-faithful Imogen had been betrayed by a scheming trickster who had succeeded in convincing her husband that he had seduced her. Jealousy, in Shakespeare's late plays, followed hard on the heels of love and overtook it in one fierce bound of the male imagination. She remembered Leontes in *The Winter's Tale* and Lear and, before that, Othello, and how their fear of losing control of their women or children unleashed a loss of self-control, a destabilization of the mind as well as their regimes.

Fears and fantasies could do all that. What was it Daniel Lukas had said to her about worry? She pushed him out of her mind.

At the theatre bookshop, she stopped and bought a *Cymbeline* poster for Becca, together with an RSC T-shirt. Whatever her feelings about the play, it had done her good to see it. Like a laboratory rat released from a relentless treadmill into the byways of the city, she felt as if she had taken a sojourn from herself and the round of her obsessive fears. Maybe, just maybe, when she went back to the loft now, she would find a smiling Isabel returned to her on the whim of a master playwright.

Leo matched her pace to that of the crowds leaving the Barbican foyer. Outside, they dispersed so quickly that, without knowing how it had happened, she was suddenly alone on the darkened street. Her heels set up an echo behind her. So resonant was their clack that she wanted to turn superstitiously to see whether she might not be following herself. At the corner, the sight of an illuminated office block relieved her of the impulse. She wound her way towards Moorgate amidst stray papers and litter driven by the wind the canyons of the streets created, and wondered again at how empty the night-time of this vast city could be. At the cemetery, she broke into a run and sped the rest of the distance home. She had an odd feeling she would be pleased to see even Christopher Norfolk.

The door of the loft stood slightly ajar. For a moment she thought her wish had been answered. She pushed it open and called out, 'Norfolk.'

There was no answer. She was about to try again when something alerted her. Was it the lack of brightness inside, or the papers oddly scattered on the floor at her feet? She picked them up. Letters addressed to Isabel. How had they found their way here? She swallowed hard and, holding her breath, tiptoed along the narrow passage. The street light cast long murky shadows across the living room, making the sofas loom. But everything here seemed to be as she had left it.

From beneath the study door came a bar of light. Surely she hadn't left one on, nor shut the door. She slipped off her shoes and walked silently towards the room. With a burst of bravado, she pushed open the door and shouted, 'Norfolk. What the hell are you doing in here?'

The sight that met her eyes made her take several steps backwards. The room looked as if it had been hit by a hurricane. A white sea of papers covered the floor. Box files floated astride them like so many broken-backed creatures. In a corner, tapes and CDs rose into a rocky hillock, banked by photographs. Isabel's drowning face stared out at her.

Who could have done this? Who? The question shrieked through Leo's mind so loudly she was certain she was screaming it. But she couldn't be because, behind her in the distance, she heard a sound. She raced out into the living room. No-one. There was no light, either from beneath Isabel's bedroom door or from her own, which stood ajar. Her skin beneath her clothes felt icy, every pore standing to attention. She inched towards Isabel's bedroom, prodded the door and switched on the light. No-one was there, but the panel of the sliding wardrobe stood open. Shoes and boots poured from it. The drawers of the mesh rack were out, too, the clothes tumbled. On the bed lay a large upended box she had never noticed before, its contents scattered beneath it. More papers, a vertigo of papers.

Suddenly the lights went out and steely hands pushed her, shoving her so hard that she was propelled against the open drawers. She screamed, sprawled forward and fell against the floor with a thud as she tried to peer back at her assailant. She had an impression of towering bulk, a gleam of hair and then the mesh stand was tumbling on top of her and her hands were over her head, anticipating another blow. She waited, cowering, waited for what felt like too long before she realized her attacker was no longer behind her. Soundlessly, she extricated herself from the jumble and rubbed her legs where she could feel the bruises forming. From somewhere she heard a click.

With an abrupt recognition of the sound, she headed deliberately towards the front door. Shut. The intruder had slipped out. Only then, as she took a deep breath, did fear jolt through her. Movement became difficult. Her heart was beating too fast. She couldn't bring herself to cross the threshold and go after him. She double-locked the door, looked around her at a loss. Like a somnambulist, she slowly undid her coat, one button at a time, her fingers strangers to the act.

Gathering her wits, she moved to the front window and peered out into the night. A man was making his way round the corner. Could it be the intruder? She could see no more than a shape and a raincoat, and then he was gone.

Clumsily, she retraced her steps. The bathroom door on her left was ajar. That was where he must have hidden when he had heard her on the stairs. She had walked right past him on her way in. She

143

shuddered again and looked around the room in horror. The medicine chest had spewed up its contents. Ransacked jars and packets littered the sink. The pots which had stood on the window sill had been toppled into the bathtub. Soot-brown earth speckled with tiny crushed seedlings lay heaped against the white porcelain.

Leo caught a glimpse of her own ashen face in the mirror, and recoiled as if it belonged to a stranger. She sank onto the nearest sofa. It made no sense. The valuables were still in place – the music system, video and television all ranged on their usual shelves. So what had been taken? Jewellery, perhaps. She forced herself to go back into the bedroom. Isabel kept her jewellery in a black lacquered box which sat on the base of her bedside table. It was still there, seemingly untouched. She was about to reach for it when she had second thoughts. The police. This time they wouldn't dare to tut-tut her.

She went to use the phone in the ransacked office. It was only as she was reporting the break-in that she noticed. She shuffled the strewn papers. No. It was gone, definitely gone. Her laptop was no longer on the desk.

One missing item and all this mess. The sentence played over and over in her mind like a refrain. All this mess for only one missing item: an ordinary PC laptop. Not even a particularly expensive one. She pulled the blind down with a sharp tug and, as she did so, it came to her with a sudden, swift clarity. This was no ordinary break-in. Someone had come here with a specific purpose, come for something he already knew existed. And it was something that could be stored in computer files or which existed on paper – Isabel's letters scattered by the front door.

Leo sat and watched the policeman make the rounds of the loft. There were two men tonight, and neither of them was PC Collins. One of them had fixed her a cup of tea, asked her whether there was any brandy in the house, and had thrown a shot into the hot brew. He had told her just to sit there and try to relax while they had a good look. Leo had obeyed. Once she'd told them what had happened and alerted them to the previous report about Isabel's disappearance, she didn't seem to have much strength for anything else.

Tears slid down her cheeks. She moved to wipe them. Her hands were shaking. Shock. That was what it was. All the adrenalin that had kept her buoyant had vanished down the plughole when she'd splashed cold water on her face in an effort to compose herself.

'Sorry to trouble you.' The policeman who had made the tea perched beside her and met her eyes. 'Can you recall whether you double-locked the door before you went out?'

Leo stared at him. His features wouldn't coalesce into a face. She made an effort to remember. 'Double-lock?' she repeated stupidly. 'No, I don't know . . . I don't think so. You see, Isabel . . . The front door, downstairs, is very solid.'

'Of course. We were just wondering if it might be an inside job.'

'Inside job.'

'You know. Someone who had the keys. There are no signs of breaking and entry on the outside door and—'

'Someone who had the keys.' She was turning into a parrot. An image of Christopher Norfolk passed

145

before her eyes. But why would he bother? He had his own computer. In any case, he was meant to be staying here. But he wasn't staying here. Her mind refused clarity.

'A neighbour, perhaps?'

'A neighbour?' The policeman's face suddenly swam into focus. He was black. It was a kind face. Not young. With generous eyes. 'Yes. Yes. The upstairs neighbour has the keys. Mike Newson. But . . . I saw a man on the street . . . afterwards. I'm not sure.'

'We'll go and have a word with your neighbour in any case.'

'I'll come, too.'

'If you're really up to it.'

Leo nodded and carefully placed her cup on the coffee table. She was grateful for the hand he put out to her as she lifted herself from the sofa. She had a sudden vision of what it would be like to be old and find your legs trembling beneath your own weight.

They walked slowly up the stairs.

'It's a little late, isn't it?'

'Just gone midnight. Still, best to find out what we can straight away.'

After three insistent rings, punctuated by pauses, Rosie opened the door the width of the latch. 'What is it?' Her voice was disgruntled.

'It's me. Leo,' Leo said from behind the police-man's girth. 'There's been trouble downstairs.'

Rosie unlatched the door. She was wrapped in a white dressing gown, a towel round her head.

'I was in the shower.' Her eyes sought out Leo's. 'What's happened?'

The policeman pre-empted Leo's response. 'Sorry to trouble you so late, ma'am. There's been a break-in. We need to know whether you saw or heard anything.'

Rosie shook her head slowly. 'You poor thing,' she said to Leo. 'Come on in. Sit down.' She looked up at the officer. 'I haven't heard a thing. I got in about eight, turned the music on, pottered about in the kitchen and watched some telly. Did they take much?'

Leo shook her head. 'But he made a terrible mess. And my laptop's—'

The policeman cut her off. 'You have the keys to the downstairs flat?'

'Mike, my partner, keeps them. I don't know quite where. He's away. On a shoot. Filming,' she corrected herself. 'He's due back on Wednesday. Thursday, if there's any delay. He'll probably ring in at some point.'

'Will you check with him? About the keys. He may have misplaced them. Or . . .'

'Sure.' Rosie wasn't paying attention to him. She was staring at Leo. 'You're not looking too good,' she murmured. 'How about if I pull on some clothes and help you clean up?'

'Not tonight, ma'am. Better to leave things as they are. We'll want the CID here in the morning. But if you can keep an eye on Mrs Holland while I pop down to the other neighbours . . .'

'She can spend the night.' Rosie gave Leo an encouraging smile. 'We can keep each other company.'

'That would be best.' A look of complicity passed between them.

'How about it, Leo?'

Leo was too tired to protest. She was also grateful. She didn't want to be alone, didn't want to sleep in

147

her bedroom, where the suitcases had been turned out and left lying where they fell. No. Nor did she want to set foot in any of the shadowy spaces through which the intruder had passed, leaving havoc in his wake.

An hour later, Leo was stretched out on a bed decked in pristine white cotton. The blind in front of her had a New York cityscape printed on it, so that she might have been at home in Manhattan, looking out at a familiar view. But the bedside lamp, a towering needle-pointed triangle, cast an altogether more sophisticated glow and, on the wall beside her, Mike Newson's eerie mannequins displayed their surreal limbs amidst refracted buildings. She switched off the light to block them out, and thought of Isabel, who always slept with the light on. Isabel, with her bright spirit and incisive wit. Isabel, who was afraid of nothing except the dark. For very good reason, Leo thought, given that her life was prey to the horror of pillaging intruders.

She was now more certain than ever that the break-in was no random act. This man had been no ordinary thief in search of valuables. He had wanted something Isabel had. But what? And who was he?

Taking her cue from the police, Leo had said none of this to Rosie, although the woman had been sweetness itself. She had given her fruit cake and whisky and tea, and had chatted all the while about her mother, who made the best cake going, and who had been burgled last year, but the insurance had come up trumps, so that she had finally got a modern sound system and a huge television. She told her, too, about her job in the Victoria and Albert Museum's costume department, and how she was sorry but she had to

148

clock in early tomorrow, though if Leo wanted to sleep late, there was no problem.

Leo closed her eyes. Sleep came swiftly, as if she had waited too long for it. And with it came dreams. A chaos of dreams as unruly as her day.

She was lying in a narrow four-poster bed, a girl's bed, all white and ruffled, in the centre of a room so large she couldn't make out its limits. Her eyes were closed, but she could clearly see two servants in Elizabethan dress carrying a casket into the room and setting it down near her. When they left, the lid of the casket opened with a slight creak. Inside it lay Isabel, sleeping peacefully, her hair strewn with wild flowers, like Ophelia. No, no, not Ophelia, dead Ophelia. Not Isabel, either, for a figure suddenly emerged from the box. A man. She couldn't identify him. He prowled around the room, stared at her supine form and bent close to her. She didn't move or let on that she knew he was there, not even when he touched her breast.

When he turned away and started to rifle through the chest of drawers in the middle distance, he suddenly grew familiar. She recognized the way his shoulders moved as he scattered the contents of the drawers on the floor. He bent to retrieve a small pile of letters. They were tied with a pink bow. Love letters, letters he had written. He. Daniel Lukas. He was very tall and brutally broad-shouldered. An arrogant smile appeared on his face as he stuffed the letters into his jacket pocket.

He wasn't finished yet. He tiptoed towards her, watched to see if she would open her eyes and, when she didn't, he was off to the other side of the large room, to another chest. He whisked it open and voided its contents, which flew here and there.

149

Becca's teddy bear and her white seal fell close to her. She almost got up then. She wanted to shout at him, but her mouth was too dry. He was holding something up to the light, a grey slant of morning light which came through the window. She could make out the object now: a small square. A diskette, that's what it was. He couldn't take that. She needed to know what was on it. Her mouth moved, but it made no sound.

He was coming towards her again. But now it wasn't him. This man had a narrow face and slicked-back hair, like her neighbour. His mouth curled in a scowl. A light flashed. He was taking her photograph. She didn't want it to be taken. She would be transformed into a mannequin with glossy unmoving limbs. Yes, it had happened. She couldn't move her legs. She screamed. His hand fell over her mouth, turning her scream into a squeal.

'Hush,' he ordered her. 'Hush now, Iris.'

'I'm not Iris,' she wanted to protest, but couldn't speak through his choking hand.

'That's a good girl. Now, you just do everything I say. Everything.'

The voice had nothing of Mike Newson's South London drawl. It had a threatening timbre. It was the toad from Origen. Or was it? The sardonic laugh that came from him belonged to someone else. Norfolk, Christopher. He dragged her out of the bed and forced her into the casket. The lid shut on top of her with a definitive click. The air was thick. It was difficult to breathe. In the distance, she could hear a sound coming closer – the sullen chopping of a helicopter's blades. Terror enveloped her as surely as darkness.

She woke abruptly, the sour taste of fear on her

tongue, the images of the dream still cascading through her. It took her a few moments to put herself together again, to realize that she wasn't in a box but merely in a strange bed in a strange room. Clumsily, she reached for the lamp switch and poured water from the jug Rosie had left for her. She was as parched as if she had just survived a trek through the desert. She drank and meditated on her dream's vivid logic, the casket she had imported from *Cymbeline*, along with the evening's more dangerous intruder. And then she was asleep again, awake only with the morning's sunlight.

Rosie had written a note to her, clipped it to a refrigerator magnet. 'Help yourself to anything you like. There's a ton of cereal in the cupboard, coffee next to it and lots of bread in the bin. Don't let cops and mess get you down. See you later.'

Leo perched on a stool at the free-standing plinth of a kitchen counter and spooned crunchy nut cornflakes into her mouth as avidly as if she were Becca on a school morning. In the midst of last night's tumult, she had forgotten to eat again. But she felt fine now, able to cope. And she knew exactly what she was going to tell the police when they arrived with their crime-detection kit.

The apartment, when she let herself in, felt a good deal less spooky than it had the previous evening. Clear spring sunshine poured through the many windows. The crimson sofa was aflame with its own colour. She averted her eyes from any of the side rooms where the signs of greatest upheaval reigned. She only went into her own room to change swiftly into a fresh pullover and trousers, then she brewed some coffee. She had just finished pouring a cup when the doorbell rang. The videophone showed a police ID card. A gruff voice announced Detective Inspector John Faraday.

He was up the stairs almost as soon as she had opened the door, a pale, thin, gangly man in a nondescript windbreaker and corduroy trousers as ordinary as his face. In a crowd, he would have been indistinguishable. He flashed his card again as he pronounced her name with careful seriousness.

'Leonora Holland?'

'That's right. Come in.' She had the inane thought that he kept flashing his card because otherwise he would feel invisible.

'Like Leonora Carrington.'

She looked at him in surprise. Carrington was hardly a widely known artist. 'How did you guess? My mother was in love with her work, so she named me after her. That's probably why I started painting. The injunction of the name.' She stopped herself. What on earth was she doing giving her life history to this stranger?

'Which should have marked me out as a great scientist.' He gave her a shy smile. It dimpled his cheek. 'Is this one of yours, then?' He gestured at the wall where Isabel's bright abstract hung.

'No. I do strips these days. Cartoon strips.'

He nodded sagely. 'Well, this isn't Leonora C, either. No sprites. No big-haired women. I'm told you had a spot of bother last night,' he finished with no transition.

'Rather more than a spot, Inspector.' She led him into Isabel's office.

He whistled between his teeth. 'Any more?'

She led him through to the bedroom, then to her own room and the bathroom. 'And this is no

152

ordinary burglary, Inspector. The man was searching for something.'

'Any idea what it was? Or who he was? His eyes had moved around each room with a kind of mechanical precision, as if he were making mental snapshots. He bent for a moment to rub some of the earth that had fallen from the fractured pots between his fingers. He sniffed it like a terrier, then carefully examined the sliding mirror of the medicine cabinet. 'Was this open when you left home yesterday?'

Leo shook her head. 'I shouldn't think so. I don't usually come in here. I use the shower room.'

He nodded again. 'I suspect your villain wore gloves. Can't see any prints, but we'll have a dust later. So tell me what's missing?'

'Apart from my laptop, I don't really know. I was told not to touch anything last night, not that I'd necessarily know, in any case. You see, this isn't my place. It belongs to—'

'Isabel Morgan aka Iris Morgenstern. I know, I've been through the files. And you think last night's burglary is tied up with her disappearance?'

Leo nodded miserably, then shrugged. 'You see, the other day I was followed by this man, Kripps, from Origen. I'll show you their brochure. I'm afraid I was pretending to be my friend. He was very threatening.'

'You shouldn't be doing detective work on your own, Ms Holland. It can be dangerous.'

He said it with a kind air, but Leo couldn't quite restrain herself. 'Your . . . your colleagues wouldn't take me seriously.'

'Missing-person cases are tricky. This, on the other hand, is another kettle. I have a particular interest in what you might call the Green beat.'

153

She looked at him with a moment's suspicion. 'You work alone?'

He laughed. 'Only sometimes. I wanted to check this out.' He waved his arm rather regally in the direction of the rooms. 'So you think this Mr Kripps might have been yesterday's intruder?'

'I don't know. I didn't see him. I didn't know anyone was here until I was pushed.' Panic clutched at her stomach as she remembered.

'Don't think about it now. But let me try a description on you.' He pulled spectacles and a notebook from his pocket and leafed through it. 'Your ground-floor neighbour, a Mr Simon Porter, told us that when he got in yesterday evening, at around seven thirty, a motorcycle messenger came in just behind him. He told him he had a package for the fourth floor and rushed up the stairs. Mr Porter thought nothing of it. As far as he could estimate, given that the man was entirely clad in black leather, apart from his helmet, which was in his hands, he was in his mid to late twenties, had sandy hair, clipped short, and was about medium height, smaller than Mr Porter in any case. Does that sound anything like your Mr Kripps?'

Leo shook her head. 'Not at all. Mr Kripps is big, fat, middle aged and looks like a toad.' It gave her pleasure to say it.

Faraday chortled. 'You didn't take to him.'

'Not at all. But, Inspector, this is the third floor, not the fourth.'

'We don't really expect villains to tell the truth. I'll be checking it out with the people upstairs.'

'I guess Kripps could easily have sent a hired hand.'

'The question is, Ms Holland, what exactly for?

Your Isabel, or Iris, hadn't been working for them. There was nothing she could have taken. Unless you . . . Is there something you're not telling me, Ms Holland?'

Leo flushed. 'I don't think so. All I have are hunches. I suspect. No more than that. I know that Isabel was investigating something. Something to do with biotechnology and genetically modified foods, I think, and the people who experiment with them. That's why she used a false name.'

'What other companies did she go to?'

'She wrote to a number. I saw the letters. There was . . . I'll check it out. If the correspondence is still here.' She suddenly remembered Christopher Norfolk. She was about to say something when Faraday went on reflectively. 'You see, it seems to me that your intruder wasn't expecting anybody. He was taking his time. He didn't think anyone would be here.'

Leo saw some of her worst fears realized. Her voice rose an octave. 'So they're holding Isabel and felt free to ransack the place. He may even have had the keys. Maybe he still has them . . .'

'We mustn't jump to conclusions, Ms Holland. Tell you what, why don't you start going through the papers? You can put them away as you go. If there's anything interesting, or anything that seems to be missing, let me know. I'll start in the office. You take the bedroom. OK?'

'OK. But there's something else I should tell you, Inspector. Isabel was in analysis. Psychotherapy. You know how people talk in that situation. Well, I just have this hunch that her analyst knows something that might help us. But I don't know what.' Her dream came into her mind, and she was about to tell

Faraday that Daniel Lukas could equally well be their thief, but in the bright light of day the notion didn't sound plausible any more. And then the inspector would stop trusting her, would label her an hysterical American. She was used to the perpetual British ambivalence about the States. A fondness for American enthusiasm, openness and energy could flick in a split-second into an arrogant disdain for their over-the-topness, their innocence, their lack of irony, their stupidity.

'According to the file, he was rung. He had nothing to tell us about your friend's whereabouts. And we can't call him or his files in unless there's a crime.'

'And this isn't a crime?'

'Not the right crime.' He said it with a droll movement of the lips.

Detective Inspector John Faraday was a distinctly interesting man, Leo thought. 'Can I make you some coffee, Inspector? Or tea, if you'd prefer.'

'Coffee would be grand. Black, one sugar.'

After she had handed him his cup, she took her own into Isabel's bedroom and set to work. As she pulled the wire-mesh stand upright and folded her friend's clothes back into the drawers, she tried not to let the hovering black mood settle over her. She had to be matter-of-fact, meticulous. She had to think. Isabel would think. She wouldn't let a break-in with a little added violence overwhelm her. If the tables were turned and it was Leo who was missing, Isabel would be doggedly methodical in her efforts to find her. She wouldn't succumb to despair.

Leo folded clothes and kept back tears. There were certainly some items of underwear missing from Isabel's drawer. There were too few here for any woman to get by on. She rearranged a lacy black frill and tucked it under a more demure white. Isabel's underclothing wasn't consistent. It moved from plain, practical Jane to femme fatale. Like her, Leo thought. But the paucity of undergarments meant that Isabel had definitely packed for a trip. As she arranged the shoes that had been flung from the bottom racks of the wardrobe in a mad hunt for something, it came to her that the boots Isabel had bought when they were together last Christmas weren't there, either. They were thick black leather ankle boots with a low heel, intended for solid walking. Would she have packed them for their planned journey? Maybe. But her summer sandals all seemed to be there, and she'd have needed them on a trip to warmer climes.

Leo poked her head into the depths of the wardrobe. On the left hung an array of suits and dresses. She rifled through them and, at the far end, came across what were distinctly men's clothes – some suits, shirts, trousers. Left over by some visitor, she determined. Or perhaps they belonged to Christopher Norfolk. She pushed them aside. On the right were shelves containing an assortment of pullovers and blouses. None of the piles was particularly disarranged. The top one above her head, however, was empty. That was where the box, now on the bed, must originally have been positioned. It would explain why she hadn't noticed it in her first cursory look round. She had been superstitiously loath to invade Isabel's personal wardrobe.

Leo looked out the window. A week ago – though it felt much longer than that – she had stood amidst the broken shards of the vase she had given Isabel and imagined a violent intruder. The police had deflected her. Now the break-in *had* occurred, differently to how she had imagined. Yet she was still no closer to Isabel.

Outside, in the crisp spring sunlight, she saw two young women walking briskly down the narrow street. Glossy hair swinging to the rhythm of their long-legged strides. One of the women raised her face and she could see the laughter on it. The other joined her, then kicked aside a stray chocolate wrapper. Two young women, laughing, busy with their sense of destination. Like Isabel and she were, way back when in that first year in London. They might even have come to this neighbourhood once in those happier times. She had an image of a comedy club buried amidst back streets where they had spent an evening hooting over impersonations of Margaret Thatcher.

Leo shook herself. She turned to the bed, with its sprawl of papers, and poised herself at its edge. Letters. Some of them old, judging by the yellowing paper. She picked one out at random: 10 December 1986, the date stated. She walked back to the window to read its fading ink in the bright light.

Dear Isabel,

Haven't heard from you for some weeks. I hope you're dressing warmly enough for what must now be the ghastly British winter. Your job sounds dreadful. Couldn't you manage a better one? Do try and keep the right kind of company. It's important for a young woman making her way in what isn't a kind world.

Things here are none too good. Martha's hip is bothering her. You should write to her, even if not to me. You know how she loves you. She's always tried to get her clutches into you, I know, but it was with the best will in the world. She's staying with me at the moment, having a break from her social work. None too soon, if you ask me. Alice Springs is no place for a woman of her age. I don't know why she bothers. It's made her a little mad.

Otherwise, the only news is that we've had a break-in. Someone stole all the tools in the shed, including the lawnmower Martha had just bought. I think it was one of the Abos who keeps following her, which only makes it worse. This place isn't getting any better. I don't mind you abandoning us. Really I don't. I'm glad you ditched that dreadful boyfriend. And I'm going to get myself a new job soon, maybe even move.

Yours, mother.

Hastily Leo placed the letter at the bottom of the box, as if to hide it from her own and Isabel's eyes. A guilty embarrassment suffused her. It wasn't her place to be reading this. She picked out another frayed sheet. This one was signed 'Martha'. Despite herself, she read it avidly. The quality of Isabel's home life suddenly materialized in her nostrils, an acrid suffocating smell of heavy wool cardigans and women trapped in emotional warfare.

My beautiful darling,

I've come to spend some weeks with Elinor, who has been far from well. She's on edge, imagining things again. Dreaming break-ins, you know how she does. The doctor's given her some tablets. But don't worry, I'll see her through. Concentrate on yourself. You deserve it. I miss your bright smile, but I'm happy to think of it growing brighter . . .

There was more to this letter, another page of chatty news about Australian politics and recent books, which Leo skimmed quickly as she tried to remember whether Isabel had ever talked to her at length about the relationship between her aunt and her mother. Nothing came to mind, so she pressed on through the yellowing sheets. These were all personal letters, old ones, which is why Isabel had stashed them out of sight. Out of mind, too, Leo reflected, though it surprised her that Isabel had kept so much of her past with her, since she talked about it so little.

She lifted a few more letters from the mess on the bed and read quickly. Here was a plaintive plea from an abandoned Australian lover called Duncan. She added it to the growing pile in the box, singled out a dozen others in the same thick brown ink and sped through them. It made sense to try and categorize the letters by their senders. There was a tiny chance, after all, that someone from the past had come back into Isabel's life and whipped her away.

Her eyes fell on a familiar hand, bold, sprawling, the strokes thickly black. Leo stiffened and glanced down at the signature for confirmation. Jeff. Embossed at the top of the stationery was the name of a hotel. In Cannes.

Gorgeous,
    You really are, you know. Emphatically.
    We should have done this sooner. And for longer. Watching you on the beach was far better than any of the films I saw.
    Why did you take off so quickly? Shall I

come and find you out in London? Nothing would be more delightful . . .

Leo stopped reading. She scrunched the letter into a tight ball and flung it across the room. Her stomach was heaving. Jeff and Isabel. Isabel and Jeff. How could he? How could he cross that particular line? Not just any woman, but her closest friend. And when? She retrieved the letter from the corner into which it had fallen and, with shaky hands, uncreased its folds. It was then that she heard the click. She froze. She knew that sound now. The door. Fear grappled with rage, a tumult of emotion. She struggled to move and alert Inspector Faraday.

Before she could do so, a voice boomed out, 'G'day. Anybody here?'

Christopher Norfolk strode towards her and paused at the threshold of Isabel's room. He was wearing jeans and a dark-blue sweater beneath a leather jacket, and he looked as if he'd forgotten to shave. His hold-all hung from one shoulder, his computer from the other.

'Hello there, Holland. You don't look too pleased to see me. Should I have told you I was going to vanish for a few days? Apologies rendered, though I didn't quite realize how long I'd be myself.' He poked his head into the room, and was about to dump his bag when he stopped short. 'Hey, what's happened in here?'

An icy voice from behind cut him off. 'What's happened in here is a burglary. I take it you have a key to this place.'

'I do.'

'And who are you?'

'I'm sure the little lady here will do the honours.'

161

'I'd far prefer you did them yourself.'

'Sure thing, Mr . . . ?'

Faraday flicked his ID a little too close to Christopher's face.

'I see. In that case, Christopher Norfolk. Pleased to make your acquaintance, Inspector. Sorry to find there have been problems in my absence.' He moved towards the study and let out a low whistle. 'Messy problems.'

Leo scrutinized his face.

'What's been taken?' He draped an arm loosely around her shoulders, as if they belonged together.

She brushed him off and felt Faraday's enquiring glance.

'You'd think Holland wasn't pleased to see me, Inspector.'

'Should she be? Where were you between seven thirty and eleven o'clock last night, Mr Norfolk?'

'Oh, it's like that, is it?' He crossed his arms over his chest and made a mockery of deep contemplation. 'I think I can safely say that I was in a red Ford – rotten car – somewhere between Totnes and London. Alone. No witnesses. Want to take me in?'

'This isn't a comedy, Mr Norfolk.'

'No, suppose not.' He turned to look into Isabel's office. 'Suppose not. What's been taken, Holland?'

'I'll just have a look at your computer, Mr Norfolk.'

Leo watched Faraday unzip the bag and shook her head.

'So that's what's gone. Anything else?' Norfolk's face was suddenly serious, his eyes a steely charcoal, as if secret thoughts had darkened them. 'Did you surprise him, Holland?'

'Leave the questions to me, Mr Norfolk.' Inspector

Faraday was curt. It was clear that he now trusted neither of them. 'You live here?'

'I'm visiting.'

'You're a friend of Leonora Holland's?'

'Leonora? Is that what it is?'

'Not a friend then?'

'A casual acquaintance, you could say. But a friend of Isabel Morgan's. An old friend. And that's enough, Inspector. I had nothing to do with this break-in. And if you stop treating me like some two-bit villain, I might even be able to help. I'm concerned about this. And Holland, here, has got me concerned about Isabel as well. I've been trying to track—' He stopped himself. 'Tell me what was taken, Holland.' He was suddenly authoritative.

'That's the problem. Apart from my laptop, we're not sure. And the letters I imagine you pinched the other day.'

He let that slide and moved suddenly past them to prowl around the apartment. He poked his head into Leo's room and glanced at the kitchen. Leo followed him. In the bathroom, she saw him repeat Faraday's gesture and bend to sift broken earth between his fingers.

'I never knew Isabel to grow things from scratch before,' Leo heard herself saying.

'She's a woman of many talents.'

'You and I need to have a conversation, Mr Norfolk.'

'Yes, we probably do, Inspector. Our talented friend may be in some trouble. The extent of it has just come home to me now. And I may inadvertently have increased it.'

'Those letters?'

'Let's go and sit down.' He slumped onto the

sofa. Faraday perched on the one opposite.

'How did you increase it? What have you been doing?'

'One step at a time, Holland. Don't get ahead of yourself. And this is all guesswork. Come and sit down, you're making me nervous.'

Leo positioned herself between them.

'Carry on, Mr Norfolk.'

'When Isabel was last in Australia, we talked at length about the biogenetic sector; in particular about the genetic engineers and their interesting new food crops. "Transgenic" they used to be called. Now the term's become less transgressive, more homely, "modified", one might say.' He chuckled. 'Isabel had leads and she was going to do some investigating – for a book or a series of articles. Not on the obvious stuff that's got everyone so excited, the soya and oil seed and corn, but the future possibilities. The dreams waiting to be realized in the labs.'

'Under the name of Iris Morgenstern?'

'I don't know about that, but I wouldn't put it past her. Anyhow, I was going to do some footwork on the Australian side, just to see who was developing what and, as importantly, who owned what. And she was going to cover Britain, and do some sniffing around in the US, too, on her trip there. Isabel had a hunch that the big players would soon be in cahoots with the drug companies, though for the moment they were hiding behind a lot of smaller research establishments, like Monsanto behind Delta and Pine Land – you know, the company Monsanto bought which developed and patented the Terminator.'

'The Terminator?' Leo heard herself croaking.

'Well, these are creative folk, Holland. Terminator

164

technology, as it's called, genetically alters seeds so they won't germinate if replanted, which is great for the patent-holders, not so good for the poorer countries and the smaller farmers. In India they're organizing against it.'

'You mean those seedlings in the bathroom were . . . ?'

'Don't know. Anyhow, the point is, Isabel is with the Greens on this. You never know what kind of ultimate effect these altered plants will have, on soil, on other plants, on economies, let alone on humans. Then there's traitor technology, a small leap into disabling germplasm, not to mention junkie seeds, which need constant injections of proprietary chemicals to keep going and—'

'Spare us the lecture, Mr Norfolk. What have you found out?' Faraday was terse.

Norfolk gave him a cold stare. 'On Friday, I took myself down to Greenpeace to see a friend I have there; a friend of Isabel's, too. She'd been in touch with them, of course, got lists from them of companies and so on, though she kept her cards close to her chest. In part because she didn't want to implicate anyone if she got into the wrong kind of difficulty. But I did learn, because they'd laughed about it, that she'd got a job as a temp with a firm near Exeter. So I hired a car and trundled down there.'

'Why didn't you tell me?' Leo interrupted.

'Easier to do these things alone, Holland. Anyhow, I wanted to get there before closing time and these English roads are something else.'

'What was the name of the company, Mr Norfolk?'

'You got one of those cancer sticks for me, Holland?'

Leo passed him a cigarette.

'A match, too. I don't carry the things.'

'The name of the company, Mr Norfolk.'

Norfolk deflected him. 'By the time I got there, the top guns had taken off for the weekend. So I got talking to a young woman. A lively Sheila.'

He winked at Leo, and she had the distinct impression he had added that comment for her benefit. She thought suddenly of Jeff. Jeff and Isabel. Her cheeks felt hot.

'What did this lively Sheila tell you then?' Her voice dripped irony.

'Well, she distinctly remembered a temp who'd worked there for two weeks or so early in March who fitted Isabel's description.'

'So how does this help us?'

'Give me credit for a little intelligence, Inspector.'

'I give you credit for a lot more than that, Mr Norfolk.'

Leo watched them perform their little power dance. Norfolk had slouched back into the sofa, his eyes half closed in an indolent disdain. Faraday sat on the edge of his seat, his body all wiry sinew, ready to discharge itself in a leap of foot or fist. They hadn't taken to each other, these two men. Faraday evidently suspected Norfolk. So did she, for that matter. He was slippery. He was hiding things behind those sleepy eyes. His whole narrative could be a fabrication, though in its larger contours it rang true.

'Go on.'

'Where were we?'

'Friday. You were talking to a young woman. Quite a long talk, from the sound of it.'

'Well, we got interrupted by a muscle man who didn't seem to like my queries. Spy cameras everywhere in that place. And he shouldered me out just as the conversation was growing interesting.'

The ring of the telephone startled them. For a moment, no-one moved. Then Leo ran for it. Faraday was just behind her. 'Leave it,' he barked and pointed to the answering machine.

Isabel's voice filled the room. Leo caught Norfolk's eye. He was tense now, listening with acute concentration, as if he might deduce something from this disembodied sound.

A woman's voice followed, heavily accented, so that it made her words difficult to grasp.

'Isabel, darling. Paola here. I need to speak to you. Perhaps with a degree of urgency. Have you been in touch with Daniel? He rang. To save you looking for my number, I remind you. Seven nine four, eight five eight five. Phone me, please, eh.'

Leo saw Faraday writing down the number.

Paola. The one Daniel Lukas had phoned yesterday just as she left him. He was up to something.

'The name of that company, Mr Norfolk?' John Faraday broke into her thoughts.

'Oh, that. Plantagen.' Norfolk seemed to have lost interest. 'Cute, eh? Merry olde England stuff. But you won't find out anything from them, if you ask – even if they did send a hired night raider over to dig out any data Isabel might have nicked. All gentlemanly and very above board, and smoother than your best claret. More Oxbridge connections than six cabinets, I'd imagine.' Abruptly he picked up his laptop and strode towards the door. 'Guess I'll be seeing you nice folks later on.'

Before either of them could hold him back, he was out the door.

7

Evening drizzle gave Upper Street a sheen which matched its recent assortment of trend-setting shops and minimalist restaurants, where bread was served with extra-virgin oil and seats were as hard as Borstal chairs. As the traffic lights turned red, Daniel Lukas pulled up short and watched a bent old man shuffle slowly across the street. In front of Daniel's car, he looked up and paused. Beneath a forest of dread-locks, Daniel spied an ashen face far too young for body and gait. It took him back to his days in the psychiatric wards of the Maudsley. The lithium shuffle. The wonder drug, lithium, which tempered manic highs and depressive lows, had its side effect in this sluggish shamble.

The man's vacant eyes seemed to accuse him. They reinvoked the helplessness he had sometimes felt in his student years, when symptoms called up treat-ments in neat pill form. Holding operations, as all the doctors acknowledged. Better than long-term wards, they all agreed. Better, yet not good enough, Daniel thought. It was one of the reasons he had started an analytic training.

The cars behind him had begun to hoot as the lights changed. At their sound, the man raised a staying hand, gave him a sly whisper of a smile and slowly finished his interminable amble across the street.

Daniel veered into a side street and parked erratically. As he got out of the car, the young-old man was right beside him. 'Couldn't spare a pound, could you, friend? I've lost my . . .' He seemed to have forgotten what he'd lost.

Daniel reached into his pocket and put a five-pound note in the man's hand, making sure he simultaneously met his eyes.

'Good on you, friend.'

'Hope so,' Daniel murmured. 'Have you got a place to stay?'

He nodded vaguely.

'Take care, then.'

Daniel hurried towards the restaurant. He was late – a certain sign that he wasn't looking forward to the encounter. But the place, as he pushed open the glass door, looked pleasant enough, with its muted pastels and long chrome bar. Paola was already there, seated at a round corner table overlooking a length of back garden in which a lifelike sculpture gazed back at the diners.

'Daniel. How nice.' She stretched her face towards him for a regulation kiss on either cheek, then scrutinized him. 'You are looking, how shall I say, a little more mature, but as handsome as ever.' She wiped a spot of lint from his jacket. 'There. Better. A woman's touch. I have already ordered us some wine. Red. I hope it suits you.'

'Very well.' She was a disconcerting woman, this Paola, he thought once more. There was a lavishness about her, an amplitude not only of form and feature, but of gesture. Her black eyes were vast, her mouth full and very red, to match the redness of the dress which billowed beneath her. Her arms jangled with the weight of bracelets and her gleaming dark head with a dangle of heavy earrings. Her teeth flashed and her eyes flashed and her jewellery flashed and she laughed with gusto. All this he should have liked, since he didn't disapprove of flamboyance. Maybe his wariness was as much to do with the adolescent boy in him who recoiled in fear from her one-time advances as it was to do with their professional differences. In any event, tonight he was prepared to be as friendly as he needed to be.

'We order, Daniel. And then we have no false pretences. I know you didn't ring me to see the beauty of my face.'

He laughed. 'The menu looks great.'

'It is. I have decided on the roast vegetables to start and then scallops.'

'Salad and rack of lamb for me.'

'A man's dish.'

'You have your predetermined ideas.'

'And you, your predetermined male ways.' She dipped her bread into the oil and chewed it with an air of triumph.

A young man in a very white shirt took their order. Daniel cleared his throat. She pre-empted him.

'Your life as a single parent is going OK?'

'We're managing.'

'Raising a child isn't a business.'

'Nor is it any of your business, Paola.' Daniel shifted into a higher gear. It was always like this with Paola. He had to remind himself that if he didn't attack, he would be perpetually on the defensive. 'I rang you because—'

'You don't have to tell me. I know. If it wasn't about an opening for me at the Marlborough, it was because of Isabel Morgan.'

'It was and is.' He met her gloating eyes.

'You're still angry with me because I stole her away from you.'

'It's not that.'

'Don't lie to me, Daniel. You are transparent. Well, maybe you have a small right to be angry. But Isabel and I, we hit if off right away. We met at a dinner party, you know, and we couldn't stop talking. It just worked between us.'

'What just worked?'

'I knew that I could help her. As soon as I told her about the group, the work I did with women, she wanted to come to me. She needed to be with a woman.' She made a prim little gesture which sat oddly on her face.

'I don't mind that she went to you, Paola.'

It was a lie and she picked it up straight away.

'Don't give me this disinterested professional garbage. If you cared about her, you minded.'

'OK, I minded.' He changed tack. 'I minded most because I wasn't informed that, for a while, we were seeing her simultaneously. But that's in the past now. Tell me how it went with her.'

'If you're asking did she talk about you, she didn't. To her credit. Only once, at the very beginning when I drew her out, she said she was very angry at you. Very angry.'

'Of course. We were just getting somewhere. The transference was beginning to bite.'

'You know these words don't mean a lot to me.' She waved a large hand in contemptuous dismissal.

Daniel swallowed rising bile with a peppery leaf. He wouldn't let her deflect him with an argument about their respective techniques. As far as he was concerned, whatever Paola did had nothing in

171

common with analytic therapies, even if it paraded under the same rubric. From his point of view, she simply charged into her patients' lives and tried to rearrange them, like some overbearing agony aunt. He chose his words and tone with care.

'We're not in a seminar, Paola, so we don't need to have disagreements. Just tell me what happened with Isabel,' he said calmly, then added, 'The police have been on to me about her.'

'The police!' Her pitch was so voluble that the people at the next table turned to stare. She gave them a warm smile and lowered her voice. There was something a little furtive in her face. 'You didn't give them my name?'

'Of course not.'

'I can always depend on you to be a gentleman. So Isabel is in trouble. In Australia, I imagine? That's why she hasn't returned my call.'

Daniel let the question pass. 'Tell me what went on between you.'

'Well, it was clear to me after fifteen minutes, once she'd told me about herself, how she lived alone, all those lovers, her inability to settle down, those seductive ways of hers, and the fact that she was dissatisfied enough to come to therapy, that she had suffered some kind of deep abuse as a child.'

'Fifteen minutes and you were certain.' Daniel bridled.

'I know these things, Daniel. I'm an experienced woman.'

'Go on.'

'I asked her straight away, was she not troubled by the fact that she had reached the age of thirty-five and didn't have a child? Wasn't her biological clock ticking away? And if not, why not? She told me she'd never wanted children. Well, we had better find out why, I said to her, before it is too late. If she didn't want children, a hundred to one it was because she didn't trust men. And if she didn't trust men, there was a reason.'

'One reason? Only one.'

'Don't be cute, Daniel.'

'So you gave her your own agenda.'

'A woman's agenda. There's no point beating round the tree, or the bush, you say.'

Her emphasis on the word beating carried a visceral charge. Daniel put his fork down. She didn't notice his reaction. She was off and running, baiting him again.

'We're not all millionaires who can lie on your couch into infinity, Daniel. Nor have we got for ever to tease out those little diamonds of truths. Life is short. Anyhow, Isabel didn't run away, so we found out why she didn't want children. I started by pointing out to her that being beautiful and seductive and independent were not necessarily virtues.'

'Wasn't that just a trifle sadistic?'

Understated irony had no impact on Paola.

'That jargon again. Unnecessary. I needed to stir her up, so we could move to the core problem.'

'So you undermined her first, turned her virtues into vices. Malevolent then, if not sadistic.'

'It's an effective technique for going places ... quickly.'

'Dangerous, perhaps, too. Your certainty astonishes me.'

'That is your problem, Daniel. You have no certainties.' She paused as a waitress cleared their plates.

'I'm certain that we're all different,' he muttered under his breath.

'What did you say?'

'Nothing. Go on.' He gave her his sweetest smile, but he was thinking of Isabel. How would she have reacted to Paola's attack. With anger, of course, but part of her would have agreed with Paola's assessment, colluded with her. The self-destructive impulse would have been unleashed.

'So she told me a little about her childhood, that terrible mother of hers, the aunt who cared – her saving grace, I imagine – the terrible schools. She told it to me flatly, not in self-justification. Which was impressive, but . . .'

'You didn't approve.'

'Not exactly. You should eat, Daniel. You will be too thin to deal with your patients.' She dug into her scallops, chewed for a moment, then made a face and called a waitress over. 'The last time I had this dish, you could taste the ginger, the shallots. The scallops were better cooked. Take it back, please. Tell your chef to pay more attention.'

The young woman looked at her in confusion, seemed about to protest when Paola uttered a stentorian, 'Go. Quickly!' She scuttled off like a whipped dog.

'They have to be kept on their toes or the standards go down. Where was I?'

'Isabel's childhood.'

'Yes. She took to the memory work very well. You know the technique I use. She closed her eyes and I asked her to go back to the first house of her childhood and find a safe space in there, one where she was happy, at peace. She described the place to me in great detail. She was good at the work. She told me about a high-up room in a big rickety house where the floorboards creaked. It was very hot, but at least there was shade. From the room there was a view across the farm. Yellow earth and sheep. She liked to watch them. There was also one doll, very battered. She loved that doll. One day it disappeared. She cried and cried. The room didn't have a key, and someone had taken the doll and flung her away. I told her, from now on that wouldn't happen. I would make sure the door was locked and guarded. Only when she wanted to allow it would others come in. It was hers alone. Voices could penetrate, of course. Once she felt completely safe, I encouraged her to tell me about these and to wander further afield.

'The voices were very loud. Always screaming. Her mother's voice was the loudest, blaming her, scolding, unhappy. Blaming her father, too, for their rotten life. There was screaming at night as well. You can imagine the kind. Isabel reproduced it for me graphically, but here is not the place.' Paola looked into Daniel's face with a faint leer. 'Oh, good. Here is my food.' She attacked it greedily, while Daniel wondered what proportion of the memories she attributed to Isabel were due to suggestion and leading questions. He had never heard about the doll, for one. He waited for her to go on.

'So, all this I imagine you know. But wait, much you don't know. She told me she had never remembered it before. In the house, apart from her parents and herself, lived another man and woman. Hired hands, I guess. Her mother spent a lot of time lying down, and Isabel would go into the darkened room and chat to her, trying to get her to smile. Sometimes, when she wanted to go into her mother's room during the day, the door was locked. But she could hear voices squealing, like cats. I told her to go back, and eventually she unlocked the door. She found her

175

mother with the hired man. I won't describe the scene to you, only that each time Isabel went back to it, it grew a little more brutal – whipping and so on – and that the man threatened the little girl who was Isabel and said he would do the same to her if she ever came in there again, and he pulled her towards the bed and her mother laughed.

'Anyhow, this is all preliminary. One day – this took us several weeks to get to – she saw her father beating her mother. Very badly. This happened on several occasions. And then her father took sick. He lay in his bed all the time in a special room and didn't work outside any more. Depression, I imagine, though Isabel called it sickness. Isabel would lie with him to cheer him up. He told her how he would take her away from her vile mother, how they would be rich and so on. And Isabel paid her dues. I don't have to go into the gory details.'

She met Daniel's eyes meaningfully, but he didn't take the bait and she carried on.

'At night, Isabel would hear the screams again from the parental bed. She didn't want to hear them, not the loudest ones. I had to urge her to visit the scene. Slowly, of course. We covered a lot of daily life in the process, but eventually she saw it. After she saw it, she didn't go back to the house any more, in memory or in fact. She was sent away.'

'What did she see?' Daniel asked. He had hardly touched his food. There was a bad taste in his mouth.

'Don't tell me you don't know.'

'How can I know whether I know if you don't tell me?' he said stiffly.

'So you don't. You surprise me, Daniel. So many months, years of working with her.' Paola paused dramatically. Her bracelet jangled. 'What little Isabel saw was her mother on top of her father. Her hands were around his throat. He was clutching at her wrists, groaning. And then his fingers went limp. He was dead. Isabel's mother murdered her father. In its best light, it was manslaughter. A sexual accident.'

Paola snapped her fingers as if she had just materialized a rabbit from a hat. 'That's why Isabel was sent away so suddenly, and then to all those boarding schools. It's why her mother would never talk about her father. Poor girl.'

Daniel contained himself. 'So, having unearthed all this, how did you recommend Isabel put herself together again.'

Paola wiped her plate clean. 'The first thing I encouraged her to do was to write to her mother or to go and see her to talk about it. We played out various scenarios and forms of letters, as well as ways for her to handle either her mother's acknowledgement or denial of the facts. I also worked with her on her self-esteem. I stressed that her mother might have been led to the act in part out of love for Isabel, to defend her from further abuse.'

'Why on earth . . . ?'

'Daniel, Daniel, as you know very well, it's not easy to love the woman in yourself if you've been abused by both parents and God knows who else. And if, on top of it all, your mother is a murderer. So one has to find love where one can.'

'Hardly easy. I agree.'

'Isabel also started to go to the victim support group.'

'The one you're linked with in Devon?'

'I didn't know I'd told you about that.'

'News travels.'

She played with her beads for a moment, taking

that in, not altogether comfortably he noted.

'No, here. She was planning to spend some time in Devon. But first she wanted to go to Australia. Then, in the midst of all this, her mother died.' Paola scowled. 'Bad timing. I imagine Isabel is still there trying to find things out. Maybe it was more than she could handle on her own.'

'It certainly sounds likely.' Daniel was so angry he could barely bring out a sentence. Paola was looking at him expectantly. 'So, she left you, too.' The flat saying of it gave him pleasure.

She didn't respond. 'What did the police want?'

'They're looking for her.'

'What has she done?' Fear flickered across Paola's face, discomposing it for a fraction of a second.

'Are you worrying that you launched her on a cycle of repetition?' Daniel's tone was acid. 'A second murder to exorcize the first.'

'Do not get cute with me, Daniel. Tell me.'

'Isabel is missing.'

'Is that everything?'

He nodded.

She patted her mouth primly with the serviette and called the waitress over. 'I will have your special short-bread with the berries, together with a filter coffee.'

'A double espresso for me.'

Daniel waited for the coffee before speaking again. He was considering, only listening with half an ear to Paola's relieved monologue about her plans for setting up her own unit. Perhaps one which could be attached to the Marlborough. She had too much work at the moment. So many victimized women knocking at her door, wanting her to be their good mother. And a television company had approached her to do a series.

In a pause, Daniel interrupted. 'Isabel's father wasn't murdered, Paola.' His voice was hard. 'To kill off the memory of someone is not to murder them.'

'Wasn't murdered? But . . .'

'You heard me. You really must beware of taking everything your patients say, or you want to hear, quite so literally. The primary rule is that we deal in psychic events which may or may not be events in the world outside the consulting room. Memory plays tricks. A child's emotional response to a scene is not the totality of that scene's factual content. Nor does suggestion help. Some patients like to please. For a while, in any case.'

'Are you accusing me of hypnotizing Isabel?'

'I'm not accusing you of anything, just giving you a fact.'

She shook her head. 'You're wrong, Daniel. I know. She told me.'

He pushed back his chair with a scrape and gestured for the bill.

She put a hand on his arm. 'We have to trust our patients. It is what we can give them. So few of them have experienced an atmosphere of trust before. Only in that trust will they heal.'

'You can enter into a contract of trust with them without taking everything they say, or you encourage them to say, as the literal truth. If a patient says to me, "I want to kill my father," I don't instantly call in the police.'

'In America, if you didn't and something happened, you would be liable.'

'In that situation, I'd stop practising.'

Her ample bosom heaved with laughter. 'You're addicted to chasing clues, Daniel. I know the

179

kind of analyst you are. You could never give it up. The Sherlock Holmes of the consulting room.'

'But I don't have a fixed model of what I want my patients to turn into, nor do I find either victims or perpetrators in every cranny. Let's hope that, between us, we haven't helped to make one of Isabel.' He rose.

She registered no discomfort, but grew reflective. Devoid of expression, her face suddenly looked weary. 'She'll be fine. She's a strong one. I insist on it. I know. Once she frightened even me. I got the feeling she would know how to drive someone mad, because she had been driven mad herself. *Adios, amigo.* You will come next week, no?'

Daniel gave her his neutral smile. He had no idea to what she was referring and no intention of asking.

The wind had come up. Stray papers scudded along pavement and street. A page of a tabloid wrapped itself round his trouser leg and refused to be shaken off. He bent to remove it, then walked briskly through the drizzling night. Testing his state of mind, he wondered that he wasn't angrier at Paola, even though he was so deeply critical of her work. It was probably because he couldn't help but feel a certain admiration for her. Yet he sensed that it was the sheer force of her that made her especially dangerous to some of her patients.

They had first met years ago at a conference. She had spoken about her work with victims of torture in Argentina. She too had been tortured and that gave her words an undeniable heft. The problem, as he'd learnt in subsequent years, was that she had never been able to shed the burden of that experience. It translated itself into her practice, into the very categories within which she worked. As he had underlined tonight, she found victims and torturers everywhere. Whereas he?

Youngest son of a London obstetrician and a doting mother, Daniel had experienced only what, in a self-critical mood, he called the banal violence of everyday life: death, disease, the ravages of mental illness, the everyday damage we do to ourselves and each other, the savagery the unconscious brings up. In Paola's book, that hardly counted. She had made that amply clear over the years when they bumped into each other here and there in the small warring world that was the therapeutic community.

Then, last year, when his wife was already very ill, by some aberration Paola had thrown herself at him during a conference. She had come to his room and told him in no uncertain terms that a man with an ailing wife needs a break. She had taken his astonished refusal well enough. The embarrassment had been all his. But now it occurred to him that the unseemly encounter must have taken place not long before Paola had taken on Isabel. A small act of malicious revenge.

Or had it been a small act? Daniel pulled the car sharply out of its parking place. He had to think now, think himself once more into Isabel's skin. What impact would Paola's intervention, her dismantling of Isabel's tested means of coping with the world, that forced journey to the manipulable child within, have had on Isabel's inner state? He drove fast. He narrowly missed braking at a red light and reached Highgate in record time. Maybe, like Isabel, he felt he needed to escape.

When he got home, he searched out the number the police had left him. He asked the man he was put on to whether the Australian police had been asked to put out a missing person's alert on Isabel Morgan.

8

As she stepped out into the milky morning light and turned automatically left, Leo had a flickering sense that she was building up habits that, by rights, weren't hers. She had felt it in the way she raced down the slightly uneven stairs of the apartment without checking her tread. She felt it again as she flung her hair back, even though it was too short to fling, before crossing the street. The familiarity with which the tiny wrinkled man in the dingy newsagent's greeted her added to the impression. His 'How are you today?', the manner in which he brought out a pint of milk, a brown loaf and an *Independent*, even before she could ask for them, all spoke of a settled life that wasn't hers.

The notion came to her that Isabel's existence was taking over her own, just as it had once taken over her husband. It was all those papers and possessions through which she had sifted and which now pervaded her mind, as much as the geography of the flat and the streets. Or was it the other way around? Had she usurped an absent Isabel's life because there was so little of her own left? She nudged the thought away and, to make the difference, bought a packet of chocolate biscuits before walking, more slowly, back to the house.

She paused where the gap in the fencing gave way to the old discoloured fire escape. There was a man she didn't recognize standing at the door of the house. He was suited and wore a soft felt hat tilted at a rakish angle. He seemed to be hesitating. A large, full keyring dangled from his hand, yet he was looking at the bells. Finally, he fitted a key into the lock and pushed the door open.

Leo came in right behind him. He turned round with a nervous lurch, scrutinized her, then moved quickly up the stairs. He had, Leo noted, extraordinary eyes, as large and vague in his face as a china doll's and more thickly lashed. Beneath them, an unsettling scar etched its way down his cheek. She kept her distance. He didn't stop on the first floor as she had expected. She could hear his footfall ahead of her as she paused on the landing and then the click of a key turning. Her heart pounding, she raced up to the apartment. The intruder had returned.

'What the hell do you think you're doing?' she shouted so loudly that he jumped back, dropping the keys as he did so.

'What's it to you?' He gave her a look of sullen appraisal.

Leo made a lunge for the keys. He did so, too. They wrestled for them and the keys fell back to the ground with a clatter.

'Having a problem, Holland?' Norfolk was suddenly at the door. 'This bloke here bothering you?'

'He's trying to break in.'

With one swift movement, Norfolk pinned the man to the wall. 'Ring the police, Holland.'

'Hold on here, hold on a minute.' The man's demeanour changed dramatically at the word 'police'. 'I rang the bell, no-one answered. And now you jump me,' he whined. 'I'll lodge a complaint. Assault. Get Isabel. She'll tell you who I am.'

'No Isabel, and I heard nothing.' Norfolk held his grip.

'Well get her. Tell her Hamish Macgregor is here.' The man abruptly lifted his arms and shook himself free. He rearranged his hat and brushed his jacket into place. There was a scowl on his face. The scar looked livid and fresh. 'Isabel gave me those keys. Ask her if she didn't.' He bent for them quickly and dropped them into his pocket.

Leo stepped forward.

Before she could speak, Norfolk intervened. 'What do you want here?'

'I . . . I came to get some things I left behind.'

'What things?'

He seemed lost for a moment, then his face brightened. 'My tools. I did some work for her.' He drew himself up to a height that didn't quite match Norfolk's. 'They're in the closet, just over there.' He pointed to the right of the door and stepped across the threshold. Norfolk stopped him. 'I'll take those keys back first.'

'And who the hell are you?'

'I'm asking the questions. Make that phone call to the police, Holland.'

'I've seen the police. So you're the bastard who put them on to me. Disturbing my old mum 'n' all.'

Leo saw the curl of fists. 'When did you last see Isabel?' she confronted him.

'That's my business, isn't it? Hey, got it, you're the bird I talked to on the phone.' He looped two keys off the ring and threw them, like a gauntlet, to the floor. 'There. All yours. I'll get my things.'

185

'I'd pick those up and give them to the lady politely, if I were you, mate.'

Macgregor met Norfolk's eyes for a moment. With a mock swagger, he bent to pick up the keys and handed them to Leo.

'Thank you,' she murmured by rote. She followed the men through the door.

Macgregor dug out an aluminium box from the midst of brooms and mops and a vacuum. He brushed his suit down. There was a flustered air about him, as if he had inadvertently cornered himself. 'I . . . I've just remembered something else.'

'And what might that be, Mr Macgregor?' Norfolk's arms were folded across his chest. Leo noticed, for the first time, that it was bare and as tanned as his face, which now wore his customary wry smile. 'Just what might that be?'

'In the bedroom.'

'Oh, yes, of course. Holland, why don't you go into my room and take that cream-coloured suit out from the far end of the wardrobe. I think that's what our friend here is looking for.'

'I'll get it myself.'

Norfolk put a staying hand on his shoulder. The grip was in stark contrast to the smile on his face. Macgregor didn't move.

'I was wondering who the suit belonged to. Is there anything else, Mr Macgregor. A shirt, perhaps?'

The two men sized each other up.

'The suit will do. For now.'

After a second's hesitation, Leo left them. When she returned, they were talking in low voices on the landing. They stopped as soon as she approached.

'Thank you,' Hamish Macgregor mumbled to her. He had grown a veneer of politeness in her absence.

186

'I'll be seeing you, then.' He nodded at her and loped down the stairs.

'What were you two talking about, Norfolk?' Leo asked as soon as the door was shut.

'This and that. Just checking him out.' Norfolk grinned. 'Not the most salubrious character. Not your type, I imagine, Holland.' He considered her astutely.

Leo stiffened. 'Not Isabel's, either, unless she was hating herself.'

'Oh, I don't know. Isabel likes taking a risk here and there. And now, if you'll excuse me, I'll go and finish my rudely interrupted toilette. You weren't, by any chance, thinking of brewing some coffee?'

Leo picked up the shopping bag she had left on the floor. For a fraction of a second she had the impression he was going to pat her on the bottom. She stood up briskly. 'I was.'

'That's grand. Could you squeeze out a little extra for your security guard? I could use it. All I seem to do around here is get into fisticuffs. It takes it out of a man who earns his keep at a keyboard.'

Leo busied herself with breakfast. She ground beans, brought out a box of cereal and thought of Hamish Macgregor. Hamish Macgregor and Isabel. There was a loucheness about the man, a ready violence that made her shudder, even though he wasn't altogether the brute she had imagined from his drunken telephone call. Obviously the police interrogation had made him hasten here surreptitiously to collect his things. She would bet her bottom dollar that Macgregor had adamantly denied being Isabel's lover. Was he hiding any more than that?

Leo's hand slipped. The milk poured over the edge of the jug.

Jeff hadn't denied it. She had rung him very late last night, when Christopher Norfolk was already asleep. She had reached him in his university office. She hadn't bothered to exchange platitudes. All she had said was, 'Did you? With Isabel?'

There had been a long pause in which she could hear him breathing. At last he said, 'So she told you. After all these years. Well, it hardly matters now, does it?' Then had come that small, artificial laugh of his which signalled grim discomfort. Leo had made no response. Inevitably, he had filled up the ensuing silence with self-justification. 'Well, she's hard to resist. And she was so willing. And you'd gone bone cold on me.' She had hung up then, gone to bed and lain there tasting the texture of betrayal, like rotten fruit exploding in her mouth.

Oddly, it tasted worse than the episode that had led to their separation. Maybe, by then, she was already subliminally removed from him. Inured. But the affair with Isabel – she had worked it out, remembering his trips to Cannes – must have dated from their year in London, or the next. It brought her back into the midst of what she had thought of as her happiness, her Garden of Eden. And the serpent lurking there had been Jeff himself.

She didn't blame her friend. She wasn't one of those women who thought it was always the other woman's fault. She and Isabel had only just begun their friendship then and she didn't owe her any particular loyalty.

A long-forgotten scene suddenly came into focus. She was with Isabel in the bar of the National Theatre during the interval of she couldn't remember which play. Isabel had given her one of her teasing looks and said, 'If you really knew me, I don't think you'd like me much. I'm not very moral about most things, you know.' She had laughed that irresistible laugh that came from the pit of her stomach and Leo had joined her.

Maybe Isabel had been warning her then, testing her. She hadn't picked up the cue.

No, Jeff apart, it was she, herself, who was at fault – for being so stupid, so trusting, so intent on happiness that she carried it with her like a blinding, rose-tinted fog.

And now the fog was lifting and she could see all the scurrying creatures beneath. Could see herself, too, placid in their midst. A small, contained woman smiling at the notion that she was creating a good family for her child, a tranquil unit, more caring and continuous than the one from which she had emerged.

Leo slashed at the bread with the large kitchen knife. As she did so, she had an image of herself standing at the bottom of a long, curving staircase. She was waiting for Jeff, who was at its top. He bent unnaturally and fell. Then he was tumbling towards her in slow motion, his body twisting, bumping, until he arrived at her side, his face white, stony, dead. It came to her that she had been haunted by images of his dying throughout the first part of their marriage. Sudden hallucinatory images. He would plummet out of a tree, or be thrown headlong by a speeding car, or be propelled by a gust from the penthouse roof. At the time, she had put it all down to her love for him and the attendant anxiety that she would lose him. But had the images been created as much out of wish as fear?

Leo lopped off another slice of bread. The voice behind her made her veer round, as if she had been caught out. The knife was still in her hand.

'Calm down, Holland.' Norfolk's tone was soothing. 'It's only me. Remember? Don't want any *Fatal Attraction* scenes here. Might ruin the sparkle of the counters.'

The knife clattered to the floor. He gave her an odd look. 'I think you need some of this coffee more than I do. Here, let me do this.'

Later, after she had checked in with Inspector Faraday, who had asked her, in an unexpectedly curt voice, how many more people he might expect to find with keys to Isabel's flat, she went for a stroll. She forced herself to walk through the cemetery at an even pace, even stopping to look at the historic graves with their disappearing inscriptions. She hated cemeteries and never visited them, even in Paris, where they had pride of place as tourist attractions. Highgate Cemetery was the only exception. Becca and Jeff had made that safe. Kept the ghosts at bay. Jeff. She forced him out of her mind and hastened her steps.

In the market street, she bought several large bunches of tulips for Rosie and daffodils for herself – so yellow that they seemed to have swallowed the sun which had now vanished from the sky. She bought some oranges, too, hungry for their colour to counter the sombreness lodged inside her.

Back in Isabel's building, she noticed the post had arrived. A sift-through produced three envelopes for Isabel. She tucked them into her bag, ran up the stairs to place the flowers and a thank-you note by Rosie's front door, and let herself back into the flat.

The door to Isabel's office was closed. From within it she could hear the light clacking of a keyboard.

190

Norfolk was at work. He really did use the thing. She arranged the flowers and fruit quickly, then ripped open the post. There was none of the earlier hesitation in her movements, she noted. It was as if Isabel's letters had become her own.

The first envelope produced a sheaf of material from Greenpeace, the second was an invitation to an opening at the Hayward Gallery. As she read it, she suddenly remembered where she had seen the name Paola – on another invitation, on her first or second day here. Had it been amidst the torrent of papers left by the burglar, which she had filed away as best she could?

Leo tore open the last envelope. It was brown and padded and bore a neatly typed label addressed to I. Morgenstern. Inside, there was a diskette. Leo stared at it. What to do with her laptop gone?

After a moment's consideration, she rushed into Isabel's office. 'Norfolk,' she called as she knocked, and then didn't wait for a response. 'Look what's arrived.'

'Hold on.' He clacked away for the length of a sentence before turning to her.

She was waving the diskette in the air. 'It's just come in the post. Can we read it on your machine?'

He groaned. 'Can't you tell when a man's trying to earn his keep, Holland? Don't they teach you manners in America?'

Leo stepped back. 'It's not mine,' she said tersely. 'It was addressed to Isabel.'

'Well, why didn't you say so?' He gave her a broad wink and took the diskette from her hand.

She stood over his shoulder to gaze at the screen. Superstitiously, she crossed her fingers behind her back. Maybe this was what they had been waiting for. Just maybe everything would come clear now.

What materialized on the screen bore no relationship to what she had hoped for. In its layout it looked like a family tree, an intricate genealogical table, with progenitors at the top, followed by branching lines of husbands, wives, children, grandchildren and great-grandchildren. Could Isabel have asked for a family tree to have been drawn up? She hadn't, as far as Leo recalled, ever known much about her grandparents. The family was a mystery, particularly on her father's side. Yet there were no names here, just initials.

Norfolk scrolled down. The next screen brought up equally incomprehensible matter. Each line was a set of figures separated by spaces, like some kind of code.

They both studied the screen.

'I suspect Isabel has sent herself a little aide-mémoire. For safe-keeping.' He pressed a key and Leo heard the printer move into action. 'Which means she's safe.'

'You mean these are coded notes she sent to herself? Under the name of Morgenstern?'

'Oh. Perhaps not Isabel, in that case.' He looked back at the screen, then picked up the papers as they came out of the printer and considered them. Leo had visions of endless enigma games.

'Maybe, just maybe . . .' He picked up the padded envelope and scrutinized the post mark. 'Dorset. Can't make out the town.' He passed her the envelope. 'Let me finish this piece here, Holland, and then I'm off. I've got an idea. I've got to work on it.'

'What idea?'

'It's too early to say.' His look was breezy.

'Make me a copy of all this.'

'Right.' He pressed a key and, as they watched the

paper slide out, he muttered, 'You're the most distrustful person I know, Holland. You could almost be Isabel's sister.'

Leo took a step backwards and met his eyes. 'Isabel doesn't have a sister.'

'You know what I mean. Now scat. Out of here. I've got to work.'

She hesitated. 'I need a favour, Norfolk. Can I use your machine to send an e-mail? My daughter . . . She's in California. And the time difference makes her almost as hard to reach as Sydney. I . . .' The tears pricked at her eyes. She could feel his on her and she moved away. 'Maybe when you're finished.'

'Get on with it, Holland,' he growled. 'I'll make some more coffee.'

Leo sat at the long glass table and looked up from the perplexing family tree she had been studying. Outside, hazy sunshine had returned. It fell on the window rails of the old factory building which dominated the far side of the car park. Standing at the window, she could just make out a shadowy figure. Light glinted on his face and, for a moment, she had the odd notion that he was directing a pair of binoculars straight on her. She walked to the window and peered into the distance. The figure moved away. She shook off the uncomfortable sense of being watched and concentrated on the small voice which emerged from the tape-recorder. It was a child's wavering voice, talking about the picture she was drawing. 'This is my dog, Woofie. My daddy took him away when he went. I miss Woofie.' Silence, and then Isabel's voice, very soft. 'And what's that?'

Leo had listened to two of the pile of tapes she had taken from Isabel's office. Both had contained interviews with children and Leo was now almost certain that all the tapes would be research material Isabel had collected for her book on childhood. Still she listened. There was a pleasure in hearing Isabel's voice, as if they might really be on the road together, heading west now under open skies.

But it came to her that this wasn't the voice she was used to. This voice was calm, solicitous, serious. It contained none of Isabel's laughing ironies or hard-edged assessments. Again she was forced to acknowledge that there were vast territories of even one's nearest and dearest that one hardly knew. An image of Jeff with Isabel leapt into her mind. She prodded it away. Maybe familiarity was a mere illusion, a flimsy, necessary comfort to fence oneself in against cold, unknown expanses which threatened to blow apart the warmth of friendly continuity.

She reached for a piece of paper and started to draw. Isabel's face leapt from her pen. A mournful Isabel, with lowered lids and downturned lips. Floating next to her was Jeff, his eyes very dark, flashing beneath a frizz of tangled curls. She edged some shadows beneath his eyes and the face turned malevolent.

That was one of the things that was wrong with her, Leo thought. She hadn't been drawing, hadn't been working. The quasi-trance of pen moving across paper, the emptying out of mind, was one of the ways she put herself together. What all the king's horses and all the king's men couldn't manage for Humpty Dumpty, drawing did for her. The lines induced containment. It didn't work with colour. Colour spread across the page, eating away definition, splodging and sprawling, vibrating with its own greedy life. Sometimes there was an adventure to that, but today she needed definition. She worked.

When the phone rang, she jumped, as if she had travelled a long distance from such everyday sounds. For a moment, she didn't know which way to turn, then she switched off the tape-recorder and rushed to pick up the phone extension next to the sofa.

Norfolk had got there before her. She heard his voice and another, stammering one. She listened despite herself.

'I may have something for you,' the unknown voice mumbled. 'Better said in person, I think.'

'Four o'clock, then. I'll come to you,' Norfolk replied.

'Right.'

Leo hung up. Too late. Norfolk was marching out of Isabel's office.

'Don't eavesdrop on my calls, Holland. We're not married, remember?'

She bristled. 'I wasn't listening, I just—'

The phone rang again and she scrambled to it ahead of him.

'Leonora Holland. Inspector Faraday here. We've come up with something.'

'Yes?' Leo felt the blood drain out of her in apprehension.

'A Visa-card trace. On the fifteenth of April, Isabel Morgan spent two nights at the Sturridge Hotel in Dorset. She booked a double room. Does that ring any bells for you?'

'No, I'm afraid it doesn't.' Her voice sounded faint in her own ears and she repeated the 'no' more distinctly.

'She arrived in a car, hired in London on the morning of the fifteenth. The car still hasn't been returned. We've got a trace on it. I'll be in touch again soon. Everything all right at your end?'

'Yes. Thank you.'

Leo put the phone down with a shaky hand.

'What is it, Holland?' Norfolk was bent over the table. He had been examining her sketches as she spoke and now twisted his head towards her. 'You're looking green around the gills again.'

She told him.

'Dorset, eh?' He straightened up, his brow furrowing. 'So I wasn't very far away. Look, I'll do some more checking around later today. Right now I gotta get my butt outta here. If I manage to finish up at a reasonable time, I'll take you out for dinner. How about it? Meet you back here at eightish. Or I'll leave a message. Got it?'

She nodded as he disappeared back into the office.

He was back a moment later. 'Sorry I can't leave this for you, Holland.' He patted his laptop as if it were a household pet. 'Never can be quite sure what you might decide to peruse, apart from your e-mail.'

Leo bristled but kept silent. She had indeed, when sitting at his machine earlier, contemplated reading through his more recent correspondence, but had decided the timing was risky.

'By the way, Holland, these sketches are bloody good. Who's the bloke?' He pointed at Jeff. 'Got it in for him, judging from these lashing strokes here.' He gave her a curious look. 'Don't think I'd relish being in his shoes. You do this kind of thing for a living?'

She nodded, then shook her head. 'Not quite this kind of thing.'

He waited for her to say more. When she didn't, he shrugged. 'Later, then.'

He was out the door before she could ask him where he was going.

Leo glanced at her watch. There was only an hour left before she would have to set off for her appointment with Daniel Lukas. She wasn't looking forward to it, but this time she would be better prepared. A strategy had come to her while she was working. On the couch, she would replicate Isabel as best she could in order to see what kind of poison Daniel Lukas had poured into her ear.

She hurried into Isabel's office, took down the file marked 'Dreams' and rifled through its contents. There was one particular sheet she remembered vividly from the last time she had sifted through the box. It had surfaced as much because of its look on the page as for the troubling nature of the dream it described. The paper was thick and a childlike script covered every square inch of it, as if paper were precious and an injunction to use all of it were in place.

Now, as she searched, the sheet was nowhere in sight. Irritation gnawed at her, and with it came a sudden disquiet. The dream could easily have been misfiled when she was clearing up after the burglary, but it could just as easily have been stolen, along with other papers and letters that she hadn't noticed. She remembered prodding open the door of the apartment that night and seeing a scattering of letters on the floor. Had these gone, too? She could no longer recall.

Perturbed, she paced and found herself standing by the floor-to-ceiling bookcase. Daniel Lukas's name leapt out at her. She hadn't noticed this volume before. She pulled it out. *On Wishing, Dreaming and Deceiving*. She looked down the table of contents and quickly turned to the section on dreams.

'Bizarre as it may seem,' she read, 'individuals'

lives have been changed by dreams. The naturalist Sir Arthur Tansley recounts how he transformed his existence because of what, to an outsider, might seem a run-of-the mill dream . . . He was not on the road to Damascus, but cycling from Grantchester to Cambridge and considering the dream when it became clear to him that he had to give up his work and travel to Vienna to visit Freud.'

Leo skimmed and flicked pages. There wasn't time to read this properly now. She would do so tonight. She paused, however, to look at a highlighted passage. Isabel must have singled it out. The gleaming yellow-backed lines jumped out at her:

'Impostors often feel most authentic, most alive, when they are in role. These are not the ingratiating impostors who wish to appease others in order to ward off their imagined attacks. Here, there is a sadistic wish in the deception. If you won't love (or respect) me as me, I'll make sure you love me as the not-me I've invented.'

The doorbell rang and stopped her reading. Cautiously, Leo looked into the videophone. A face leered at her from the tiny screen. A face with a livid scar.

'Yes,' she said faintly.

'I've brought you a present. Think you'd better come down and fetch it.' Hamish Macgregor's voice carried a hint of menace.

'What is it?' Leo asked, but the man was already gone, the screen a blank.

She stared into the emptiness, her skin prickling uncomfortably. What kind of present would a man like Hamish Macgregor leave? In a swoop of panic, she thought of severed limbs, an ear lavishly wrapped in gilded paper, or a lock of golden hair. She forced herself into reasonableness. It was broad daylight in a civilized city in a civilized country. She took her keys from her bag and walked resolutely down the stairs to the front door.

On the top step stood a medium-sized cane hamper, like the kind one might take out to the heath for a picnic on a warm summer's day. Leo looked around to see whether Hamish Macgregor was still visible, but the only sign of activity on the street was a motorbike revving round the corner.

She bent to the hamper. An acrid pong attacked her nostrils. She straightened up with a tremor. Had her initial fearful imaginings been the right ones? Swiftly, she raised one of the hamper's lids. Before she could stand away, a furry form streaked between her legs and up the stairs. She lurched backwards, almost tripping over her feet, then picked up the hamper and raced up the stairs.

The cat was waiting for her by the door, a taut bundle of mustard and soot. Its head cocked, it examined her, as if it was weighing up the chances of mistreatment against its desire for entry. 'Hello, Beast,' Leo murmured in wonder. She stroked his fur, ruffled his ears, then opened the door. He bounded through it, raced into the large room and, from there, into the study. 'No Isabel, I'm afraid,' Leo heard herself calling after him. 'Poor Beast.'

She took the hamper into the kitchen and cleaned out its insides, scrubbing the bowl she found there, tossing the wet pillow into the washing machine.

When she went out to look for him, she found him sitting on the ledge in Isabel's bedroom and looking wistfully out the window.

So the police had been right, Leo reflected. She unlocked the window and pushed it up until the bolts would let it go no further. With a miaow of pleasure, the animal leapt out onto the fire escape. Leo watched its antics and wondered what on earth had led Isabel to leave her beloved Beast with a man like Hamish Macgregor, if that was indeed what had happened. The thought came to her mind that perhaps, for Isabel, the animal was a replacement for herself.

She banished the notion and told herself that if Beast was back home, Isabel might not be far behind, though the part of her that lived in dread sensed simultaneously that this was mere wishful thinking.

9

As the murmured 'come in' released the door and she slowly climbed the steep staircase, Leo had an acute sense of repetition, as if she had already spent months trudging up these stairs to the long narrow room at their peak, where that lean man sat like some hungry spider waiting to trap her in his elaborate web. She reminded herself that she was doing this for Isabel, and then corrected the thought. She was doing this because anything was better than doing nothing at all.

Despite her foreboding, the room looked pleasant today. Sunlight streaked in through the far window. The heaped books glowed. Motes of dust danced in the air. Two worn leather armchairs curved in comfortable Edwardian elegance had appeared where she didn't remember noticing them before. Their age made them seem steeped in accumulated memory, as if they were carrying on a conversation with each other across the other objects in the room, even though their sitters were nowhere present.

Daniel Lukas sat on the sofa between them, exactly as he had on Monday. This time he didn't get up to greet her. His lips arched into what was not quite a smile as he gestured her towards the couch opposite. He looked tired, she thought. There were sooty rings beneath his eyes.

As she realized that he wasn't going to speak, she cleared her throat. 'I thought I'd try to be good today. Follow the conventions, I mean.' She met his eyes and he nodded.

She took off her shoes and stretched out on the sofa, facing the window today, to mark the difference. 'Trouble is, lying here makes me feel I'm about to undergo surgery,' she muttered.

'Why surgery?' he asked in a low voice. 'Why not sex, or giving birth, or simply sleep?'

'You know perfectly well why,' Leo snapped. 'You lot want to cut us open.'

His short, sharp laugh astonished her. 'The cutting might hurt. But the openness can't be all bad.'

She shivered the remark away with its implied admonishment to be open and tried to collect herself. On the wall next to the window hung a large-faced clock. For a moment she had the impression that its hands were moving backwards, like the clock she had at home. She should send it to him. The perfect clock for a shrink. Time moving backwards. She lopped off the ensuing thought of Jeff and rattled out, 'I thought I'd begin by telling you about a dream I had. I think it's connected to childhood. That's the right place to begin, isn't it?'

She raised her head to look round at him, but he had moved out of easy view, so she lay back and closed her eyes to remember.

'In the dream, I'm very small. At least no-one seems to see me, even when I open my mouth to call out. A strangled sound comes out, not my voice. Yet I know it's me. I'm very close to the ground. It's rough and very hot and there is a lot of it. Maybe I'm a beetle. My skin is hard and has edges like a carapace. No, not an insect. I have toes and the earth

202

gets caught between them as I walk. In the distance, which is wavy with heat, there's a large white creature. A sheep maybe. It has a white coat and a black face. I want to get to it, but something keeps tugging me back and I have to walk in the other direction. It takes a long time. I walk and walk. The sky is very blue, so blue it hurts my eyes. I trip. The earth gets into my mouth, all dry and gritty. I cry. No-one comes.

'On the ground there's something thick and hairy. I follow it. Follow it to a big pole. And then I'm frightened and I run away towards the sheep, which is there again. My head hurts. It's grown big with explosion. I can't breathe properly. The sheep will help me. But no matter how hard I try, I can't get to it. My bracelet hurts. I look at it, rub it. It's not a bracelet. It's that thick and hairy thing. It's wrapped round my arm like a snake. It won't let me move. I scream. I wake up. My arm hurts.'

Leo waited for the sound of his voice. It didn't come. Surely he would say something now. She wriggled on the sofa and opened her eyes. Outside, in the distance, smoke was billowing from some invisible fire. It gusted into the sky, first thick, dark swirls and then lighter and lighter into evanescent tufts. She watched them and waited.

Daniel took his time. He was in a quandary. He had recognized the dream, seen its resemblance immediately to a dream or memory Isabel had recounted to him as a dream. It had formed a key moment in her analysis. The child tied by its wrist to a pole outdoors in the hot sun – brutally tied, or simply tied in a moment of unthinking practicality, a makeshift playpen. They had teased out its meanings, translated them. He had urged her to revise them in the light of present and adult understanding, as well as future significance. Had Isabel recounted the dream to her friend Leonora Gould? Had the woman so interiorized it that it had become her own, or was she using it as yet another ploy to get him to talk about Isabel?

He suspected the latter, but his instincts and her nervous posture told him this wasn't the moment to take her to task. Instead, when it became clear that she was going to say nothing more, he asked, with classic neutrality, 'What does the dream make you think of?'

'Vulnerability, defencelessness. Poor child,' Leo answered without a pause, as if she were sitting an exam.

'Is that how you feel here? Vulnerable, without defences?'

Leo was hardly listening. Her hearing was only attuned now to the sound which had started up outside. The hideous whirring of rotating blades cutting the sky, chopping. They were coming closer, louder. She put her hands to her ears. She could see it now, like some giant dragonfly challenging the elements. Perspiration gathered in her armpits and on her forehead. She leapt off the sofa and turned her face away from the window.

That man was watching her. 'The helicopter disturbs you?'

'What does it look like?'

'It does look like that.'

'Bravo. Great insight. Next you'll tell me it's a phobia, a result of some deeply buried and forgotten trauma which I've displaced onto ... onto ...' She was sputtering, waving her arms. 'Well, it's not like that. I know precisely why I hate the damn machines.'

204

'Why don't you tell me too?'

'My father was killed in one, killed by one.'

'I see.' His voice was soft as he met her eyes. His were warm now. They seemed to hold her up and then direct her towards the couch. She lay down.

'Tell me about it, if you can.'

'I don't know about it.' Leo's throat felt tight. 'I only saw the photograph. A lot of men traipsing through a dark jungle somewhere. Malaysia.'

'Yes . . .'

She told him about it then. She didn't know what words she used, since none of them sat well on her tongue. And the story was all mixed up with feelings and responses which he prodded out of her, so that somehow she was living them as if for the first time through words. There hadn't been words before, nor, for a long time, any thought. There had been silence, or the flat phrases which go into making announcements. 'My father died when I turned fourteen.'

It was indeed just before her fourteenth birthday. She was at school in Cambridge, it was her second year there. The autumn was beautiful. In the gardens the hydrangea wore burnished red, the chrysanthemums gold and russet. The girls waved their lacrosse sticks at them as they strode in jagged files across the lawns. She had been ill for a few days with a bug of some kind, but Matron had taken care of her. And now half-term was coming up. It was to be a special half-term. Her parents were flying over and taking her off to Paris for a whole week. She had never been to Paris before, though she had been to Bali and Jakarta and Goa, and even lived briefly in India, not that she remembered much of that. Paris was to be her birthday present.

She had seen her mother just before the school year began, but she hadn't been with her father since the first week of the summer holidays. It felt like a long time. She missed her father; her mother, too, of course, but her father most, though she knew that was wrong and that she should miss them equally. Her father was special. He was tall and lean and tanned, and her friends had whispered to her that he looked like an actor. In her mind he was an adventurer, like the hero of *Lost Horizon* who had found his Shangri-La in the Tibetan hills.

Her father didn't speak much, her mother did all that, but she knew from the way he looked at her that he understood her and thought she was special, too. The last time they had met, he'd said he felt a little shy with her now that she was turning into a woman. That had made her blush. It was a pleasant blush.

Her travel bag was neatly packed for a week before the planned departure. She tucked it under her bed, and every night she would secretly peek at it, just to make sure it was still there, and to count down the days.

On the day before the anticipated arrival of her parents, she had been called to the headmistress's office. She had walked nervously down the corridor and wondered what she could, unknowingly, have done wrong. There had been only one prior interview with Dr Brody and that had been at the very beginning of her first year. Dr Brody was large and bony and always wore plaid skirts and stiff woollen jackets with a long flower-shaped pin stuck in the lapel. But her voice was nice. It had a soft, Scottish burr, even when it pointed out that a skirt had been turned over a few too many times at the waist to reveal a greater-than-permissible extent of leg.

Dr Brody had smiled at her affably, so she knew she hadn't done anything terribly wrong, and had urged her into the chair on the other side of her impeccably tidy desk. 'Now, Leonora,' she had begun, 'I'm afraid I have some sad news to convey to you. Your mother telephoned me earlier to say that, unfortunately, she won't be here to pick you up tomorrow. Arrangements have been made for you to spend your break here. I hope it won't be too unpleasant for you. Miss Henderson will be in charge and will look after things.'

The tears had crept into Leo's eyes, but she had forced them back. Dr Brody must have seen them, because she came round to pat her on the shoulder with a 'There, there, now. Your mother will be here soon. She told me to tell you that.'

In her room that night, Leo unpacked her bag slowly and then, with a kick, sent it flying back under the bed. She had cried herself to sleep, all the while telling herself there was no reason for the tears. But at the same time it came clear to her, in a jumbled way, that her parents didn't love her, didn't love her enough to keep their promises, maybe didn't love her enough because she was no longer a sweet little dimpled girl who could be paraded before cooing acquaintances. The world felt smaller than her grief.

The next day, or maybe it was a few days after that, she was walking through grounds made desolate by her schoolmates' absence when she came across one of the youths who helped with the gardening. She didn't know what led to her boldness, but she started to chat to him. Two days later, and for the rest of that fleeting week, they made love in one of the isolated sheds. She neither enjoyed it nor disliked it, but it made her feel better about things.

It was the first time she slept with the boy – Pete was his name – that the intuition came to her. It was like a knife piercing her ribcage, looking for the soft flesh beneath. What she saw was an avalanche of snow toppling from a peak and covering her father in a feathery vastness so thick and smooth and white that no trace of him remained. The vision passed in an instant, leaving behind it only a sense of a profound absence and a lingering anxiety.

A few days after the end of the half-term break, her mother arrived. She looked strained, her lipstick jagged, and she didn't speak much, which added to the oddness. She was staying in a hotel near the centre of town, and she took Leo there for dinner. They sat, not quite looking at each other, Leo answering desultory questions about her schoolwork, until the soup came, at which point her mother burst into tears. She wiped them away with a starched white napkin. Mascara smudged her cheeks and left dark stains on white cloth.

'I wasn't going to tell you until we had finished,' she sobbed. 'Your father's dead, Leonora. Killed.'

More tears flowed as she reached into her bag and brought out a crumpled, folded sheet of newsprint. 'There.' She passed it to her. 'A helicopter crash.'

She was blubbering, and it was hard for Leo to make out her words – or maybe it was the sudden pounding in her own head. Her mother said something about how long it had taken for her to hear about it and make her way there, only to see the charred ruins of the wretched machine. The three bodies, what remained of them, had already been buried by local villagers. It didn't make sense to unearth them, but she had managed to arrange for some kind of grave marking and . . .

Leo had stopped listening. She watched her mother weep. It was as if she were usurping the entire world's quotient of tears. Leo didn't cry. Methodically she ate what was put in front of her. Her lips felt numb. Her mouth felt numb. Only her jaw ached, as if it had grown rigid with biting at food and news.

Her mother wanted her to go straight back to New York with her. Tomorrow. The next day at the latest. It would do them both good to be at home, amidst friends.

'Home?' Leo had queried. 'I don't think so.'

She had refused to go. She had barely managed to give her mother a goodnight hug.

When she left for New York, her mother handed her the newspaper clipping. Leo was glad she was gone. She was angry at her. Angry at her for not telling her sooner, for not filling in the facts so all she was left with was an image as vague and blurry as the photograph, not even a date or a precise place. Angry at her for not having the strength to keep Leo's father alive. If Leo had been there, it wouldn't have happened. No, she wouldn't have allowed him to go off like that. No.

Part of her also felt a kind of guilty embarrassment at not having complied with her mother's wish to accompany her. But the guilt was only a low thrumming. What she felt, above all, was cold and listless and numb. She must have gone to classes and done her prep and played games and spoken to friends, but she couldn't remember anything about those days. She was absent, frozen.

What she remembered were the nights. She would

go to her room and stare at the photograph, trying to conjure sense out of dense trees and undergrowth and a few hazy figures bent over an invisible object. When she closed her eyes, she would see giant helicopters whipping through air heavy with a viscous jungle mugginess. Sometimes the 'copter crashed into a treetop and burst into flame, only to plummet slowly to the ground amidst curdling screams and a thrashing of blades. Sometimes her father jumped from the tumbling craft and whirring blades lopped off his head and limbs, only to cut through neighbouring trees and plunge to the ground in an explosion of fire. She would try to imagine him, his handsome face gaunt with sudden fear. Had he thought of her at that moment? No, no, she had already betrayed him, and now she could never make it up to him.

Her periods stopped. She thought she was pregnant. She didn't dare tell anyone. It didn't matter anyhow. Nothing felt real, neither the kindness of friends nor the sympathy of teachers who complimented her on her mature behaviour. Nothing felt real except at night in her dreams. Then the helicopters came back, whirring, thrashing, plummeting, curdling her blood.

Leo stopped. Her hair was moist, her cheeks wet with tears. 'I don't know why I'm telling you all this,' she murmured.

Silence fell.

'Curdling your blood.' The words floated towards her softly, as if she were still in a dream.

'Curdling my blood,' she repeated. Then, after a moment, she saw his sense. 'No. I wasn't pregnant. Just shock, I guess. A shock to the system.'

'The turning-into-a-woman system.'

'What do you mean?'

'Your father said that to you.'

'It came back. The periods came back.'

'When?'

'After I went to New York.'

'Back to your mother.'

'Back to my mother and my new stepfather.' Leo spat the sentence out.

'So your mother was a woman again and you could dare to be one, too?'

'Nonsense. It's not that simple.' Her words carried a conviction she suddenly didn't altogether feel. She was seeing herself in those first weeks in Manhattan, the muddled state of her emotions. Her mother had a glow about her which Leo felt sat grotesquely on what should have been widow's weeds, whereas she, she was an ugly duckling. For the wedding she had gone and had all her hair lopped off, a forest of childhood growth. To her astonishment, it looked good. Her stepfather had commented on it in his unctuous way. 'You look beautiful, Leonora, now that we can see your face.'

'No, never that simple.' She heard his voice. 'And the repeated whirring and thrashing of the helicopter, that must be hard to bear.'

'Like killing my father over and over again.' She said it so softly that she wasn't certain she had spoken out loud.

'And keeping him present.'

'Keeping him present?'

'Alive, perhaps. Still powerful.'

'But dead.'

'The dead are very demanding. We keep in touch with them. We can keep them alive by imagining they

211

still want something from us. Does your father still want something from you, Leonora?'

She didn't know whether she translated it into words, but she suddenly had an image of her father and herself. They were walking in some exotic park. The leaves on the trees were very thick and shiny. And then came the orchids, an infinite variety of them, a little scary with their forked tongues emerging from lustrous mouths, brashly pink or magenta, or a blushing, fragile white. They stopped to wonder at one of them. They were so happy. Her father's large hand stroked her hair. She turned to look up at him. 'Almost as lovely as my little girl,' he said, and his arm encompassed her narrow shoulders. She felt so small and safe. Very small and very safe.

'He wants his little girl.' Her voice echoed through the stillness. Its piping childish sound confused her.

'She's still there, though grown up,' Daniel said softly. 'And the helicopter, with its thrashing and whirring, like all those feelings you must have had – fear, loss, despair, rage – at your father, too, for abandoning you. Does it want something from you?'

Leo didn't answer. She was very tired. She could sleep now, she felt. Sleep for a long time. She curled into the sofa.

Daniel watched her. She had taken on the posture of a slip of a girl, her legs slightly awkward, feet pointed out. She was chewing at her fingernail. He hesitated. They had covered so much ground already. He sensed the moment wasn't altogether right. But she had forewarned him there wouldn't be many sessions, and she was an intelligent patient. He took the risk and plunged. 'The child in your dream, the one who wasn't able to move forward, who could only walk round in circles, was that you?'

'The child . . . ?' Leo roused herself. 'No, no. Not me.'

'Your daughter then, whom you're worried about, whom you'd like to tie to you, stake close to yourself?'

'Of course not.' Leo leapt angrily to her feet. How had she let him embroil her in herself so much? That wasn't what she was here for.

'Don't you know anything?' She waved her arms at him. 'Don't you even remember what your patients say to you? That child was my friend. Isabel.'

'You're certain of that?'

'Certain? What do you mean?'

Leo had a sudden dreamlike sense of figures melting into one another as they went round and round that stake, taking on each other's gestures in a kaleidoscope of fusing and splintering shapes. Isabel, Becca, herself, her father, round and round. For a split-second the kaleidoscope paused at a new distillation: a girl, not Isabel, yet with a mass of honey-gold hair. A wild girl with long limbs and yellow-green eyes. Laura, yes Laura. The name leapt before her. Laura who had been her most intimate friend at school in Cambridge. She hadn't thought of her for so long.

Leo flopped back onto the couch.

Laura who had secretly tucked up next to her in bed so that they could whisper into the early hours. Laura who had suddenly and unexpectedly vanished after that half-term break. That dismal break in which Leo hadn't gone to Paris. And then had never returned. Rumours flew about her disappearance. Teachers offered no reasons, only said, 'Laura won't be back with us this term.'

In her state of numbness, Leo had registered the

loss only to bury it with the greater one. Laura was gone. Her father was gone. Both had entered the shadowy realm of the unsayable.

And now Isabel . . .

The noise of the helicopter was back, whirring and thrashing. Death.

'Are you certain that child in your dream was Isabel?' Daniel repeated.

'Stop mixing everything up. Stop it,' Leo shouted, jumping up again, glaring at him.

If she could, Daniel thought, she would hit him now. She was incandescent. That was good.

'Your time is up, Ms Gould,' he said softly. 'I'll see you on Friday.'

He rose, put a distance between them. He watched her look awkwardly around, then scramble for her bag and take out an envelope. 'I've brought your fee.'

'Just leave it on the table over there.'

She whipped the envelope onto the table, like the slap that hadn't been delivered, and marched down the stairs.

Daniel closed the door behind her and went to jot down a few notes. It took a few moments for him to realize that he hadn't heard the expected slam of the front door. She had certainly been angry enough for that.

He listened. Nothing. Had he overdone it? Was she sitting in a heap on the stairs, unable to open the door on to the world. He ran down the flights. No sign of her. Odd. She must have slipped out as silently as a ghost. Only Eva had ever had that kind of quiet consideration. He was about to make his way back up the stairs when a sound from the living room alerted him. He pushed open the door. Leonora Gould was bent over the bottom drawer of his

214

filing cabinet, oblivious to anything but its contents.

'You won't find anything of interest in there, Ms Gould, I can assure you.'

Leo veered round. Her pupils were as round and black as a trapped animal's. 'I . . .'

'You were looking for a file on Isabel Morgan. I know.' Daniel's tone was caustic. 'There's nothing in there, unless you're interested in my accounts.'

'Well, if you won't talk to me like an ordinary human being . . .' Leo justified herself. Her cheeks were hot. 'I'm desperate. There's been no word from Isabel. Nothing.'

'I told you, I haven't seen her for some months.' Daniel restrained a sudden rush of anger. 'I think you'd better leave now.'

'But if only you would tell me something of what went on between you, it might provide a clue. For example, did Isabel talk to you about her work, a project to do with genetic engineering?'

'Isabel talked to me about many things. If I thought there was anything of use within that for the present situation, I would communicate it to the police.' Daniel's choice of phrasing sounded pompous even to his own ears. He added, 'I have communicated with the police.'

'But they don't understand her as I do. She may have had some kind of breakdown. She may be—'

A loud voice interrupted her protests and stopped her from saying what was tumbling off her tongue. Isabel dead. She tried to collect herself.

'Dad. I'm home.' A small boy burst into the room and stopped in his tracks as he saw Leo. 'Hello.' He peered up at her with evident curiosity.

'Hello.' Leo gave him what she hoped wasn't too nervous a smile. Behind him stood the young blonde woman she had seen before. She had a protective hand on the boy's shoulder. Could this be the boy's mother? Daniel's wife? Leo's discomfiture mounted.

'Have you come to look at my mummy's pictures?' the child asked. 'That's my favourite.' He pointed at a canvas which was a swirl of forest greens. 'Can you see the owl? He's called Hooter.'

'Hooter. That's a good name.' Leo looked at the painting. Amidst the darkly vibrant greens, she made out a white hieratic bird with staring eyes of molten yellow. 'A very good name. Mine's Leo. Leonora,' she corrected herself, and glanced quickly at Daniel Lukas as she bent to give the boy her hand.

'I'm Robbie,' he said with solemn emphasis. 'And this is my nanny, Martina. Are you staying for tea?'

Daniel shook himself out of the raptness with which he had watched the scene. 'Ms Gould was just leaving. Weren't you, Ms Gould?'

For a moment, as she nodded, he was tempted to ask her to stay. But given her status as a patient, let alone her questionable motives, that would hardly do. Yet his son rarely manifested such instant interest in adults. Was that his doing rather than Robbie's? Over this last year, he had been so intent on shielding the boy that, apart from his close circle of friends, he had never let anyone in.

'That's too bad.' Robbie looked crestfallen.

'Another time perhaps,' Leo said. 'I'd like to come and visit you and Hooter again.'

'OK. That would be good.'

As Daniel saw her to the door, she gave him a glance which he read as a mixture of embarrassment, contrition and challenge. The challenge won.

'Rules of confidentiality can't possibly govern all situations,' she said, turning back at the threshold.

'So if I bump into your husband, you won't object to my telling him what passes between us?'

'My ex-husband,' Leo said, disliking them both. 'He'd probably tell you that I'd only come to you because I'd discovered he had an affair with Isabel,' she added, startling herself. 'Which would be as wrong as everything else.'

Daniel watched her walk quickly down the street. There was a resolute thrust to her shoulders. She didn't look back. He mused for a moment, then returned to his son. They sprawled on the floor and played two games of concentration, the cards spread between them in a wide arc.

After Robbie had trounced his father, Daniel tousled his hair and excused himself. He walked slowly upstairs to his desk and pulled out the bottom drawer. A haphazard stack of brochures and theatre programmes confronted him. With lightning irritation, he upended the drawer and spilt its contents onto the floor.

A penknife clattered onto the pile. He picked it up. He had forgotten that was there. It was so long ago. The youth's name was Daniel, just like his. That had played a part in things. Daniel Roper. The boy had pulled the knife on him one day and slashed menacingly in his direction. 'Who is it that you really want to harm?' Daniel had asked him softly. 'Me? Your father? Yourself?' Towards the end of the session, the youth had handed him the knife, telling him to keep it. He hadn't meant it anyway. Not really.

As he handled the penknife, Daniel suddenly felt the fear that had flooded through him at the time. His fear, and the boy's, bound together for a split-second. He placed the knife carefully in the corner of a high shelf and turned his attention to the brochures.

The one he wanted was now close to the top of the pile. He punched out the number. A jolly voice responded, one which spoke of hockey fields and sweaty rides across the countryside.

'How can I help you?'

'I'd like to know whether you have an Isabel Morgan staying with you, please.'

The voice replied with the same automatic jolliness. 'I'm very sorry, sir. We don't give out the names of our clients.'

Daniel swallowed his frustration.

'My name is Daniel Lukas. Dr Daniel Lukas. Can you put me through to your director, please.'

'He's not here today. Thank you for calling.'

When he heard the dialling tone rebound in his ear, Daniel let out a low laugh at the irony of the situation. He thought of Leonora Gould. She would have enjoyed him falling prey to his own rules of confidentiality.

Leo walked slowly down Highgate Hill. The squeal and giggle of brown-clad girls accompanied her as she passed the school Becca had attended. She quickened her step. What did that know-it-all Dr Lukas with his babe of a nanny mean by colliding Isabel's dream with her own life and suggesting that she wanted to keep Becca staked to herself? Of course she missed her daughter. That was hardly unnatural.

His voice played itself over and over in her inner ear. She had the odd sensation that it was becoming a part of herself. She shut it out, like she had shut out her mother's voice in those months after her father's death. The internal gesture was the same, she suddenly realized. All she had to do was visualize a flap, like a square of thick velvet curtain, coming down over the inside of her ear. It muffled the sounds, drowning them out so that they became merely an incomprehensible burble, a low droning without words.

Had she done that to her father's voice, too? No, she liked to hear his voice, the cooing tone he had used with her when she was small. But somehow that voice, too, had made her angry, and it had brought in its train the hideous sound of the thrashing helicopters which beat it out of recognition. All the panic and pain and tangled feelings of that time came back to her, as if that insidious doctor had switched on an ignition key and then abandoned her to a vehicle whose gears she was unfamiliar with, so that it threatened to rush out of control. She slowed her steps.

The sprawl of the Whittington Hospital was now on her right. She noted the big sign announcing Accident and Emergency and had a vision of checking in and being placed between starched white sheets. A soft-spoken nurse would bring her a cup of tea and tut-tut over a thermometer.

That's what the know-it-all doctor was doing, turning her into a patient. An impatient patient, she told herself, and walked hastily towards the tube. Like any other ordinary commuter, she stopped to buy an evening paper. Like any other ordinary commuter, she perched on the steep slope of the escalator and skimmed the array of posters stretched on her left. A glistening, silver-laced helicopter leapt out at her and came back at regular intervals, as if the world had been designed to force her back into the universe of the analytic session, a universe where everything became significant. The posters were only there to advertise a book, Leo reminded herself, determinedly focusing her eyes in front of her.

But was Daniel Lukas right in intimating that her fear of helicopters had come to stand in for all the jumbled and conflicting feelings of that distant time? That her panic at the machines kept her father present? Was that what she wanted? Her perfect, irreproachable, always-absent father? And her friend. Her friend Laura. Her friend Isabel. She remembered how her anxiety about Isabel's non-appearance that evening in Manhattan had catapulted into panic with the sound of the 'copter.

Leo listened to the roar of an oncoming train. Her hair flew. She turned her eyes away from the scatter of grit and bumped into a stranger as she made her way towards a door. She murmured apologies and sank gratefully into an empty seat. The stale odour of the carriage attacked her nostrils, a mixture of rank, sweaty bodies and century-old dirt.

Too bad she hadn't found anything in the file neatly labelled 'Isabel Morgan'. Too bad he had caught her at it, too. That had been deeply shaming. There was probably no point in going back to see him now. He wasn't going to divulge anything.

The child had been sweet, though. Robbie. She wondered what his mother was like. A painter. She closed her eyes and saw Daniel Lukas in the room that bulged with canvases, his boy at his side. A woman came in and gave the child a kiss on the top of his tousled head, then she turned to look up at Daniel and sauntered towards him with a wide smile.

Isabel.

Leo's eyes snapped open. She felt heat rising into her cheeks. Isabel and Daniel. That gave her an idea. Why not? She was, she acknowledged, willing to try anything.

10

For once the street on which Isabel's building sat like some industrial monster transplanted into the cyber age gave signs of city life. Office workers streamed out of a neighbouring block, eyes and shoulders thrusting towards home or the nearest pub. Traffic edged forward at caterpillar pace, blocked by the line emerging from the half-gutted car park. Bicycles wove their way precariously through the crush, all but scraping the pavement. A traffic warden stood beside one of the two meters, punched out a ticket and stuck it to a window, just as a red-faced man ran up to her and started gesticulating furiously.

Leo let herself into the building. Halfway up the stairs, she met Rosie carrying a tote bag.

'You OK, Leo? Can't stop now. I'm meeting some-one at the gym and I'm already late.' She blew her a kiss. 'Pop round for a drink later, why don't you.'

'If I can.' Leo smiled in response and took the rest of the stairs two at a time. In lieu of the gym, she told herself.

Despite herself, she paused before pushing open the door, as if the apartment had become an un-predictable and treacherous space. A sudden rubbing against the bottom of her legs made her jump.

The cat miaowed beneath her. 'Silly Beast,' she

murmured and stroked his fur until he set up a comforting purr. He followed her into Isabel's office, pounced onto a chair and watched her as she checked the answering machine.

'Greetings, Holland,' Christopher Norfolk boomed at them. 'Looks like I'm not gonna make it tonight. Rain check, please. See you anon.'

Leo didn't like to recognize that she was sorry. She lifted the cat into her lap and stroked him thoughtfully. She was at a loose end. A moment of inaction and all the matter that Daniel Lukas had stoked up flared before her. She pushed it aside and tried to concentrate on plans when the phone rang. She reached for it with alacrity.

'Mom? Just picked up your message about your computer being stolen. You poor thing.'

'Becca. Hello, darling. Thanks for phoning.' Warmth flooded through Leo. 'You're back at Stanford?'

'Yeah. Had a good time with Dad.' She paused. 'Did you know I was going to have a little brother or sister?'

'Jeff told me.'

Another pause. 'You OK about it?'

'Yes. Think so. How about you?'

'Feels a bit weird.'

Leo laughed. 'That, too. But who knows, you might end up enjoying it.'

'Yeah. Who knows.' Becca abruptly changed tack. 'Did I tell you about this boy in my English class? He's cool. We're going to see a movie on Saturday.'

Leo put a brake on the questions which were about to tumble off her tongue. 'That sounds good,' she said with more enthusiasm than she felt.

'Yeah. Any news of Isabel?'

Leo kept her voice calm. 'Not yet. Soon, I hope.'

'You've been checking in on the Manhattan number?'

'Will do again. Tell me about your classes.'

They chatted for a few more minutes and, when she hung up, Leo realized that the pleasure she'd felt at the sound of Becca's voice was edged with disquiet. For a moment, she pondered the impact Jeff's new child would have on Becca's journey into womanhood, then reminded herself that she needed to follow Becca's nudge and check her New York answering machine. She hadn't done so since the weekend. She started to dial when the sound of the doorbell deflected her.

Inspector Faraday's face bore all the solemnity of a vicar's at a funeral service. As he settled himself stiffly on the edge of the sofa and clasped his hands together, Leo suddenly saw him in black tails and a stiff collar administering a Victorian funeral service. He wouldn't altogether meet her eyes.

'Is something wrong, Inspector?' she asked nervously.

'Tell me about your relationship with Christopher Norfolk, Ms Holland.'

The demand surprised her as much as the steeliness of his tone.

'That really isn't any of your business, Inspector, but, since you ask, I can tell you that there isn't one.'

His gaze fell on her, then was quickly averted. 'On Monday evening, the night of the break-in, you failed to mention to the officer in charge that Mr Norfolk had the keys to the house.'

Leo shrugged off the accusation. 'It must have slipped my mind.'

'A useful slip.'

'Norfolk would hardly need to make such a mess if he were looking for something. He had easy access.'

'Doesn't it occur to you that he might want to throw us off his scent?'

'It doesn't,' Leo said flatly, though, as she said it, she realized that she didn't know quite why she was defending Norfolk so adamantly.

Inspector Faraday scrutinized her. 'And where is he now?'

Leo shrugged. 'I don't know.'

Slowly Faraday reached into his pocket to draw out his spectacles. He opened his notebook with the air of a methodical tax inspector. 'I interviewed Hamish Macgregor earlier, and he confirmed that he had been here. That he had seen you and Mr Norfolk together.' He threw Leo an admonishing glance. 'And that your friend had roughed him up.'

'But that's . . . Macgregor was trying to break in,' Leo spluttered.

Faraday shook his head solemnly. 'He told me that Ms Morgan had given him the keys months ago, since he did work around the house for her, and that he'd come today to collect some money she owed him. One thousand, two hundred pounds, to be exact. In the normal course of things, she left his payment in an envelope in the bottom drawer of her night table. However, this morning, you and Mr Norfolk refused him access.'

'That's a lie. He'd come for his tools, and clothes. A suit he'd left here.'

'Mr Macgregor insisted that your Mr Norfolk did indeed fob him off with a suit. Not a suit of his own.'

'That's complete and utter nonsense.' Leo stopped

224

herself and tried to replay the scene in her mind. What had the two men talked about while she went to fetch Macgregor's clothes?

Faraday broke into her thoughts. The glasses were off now, and he was staring at her with a glint of menace. 'I've had access to your friend Ms Morgan's bank accounts. She was hardly a struggling writer or journalist. Her account showed a very tidy balance. And on the fourteenth of April, she drew out, in cash, the hardly minimal sum of three thousand pounds.'

'I don't know anything about Isabel's finances,' Leo murmured. 'Maybe she inherited some money from her mother, who died earlier this year. But if she took out that much, it explains why you found nothing drawn on her Visa card after the fifteenth, which means she's still alive.' Leo heard her own words reverberate around the room with a clang of triumph. She met Faraday's invasive eyes.

'So you presumed she was dead.'

Leo shook her head vehemently enough to blot out her own imaginings. 'I worried, that's all. Don't use that word.'

'Shall we have a look for that money?'

'You look, Inspector, since you don't seem to trust me. I'll go and get myself a drink. I need one.'

She watched him walk towards the bedroom and heard the rattle of drawers. After a moment, she went to pour herself a glass of burgundy and followed him.

His beanpole of a body bent double, Faraday was rifling through a bottom drawer filled with tights and stockings. He stood up with a muted smile on his bony face. He was holding a long, white envelope. 'It says Hamish M. right here, but there's nothing inside. Any ideas, Ms Holland?'

Leo took a long sip of her wine. 'Lots of ideas,

Inspector. How about the burglar? How about Isabel didn't leave Hamish Macgregor any money this time, though that could be the usual deposit place? Or how about she didn't owe him anything and he made it all up? Or he's already been to get it before this, maybe even before I arrived, since when I did there was a shattered vase just where you're standing. And maybe you should check out his bank balance. Or how about I stole it 'cause I'm so desperately in need of funds? You can check my balance, too. I'll get you the account number.' The sarcasm dripped from her voice, drier than the wine.

'Or how about your Mr Norfolk?'

'Well, you'll just have to ask him. I really don't see how this is helping us find Isabel. And that's the important thing, Inspector. The burglary doesn't matter. Just find her.'

'We're trying, Ms Holland. Calm yourself.' He paced, uncomfortable with her sudden emotion. He paused at the dining table and pulled out his glasses. He was studying the papers she had left there before going to see Daniel Lukas.

'What is this, Ms Holland?'

'You have me there, Inspector. I've been trying to work it out myself. A family tree, perhaps.' She hesitated, then rushed on, feeling herself grow hot as she spoke. 'It was in Isabel's post this morning. There was a diskette. That's what was on it.'

'And you printed this out on Mr Norfolk's computer.'

Faraday missed nothing.

'Yes.' Leo swallowed.

'I see.' He gave her an admonishing glance. 'I'll just take this, if I may, Ms Holland.' He folded the sheets carefully into his jacket pocket. 'I'd like to have another look at the papers in Ms Morgan's office, if I may.'

'You may.'

He preceded her stiffly into Isabel's office. The cat, sprawled in the chair like some luxuriating emperor of fur, roused himself at their entrance.

'New pet?' Faraday asked, relaxing visibly as he gave the animal a series of practised strokes.

'Didn't your dear Mr Macgregor point out that he'd made a second stop here today to deliver Isabel's cat?'

Faraday suddenly looked uncomfortable. 'No. He didn't.' He sat down at the desk chair, his back to her. 'Where was the envelope in which the diskette arrived posted, by the way?'

'Dorset was all we could make out.'

He nodded. 'You can leave me, Ms Holland. I won't take anything without your permission.'

'What are you looking for, Inspector?'

'Oh, this and that. Bank statements, bills. Whatever turns up.'

'This and that,' Leo murmured and went to stand by one of the living-room windows. Yes. Life reduced to a random assortment of this and that. Her own life, too. Everything had taken on a randomness since Isabel's disappearance, as if Leo was totally at the mercy of events. She hardly even recognized herself from day to day, let alone from minute to minute. She didn't know what she was going to say or do next.

An image of herself scurrying, like some furtive criminal, into Daniel Lukas's private rooms bounded into her mind. It was so wholly uncharacteristic that it took determined force to erase it.

She held back tears, went into her room and stared in the mirror. Did that face with its stray locks of auburn reposition her as herself? Eyes, darkly blue and slightly too far apart, gazed back at her. The skin over the cheekbones was stretched tight so that there were curved hollows in the cheeks. The mouth was generous to a fault. It was her face, yet it had nothing to do with her. She looked at the self which might as well not be herself, and from somewhere in the mists of memory she remembered examining herself like this when she was young – an adolescent staring in the mirror and seeking some definition.

It was when she had just returned to Manhattan from England. The unfamiliar surroundings didn't return a recognizable self to her. Everything was in flux. Sensations carried her along, like some leaf unfettered by a staying branch. If the wind blew one way, she might end up at the Whitney, sauntering past pictures, if in another, in some SoHo bar. She relished the freedom, yet also feared it, not knowing who she would wake up to be the next day. She had even slept with two men in those months. Random men. Her life was determined only by chance. Until she had met Jeff, whom chance had brought but who erased the sense of randomness.

Jeff had bestowed an identity on her in those early days and she clung to it as if it were her salvation. In her quietness, he saw sophistication and a worldly, much-travelled woman – which she was, of course, though she had never seen herself in that light. Whereas he had never yet left the United States. From the vantage point of his nether-end-of-Brooklyn childhood, her Park Avenue family were mysterious beings, lapped in the privileges he aspired to. In the hectic glow of his regard, she had ceased to float like a bit of flotsam on the ocean of life and taken on ballast. Certainty, too. Even her talents seemed more definite. Real. He had been her greatest good luck.

Not for ever.

Leo went back into the living room and leant into the sofa. Above her, the lavish colours of Isabel's chosen canvas sprawled as vivid as a sunset in the desert.

'I've done now, Ms Holland.' Inspector Faraday's voice roused her from her reverie. 'I'll keep in touch.'

She caught up with him at the door. 'Did you manage to get hold of the woman who left a message, Inspector? Paola someone.'

'I left a message for her; it hasn't been returned yet.' His bland face creased into a frown. 'Do take care, Ms Holland. You've been pushed about once, the next time might be more serious. I really suggest you leave this to us.'

But this doesn't leave me, Leo reflected as she went back into the empty room. She rubbed her legs where the violent fall had left them sore and looked out on the cluster of roofs. In the distance a statue poked above the buildings. It glistened in the gathering dusk, which was tinged with palest urban pink. She should go up and see if Rosie was back and put an end to her desultory thoughts, but she didn't feel like chatting. Not really.

With a vocal sigh, Leo decided to scramble some eggs. As she whisked she remembered the inspector's words about the size of Isabel's bank balance. Had an inheritance come her way? Or was it something else? The Australian aunt might know. How to find the number? She didn't feel like digging back into the box where she had come across Jeff's letter. Then, too, those were old letters. People moved. Norfolk might know. She would ask him when he got back.

The flat grew dark as she ate her eggs and toast.

The darkness set up a tremor in her. For the last two days she had repressed her sense that the place had grown hostile, a site of violent visitations and gloomy foreboding. Where could Isabel be? She conjured her up again, watched her stride across the room, her hair swinging. She sat down opposite her with a swish of silk trousers. A grin illuminated her features. She laughed her booming laugh. 'It didn't matter about him. Neither of us cared. I was just curious. Curious about you, too. Through him. And curiosity ran away with me. I like events. You know what I mean.'

Isabel faded to be replaced by the vase of vibrant daffodils. Did she know what Isabel meant, Leo wondered. Really know, as an experience within herself?

She washed her lone plate and dried it to an impeccable sheen, then watched herself aghast. She was turning into an old woman. What she needed was the sound of human voices. But she didn't want to go out. She checked that the front door was double-locked and wandered through the apartment. The television, that would do. Other people's lives to put one's own into relief.

She went into Isabel's room and rapidly switched on the TV to blot out any memory of the hands emerging from the darkness to shove her violently to the floor. She stretched out on the bed and watched colours form into a landscape – pools of crystalline blue dotted by ice caps, and then a plateau of untouched snow, ridged and heaped only by wind. A soundtrack – was it Grieg? – scored the images. And then came a whirr. A helicopter flew into the frame. Leo leant on her elbows, her hands firmly clasped beneath her chin. For a split-second she thought of

Daniel Lukas. She didn't reach for the zapper. She forced herself to watch.

The machine glided and became a fragile, glistening form against the expanse of white. A cut brought the pilot's face into relief. Not her father's face. Definitely not her father's, but a burly, curly-headed man in a lumber-jacket. Beside him sat a woman with the pure face of an ice princess. She clutched his arm in mute panic.

Leo couldn't tear her eyes from the screen. She watched the man give the woman a consoling smile. A moment later, he was peering into the distance, his face resolute.

She was outside the cabin again, the helicopter a bobbing form moving closer and closer to the ground, then up again, until finally, as the music reached a frenzied crescendo, it landed with a lurch, its insect form half swallowed by snow that was too soft for its weight. In mid-shot, she watched the pilot emerge, push against the partly buried door, then drag his sinking feet to his partner's side and let her out. She fell into his arms.

Leo turned away. A howl of pure rage seemed to be building inside her, demanding explosion. She reached for a pillow and threw it at the far end of the room. Then followed it with a second. Why couldn't her father have stayed alive? Stayed alive like this man. He was strong, too. Powerful. He could have stayed alive. Stayed alive for her. He had promised to come. Had promised. And he had betrayed her.

Tears flooded her cheeks. Copious tears interrupted by great heaving sobs, like a child's. She couldn't stop them.

Through their blur, she half watched the screen. The helicopter had started up its whirring again.

Inside there was a second man now, his eyes closed, his face contorted with pain. Blades rotated through the air, growing invisible with speed. The machine lifted, leaving a gully in its wake.

Leo closed her eyes. She let the weeping take its course. As it ebbed, a profound hollowness came in its place, as if she had been gutted out. A hollowness of loss. The loss carried her into sleep.

She didn't know whether she was dreaming or awake when she felt the hand on her hair. It stroked her, consoled, rumpled her a little. Her father's hand, she thought. She covered it with her own small one. The skin felt hard and cool.

A voice whispered in her ear. 'Nice of you to wait for me, Holland.'

Leo turned and saw Christopher Norfolk perched beside her. He looked big and solid, not a dream. She couldn't quite read his expression. 'I'm sorry. I didn't mean . . .' she croaked.

'Shhh.' He continued his stroking, but now it was her features his fingers outlined.

She met his eyes. His were very clear and blue in the half light. His face moved towards her. Lips brushed hers. Her arms curled round his back of their own accord. The gesture surprised her, as did the force of his kiss. It set up a tingling in her body. She had forgotten that sensation, its warming glow, had never really expected to experience it again. She gave herself to it, gave herself to him, wanting the soft ardour of his gaze as he unbuttoned her shirt, the firm moulding of his hands on her skin, the weight of him against her body. When her hands burrowed beneath his sweater and shirt to find the smoothness of his back and he rose, she felt bereft. But he was pulling off his clothes, leaving them in a heap on the floor. She watched him covertly. The broad back made darker by the pallor of buttocks untouched by the sun, the tawny legs. Like a shy schoolgirl, she closed her eyes when he turned towards her.

'Your turn, Holland.' It was a command. But when she didn't move, he did the undressing for her in swift, certain movements, curving against her before she could feel the coolness of the night air on her skin. She stopped thinking and abandoned herself to the pleasure of him, astonished at her own when he moved inside her or rolled her on top of him. For a moment then, as their eyes clung to each other, she thought of Isabel. Him and Isabel, for they must have been together like this. And she was glad. She arched her back and swung her hair savagely and dug her nails into his shoulders and a moan reached her lips. It flowed around the room and came back to envelop them. And then Isabel was gone and it was just Leo and this man, this stranger. This Christopher. This Norfolk. Inside her, outside her, beneath, above, so that her blood seemed to flow to a new heated beat. Uncurdling, the word popped into her mind and disappeared as quickly, replaced by his name. Spoken now, or cried, a wave in her mouth to challenge the waves which encircled her from below.

Later, as they lay together, there was uncertainty.

She didn't quite know how to take his 'You're a fierce little thing, Holland.'

'Am I?' She moved to hide her nakedness beneath the duvet. She drew it right up to her neck. He edged it down again.

'I like looking at you. There's a lot more of you with your clothes off. Like those French women.

233

Speaking of which, how about a glass of something?'

He rose before she could answer, and came back a moment later with two glasses and a bottle. He poured the wine and then held up his glass to her. 'To Holland. A step forward from the truce.'

She met the irony of his smile. 'To Norfolk.'

He came to lie beside her, his hand smoothing her thigh. 'Where did these come from?' He touched the ugly bruises on her legs.

'From our intruder. Monday night. He pushed. I fell. Against the drawers.'

'I'm so sorry.'

For a moment she thought he was apologizing for something he had done. She banished the thought. 'And this?' She pointed to the welt on his shoulder.

'That, my darling Holland, is all your doing. It's what I mean by fierce. But I guess it's better than your attempt at bashing my brains in.' He gave her a slow wink and curled in beside her.

She liked his face, Leo decided, the leathery etching of lines in it, as if he had spent his life narrowing his eyes against the sun.

'I had a distinct feeling, while you were administering this little wound,' he fingered his shoulder, 'that you were possessed by . . .'

'Oh . . .' Leo inched away from him.

'Or maybe just pretending to be our mutual friend. It was the way you shook your head. Am I right, Holland?'

Leo could feel his gaze on her, as incisive as Daniel Lukas's. 'Maybe I was,' she acknowledged. 'It just came over me. I don't know why. I've been thinking about Isabel so much.' She paused. What came to her lips next startled her. 'Isabel slept with my husband. My former husband,' she corrected herself.

234

'Is that it?' He wound his arm round her, caressed her gently, then laughed, a brief, droll sound. 'She's a rogue. But that's our Isabel. Of course, you forgave her.'

Leo, suddenly, wasn't altogether sure. Anger flashed through her. Anger at Isabel for betraying her with Jeff. Anger at the second betrayal for standing her up with no warning. But with that came a tangled sense of guilt, loss and fear which swallowed up the anger.

'We always forgive Isabel her misdemeanours. Not to is like asking lightning to feel responsible for striking.' He laughed.

She joined him and rose to pour them both some more wine. She didn't feel so shy now, she realized. She rather enjoyed his passing scrutiny. She returned it and let her eyes rove over his body. She saw his penis begin to bulge. She had an uncharacteristic desire to take it in her mouth.

'The difference is, Holland, if you're contemplating a smidgen of revenge, I was never Isabel's husband. Isabel's not the staying kind. She bores too easily.'

'And you?'

'We share that.' He grinned.

Leo had the impression he was giving her a sign. 'So you're bored already.' She had intended to say it lightly, but it didn't quite come out like that.

'Don't be a sensitive ass, Holland.' He pulled her down beside him and stroked her hair. 'I'm just beginning to get interested.'

'Why do you insist on calling me Holland?'

'I like it. Like the place. Lived there once. Even got married there.'

'Once?'

235

'Yes. Did that again, elsewhere.' He was deliberately vague and she didn't press him.

'What did you do in Holland?'

'Played. Worked. In a chemical firm.'

She thought she saw a shadow cross his face. She didn't pursue it. His lips were on her breast. She abandoned herself to sensation, the heady play of limbs and lips, wondering only at some point at her sheer avidity for him.

Afterwards she said, without quite knowing why, 'I haven't, you know, done this for two years. Maybe more.'

He chuckled. 'I hadn't realized I'd got myself a virgin. Difficult women, virgins.'

Her face fell. She looked round for her shirt. 'I guess I'd better get back. To my room. My life.' She buttoned her blouse and tugged on trousers. He was watching her, but she wouldn't meet his eyes.

'Holland.' His voice was suddenly gentle. 'We all have our fallow periods. And I'm not altogether the crude bugger I sometimes pretend to be. Now just stay here. I have something to ask you.'

'What?'

He tugged her down beside him. 'What did that copper tell you today? That Inspector Faraday?'

'How did you know he was here?'

'I guessed. I'm beginning to know you a little.'

'He doesn't like you.'

'You surprise me, Holland. What else?'

'Do you know Isabel's aunt. The one she liked.'

'Aunt? Isabel never talked about her family.'

'That's odd.'

'Is it? We had rather more interesting things to talk about.' His grin was all mischief.

'I need to find her.'

236

'I know. That's what we're working on.'

'I mean the aunt.'

'I'll check it out down under. But why? Do you think she might know something?'

Leo shrugged. She scrutinized him. The rough-hewn face gave little away. But the body was generous. She ran her hand over his chest. He caught it. 'Tell me.'

'It seems Isabel had a lot of money in her account. More than is reasonable, according to Faraday.'

'So he thinks someone was paying her? That she was working for someone. Mata Hari in the world of terminators.'

'He didn't say that.'

He was silent for a moment. 'We're going to have to move quickly, Holland. Before those bumbling cops blunder in and make things more dangerous all round.'

'The good news is Isabel withdrew a large sum from her account in cash. Which explains why there have been no credit-card traces for her in all this time. So she's probably OK.' Leo's voice cracked as she said it.

He considered this, then frowned. 'Did Faraday check for any video snoopers that might have been planted on us?'

'What do you mean?' Leo asked, realizing as she said it that he meant hidden cameras.

'Look, Holland, someone broke in here. I may inadvertently have tipped them off by talking to that lab technician – we can't be sure of that, but let's presume it for a moment. The blokes at Plantagen, or wherever, were looking for any sensitive material Isabel may have walked off with. The likelihood is they didn't find it. But they may still think it's worth keeping an eye out.'

He got up and roved around the room, pausing at lamps and window frames, then pulled on his shirt and shorts.

'But if they're trying to tail Isabel, that means they aren't holding her, that she's OK.'

'Let's hope so.' He came to plant a kiss on her forehead. 'Let's hope she's just living it up somewhere. But I didn't like the look of this place the other day.' He touched the bruises on her legs. 'Now you just curl up and go to sleep. I'll join you when I'm done. Soon.' He smiled.

'Norfolk.' She held him back. 'What did you find out today?'

'One thing I discovered is that none of Isabel's and my mutual contacts have seen much of her since Christmas. The rest . . . well, I'll tell you tomorrow. How about coming with me? Bright and early.'

She smiled. 'Nice of you to ask. But I was planning to hire a car and drive down to Dorset. To have a look at that hotel Isabel stayed in. See if I can find anything out. I can't bear this waiting.'

'Great minds, partner. We'll drive together. Though it wasn't hotels I was planning on. Now, get some sleep.'

Leo didn't sleep. She lay there in Isabel's bed and touched her body. It felt taut, rosy, as if it had acquired definition, distinct outlines. As if she had been returned to herself by a patterning of another's hands and limbs. The thought came into her mind that she was too old to be finding definition through a man. But how else did one know oneself except through others? Mothers and fathers, Daniel Lukas had insisted. One gradually became who one was through their imprint, a tugging and a pulling, not a simple stamp. Maybe Jeff had come along and allowed her to stop longing for her dead father, to make some sort of uneasy peace with her mother. And then he had gone, well before he had in fact moved out. And Isabel? Did she find definition through the various men in her life? No, not Isabel. Maybe not. She refused definition. It was a kind of confinement. She was all vivid colour spilling over into neighbouring spaces.

The dream Leo had chosen to tell Daniel Lukas leapt graphically before her. She saw a hot place, almost a desert. Sparse grass tufted here and there from the ground. Abandoned in that space stood a child, roped to some sort of peg, a toddler desperate to move and wander, unable to do so. The child was crying. Salt tears wet its cheeks.

It occurred to Leo with a terrible urgency that, more than anyone, Isabel would find confinement impossible to bear.

PART THREE

NOTES TOWARDS A CASE HISTORY (II)

Anna paid me to listen to her stories and feel besmirched by them. The stories themselves had the effect of rendering me helpless. Once I had swallowed this fact, I set out to discover why, and to uncover who in her life she was paralysing through me. The analyst is, after all, a mere stand-in for more potent players.

Anna is lying on the couch. She is in deepest black today. Dramatic layers of it – black trousers, black shirt, black silk waistcoat, black jacket, a chiffon cloudiness of scarf which might as well function as a veil the way she wraps it round her hair and her hands. Since I know by now that she dresses for her performance, I ask her why she is in black. She tells me she is in mourning, in solidarity with a friend. Yet another friend who has been abandoned by a lover, which seems to be a recurring theme in her friends' lives, or certainly in her stories. Anna herself, it seems from the way she tells me these things, is never abandoned. But she doesn't let me press her on this, which is what I am primarily interested in.

She goes on to tell me her friend's story in full dramatic detail. In her characterization, her friend is an innocent who has allowed herself to be beguiled by a married man who has promised her everything, including eventual marriage. They spend almost every weekday night together, but not weekends. On weekends the man goes home. Her friend grows to mind, in part because of the fulsome promises, in part because of the imposed secrecy. She wants full commitment. Honesty. One Saturday, because she feels she has to hear his voice, her friend rings his home number, which she has covertly extracted from his place of work. A woman answers the phone. Anna's friend swallows hard and asks for Mr Sutton. She is told he isn't in so, taking her courage in hand, she asks whether she is speaking to Mrs Sutton. There is a pause and the woman announces that there is no Mrs Sutton. She is the housekeeper. Who is she to say called? Anna's friend hangs up. She is devastated. She confronts her lover with his lies, and he leaves her, just like that, from one day to the next. Anna consoles her friend and suggests a wake to celebrate his passing.

Anna tells me this story with a great many details and flourishes, which include a vivid evocation of the couple's sex life. This last, I know, is conveyed in part to tease me, in part to prove her status as an informed analytic patient.

When she has finished I wait for a moment, then ask, in good transferential mode, whether she is telling me this story because she feels that, in some way, I have let her down or left her feeling abandoned, or perhaps been too secretive about my own status.

She laughs. 'Nonsense. The reason any of us ever come to shrinks is that you never abandon us. We pay you, after all, like prostitutes. You're in our thrall.'

I let this pass and, after a moment, find myself

asking her, 'When you were little, Anna, did people believe what you told them?' I do not know quite why I have said this, but as I say it I realize that the time has come for me to be a little more confrontational. Unlike most patients, Anna rarely mentions her childhood. We need to find out why. Then, too, I want her to know that, although it doesn't particularly matter in my understanding of the analytic context, I do recognize that she fabricates.

She doesn't answer me. Her silence, in itself, is unusual. I wait, and at last she says in a dreamy voice, 'They did and they didn't.'

I wait, and when nothing more comes I ask, 'Who do you identify with in this story, Anna? Who are you? The man, the housekeeper who delivers the truth, your vulnerable friend?'

'No-one ever leaves me,' she says with a note of harshness.

'Because you do the leaving first,' I say without thinking. 'Because you're unwilling or afraid to meet the challenge of commitment.' I realize as I hear myself that I am irritated. Otherwise I would hardly be so direct.

'Death,' Anna says. She seems surprised by her own enunciation of the word, for she is then quiet for a long time. She covers her face with the veil. She is more troubled than I have ever seen her.

'Staying means death. Boredom, repetition?' I eventually hazard.

'Death means death,' she says. 'Just death. A cigar is sometimes just a cigar.'

Suddenly I feel her restlessness. She tosses her scarf, fiddles with buttons. Staying still is indeed death. She needs to get up.

I need to keep her there.

'What do you see when you say death?' I ask.

She fidgets some more and then, all at once, she is very still. 'A man in a bed. His eyes are as wide as saucers. He's skinny, like a skinned cat. Horrible. He can't move. He is death. I love him.'

She says this with the creaking slowness of a tape whose battery has run down and then makes a sucking, swallowing noise. Then in one swift gesture she is off the couch. Her own eyes are very wide. I know at once that she has said something she didn't intend to say. It has made her nervous. And angry. Before I can stop her she has planted a kiss on my lips and is out the door. My watch tells me we still had some fifteen minutes to go.

I have an intuition that Anna will not be back for her next session. I am right, though the rightness is not altogether consoling. I feel we may at last be getting somewhere and that this is the point when Anna will choose to leave.

In fact, she doesn't turn up for five sessions, at which point she rings me to say she won't be coming back. But the next day, as if she has been carrying on an argument with herself and the Anna who phoned me has lost, she shows up at her usual time. I am on edge. She doesn't seem to be. She neither apologizes nor explains. She simply lies down on the couch and says, as if she were me, 'Where were we?'

'We were talking about a skinny man. A very skinny man on a bed. Death.'

'Oh that!' She gives me one of her fluttering, inconsequential laughs. 'I want to tell you about a friend of mine, a very interesting American friend, who quit his job on Wall Street yesterday in order to go and work for the Greens. Left his wife in the process, but that's secondary.'

246

She isn't dressed for any dramatic part today. She looks, for her, rather ordinary. Perhaps that gives me courage.

'Anna.' I stop her. 'I don't want to hear any stories today.'

'You're paid to listen.'

'That may be. But today I want to explore why it is that you've told me so many stories, true or false, over the past months.'

'To give you pleasure,' she says, as if it were self-evident. 'I've told you that.'

Something clicks inside me. I have been blind. I have interpreted every aspect of the content of her stories in terms of the transference, except the whole storytelling process itself.

'But I'm not enjoying it,' I say. 'Perhaps you tell me stories because, without them, you feel I won't be interested in you. Without your stories, you're no-one. Nothing.'

'Nothing,' Anna repeats, as if she is tasting the word, then laughs. 'That's right, a boring, dirty little nothing.'

'Dirty?' I prod.

'A dirty little beast. That's what she called me.'

'Who?'

She doesn't answer.

'Your mother?'

Again no answer. She is lying very still and I wait. I don't wait too long, since I don't want to lose the moment, then I try again. 'Who are you trying to please with your stories, Anna?'

'Who?'

'Yes, who? A bullying brother? A bored carer? A depressed mother who needs cheering? Your father?' I flap about wildly.

'My father died before I can remember,' she says flatly.

I can feel her sudden heaviness.

'You were four, I think you once told me.'

'Thereabouts.'

'Not too young for stories,' I press her. 'He told you stories.'

Her face suddenly takes on a look of acute disgust. 'No, no, I told him. He was so skinny. And he smelt bad. It was so hot.'

'So that skinny man, the one you associate with death, is your father.'

She is silent. She squirms about on the couch and then starts to speak in an uncharacteristic, disjointed way and I know that we have finally broken through to something. A picture begins to emerge of a family. An angry, often railing mother, a small child and a sick man. Every evening the child goes to sit with her ailing father in a darkened room and tells him stories. In her eyes, the stories keep death at bay. His death. He tells her that, too. He loves her stories. As long as she can keep telling the stories, he will stay alive. Scheherazade in reverse. So she tells him anything, everything, fabricates, recounts, dramatizes, excites.

One day she is unwell and her mother won't let her go to him, however much she pleads. Her illness gets worse. She is feverish, delirious perhaps. And when she emerges from the fever, he is gone. He has abandoned her. He is dead, her mother eventually tells her, and sends her away from the only home she has known. She feels she is being punished for his death, for failing him, but the fault is shared by her mother, who has prevented her from going to him. Whatever the fault, she is devastated. She loses the ability to speak. She doesn't know for how long, but she knows her voice has gone. Gone with her father. She is mute.

Anna lies absolutely still. She doesn't speak. In her silence it becomes crystal clear to me that her exuberant and compulsive storytelling is also a way of warding off her own anxiety about annihilation.

When her hour is drawing to a close, I say, 'That was then, Anna. This is now. And now we know a little about why you've been entertaining me all these months. Let's hold on to that. It's a big step.'

She gets up. Her look is a little dazed and then, with a touch of her usual spirit, she says to me, 'It may be crap.'

She is rubbing her wrist, and I remember her story of the little boy who couldn't speak and caught her there, on the wrist.

'That, too,' I say. 'A gift from you to me. A veritable gift.'

11

Rain drummed on the car roof and pelted against the window. The wipers struggled against its force. Red brake lights punctuated the wet blur of the motorway world.

Norfolk drove with total concentration, drove fast, despite weather, and as if he were alone. He had barely exchanged a word with her since they had hit the open road.

'Two weeks today,' Leo murmured, switching off the crackling din of the radio. 'Isabel should have arrived in Manhattan two weeks ago today. Same rain. Everything else different.'

Norfolk flashed her a look, but said nothing.

'By now we might have been in New Mexico. Big skies, tumbleweed, adobe . . .'

She felt the inadvertent welling of tears. So much hope had been vested in her holiday with Isabel. It was as if her friend's fearlessness, her openness, her electric proximity would somehow take Leo over and out of herself and deposit her in a better place. And now she had been landed emphatically back in herself. And her fears for Isabel grew with each passing day.

Leo forced herself into composure. She should be focusing on what Isabel wanted out of their

250

joint adventure. It might provide some kind of clue.

She tried to recreate the moment in which the plan had been conceived. They were sitting together in the half-light of the loft, murmuring, while Becca watched a video in the bedroom. Isabel's face, as it came to her now, was shadowed with something Leo didn't altogether understand. A burden to be shed, perhaps. Her shoulders were tensed with the effort of holding it up. She didn't have her usual easiness. Her gusto. No, Isabel hadn't been at her best over Christmas. That's what must have cued Leo's present insistence that Daniel Lukas might know things.

It was Leo who had come up with the notion of setting off across America. Two women in a car on the open road. Easy riders. Isabel's face had lit up with animation.

'But if you were in New Mexico, Holland,' Norfolk broke into her thoughts, 'you wouldn't be here with little ol' me in the glory of the English hills and dales. Look on the bright side.'

'I'm working on it,' Leo mumbled.

'You're not working hard enough. And Isabel might have taken you to a few of the kind of places we'll probably end up in today. She told me she intended doing a little of her gene-tech research while you were holidaying. Not altogether a holiday, therefore.'

'Did she?'

He was off, no longer paying attention. Jeff tumbled into her mind. He used to drive like this on those weekend journeys from Boston to New York. She would often choose to sit with Becca in the back seat. Becca with plump legs kicking into the air and a dreamy baby smile on her face. Past now. All past.

She stole a glance at Norfolk's profile to reassure

251

herself about the present and heard a siren come up from nowhere. A police car overtook them, its blue light punctuating the gloom.

'Relax, Holland. I'm not driving too fast.'

'I wasn't—'

'You were. But at least you have the grace to be silent.' He chortled. 'Rare tact.'

She would have liked to continue the conversation, liked, too, to have touched the hand which quickly pressed her knee, but his attention was on the road again and she was back in her solitary bubble.

Rare tact. She had a sudden image of herself reporting those words to Daniel Lukas, as if she needed to prove to him that she wasn't the demented creature who babbled on his couch or that other furtive being who invaded his files. Ridiculous thought, she chastised herself. She hardly needed that man's approval. Yet she had to admit that she felt an intimacy had grown up between them, despite her intentions, despite everything. That was odd.

She mused for a moment on what he had said about her helicopter panic, and then remembered that during her pregnancy and while Becca was small, the panic had receded. That was odd, too. Maybe Jeff had filled a lack her father had left, a strong and solid presence to replace Daddy. Or maybe it was due to Becca herself, who needed her to be in charge. And then Jeff wasn't there for her any more. Gone before the actual separation, and that tangled fear, that abandonment and anger which the helicopter represented had reasserted itself.

Leo caught the unfurling of her thoughts, the hunt for reasons, and wondered at how much Daniel Lukas's ways of thinking had taken hold of her.

* * *

The rain spluttered itself out with the end of the motorway. Through the greyness ahead, Leo glimpsed the tracery of pale honey-coloured spires. Exeter Cathedral. Its startling beauty made her rue the fact that, on their way out of London, she had argued with Norfolk about heading here first. He had insisted, had told her that it made geographical sense. He had discovered that each of the series of mysterious numbers on the diskette sent to Iris Morgenstern was not code but referred to Ordnance Survey map locations. They were evidently sites to do with Isabel's investigations – sites possibly leaked to her in her clandestine guise, sites of experimental plantings or labs. Exploring them would lead them to Isabel. He had been excited, adamant. The Sturridge Hotel could wait for the evening.

Now, as they walked up a lane bordered by the towering red brick of the city wall and turned into an old church close, from the end of which the cathedral emerged in all its ancient magnificence, Leo was glad that she had allowed herself to be persuaded. She paused to take in double-ranked buttresses and castellated parapets. Norfolk's arm tugged her along.

'Wonderful, I know, but we should make use of our time. Unless you want to hang out here while I get us maps and some other bits and pieces. We could meet in the pub along the lane. Just over there.' He pointed across the square, towards the end of a Georgian row. 'Half an hour. OK?'

Leo nodded. She walked slowly towards the front of the cathedral and gazed at sumptuous stonework saints and the delicacy of a rose window. At her side, a determined busker in Renaissance garb plucked out a tune on a lute. She gave him a pound and made her way in, then sat on a chair and absorbed the beauty of arches and structure and echoing silence. After a moment, she found herself superstitiously offering up a prayer. A prayer for Isabel. 'Please let her be returned to me. To us.' The words formed themselves of their own accord and, realizing they weren't quite right, she added, 'Above all, let her be safe.'

A child's howl shattered her thoughts. It reverberated through the aisles, rising higher and higher, filling the nave with a cacophony of pain, like an omen.

Leo couldn't identify its source. Then she saw a toddler hurtling along, dashing blindly, his face a stream of tears. She was about to go to him when a man emerged and scooped him into his arms. He planted a resonant thwack on the child's bottom. The howling grew louder, then ceased and turned into a hiccuping whimper. The child's eyes were round with incomprehension.

Leo slid out of her seat. The man misinterpreted her motion and hissed, 'Sod off, cow. Mind your own business.'

She stopped in her tracks. She stood there, unable to move until well after they had left the church. Foreboding coursed through her, as if it were once again intent on taking up permanent residence in her blood.

Norfolk was late. Leo sipped tepid coffee and waited in a pannelled room beneath ancient beams. To still herself, she picked up a newspaper from a side counter. It was a local paper filled with Devon news of uncertain interest. She scanned the front page erratically. A smallish headline at the bottom caught her attention: UNIDENTIFIED WOMAN DEAD Leo read swiftly.

A woman's body had been found in a red Ford Escort, registration number L42 TBR, which had careened off a small road in the Barnstaple area. It wasn't clear when the accident had taken place. The car did not belong to the driver. The police were treating the matter as suspicious and were carrying out inquiries. Any information leading to identification of the young blonde woman was welcome.

Leo's heart set up an erratic beating. Isabel. Isabel driving down a lonely night-time lane, one of those single-track roads with a grassy strip at its centre. Isabel skidding into a ditch. No, no. A car, or a van or a tractor, coming up behind her, or in front. A car driven by the brute who had broken into the loft. Deliberately pushing her off the road onto a treacherous slope. Isabel, her body mangled. Isabel, dead.

Leo read the article three times, and with each reading her certainty grew.

Tears welled in her eyes. She tried to convince herself that she was jumping to false conclusions, but all her unspoken fears of the last weeks pointed to this. Only to this. It was fine and well for Norfolk to insist that Isabel had simply gone underground to carry out a delicate investigation, perhaps to acknowledge that she might have got into some kind of trouble. But Leo's intuition, the intuition she didn't want to confront, was this: Isabel's life shattered by a terrible violence beyond her control.

'What's up, Holland? I'm not that late.' Norfolk dropped a bundle of pink-backed maps on the table. 'These are for lunch and this is for later.' He waved two large plastic bags in the air before depositing them on the floor. 'What are you drinking?'

'I'll get the drinks. You read this.' Leo's voice cracked as she pointed to the article.

'Yes, sir. Make mine a pint of bitter, and I wouldn't say no to a couple of rounds of something between brown bread. Smile, Holland,' he cajoled her, 'the day's only beginning.'

'Read.' She gave him her back.

When she returned he was drumming his fingers on the table. 'And you think this unidentified woman is Isabel?'

Leo nodded.

He took a long sip of his beer and stared at her reflectively.

'We have to get over to Barnstaple. If you don't want to come, I'll go on my own.'

'Have I said anything yet?'

'I could feel you objecting.'

'Stop feeling.' He ruffled her hair gently. 'I just don't like having to alter my well-laid plans.' He gestured at the maps. 'All those sites in there are longing to be investigated. But you're right, though we should phone first, just to check whether an identification has been made since the paper went to press.'

Leo nodded, but didn't move.

'Right. I'll phone.'

She watched him stride over to the bar, exchange a few words with the woman behind it, then disappear through a door. A bleak numbness overtook her, so that when he returned she could barely make out his words.

'All set. We can go straight to the morgue. At the hospital. We're to ask for a DI Rawlence. Grab those sandwiches, Holland. We're going to need sustenance.'

The road curled and stretched and climbed before

them like a ribbon blown into erratic activity by the wind. They drove through rolling, sheep-strewn fields, which on a different occasion would have provided yelps of pastoral delight. Sleepy villages, studded with thatch, grew straight out of steeply banked hedgerows bursting with spring green. Beyond, hills and valleys offered a patchwork of irregular shapes. Brashly yellow gorse sat astride rounded slopes and competed with neatly ploughed furrows.

Near Barnstaple, traffic ground to a standstill. It increased their impotent tension. Leo couldn't find words. She was floating in the realms of the unspeakable, her hands clenched, her nails digging into soft flesh. Norfolk flicked radio stations. At each new light, inane chatter burst into pop songs and back again in an interminable cycle.

Suddenly he pointed to a road sign announcing 'Hospital' and veered sharply to the right.

It took some twenty long minutes to reach the set of sprawling buildings situated in a dip of the hills at the far edge of town, another twenty to locate the morgue. Still more time to convince a recalcitrant nurse that they had to see DI Rawlence. Finally, they were shown to a creaky leatherette sofa at the edge of a bleak corridor. They perched and waited.

A tiny woman with mottled skin emerged from a door. She walked slowly, pausing every few minutes to lean against the wall, as if only its solidity could contain her bewilderment. Minutes later, a man came out. He was sturdy, his cheeks pink from weather or drink. The look he turned on them was sour.

Norfolk didn't give him time to speak. 'Detective Inspector Rawlence. We've been sent by Faraday of the Metropolitan Police. There's a very real possibility that the dead woman you've found may be our missing friend. We're her only contacts in Britain. We've come for an identification. I take it she hasn't been . . . yet.'

The officer scrutinized them. 'That's all right, then. But the lady stays out here. The last one fainted on me.'

Norfolk met Leo's eyes.

'No. The waiting is worse. I'm coming in.'

'You heard her, Inspector.'

The policeman shrugged. 'Don't know what it is, but the entire population of the south-west seems to have developed a taste for cadavers. Suit yourself,' he grumbled. 'And I need some ID.' He pressed a bell on the door and a medic appeared, a long plastic bib over his white coat.

'You see to this, Doctor. I've had enough.'

The man ushered them into a long room illuminated only by one powerful lamp at its far end, where a uniformed woman stood. The air was chill and reeked of chemicals. Leo's grip on Norfolk's hand grew tighter.

'I'm working on her now,' the doctor offered as he led them towards the light.

In its glare, Leo saw a slab of a table, with a naked body on its surface. The woman's hair was copious and brightly golden, the neck at an odd angle, so the face looked away from them. Leo could feel the blood draining out of her as quickly as her courage. Her heart was thudding loudly. It seemed to echo from the ceiling of the room back into her ringing ears. She leant heavily on Norfolk.

'Come round here,' the doctor urged them forward, then, remembering himself, quickly pulled a sheet up to cover the body's nakedness. 'She doesn't look too bad.' Leo had the odd sense he was inviting them to examine a picture in an exhibition. 'Except for the cuts on the face. Not much blood, which is what's odd.'

Leo couldn't bring her eyes to the table. Images of Isabel raced through her mind, obliterating everything around her. Isabel dancing at a party; Isabel sitting across from her at a food-strewn table, her face animated, her mouth curved in laughter; Isabel stroking Beast, her features soft with tenderness.

'It's not her.' Norfolk's voice penetrated her consciousness. He was guiding her closer to the body. 'Much too young. Poor kid.'

Leo raised her eyes to take in the full face of a girl not much older than Becca. She shuddered. Thick lashes shadowed cheeks that were too pale. Lips that bore the traces of dark lipstick arched over slightly gapped teeth, giving the face an air of surprise. Surprised by a dream, or a nightmare. Tiny lines like imprints on old porcelain marked the cheeks.

'Did the impact kill her?' Norfolk's voice seemed to come from a long way away.

'That's what's curious. There wasn't that much of a bang, but the windows of the car were shattered. We're just running the tests. Looks like drugs. And the position of the body was odd. There's a bit of . . .' He stopped his garrulous flow. 'You'd better talk to the police.'

Leo felt Norfolk's arm urging her on, but her feet wouldn't take the necessary steps. She stared at the girl, transfixed. So this was death. Like sleep, but utterly unlike it. There was no breath. An intangible substance that separated two such different states. Separated them permanently.

'Come on, Holland,' Norfolk whispered. 'Let's get out of here.'

The door of the hospital had just hissed shut behind them when Norfolk stopped abruptly. His fingers dug into her shoulder.

'Holland, I'm an A1 arsehole.' His face had turned a sickly white beneath the tan. 'I know that woman. It's just come to me. The nakedness . . . it confused me. And I was so shit-scared of finding Isabel. Come on.'

She held him back. 'What are you talking about?'

'The woman. The dead girl. She's the one I talked to at Plantagen. Last week. Jill Reid, that was her name. I don't believe it. They wouldn't . . . Not that.'

'What are you talking about, Norfolk?'

He wasn't listening. He was dragging her back into the interstices of the hospital. 'She could have been the one who sent Isabel the diskette. But they wouldn't . . . they wouldn't go that far.'

Leo stepped in front of him and blocked his path. 'Who wouldn't? Wouldn't go what far?'

He paused, his expression grimmer than she had ever seen it. 'The biotech companies. Plantagen. They might indulge in a little burglary, spying, coercion, indirectly provoke famines. But murder . . .'

'Who mentioned murder, Norfolk?' Leo's voice was shrill. People turned to stare at them. Leo took hold of her tone. 'Nobody said anything about murder,' she whispered, realizing she was contradicting her own earlier instincts. 'It was an accident.'

'You weren't listening to the doctor, Holland. Come on.'

She pulled back. 'I . . . I don't want to go in there again.'

'OK.' He met her eyes for a moment and gave her

a quick hug. 'OK, you wait outside. Take some deep breaths. No, wait a minute. First of all, go and ring Faraday. Just alert him to this.'

'Why? You think Isabel . . . ?' She couldn't finish her question.

'I'm not thinking now. Just tell him. Jesus. The poor girl told me she was just going off on a short break, too. I hope I didn't step in there with my big feet and provoke something.'

He was gone before Leo could press him any further. She did as he had said. She found a payphone and left a slightly incoherent message for Faraday, remembering only at the last minute to mention names, Jill Reid and Plantagen and DI Rawlence and Barnstaple. Then, she went and sat on a bench in front of the hospital and listened to the wail of ambulance sirens. But all she could see was the dead girl's scratched, ashen face.

When Norfolk returned, he was terse and in a hurry. He deflected her questions. 'DI Rawlence got in touch with Plantagen. Jill Reid was due back yesterday. She didn't turn up. Let's go, Holland. We've got a lot of ground to cover, and very little time.'

In the car, he drew out the maps he had purchased and, consulting the sheet of reference points, circled areas.

'Can you map-read, Holland?'

'Of course. But—'

'No buts.' He jabbed his pen so that it made holes in the sheets. 'One, two, three, four, five. We'll see what these yield and take it from there.'

He lurched the car into motion. The town fell away behind them. Dappled cows watched their passage with mournful eyes. Sheep grazed, as if grazing would never end. Leo took a deep, uneven breath. 'I don't know if this is the best way to find Isabel.'

'You got a better idea?' He took a curve too swiftly so the tyres squealed.

'We could start with that hotel.'

'We'll stay there tonight. I want to use what light we have.'

'You think Jill Reid sent Isabel the list of locations, don't you?'

He shrugged. 'Could be.'

'But when you talked to her, you were looking for Isabel Morgan. And the envelope with the diskette was addressed to Iris Morgenstern.'

He threw her a scalding look.

Leo persisted. 'What exactly did Jill Reid say to you?'

'Patience, Holland,' he growled. 'I'm just trying to reconstruct it for myself.'

They drove in silence. They were on a single-track road now, like the one Leo had imagined so few hours earlier as the location of Isabel's 'accident'. Their view was blocked by the steep hedgerows, but at the first left turn everything opened up. They were on the edge of a valley. A flat expanse of plain lay beneath them.

'Not much further now for point one,' Leo murmured.

A long stretch of metallic wire fencing some seven foot high appeared to their right. Beyond it there was a desolate stretch of land, bereft of sheep, cattle or humans. The fence reminded her of the Origen premises outside Oxford, but here, in the distance, there were strange sounds, like cars backfiring.

She was about to say all this to Norfolk, when he

shouted, 'Bingo. Now we're getting somewhere.' He slowed the car and pointed to a sign. It warned of Ministry of Defence property.

'What do you mean we're getting somewhere? What's this got to do with anything?'

He didn't answer immediately. 'I'm not sure,' he said at last. He waved the printed sheet of map co-ordinates in the air. 'But if any of this has military involvement, it explains Isabel's secrecy. And that of her informer. Maybe Isabel inadvertently stumbled onto something. There would be little point to all this cloak and dagger if these map sites simply referred to some of the four hundred officially registered testing grounds.'

Icy fingers crept along Leo's spine. 'I can't see what interest the MoD would have in growing experimental foods?'

'Can't you?'

She shook her head vigorously, wanting to rid herself of the sudden tingle of fear.

'They may not be what you and I normally think of as foods – except that they're grown. They could contain specific toxins or bacteria or contraceptives designed to make certain groups of people infertile. Or slow poisons. Chemical weapons under a different name.'

Leo looked through the stretch of wire mesh which gave the landscape an eerie quality. 'You're not to try to go in there now, Norfolk.'

'No. Keep your eye on the map. We'll head for the next point.'

'Have you remembered what Jill Reid said to you?'

He nodded. 'But maybe it's taken on a different light in . . . in the present circumstances. First I just described Isabel to her and she was a little hesitant, as if she couldn't quite recall her. Then I came out with her name, Isabel, and she relaxed a little, as if she was relieved. Relieved I hadn't said Morgenstern, perhaps. The undercover name. I put on the broad Aussie and had her laughing, told her Isabel was an old friend and we were a bit worried about her whereabouts, and she kind of consoled me and said she was sure Isabel was fine. With quite a lot of certainty. As if she knew something I didn't. And I said this was kind of a weird place for Isabel to have been working, given that she was a Green from way back, and what kind of work did they do there, anyway? She then launched into a riff about antibiotic resistance marker genes, their links to GM stuff in animal feeds. And that's when we got interrupted.'

He grated fingers through his hair and moved the car into a higher gear. 'I think she and Isabel were secretly working on something together, but I don't know what.'

They passed a village of clustered stone which looked as if it were simply a more solid version of the surrounding vegetation. Not far beyond it was their next site. They parked in a muddy lay-by. Norfolk brought out two pairs of wellies, a small rucksack, a spade and some planting pots from the bag he had stored in the boot.

He tucked the equipment into the sack while Leo pulled on her boots. 'If anyone asks, we're just having ourselves a little ramble. Right?'

She nodded.

The sun peeked out from the covering of clouds. 'At least the weather's on our side, Holland.'

For the next few hours they walked and drove

between sites. On two occasions, Norfolk's surreptitious collection of soil and plantlings was halted by plastic-sheathed and electrified obstructions. On two others, they found fields where sheep or cattle grazed peacefully. No planting had taken place, and Norfolk wondered aloud whether these were fields for future use or had something to do with feed or drug trials on the animals.

On the whole, they didn't talk much. Maybe it was the edge of danger which trailed them. Or the aftertaste of death. Leo found her mind returning time and again to that naked body, so waxy in its stillness, cut off too soon from a future. Like her father, all those years ago. Dead. Gone. And she thought about Isabel, trying to muster hope, but she couldn't prod away her ever-mounting fears.

'I don't understand why Isabel would be doing this,' she stated, anger in her voice, as they got back into the car again. 'It makes no sense. And if she were about to embark on something like this, something risky, surely she would have alerted me before heading off. She's sensible.'

Norfolk glanced at her and rubbed the back of her neck for a moment before switching on the engine. 'Maybe she couldn't, Holland. Or maybe she alerted someone we don't know. Or maybe you just don't understand her. Her love of risk. Or the nature of her concern, her commitment.'

That, Leo had to acknowledge, if only to herself, was true. She had no real sense of why Isabel would have taken up this particular cause rather than any other.

There were so many causes, an overwhelming number of causes. The way women were treated by the Taliban in Afghanistan, for instance. Or the

Albanians in Kosovo. Or the perpetual poverty in Bangladesh. Or the victims of human-rights abuses in China or East Timor. Or, closer to, the homeless, the aged, the mentally ill.

Leo mentally ticked off a list and wondered again why Isabel should have focused her attention on an uncertain campaign which had already received so much publicity. After all, the United States considered GM foods perfectly safe, no different from hybrids. Some 75 million acres were given over to them. Maybe that was it. The anti-GM protest was a new form of anti-Americanism, a reaction against American power. But Isabel didn't think that way.

Leo could understand the surface reasons, of course. Terminator genes would harm the poorest countries. Modified genes could spread horizontally and affect ordinary plants, genetically pollute the countryside, kill birds. Affect animals and humans in unknown ways. Pollution was a bad. But Isabel was hardly a technophobe. Her gut reaction wasn't ever and always to protest at the products that modernity brought with it. She ate meat, she drank whisky and wine. She didn't pore over labels at supermarkets or drug stores.

And yet, now that Leo considered it, there was a part of Isabel that wished for purity. Particularly of late. Leo thought of the loft with its lack of clutter, its bareness. Nor did Isabel run her own car any longer. But why would a person develop a desire for purity.

Because she felt tainted, Leo concluded.

Something else occurred to her. Isabel liked to dig into the hidden – that's what her writing was about. And what was more secret than these clandestine experiments with transgenic plants, barricaded by the wealth of multinationals? Isabel herself was secretive, too, Leo had to acknowledge now that she came to reflect on it. Indeed, she thrived on secrets – or was this only a notion triggered by her recent discovery about Jeff and her friend.

Suddenly Leo felt annoyed with the progress of her own thoughts. That shrink was making her reason strangely, inducing her to search out internal explanations rather than external ones. Isabel could simply have taken on this cause for political motives, out of a sense of justice. There was no need to look any further or deeper. Everyone was secretive. If Isabel were here, would Leo have told her about Norfolk and herself?

But then, Leo corrected herself, if Isabel were here, nothing would have happened. There would be nothing to tell.

'Having foul thoughts about me, aren't you, Holland?' Norfolk broke into her thoughts. 'Gonna run off with the car at the next stop and abandon me. I can feel it.'

'No, I was just reflecting that perhaps I don't know Isabel as well as I imagined.'

'One never knows other people as well as one imagines.'

'Maybe not even oneself.'

'You're not to get philosophical on me in the middle of this bleating countryside, Holland. The only essential to know about Isabel is that she always wants more than she wants.' He let out an abrupt laugh. 'She was always like that. Even way back when. Back then, she had the hunger of those who move from the periphery to the centre. She wanted everything: sex, drugs, rock 'n' roll. And knowledge. She wanted to experience the whole world and more. She hasn't changed all that much. It's as if, inside her, there's this big hole that can never be filled.'

'You love her, don't you.'

He gave her a swift glance. 'Guess I do. In a way. And I'm getting just a little fond of you, too, Holland, given our brief acquaintance and your foul temper.' He grazed her cheek playfully with his knuckles. 'And I'm distressed about that girl.'

'I think we've had enough of these fields for one day.'

Norfolk nodded. 'I'm with you. I can get some more samples tomorrow, if there's any more to get. What I'd like to do now is go and have a look at the place where Jill Reid's car went off the road.'

Leo tensed.

'We're not very far now. I got that cop at the hospital to tell me where it was. Right near the coast.'

'But the hotel . . .'

'Don't worry. We'll get there.' Suddenly he slammed his hands on the steering wheel. The car swerved, barely missing a hedgerow. 'Holland. It's just come to me. That sheet we thought was a coded genealogical tree, where is it?'

He rifled through his pockets as if he had struck gold after a lifetime's mining. 'Here.' He passed it to her. 'Read me the letters in the first entry on the left.'

'B–W–I–S.'

'That's it. Bioworld International, Seattle.' He whistled beneath his breath. 'What's next?'

'PLIL.'

'Plant Life International Limited. Find another one with a P.'

'PTGD. Five down on the left.'

'That's it. Plantagen, Dorset. Holland, what we've got here is a list of holdings and acquisitions. Who owns whom in the sector. Isabel's got herself a high-ranking snoop.' He threw her a euphoric grin.

'What we haven't got is Isabel.'

'Soon. I'm starting to feel lucky.'

He didn't look as if he felt particularly lucky when they began to climb a fog-bound road as narrow as a roller-coaster gauge, and with more hidden twists and turns. Craggy branches scraped the roof and sides of the car. To the right, an occasional break in the trees showed a sharp drop. Beyond, though mist and angle made it invisible, the sea roared and pounded against rock.

To Leo, the sudden savage drama of the coast, as wild as any Pacific, was totally unexpected. 'According to the map, we should almost be there,' she said to reassure herself as much as Norfolk.

'We are.' He gestured towards a tiny dip in the road where police tape fluttered. There was nowhere to pull up, so he switched on his high beam to alert any oncoming traffic.

Cold wetness embraced them as they scraped past the stationary car and looked down the wooded verge. Jill Reid, they concluded, must have gone over just where the road curved and there was a break in the short, gnarled oaks and scrubby trees. The car had been towed away now, and the ground beneath them was muddy with tread marks. Its plunge had been broken by stout tree trunks a few yards down. Two of them showed indentations. The bark was freshly chipped, gouged into stark pallor. Stray branches littered the ground. The car's hurtling force had perhaps severed them from the trees. A little way on, the precipice gave way to nothing but air. From the distance came the massed call of gulls, as mournful as an elegy.

raw as the wind which lifted and carried her words. 'Though no-one seems to come along here anyhow. You notice we haven't met a single car.'

'Someone pushed her.' Norfolk's face was distorted, his mouth twisted into a hard line. 'She had no ID on her and no shoes, unless they were stolen afterwards. How often do you go out without shoes in this weather, Holland?'

It was true, Leo thought. There was no particular need for the woman's car to go down just here except that the gap in the trees provided a convenient point for a descent.

Her eyes hovered over the gouged trees. Had the assailant known the trees would break the car's fall? She couldn't have been driving very fast. In a way it was surprising that, if she hadn't gone right over the precipice, the crash had killed her at all.

'What do you bet all those broken branches on the ground were used to hide the car, just in case anyone drove by?'

Leo shuddered. 'Poor woman. Do you know how long before she was found?'

Norfolk shook his head, then put his arms around her. He held her close for a moment, as if the heat of their bodies might dissolve the chill proximity of death.

'Let's go,' he whispered at last. 'Nothing more we can do here.'

12

Fog obliterated the landscape. It obliterated time, too, marked out now only by the repetitive rhythm of the creaking windscreen wipers. The road twisted and turned and climbed, only to descend sharply and climb again. And again. In the murky greyness the map was as unreadable as the eerie caw of invisible gulls.

Leo had a feeling that, however much they moved, they were getting nowhere. Activity was an excuse to banish a sense of helplessness and its attendant guilt. Isabel was receding into an impenetrable distance.

When they finally reached a crossroads and turned away from the sea, she took a deep, ragged breath and tried to conjure up hope from the slightly wider road and slight increase in the car's speed. Suddenly the faint lights of what could only be the bulk of a car loomed above them on the horizon. They approached at a terrifying speed. Norfolk hooted, swore and pulled over as far as he could beside a towering bank of hedgerows. The vehicle charged towards them, heedless, and, with a loud scrape, carried away their wing mirror.

Leo had a fleeting impression of a bull of a man at the wheel, a huge head on a powerful neck. Behind him was a woman, a tangle of golden hair fanned out against the window. She blinked and the vision was gone. Shaking, she followed Norfolk out of the car. He was shouting obscenities, waving his fist, running. But the large black vehicle had already disappeared, swallowed up by a bend and mist.

'Bastard! I didn't even get a glimpse of his licence plate.' Norfolk smashed his fist on the roof of the car.

Leo gazed into the distance. Above the rise of the hill a light appeared. The blurred contours of a large stately house materialized between wind-lashed trees. She rubbed her eyes. 'Maybe that's a hotel, Norfolk. Maybe he was heading for it. We could follow him. Get a drink, too. We need one.'

He gave her a bleak look and shrugged. 'Not much point, Holland. It's too late for fisticuffs. Even if he's there, the bastard will deny it. And there's nowhere to turn round here.'

She was about to insist when the light, the house she was certain she had seen, disappeared, leaving behind only a residue, a spectral outline in her memory, instead of solid stone. Her eyes were playing tricks on her. 'Did you notice a woman in the back seat of the car?' she asked in a quivering voice.

He understood her immediately and, as he shook his head, he stretched a reassuring arm across her shoulder. 'We've had a long day, Holland. This fog doesn't help. Let's carry on.'

As if it were under the sway of engineers, the fog lifted with the appearance of a double-lane road. Leo found a classical music station without the crackle of interference and tried to put order into the frazzle of her mind. Now that the minutely metered world of the Ordnance Survey map was behind them, they made good time, travelling south-east. Some thirty minutes brought them to a signpost announcing the Sturridge Hotel two kilometres on from the next right. The building itself first emerged as a glow in the darkness. They dipped down into a steep valley, and then up again, almost missing the tree-lined drive which eventually led to an old Jacobean manor, forbidding in its severe symmetry of hewn stone.

But at least it was there, Leo thought, not an illusion borne of fog and dread. Real pebbles crunched beneath their feet, loud in the night-time hush. The air was moist and chill and smelt slightly of rank vegetation. From above came the swoop and call of a predatory bird.

The heavy door opened with a slight creak to Norfolk's push and revealed a small, dimly lit reception area, adorned with faded furnishings and gilt-framed oils. There was no-one behind the counter at the far side, but a bowl of lavish spring blooms signalled some kind of welcome. Norfolk pressed the old-fashioned bell beneath it and, after a few moments, a tall, spruce grey-haired woman came to greet them.

'So sorry. We're busy in the dining room tonight. But there's still time.' She gave them a tight little smile as she glanced at her watch and looked them over.

'We'd like a table and a room, please, ma'am.'

Leo noticed that Norfolk had put on his broadest Australian. It seemed to relax the woman. Her smile widened. 'I've got a lovely room on the first floor with exceptional views.'

'That's just what we've come for.' Norfolk worked his charm and, by the time the register was signed and the key handed over, the woman seemed to have shed twenty years and was telling Norfolk about her single visit to Australia and urging them to hurry to dinner or the best of the day would be gone.

Leo cleared her throat. 'A friend of ours from Australia stayed here a few weeks back. On the fifteenth of last month. Isabel Morgan. I was wondering if you'd talked to her. We're a little worried about her. A tall woman. Blonde.'

'The fifteenth. Let's think.' The woman traced a well-manicured finger along a calendar. 'Oh no. That was a Wednesday. I only do Thursday and Friday evenings. Mrs Donald will be here in the morning. Why not talk to her.' She suddenly stiffened. 'Is that the woman the police were inquiring after?'

'Maybe,' Leo murmured.

The woman gave her a disapproving look, as if she had suddenly discovered a nest of dirt swept under a good carpet. 'I don't think—'

Norfolk cut her off. 'Now you go and tell them to keep a table for us. We'll put these bags upstairs and be down in a jiffy. I could eat a whole sheep all by myself.'

The room was large and floral and comfortably shabby, with a plump duvet on a soft bed. It creaked a little with Norfolk's tentative bounce. The recessed window was wide and gave out on to shadowy trees. Leo watched them bend and flutter and had an uncanny feeling that Isabel had stood in this very place and listened to the low moan of the wind.

'No gloomy thoughts for the next two hours, Holland.' Norfolk's arms curled round her, as if he could read her mind. She snuggled into him.

'I took a peek at the register while you were grilling the old dear. No I.M.s in any permutation in the last two pages, which take us back to January.

So they're a little erratic with their formalities.'

Leo looked at him open-mouthed.

He gave her a slow wink. 'I'm in the business, remember. Kind of. What I did notice, way back in late January, was that Jill Reid stayed here. She must have told Isabel about the place. No.' He put a finger on her lips. 'We'll talk over dinner. Now hurry along, as the lady ordered, or I'll beat you to the shower.'

The restaurant had a dusty formality about it, but the rolls were hot and the claret Norfolk chose was mellow on the tongue and wiped out a little of the bleakness of the day. The guests were largely an assortment of elderly couples: tweed-jacketed men with pocket watches and comfortable stomachs, accompanied by rouged, silver-haired women, who looked as if their single care in the world might be the tending of their roses. They spoke, if they spoke at all, in hushed voices.

It wasn't Isabel's kind of place, Leo determined, unless she no longer had any idea what kind of place Isabel liked. She shook away a momentary vertigo and tried to concentrate on their order, and then on Norfolk's words.

He was speculating about Isabel's links with Jill Reid and what it was they had been involved in together. He conjured up visions of the two women engaged on an intrepid investigation into a science which, to Leo, had all the signs of a future fiction. The technical terms tripped off his tongue with a practised biochemist's speed, as did the names of companies he had now identified from the list of holdings. Leo couldn't altogether follow but, as she pushed the mint-fragrant lamb round her plate, she had the sense that she was being tangled in a web of conspiracy so vast that it covered the world. From the midst of its sticky paths and convoluted loops, its drugs and plants and genetic manipulations, it came to her that Norfolk was evoking an Isabel of his own creation. Just as she did, she imagined. Which one of them was right? Or was Isabel large enough to contain them both?

She was speculating about this when a squat, broad-shouldered man approached their table. His girth blocked out the rest of the dining room. He examined them with pebble-hard eyes. Above his fleshy cheeks, his forehead was puckered into a permanent frown. He prodded the knot of his bright tie, as if he wanted to yank it off his neck.

'You the people who've been asking about Isabel Morgan?' He addressed them in a coarse whisper.

'We were.' Norfolk was smooth.

'I've told the police everything I know. I don't want them back here.'

'Do we look like police?' Norfolk laughed.

'What are you after?'

'Isabel is a friend.' Leo's voice soothed.

'Well, I don't know her from Adam. She stayed here two nights, and she left. That's the whole of it. This is a hotel. People come, people go. Don't even remember what she looked like.'

He gave them a menacing look and turned on his heel.

'Methinks he doth protest too much,' Norfolk muttered, looking after him.

'So he's hiding something.'

'You'll have to find out what tomorrow, Holland. And about Jill Reid.' He studied her for a moment. 'I've been thinking. I looked at those maps again. I want to set off at the crack of dawn. Why don't you have a lie-in and then talk to this Mrs Donald when she arrives? Try to get her on her own, without big boy there. I'll come and fetch you around eleven, say. I haven't much time left, and I want to make use of it. I've got a plane to catch first thing Saturday.'

'You're going back to Sydney?' Leo's voice caught.

'No, not that. Not yet.' He hesitated. 'I'm due in Amsterdam.'

'Oh.'

'I've got a date with my daughter. Unbreakable.'

'You never mentioned a daughter.'

'Didn't I? Well, that's the way it goes.' He grinned. 'You understand that.'

She didn't know quite which 'that' he was refer-ring to, but she nodded. 'How old is she?'

'Fourteen. And she's a stunner. Though I haven't seen her for some eight months.'

She watched the fondness play over his face, the blue glint of his eyes grow soft, and she suddenly felt like kissing him.

'And yours? Becca, isn't it?'

'As tall as our waitress.' Leo smiled covertly as the trim young woman took their plates, watched the swing of a glossy ponytail and felt what she could only describe as a jab of pain round the area of her heart. She found herself swallowing hard and telling Norfolk that Becca had now flown the coop. She missed her. Then, forcing her tone to lightness, she rushed on to ask him how he got on with his former wife, or wives.

'Just fine, now that we don't live together.' He chuckled. 'We're friends. They've both remarried and had more children. I've even been named godfather to one. Dogfather more like.'

Leo met his laugh and mused about the vagaries of

modern life: the way in which one carried on having relations with former spouses, out of need, because of the children. Or maybe, too, because there must have been something in all those years that kept you close, kept you together. Something to which it was necessary to pay respect, beyond the inevitable acrimony of parting. She was trying, but she knew, as she thought of Jeff's new child, that she hadn't yet altogether succeeded.

Later, in bed, her hunger for this man she hardly knew surprised her. Maybe it was the shadow of that dead young woman hovering over them, urging them to seize the day, to live while there was still time. She had a fantasy, too, of Isabel whispering in her ear, saying with her wry laugh that she was glad Leo was enjoying Norfolk, a gift from her, a gift to make up for their spoilt plans, or perhaps to make up for Jeff.

Still later, as they smoked a companionable cigarette and, like young ones, shared wine from a single glass, she wondered whether she would have been as open to Norfolk in New York. Or was this one of those holiday phenomena, a different self to match the different setting? Daniel Lukas sprang into her mind. Despite her hostility, she had to acknowledge that he had something to do with her new-found openness. That first breaching of the barricades of intimacy had been his. It had left her more susceptible than she would otherwise have been.

Leo's thoughts floated randomly and deposited her back in Norfolk's arms. Maybe the roll of reasons wasn't necessary. Maybe it was simply him.

She woke to a stream of crisp light poking round flowered curtains. He was no longer beside her. She lay still, trying to hold on to a fragment of a dream. She couldn't quite keep it at rest. As it fled, she was filled with an uncanny sense that Isabel had slept in this very bed, had lain here like her for a moment, trying to catch hold of a fugitive image.

She stirred herself into activity. It was already after eight. Norfolk must have left on cat's silent feet so as not to disturb her. She showered quickly and made her way downstairs. There was no-one at the small reception desk, nor in the office behind.

In the dining room, the waitress with the sleek ponytail gestured her to a windowside table and pointed out a buffet. Leo helped herself to fruit and cereal and, as the woman poured her a cup of coffee, she asked softly, 'Has Mrs Donald arrived yet?'

'Oh, she's around somewhere. In the garden probably. She loves her garden. She's usually out there of a bright morning.' The woman didn't seem to approve.

Before Leo could ask her any more, she had disappeared into the kitchen.

Leo headed out into the grounds. Clumps of daffodils, bright against the rich red earth, lined the path. Beyond stood the camelias and rhododendrons, their fat buds ready to burst. She peered through each break in the sun-mottled greenery for a sign of Mrs Donald. At last, she crossed a stretch of moist grass and made her way towards the back of the house. To the side, she noticed a high wooden fence. After a second's hesitation, she pushed open the door at its far end.

She found herself in a well-tended kitchen garden. Oblivious to her presence, a woman in a large straw hat was bending over plants.

'Hello,' Leo called.

The woman rose to reveal a crinkled face surrounded by strands of grey hair. Her cheeks were flushed. She threw Leo a winsome smile. 'Oh hello, dear. Just doing a bit of weeding. Did they send you to fetch me?' She waved towards the house in an off-hand way, then, remembering herself, took off her grubby gloves. 'We weren't expecting anyone to check in until later. Sorry. It's just that I like to get on with things here while I can.'

'No, no. That's all right.' Leo smiled back. 'I just wanted a word. The lady at the desk last night told me you might be able to help.'

'Miss Grey? Well, that's a surprise.' Periwinkle eyes turned impish. 'How can I help, dear?'

'It's about a friend of mine who stayed here some weeks back. Isabel Morgan. I'm worried about her.'

'Oh yes, that nice blonde girl. Friend of Jilly's. I was worried about her, too, dear.' She suddenly clamped a hand over her mouth.

'What is it, Mrs Donald?'

'Oh, nothing. Nothing at all.' She giggled girlishly, but the eyes that surveyed Leo were astute. 'It's just that Andrew – that's my son – he's the boss, now. Good one, too. He's doing everything to modernize this place and keep it going. Yes.' She bent to her plants, as if she had forgotten Leo.

'It is very nice here,' Leo said emphatically. She wondered if Andrew was the squat man who had come to their table last night. She waited for a moment, then tried again. 'I just wanted to know, how was Isabel when you saw her? I'm so worried. You see, she's vanished.'

Her voice broke and the old woman looked up at her.

'You're not with the police, are you, dear? You're

American. I can tell. I went to New York once.'

'That's where I'm from.'

The woman nodded.

'Your friend came when they were having one of those meetings. Andrew likes hiring the place out for all kinds of meetings, friends of this and that, with dinner thrown in, but none of it quite pays for the upkeep, you know. Things are so expensive now. And I'm not much good any more.' The woman gave Leo her sweet smile again. 'Sorry, I'm rambling.'

'Meetings of friends of this and that, you said?'

'Yes, you know, cyclists and birdwatchers. Bit like a village hall, really. But more serious. They talk a lot. Argue. Jilly comes sometimes. Not that time, though. But your friend spoke to her. They were going to meet up.'

Leo stiffened. So Norfolk was right. Isabel had probably come here for a meeting of Greens. A secret meeting, perhaps, since the squat Andrew didn't want the police to know.

'But that nice friend of yours didn't go to the meeting for more than ten minutes.' Mrs Donald prodded at a weed and burbled on as if to herself. 'She . . . she just sat by the fire in the bar and drank. She drank a great deal. Looked into the flames and drank.' The woman shook her head sadly. 'I thought she could do with a cup of tea, so I took her one. There were tears running down her cheeks. And the next day, she planted herself on the bench beneath the oak. Thought she'd grow moss. Sat there, even through the rain. She said she was fine when I asked. But she didn't look fine. Poor dear. So much sorrow . . . I don't know.'

Tears bit at Leo's eyes. 'Did she say—'

The woman cut her off as if she hadn't heard her.

281

'And then she left. Don't know if she was in a fit state to drive, but she left.'

Mrs Donald stood up, her parchment face even more wrinkled with the force of her frown. Her eyes suddenly lit up. 'Yes, I remember now. We talked about the sea. She said she wanted to be by the sea. I said I had stayed at the Lynton Arms once with my husband and she asked me whether he'd been a good husband. Funny question.'

The gate of the garden creaked and the woman stiffened. 'That'll be Andrew come to fetch me.'

Leo planted a quick kiss on her cheek and whispered a thank-you just as the door opened. She strode towards it and paused as she passed the rotund figure. 'Nice garden you have here. Sorry I have to leave. Is there anyone who could order a taxi for me?'

The man looked from Leo to his mother, who was innocently turning earth with her fork. He seemed about to say something, then thought better of it. 'Gaby's in the office. She'll ring for you.'

Leo sat in the back seat of the taxi. Her hands were clenched, her palms as clammy as if she'd dipped them permanently into a cold sea.

The good thing, she told herself, was that the sky was high, a clear blue backdrop for scudding clouds. The other good thing was that she had managed to persuade Norfolk during the night that he needn't waste time by coming back for her, so she hadn't had to hang around and wait for him or leave complicated messages. The last good thing was that she had a precise destination, even if it was one the driver was loath to take her to because of the distance.

The bad, the frightening things were too numerous

to detail. Mrs Donald's evocation of Isabel had heightened Leo's dread, so acutely did it dovetail with her own muffled fears about her friend. She had been tempted to ring Daniel Lukas before heading off, in order to shout at him and pour venom in his ear. But there was little point in hurling abuse at an answering machine which provided no answers.

She tried to make sense of the information the last two days had brought to the fore. Jill Reid had been a friend of Isabel's, though not one she had ever mentioned to Leo. Jill Reid was dead, either as the result of a random road accident or as the result of something nefarious. If it was the latter, then it probably had something to do with the secret delving both she and Isabel had undertaken. Isabel was drinking heavily. This wasn't the norm. She was in a state of distress. The distress was linked to her disappearance. It perhaps explained why she hadn't alerted Leo to her altered plans. What was the distress about?

She had asked Mrs Donald about her husband. It was an odd question for Isabel. Could disappointment over a man be the reason for her distress? Was that the force that had propelled her into taking some kind of unnecessary risk, a risk which had cut her off from everyone who knew her?

Or, alternatively, was her despair the result of the investigation itself? Perhaps she had got into hot water and couldn't extricate herself. It came to Leo that if the hot water was of Isabel's making, it might somehow have spilled over to envelop Jill Reid. No. No. She forced away the thought of Isabel's substantial bank account. Isabel wouldn't have betrayed a friend.

Jill Reid had been alive two weeks after there had

been any definitive sign of Isabel. When Norfolk had questioned the young woman at Plantagen, had she known where Isabel was and kept it from him? That wasn't unlikely. Norfolk had said she had given him the impression that she was consoling him, telling him that Isabel was fine. But now?

The thoughts went round and round in Leo's mind in an ever-more-tangled web. She was oblivious to the changing countryside around her, and when the driver announced that they were in Lynton, she sat up with a start.

They were making a steep ascent on a tree-lined road. At its crest the road veered, and beneath them the sea appeared. Foam-tipped indigo curved between stony precipices, sheer on one side, dotted with houses on the other.

'I'd rather take you to the edge of the road and wait,' the driver announced. 'The Lynton Arms is up that way.' He pointed along a dizzying track. 'The car hates going up there. And it's a job to turn round.'

Leo nodded. 'I don't know quite how long I'll be. If I'm over an hour, just go.' She took out the sum she had promised him, saw the smile curve his lips, and wished she could meet it.

The wind whipped at her hair as she trekked uphill. Its whistling moan competed with the pounding of the sea. Her head set up a throb to its rhythm. She drew her jacket more firmly around her and paused to look out at the waves, then quickly turned away, blinkering her vision. She passed a woman walking a pencil-thin greyhound. Her tartan scarf matched the animal's coat.

The woman nodded at her in friendly enough fashion and mouthed a 'Beautiful day'. The wind carried the sound into the void.

Leo hurried on. 'A beautiful day,' she repeated to herself. She must hang on to that.

The buildings, all on the left, were mostly hotels. Some of them looked as if they were boarded up, waiting for a more clement season. Others bore signs announcing vacancies. For a brief moment, Leo's mind played with a happy vision. She would find Isabel at the Lynton Arms. A troubled Isabel, but an Isabel who was safe in front of a warm fire. An Isabel who was sipping whisky in a secret sanctuary she had found for herself at the edge of the world. Leo would throw her arms around her and Isabel would weep out her cares. They would spend the night there together and, in the morning, stealthily, Leo would wing her far away to Manhattan, where genetic meddling of whatever description was far down the list of everyday concerns.

Yes, she would take Isabel away and keep her safe.

As she would have kept her father safe, if only they had let her.

Leo caught her thought and examined it. Why had her father leapt into her mind?

She heard it then, a low mechanical droning, different from the lashing of the wind and sea. It was coming closer, louder. She broke into a run, waiting for the panic of perspiration to overtake her and freeze her movements. It didn't come, though the helicopter appeared above her, its black body droning menace. She watched it for a moment and followed its swoop as it disappeared from view.

She took a deep breath. Perhaps she had outdistanced her dread. All she was left with, as she saw the arched sign of the Lynton Arms emerge from a tangle of wisteria, was a kind of residual fear, like a habit or a premonition.

The hotel was a gabled Victorian structure, half-Gothic castle, half-seaside resort, set so steeply into the cliffside that it might have been an overblown façade. The paint on the windows and shutters peeled slightly. The wrought-iron gate, as she pushed it open, creaked on its hinges. The steps were abruptly raked and slippery with lichen. For a moment she had the impression that she was entering an alien dream, long-since abandoned, but the door gave to her push and released a cow-bell clatter.

A slightly dilapidated but comfortable lobby met her gaze. Signed photographs of unknown faces cluttered the walls and competed with sea views and prints of the town. A plump flower-decked sofa stood next to a rack of tourist brochures advertising pleasures.

Leo made her way softly along a floor of lavish Edwardian tiles towards a mahogany counter.

'Hello.' A high-pitched voice came from behind her.

She turned to see a tiny woman descending a staircase so elaborate that it called out for a larger scale. The woman had the blond, poodle-curly hair and winged glasses of another epoch. She walked ramrod straight, her bosom a perfect triangle beneath the sheen of her blouse.

'Hello,' Leo echoed.

'Welcome to the Lynton Arms.' She smiled a swathe of coral lipstick and looked down at the floor beside Leo as she propped herself on a stool behind the counter.

Leo realized she was wondering at her lack of a case. 'I'm not sure I'll be staying the night,' she stammered slightly. 'But I was wondering if you did lunches. I know it's a little early.' She paused, at a loss for a moment. The woman's demeanour had taken her aback. There was something else, too. It was as if she couldn't smell Isabel here, as if, for all her earlier certainty, she had suddenly lost the trail. 'Really, I was wondering if a friend of mine might be here. She said she was coming this way.'

'If your friend is Mrs Seale or Mrs Granger, then she's here.' The woman was slightly tart. 'Lunch today is mushrooms on toast, followed by fish and trifle.' She was peering at Leo strenuously, her pupils vast beneath the thick lenses.

Leo suddenly realized that she was far older than her demeanour. She smiled. 'That sounds just fine.' She cleared her throat. 'My friend, Isabel Morgan, would have arrived here on the seventeenth of April. I'm sure you'd remember her. She's Australian, rather striking, tall.'

'Australian.' The woman moved the register closer to her and shifted her glasses. Her finger moved slowly down a sparse list of names. 'No. No-one here by that name.'

Leo read upside down. The syllables of Morgenstern leapt out at her. 'Of course. How silly of me. She wasn't using her pen name. She was here as Iris Morgenstern. I should have thought of that,' Leo babbled. 'She does that sometimes.'

The woman threw her a suspicious look. It creased her make-up. 'That's it, then. She was only here for the one night.'

Leo had the distinct sense that the woman was pleased Isabel had only stayed for the single night. 'I was wondering—'

The woman cut her off. 'Pippa, we've got another guest for lunch. Can you manage?'

Leo turned. A woman in soft-soled shoes, mannish trousers and a burly sweater had come up behind her. She had short-cut, steel-grey hair and a pug nose in a weathered gnome's face, but her smile was warm as she surveyed Leo.

'Of course we can manage, Bea. We can always manage. Come on through. I heard you say you wanted to eat early.'

Leo followed her gratefully into a generous dining room. A row of windows gave out on to the sea, as if nothing but air and height separated them from the distant, churning indigo. The tables were formally laid with sparkling white cloths and silver.

The woman led Leo to one in the far corner.

'This is where your friend sat,' she said softly. 'Don't let Bea upset you. She gets nervy with strangers. She barks a little.'

'You . . . you talked with Iris?'

The woman nodded. 'In a way. Call me Pippa.'

Leo sank into the proffered chair.

'Let me get you a drink. There's tea at the ready. Or something stronger.'

'Tea would be wonderful.'

She looked at her speculatively, then marched off, only to return moments later with a tray laden with teapot and crockery. 'I'll join you, if I may. I was ready for a cup myself.'

'Please.'

'You really want a chat, don't you? Not lunch at all.'

'Have I made it that obvious?'

"Fraid you have.'

'I . . . my friend. She's . . . well, she's gone missing.'

The woman nodded sagely. 'I think she wanted to. Even from herself. I'd leave her to it, if I were you.'

'What do you mean?'

'Sometimes we need to disappear.'

Leo stiffened. 'Was . . . was she drinking a lot?'

'Not particularly.' The woman studied her. 'I like a drop myself, sometimes.'

'I didn't mean—'

'No, no.' The woman smiled. 'I had a feeling she was trying to blot something out.'

'What made you think that?'

'I don't know, really. I was walking and I came across her on the path. She was staring out to sea, not really seeing it, but staring. Oblivious to everything. Statue-like. As if she was contemplating a jump. It took her a while to hear my greeting. I made her walk with me. She asked me if I'd ever lost anyone.'

'Her mother,' Leo murmured.

'I don't know. I told her, by the time you get to my age, there are more losses than living. She gave me a vague smile and turned back to her staring. It was clear that she didn't want me about. But I stayed close anyhow.'

'Do you think she was having some kind of breakdown?'

'Maybe. Though I wouldn't put it quite like that. She just felt . . . well, driven. Bea and I talked about it . . . speculated. We do that, you know. Particularly in the cold months. There aren't that many guests around and we like to get to know them. And there was something mysterious about Iris. Bea thought . . .' The woman glanced behind her and lowered her voice. 'She thought that your friend might be a film star travelling incognito, trying to evade the limelight. Particularly after that chauffeur came to collect her. Uniform and all.'

'Chauffeur? But Isa— Iris drove here.'

Pippa refilled their cups. 'Are you sure? We have room for a few cars round the side and hers wasn't there. I guess she could have used the public car park. I have to tell you, I was sorry to see her go. I thought we might take care of her for a bit. We like doing that and I felt she needed it.'

Leo studied the woman's weathered face. She had a sudden acute sense that the woman had become involved in the romance that was Isabel. How much of what she conveyed was fantasy? How much an accurate reading? She hesitated. 'Do you think I might have a look at the room where she stayed?'

'Of course.' The woman didn't get up. 'She made me remember, you know. All those difficult moments in one's own life.'

'Pippa. Isn't it time to be getting on with lunch?' A piercing voice interrupted them. Leo turned to see the woman with the winged glasses and fluffed hair. 'Mrs Seale's just come back from her walk.'

'I was going to show this nice young woman the room Iris Morgenstern stayed in. That's all right with you, isn't it, Bea?'

Bea's look was admonishing, tinged with some-thing like jealousy.

'If you're quick,' she said. 'You can give her the pot plants, too. We don't want them.'

'Oh, yes.' Pippa's eyes creased into a tender smile. 'Iris left two little plants behind. We kept them for her. I thought she might come back for them, since she'd taken the trouble to set them up on the window ledge.'

'Pot plants,' Leo echoed.

She had a vision of rampant tendrils shooting up to block out the light which had momentarily dawned in her mind.

13

The train from Bristol ate up the miles at high speed. Leo looked out of her window, only dimly aware of their passage. She was trying to reconstruct in graphic detail every minute of the last days she had spent with Isabel. Surely within them lay clues to the troubled state the two strangers she had talked to this morning had witnessed.

Life was such a blinding affair. One took in only what one wanted or needed. And during that brief pre-Christmas visit, Leo had to acknowledge that she had probably been more alert to Becca than she had to Isabel. She hadn't seen Becca since the previous September, and was intent on making sure she enjoyed her holiday with her mother. In a way it had been more than a holiday, Leo now admitted to herself. Leo had taken Becca to a few childhood haunts in a ridiculous attempt to recapture the closeness that had existed between them in that happy year in London when Becca was a mere eight-year-old. And Isabel? Isabel whom Leo had longed to see. Isabel had tagged along, largely a third party to mother and daughter. A necessary third party, Leo chastised herself, an eye to help create the mythical tableau that was mother and daughter.

A scene came back to her with a rebarbative

aftertaste. They were in a noisy, low-ceilinged restaurant which was one of Isabel's new favourites. It was close to the loft and had the slightly brutal bareness that Isabel seemed to appreciate of late. Leo was eating a warm goat's cheese salad. Becca's plate held a sculpted mound of risotto, flecked with exotic mushrooms. Isabel was pushing spinach topped with thin slices of Parmesan round her plate. Leo watched. The fork rarely rose to her mouth.

Isabel was talking, addressing Becca. 'It must feel wonderful going off to university and leaving the ageing, invasive parents as far behind as one can.'

The statement had a lilting enthusiasm, but it was laced with an acerbic edge. Leo hadn't paid attention then. She was too intent on Becca's response, which had reassured her. Becca had flushed slightly and said, with a shy smile, that in fact she missed her mother sometimes. Her father, too, she had rushed on to add. 'But you're right, it's great to feel independent.'

'Yes,' Isabel had continued. 'Independence is the thing. You can never really trust mothers or fathers to have your best interests at heart.' She had glanced at Leo as she said this and laughed a little brittlely.

At the time, Leo had interpreted it as Isabel's way of making a pal of this new, grown-up Becca, but not hitting quite the right note. Now she reconsidered. Some force she wasn't altogether in control of had been driving Isabel's remarks. She had been over-the-top. She had gone on to give Becca advice about men, while Leo sat nervously by. Her advice had focused on how to keep men at bay – by acting as intelligent as one really was; by refusing to mother or cajole them or listen for hours on end with a fascinated look on one's face.

'At heart they're all deceivers. Boys, lovers, teachers, even fathers. Not one of them is to be trusted for more than ten minutes. Keep yourself independent, Becca.' Isabel's voice had trailed off in a peculiar way.

It came to Leo that this statement was hardly in character. Isabel had never cast women, certainly not herself, as victims.

Nor was she eating with her usual gusto. Her plates went back to the kitchen virtually untouched.

Yes, something must have happened to Isabel in the months since their last meeting that she hadn't had the opportunity to confide in Leo about. Some deception or terrible awakening.

Pain cut through Leo with the slow scratch of a serrated knife. Pain and guilt. She had failed her friend.

She looked at her watch. If the train was on schedule she could arrive at Daniel Lukas's office no more than five minutes late. This time she would press him more astutely. He had to be implicated in Isabel's state. After all, therapists were all too well known for their habit of suggesting to women that they understand themselves as abused.

Even if Daniel's claim that he hadn't seen Isabel for some months were true, it could well have been December when he stopped seeing her. Whatever the reason – whether Isabel had attempted, succeeded or failed to carry out her proposed seduction – the end of analysis would have been a brutal closure, like a door shutting on your fingers. Compounded by the death of her mother, it could easily have precipitated her into taking extreme risks.

Somewhere inside Daniel, perhaps even without his knowledge, there must reside a key which would open the lock to her friend. Nor for the moment, now that she had left yet another message for Faraday at Bristol station, was there anywhere else to turn.

Beneath the old church at its crest, Highgate High Street was choked with near-stationary traffic. Leo abandoned her taxi and simultaneously noticed a chocolate shop. Yes, that would be a good idea. She popped in and bought a pretty golden box crammed with delights. Her purchase as securely in hand as a weapon, she quickly walked the remaining distance and pressed Daniel Lukas's bell.

There was a large bowl of flowers visible on the basement table today. His wife had a gift for arrangement. The lock, she noted, bore the word 'Union'. Had they chosen it for that reason? The notion suddenly made her feel intensely alone.

'Yes.' The answering voice sounded disgruntled.

'It's me. Leonora. Leonora Gould.'

'I see.' After what seemed like a pause, the buzzer released the door.

Leo raced up the stairs. She arrived slightly breathless. Daniel Lukas was standing beside a desk scattered with untidy heaps of paper. He was in shirt-sleeves, his hair decidedly dishevelled. It gave him a boyish air which caught her off-guard. In her imaginings he veered between monster and sage, with no intervening moment of ordinary humanity.

'You . . . you weren't expecting me.'

He didn't respond, but he gave her a look which was halfway between concern and admonishment as he gestured her towards the couch.

Leo hesitated. 'I'm sorry I'm late. Sorry about last time, too. Stupid of me to do that. Here' – she stuck out her hand awkwardly – 'I brought you these. For your little boy.'

'You don't need to give me presents, Leonora. You already pay me for my time.'

She felt caught between his sudden intimate use of her first name and the sense of what he was conveying. A reiteration of the rules. With a wave of irritation, she put the box clumsily on the table. 'For your son, I said. Not for you.'

Again he pointed her towards the couch. She made, instead, for one of the two leather armchairs and forced herself to look at him directly. 'I want to see your face today.'

He nodded and sat down opposite her.

'I . . . I've been thinking about food. I can't bear the fact that we're playing around with it: tampering with seeds, modifying genes. It's not as if there isn't enough of it – in the First World, in any case. All these unknown products going into packages, cans, our mouths.'

Daniel watched her. It was another riff in the supposed guise of Isabel. On that level, at least, she was transparent. She was also desperately determined. He allowed himself a little sigh.

'Do you want my theories, Leonora? Or analysis?'

'I'm not sure. Both maybe.'

'Unknown things going into your mouth. Is that what you can't bear?'

He was doing it again, Leo thought, turning everything into a personal event. A bodily event. She went along with it and nodded.

'You want to control what you take in?'

'Are you telling me I'm becoming an anorexic?' An image of Isabel not eating flashed through her mind.

He shrugged. 'I don't really like bandying labels about. It's never quite that simple. But I guess we do live in an age which has anorexic properties. In the midst of plenty, of speed, of high technology, of open markets in goods and people, of a life distant from the sources of food, of a world too vast for us to control, we try to create a kind of controllable scarcity. We diet, we label, we worry ourselves into scares. The body can appear to be our last possible field of control. So we want to be a little more certain of origins, of provenance, of roots – the human kind as well.'

'Is that the theory?'

He laughed. It was the first time she had heard him laugh.

'Hardly that. Let's call it instant speculation.'

'And genetic tampering?'

'What frightens you about it?'

'What it can do to the environment, to eco-systems.'

'Nothing else?'

'Unknown things going into your mouth, you said.'

'You said,' he corrected her. 'Penetration by the unknown. Things you can't identify, aliens making their way into your body. Taking up residence there. Reproducing.'

'Sex,' Leo murmured. 'Mutants.' She lost her thought. A sequence of images had started to speed through her mind. An IVF laboratory, a hypodermic moving sperm cells into an egg. Bright-eyed semen navigating up the birth canal, captain in the lead, like in those cartoon body programmes for children. Then Norfolk. He had said something to her about Isabel. Her perpetual hunger, a hole that couldn't be filled. And something else. She closed her eyes.

Isabel and she, sitting on sofas opposite each other in the loft. That bare loft, because Isabel had changed, mutated. She wasn't eating. Like Leo at home, not letting anything in.

The lights were low. It was late. There was an almost-empty bottle of wine on the table. From next door came the muffled sound of the television: Becca watching a video. Leo murmured, a little sleepy with the wine, 'What's wrong, Isabel? I sense there's something wrong.'

Isabel made a shrill sound, like a scoff. 'Oh, it's nothing. It's a stupid idea my shrink put into my head, that I can only know people by sleeping with them.' Their eyes met, a jolt of electricity passing between them. 'Maybe we should. In the heat of Savannah.' Isabel laughed. A joke. 'Then I can penetrate your wonderfully ordered life.' Leo got up, laughing too, uncomfortably, clearing the table. Dusting it all away. Under the carpet. Until Savannah.

'Sex? Mutants?' Daniel Lukas's voice urged her back into the present.

Leo's eyes flew open, and with them the attack she had been hoarding. 'You slept with Isabel, didn't you?'

She watched him, watched for a tensing of hands or face, or a revealing flicker of an eyelid. But he didn't flinch. Dark eyes surveyed her with unnatural calm. He was waiting for her to say something more, so she repeated her statement. This time there was no question mark. Her tone was heavy with accusation.

'Is this sleeping with me, this mutant penetration, something you would wish for yourself?'

Leo gasped.

'Because otherwise it seems to me that your un-inhibited desire to know about your friend is the only desire you manifest. Is it only through her – and

297

perhaps your daughter – that you feel real to yourself?'

The attack was frontal. He was a monster, after all.

She looked away, wishing herself behind the chair rather than hideously visible in front of him. What did he mean? Did she really only gain a sense of solidity, of three-dimensional life, through Isabel or Becca?

No. She mustn't let him get to her. That wasn't why she was here.

'I have no desire whatsoever to sleep with you, Dr Lukas.' She announced it in a mimicry of his clear, flat tones, though as she said it, her pulse raced oddly. She hurried on. 'As it happens, I have a particularly satisfactory lover at the moment.'

The statement, spoken so adamantly, sounded like a boast. She averted her eyes again. On the carpet beneath her, she noticed a stain. Like track marks. Sperm, she thought, and looked up quickly.

'I take it he is neither Isabel's lover nor your daughter's, but your own?'

He said it so softly that, for a moment, she was confused, unsure whether he had spoken or she herself had silently posed the question. Becca with a lover. The idea had rumbled in her ever since Becca had mentioned the 'cool boy'. It wasn't the first time, of course. The thought had played through her subliminally for years. A man to displace her for ever. Like she had displaced her parents with Jeff. And now she was displaced twice over. No wonder she clutched at Isabel.

'I knew you'd bring me round to sex sooner rather than later,' she muttered.

'I was following your lead. But since we're here, let's talk about it.'

'It's personal.'

'That's fine. That's good.' She thought she heard a smile in his voice. Hearing it rather than seeing it made her realize that she had moved to the couch and was stretched out on it. She didn't remember doing that.

'Perhaps you'd like to tell me about your former husband, then? The one who made love to Isabel.'

'What?' She was shocked at having it spoken out loud like that by someone else. Impersonally.

But, as if he had pulled some kind of lever in her, she responded, despite herself. Incoherently, she found herself talking about Jeff, telling him about those last years, how she had closed herself off in a little casket of safety and beauty, and obliterated what she didn't want to know. Rage leapt out of her, at Jeff for his betrayals and at herself for letting all those years pass in a limbo of virtuous unfeeling. She felt incandescent, as if she would burn up in her own fury. There was rage at him, too, at this know-it-all doctor who pulled levers in her psyche. Tears poured out of her but only stoked the fire.

At one point, she heard him say softly, 'So, as you tell it, it would seem that since your father's death, or was it since a few years before your husband's departure, you've kept yourself locked up, a little afraid of living. Your friend and your daughter do that for you, while you wait in abeyance, nursing your hurt, your loss, your integrity. It's not a bad kind of living. Pretty good, really. It makes cardinal virtues of friendship and mothering. It allows you to love through them. But now you want more. You need to move on, perhaps?'

Leo's anger burnt. 'You're twisting things again. Twist and turn, that's all you do, so that I lose things, lose the thread, find it in the wrong place.'

'Or just another place.' He waited for her. When she didn't speak, he went on. 'Maybe life is about loss. Or about violation. We all feel violated by it sometimes. Violated from the inside by unruly desires. Violated from the outside by deaths, betrayals, incursions by others – even strange foods. Defensiveness is a reaction to that, a way of protecting ourselves in order to go on living with sufficient pleasure. But we can't deny it all. We can't deny all the loss or the sense of violation or the pain. We're not inviolate. We can't lock ourselves away for ever. Loss and violation may be what keep us moving. They land us in another place. A good place, perhaps. You have a lover. You're moving. That may be a good.'

As Daniel made this long speech, he wondered whether he had already taken the decision not to see her again. It felt like a summing-up. But he didn't have time to think. She was suddenly bolt upright, her cheeks blazing.

'Isabel told me you had slept with her. Did she have some kind of breakdown after that? Where is she? I saw one dead woman this week. I don't want to see another. Not another.' She was crying again.

Daniel looked at her, felt pain and confusion fill the room. A recent death to bring the first one in its train. All that compounded with the fear about Isabel. She hadn't told him about the recent death. Too late now.

He kept his voice even. 'I share your concern, Leonora. I know that, apart from everything else, it's also deeply felt. But here, in this room, we have to talk about you, about your relations with Isabel, if you like. But not about what Isabel may have told

300

you about me. The statement you attribute to her is a subject for her analysis, not yours. I'm sorry, I wish I could help. What I can do doesn't form part of your hour.'

'I could report you,' Leo hissed.

He shrugged. He suddenly felt very tired. 'I don't really think that would help you locate your friend. But perhaps we should say goodbye now. Your hour's up. I can refer you to someone else, if you like.'

The door, this time, sounded with a noisy slam. Daniel stayed in his chair. All his energy had flown out of the room with her. He looked out the window. Beyond the brick of the back wall the chestnuts in the park were bursting into vibrant bloom, almost too full of life. Eva had lived to see their flowering. It was one of the last things she had commented on. She had loved their beauty, heavy, yet somehow fragile. And then pain too intense for the morphine had swallowed her up and she was gone. Almost a year now: 11 June 1997. The minutes of the intervening months had passed with a dull, aching slowness. Yet their accumulated dailiness added up to speed: sitting here now, it was startling to think that almost a year had already passed. A fifth of little Robbie's life.

It was at the very abyss of that year – the point at which the unending reality of Eva's absence had finally hit home – that Isabel Morgan had un-expectedly turned up. Christmas could only have been some ten days away. Robbie and he had decor-ated the tree together, and the boy had said to him in a flat little voice that it wasn't half as good as when Mummy did it. Then his grandmother had whisked him away for a weekend of shopping and adventure.

Daniel was sitting in front of the less-than-perfect tree

and nursing a solitary whisky when the doorbell rang. Already awash with the self-pity the Scotch so skilfully encouraged, he was in no mood for contact with the living world. But the ringing was insistent. He had lifted himself heavily from the fireside chair and, with a curse at whichever friend of Martina's it was who didn't know she had gone home for the holidays, he had at last opened the door.

On the threshold, Isabel had looked like an apparition, a present delivered by some beneficent Scandinavian Santa. Her hair bounded from beneath a tiny embroidered toque. Her cheeks were glowing, her eyes as electric as her hair. She was wearing a long suede coat in recreated hippy fashion, tight at the waist and trimmed in some flurry of wool which moved with her. And she moved quickly. She was in the house before he had uttered a word, her coat flung on a chair, a bottle of wine proffered.

'I was in the mood for a friend. And, in retrospect, you felt like one.'

He couldn't quite read whether the irony in her face was directed at him or herself. Maybe he wasn't paying enough attention to her face. But for its abundant roll of a collar, her dress was minuscule, a black second skin above an infinity of leg. He had forgotten how striking she was, or maybe the limits of the consulting room had provided a small measure of immunity. Now he felt like rubbing his eyes.

'Wine would be nice.' She pointed to the bottle he was still holding and walked around, pausing at objects and pictures. 'Whisky's fine, too, if that's what you're drinking.'

He found a glass in the cabinet and poured her one. He hadn't seen her since that session in

September when she had walked off without telling him she wasn't intending to return. That terse message had come in a phone call. And now she was sitting in the chair on the other side of the fire, her legs lavishly crossed. He didn't quite know how to handle the situation.

'It's nice here. Warm,' she said in a low voice. Perhaps he didn't respond quickly enough, for she then added, 'Now don't get all rule-bound on me, Daniel. Life is too short.'

He had eased himself back into his chair and swallowed a large glug of his topped-up Scotch.

'That's better.' Her smile teased him. He returned it a little wistfully. So her next comment took him by surprise. 'Why didn't you tell me your wife had died? You should have told me.'

'Should I?' He shrugged, considering. 'It didn't feel appropriate. And then there was the summer break. And then you left.'

She let out a noisy guffaw. 'Appropriate! I had to find out from Paola. I've just found out.'

'You talk to her about me?'

'Not much. Only when it's appropriate.' She mocked him.

He tore his eyes away from her and gazed into the fire. The flames were golden, then tipped with blue. They leapt and crackled in the stillness. Like her. 'How have you been?'

'Up and down. Quite a lot of the latter. She's one tough woman.'

'I don't really want to know.'

She was suddenly out of her chair and standing behind him. 'No, but I know that I need to make amends. Need to.'

It was the way she said that word, a low hoarse

sound, like the sound of need itself. It awakened his own, made him aware of a dark gaping hole somewhere inside him. The brush of her fingers and lips on his neck acted like kindling. She could burn darkness away.

After that the need took over. It made them anonymous. Any man and any woman clasped together on a rug in front of a fireplace, their limbs moving, their backs arching, their lips and fingers enmeshed in a dance of hunger that grew with the eating. She was so beautiful, her skin tawny, her eyes lit by fire. And he was alive with desire. The depth and extent of it astonished him, as if he were an untouched youth again, free of the burden of second thoughts.

Later, when they were dressed, it was more difficult.

He felt she was eager to leave, nor did she want him to see her home. She rang a cab for herself. 'You've made ample amends,' he said to her at the door. Maybe he said it too stiffly, because she gave him a peculiar look, as if she had no recollection of her own words. Or perhaps the giving of herself wasn't what she had meant by them. Then she was off into the waiting car with a little wave of the hand. Cinderella disappearing into the night, with not even a dropped slipper to mark her passage.

He was left with the sense that what had passed between them wordlessly bore no relation to any words they might exchange. He thought about her for the rest of the night. His mind was a ring of wrestling emotions. He tried to understand what, if anything, had happened between them. At one point he told himself he might have experienced a hallucination. But his sense of having committed a wrong increased with each passing minute. More than a wrong, it felt like sin. He had never committed this particular one before.

At lunchtime the following day he rang her, only to be answered by a machine. He asked her to pick up if she was there. When she didn't, he made a little speech which sounded far too dry and stumbled along ineptly. 'You were generous last night, Isabel, thank you. If you want to talk, I'm here. But I know, as you do, that it was a one-off. Unrepeatable. Like a miracle. And a grave wrong in my small world of rules. For that I'm sorry.'

Her response didn't come until a few days later. It, too, was a message – light-hearted to begin with. 'There's nothing to talk about. No significance. No heavy meanings. I was curious. Simply that.' And then the voice changed, took on a steely, malicious edge. 'You should know that I'm writing two books at the moment. The first won't interest you. The second might. It's called *On Being a Patient.*

The slam of the receiver wasn't recorded, but he heard it. Its menace reverberated through his days like a guillotine poised to drop. He felt angry and helpless by turn. And though rationally he recognized the fault was all his, her vengefulness ignited his own. The fitful pendulum logic of an eye for an eye infested his dreams.

And now this Leonora Gould had turned up to reactivate the threat. A part of him was distinctly ambivalent, he noted, about the need for locating Isabel Morgan.

Leo walked. She walked across the leafy green slopes of the park and skirted the ponds with their mirrored shrubbery and ever-hungry ducks. She walked with no sense of destination. There were hours to kill before she could hope for Norfolk's return to the loft. She needed to talk to him. The contending voices in her head had grown too noisy.

Daniel Lukas hadn't denied her accusation. He had merely deflected her. That must mean he really had engaged in some kind of murky affair with Isabel.

But what difference did it finally make? And why was she so intent on knowing, since it seemed increasingly likely that, whatever her inner state, Isabel's disappearance was somehow linked to the savage secrecy of rapacious multinationals who had chauffeurs at their disposal? After all, the respected Dr Gould had slept with her mother, and she had neither suffered a breakdown nor vanished into the ether. That was different. He had married her. Yet Isabel was not the marrying kind. Still, she had wanted Daniel to know that, whatever had happened to Isabel, Leo, for one, knew he was implicated. Guilty by implication.

She could hear him turning it all round for her, landing her in another place, telling her that he was a mere stand-in for Jeff or her father, men she wanted to implicate in her own plight and hadn't dared, so that she could more easily and eventually live in her own skin, not Isabel's reckless one. The man had her hooked.

Leo paused with a sigh in front of the ivy-clad fence that separated the park from the cemetery. If she stood on the ledge, she could see the tip of Karl Marx's bulbous stone head amidst a sea of leafy growth and ornate, crumbling tombstones. Her eyes roamed through dappled light and deep shadow and stopped abruptly. Lying next to a stone with a broken-winged angel at its crest was a man. His head was a mass of long curls, as tangled as the ivy and as grimy as the earth beneath him. He was wearing an ancient checked jacket and, beneath it, a ragged pullover. Baggy cord trousers, tied at the bottom with rope, covered his legs. Only one foot had a shoe on it.

A wave of nausea attacked her stomach. Dead, but unburied. A destitute old man. She had to alert someone. She gripped the iron railings and closed her eyes for a steadying moment. When she opened them, the man was upright. He was pissing onto a neighbouring grave, whistling tunelessly as the great arced stream fell on stone, splattering leaves and gathered grit. The gesture was so anarchic, so free, that Leo felt a laugh of relief rise to her throat. At its sound, the man turned and waggled his penis in her direction with an inane smile.

She strode off purposefully. The old man had given her a brief respite from the prison of her mind with its bevy of chattering monkeys who could only ask questions, cast doubts and dialogue endlessly to no avail. For all her mental juggling, she really moved as blindly as a mole, driven to dig and tunnel because there was nothing else she could do.

Maybe the old man was a sign. Isabel would arise, just as he did, from the death into which Leo's imagination over these last days had too often cast her. She would return to her loft on the very day she had intended to return from their journey across the States. Isabel had simply gone east rather than west. Her mother's death had scratched old scars. She needed to pour native balm on them. Alone. Privately – as she had intimated to that Pippa woman. Once back, hers and Isabel's lives and diaries would once more be enmeshed. They would travel together,

14

The light on the answering machine flashed red. With a tremor of anticipation, Leo pressed the messages button. Norfolk's voice boomed out at her.

'Holland? You not there yet? OK, here's the low-down. Isabel's almost definitely down here somewhere in the south-west. I met up with these Greens in Exeter who talked to her at that hotel we stayed at. They're engaged in some mutual muck-raking.' He paused for a little too long. 'The thing is, they're worried about her now, too, 'cause she hasn't reported back. She said she'd be staying with a cousin in the area. They don't have a contact. I won't be back tonight. Need to do some more exploring. I'll go straight to Heathrow in the morning. I'll try to ring in later. Miss you. Oh, yes, that aunt's number has come through on the Aussie e-mail. Here it is, code and all.'

Leo reached for a pen and jotted down a long row of digits. No sooner had she finished than a new voice came on.

'Ms Holland, Faraday here. We need to talk. I'll drop in on you about nine thirty on Saturday morning, unless I hear that isn't convenient.'

Faraday's voice was clipped. He wasn't happy about something. She ran through the two messages she had left for him, one about Jill Reid, the second about the hotel in Lynton. She wished she could speak to him immediately, but it was already after eight. She had been anticipating a late dinner with Norfolk. The groceries she had picked up were still standing in their bags in the kitchen, next to the two tiny potted plants Isabel had left at the Lynton Arms. Why had she left them behind if they were in any way significant?

A voice she didn't recognize interrupted her thoughts. 'Isabel, dear one. You must be angry with me after our last conversation. You said you'd write, but nothing's come. Not for weeks. I'm sorry if I did the wrong thing. Do please phone, even if it's just to shout at me.'

Leo replayed the message. The voice, which didn't identify itself, had an Australian lilt. Its tone was intimate.

Without pausing to think, Leo dialled the number she had taken down from Norfolk. It was only as she heard the tone that she realized she didn't know the woman's full name. It wouldn't be Morgan. Nor had she calculated the time it would be in Australia.

'Is that Martha?'

The question played itself back in Leo's ear, jumping off satellites.

The voice that answered her held a muffled, sleepy note.

'Yes. Who is it?'

'My name's Leo. Leo Holland. I'm a friend of Isabel's. I hope I haven't rung too early.'

'No matter. How is she?'

Leo could feel anxiety battling with hope in the woman's voice.

'Well, that's just it. I can't tell you. I thought you

310

might be able to tell me. You see' – Leo censored the word 'missing' – 'none of us knows where Isabel is. Where she might be.'

There was a long silence, interspersed by crackle and what Leo sensed was a judder of breath. 'How long has it been since you've seen her?'

'No-one has seen her for at least three weeks.'

The breath was audible now.

'Where are you phoning from?'

'I'm in Isabel's flat in London. She hasn't been in Australia in that time?'

'Not as far as I know. And I'm sure she'd contact me. Yes, of course she would.'

'The last place at which she was seen, she was using the name Iris Morgenstern.'

'What?' The woman's voice caught, and Leo repeated what she had said.

There was a long pause. 'Look, I'm going to fly over. I've been so worried. I tried ringing, but there was no answering machine. Not for weeks. And then I had to . . . never mind. Where can I reach you?'

'I'm staying in Isabel's apartment.'

'Tell me your name again. Of course. Isabel talked about you. Yes. I'll let you know as soon as I have my flight fixed. I might be of some help . . .'

Inspector Faraday paced the loft and gave Leo the full force of what she could only call a polite scowl. She decided she wouldn't like to see it without the constraint of politeness. As it was, poised here with a strip of sun beaming down on her, she felt she was in an interrogation chamber. She stirred herself to pull down the blind.

'I warned you that this could prove dangerous, Ms Holland. I don't want you interfering in our

311

investigations. We have one woman dead—'

'So you've concluded Jill Reid's death was no simple accident?'

'There were drugs involved. We're not sure of their source yet. They might have been self-inflicted. But that really is no concern of yours, Ms Holland. Nor is it any business of yours to trespass on private property.'

Leo was about to interrupt, but he stopped her.

'Yes, yes. Of course I know you've been exploring those map sites. We're not fools.'

'But your men didn't trace Isabel to the Lynton Arms, did they?'

'No.' He had the grace to look a little abashed. 'But we have now located the car she hired.'

Leo reached for a cigarette, then stopped herself from lighting it. She poured coffee instead. 'Where?'

'In the Lynton car park. Yes, yes. As you suggested. Where is Mr Norfolk?'

'In Amsterdam by now, I imagine. Or on his way. Why?'

'Don't you find it just a little convenient that he was the last person we know to have seen Jill Reid, as well as the man to identify her?'

'Convenient? What are you suggesting, Inspector?'

'I must ask you again, Ms Holland, how well do you know Christopher Norfolk?' He had stopped directly in front of her and was peering at her as if she were in a line-up.

Leo sat up straight. 'Well enough, I imagine.'

'Well enough.' Faraday echoed her with a growl. 'Do you have any objective confirmation that he's a friend of Ms Morgan's? Do you know where he got the keys to this place?'

'No, but—'

'No. Can you tell me how he knew to go directly to Plantagen where Jill Reid worked?'

Leo shrugged. 'I think Isabel—'

'You think. You don't know. You probably don't know where he was on the day Jill Reid died, either.'

'When was that exactly?'

He didn't answer. Nor did his eyes leave her. 'Where can I find Mr Norfolk in Amsterdam?'

Leo got up. 'I didn't know I was on trial, Inspector. Nor do I have a contact number.'

She said it coolly enough, but she could feel the tears pricking at her eyes. Faraday was right. She knew nothing about Norfolk except that she liked the pressure of his arms around her. Could she really have allowed herself to be duped like some hapless girl, avid for adventure? No, more like an ageing, besotted spinster, all too grateful for advances that bore the semblance of passion. Luckily she hadn't allowed too many emotions to follow in her body's witless path. Or had she?

The coffee scalded her tongue. Pain jarred her back into an approximation of reason. She had to trust her instincts. Faraday was on the wrong track.

'Shouldn't you be concentrating on finding Isabel, Inspector? I've told you what I discovered. If I had your resources, I wouldn't be chasing after a friend of hers now; I'd be interviewing all the chauffeurs in hitting distance of the northern coast. Maybe even further afield. I don't have to do that myself as well, do I? When Norfolk phones, I'll tell him you want to speak to him.'

'That would be kind, Ms Holland.' He inclined his thin body slightly in a mockery of a bow. 'There isn't anything you've omitted to tell me, is there?'

Leo considered. 'I spoke to Isabel's aunt in Australia. She's flying over.'

'Good.' He gave her a quick smile. 'It will relieve me to know you've got suitable company here.'

'You might as well take these, too, Inspector.' Leo strode into the kitchen and brought out Isabel's two plantlings. 'Isabel left them at the hotel where she was last seen.' Leo frowned. 'I can't imagine what they'll reveal about her whereabouts.'

Faraday took them from her with a marked alacrity. 'You leave the imagining to me, Ms Holland.'

Leo grimaced at him. 'I hope your nights are better than mine, Inspector.'

'If these plants are what I think they may be, then my nights will be full, Ms Holland. Whoever sent Isabel that list of sites may also be paying her. Paying her to procure just this. A little hi-tech thieving.'

'Yet she left her ill-gotten gains behind, Inspector. So they can't have been all that important. At least not to her.'

Leo was at a loose end after Faraday left. Stroking Beast, who had taken up position on her lap as soon as Faraday was out the door, was no help. Inaction turned the rumble of anxiety into a thunderclap. Needing to move, she went into the study and took down a series of box files. There might be something from Isabel's aunt that she had overlooked. Martha had implied that Isabel and she had argued over something. It might help if she knew what.

Near the top of the file, she came across the invitation she had vaguely remembered and then mislaid in the chaotic rearrangement of papers after the break-in. Paola Webster. She had never followed up the Paola lead. The invitation was for the launch of a book called *Scar Tissue* the following evening. Leo fingered the card and pressed the messages button on the answering machine. She hoped the message from Paola hadn't been wiped. It must be the same woman. Yes, the message was still there. She took down the phone number and gazed at it for a moment.

She had nothing to lose and nothing else to do. She prepared a little speech, but there was no answer to her ring. Odd in these days of answering machines. Maybe the woman had forgotten to switch it on.

Irritated, Leo sifted through the box files some more, then remembered that when she had finally spoken to her mother last night, she had promised to ring Aron Field, a mutual friend who was in London.

She had phoned her mother immediately after she had spoken to Martha. The woman's fretful longing to make contact with Isabel had stirred a generational guilt in her. Her mother, too, would be worrying. Leo hadn't rung her in days; nor had she given her Isabel's number. Remembering the debt that Daniel had underlined she owed her mother, she had for once managed to keep her voice even. And despite an initial bout of plaintive recrimination, her mother had indeed been both relieved and grateful. She had finished by saying in a soft, oddly vulnerable voice that they all missed her and looked forward to seeing her back in Manhattan.

Her mother's tone had surprised her. It had also made her think of Becca. The generational equation would be complete if she now rang her daughter only to be barked at abruptly in the way she normally did at her own mother. She didn't ring. The time was wrong. Becca would be in classes. In any case, Becca didn't bark. Not yet. Not quite. But she had made a mental note that the situation could provide a strip.

With a sudden lightening of mood, Leo pulled out a sheet of blank paper and started to draw. When she had finished, like the good daughter she rarely was, she rang Aron Field.

The address bore no relationship to anything Leo had expected. Behind a well-trimmed privet and small garden stood a respectable red-brick family house, largely indistinguishable from its neighbours on the quiet, sloping street. A lofty central bay was flanked by two solid wings. A series of attic windows protruded from the tiled roof. Only the round blue plaque discreetly positioned between the sash windows indicated a difference. It read, 'Sigmund Freud, Founder of Psychoanalysis, lived and died here'. This was the house Freud had inhabited for the last year of his life. It was also the museum the invitation to Isabel from Paola Webster had led her to.

Leo took a deep breath and pressed the bell beside the freshly painted door. It opened instantly to reveal a suited man of Mediterranean aspect seated behind a small desk. She flashed the card at him and he waved her in.

She was standing in an airy hall, through which light poured from the high windows above. The stairwell was graceful, the banister highly polished. A small table beside her held a beckoning guest book. She was about to sign when she thought better of it. In front of her, beside a door from which a babble of voices emerged, hung an engraving. She examined it, not quite ready to confront a room full of strangers. A robed, wild-bearded man holding aloft two stone tablets etched with Hebraic script looked out at her.

Moses. Leo wondered which of the commandments were etched here. Thou shalt not kill, she thought, with a sudden nervous tremor.

She shunned the room in front of her and turned instead into one at the side. In the sudden gloom, she had the feeling that she had entered a time capsule. Heavy leather-bound tomes lined the walls, interspersed here and there with photographs and prints. Crowded everywhere on shelves, tables and behind glass, and in an assortment that defied order, were antique figurines and funerary objects. Too many to let the eye rest at first, though she thought she recognized a winged Eros and a handsome Athena, as well as a host of other mythological deities, Greek and Egyptian.

The desk, too, swarmed with shapes, ghostly in their frozen movement. But here, as if its occupant had only momentarily left the chair which echoed a human shape, there were also items of everyday use. A pair of rimless spectacles lay on a sheaf of paper. Inkstand and pen, cigar box and ashtrays awaited their owner's return. Opposite the desk stood the couch, covered with Persian rugs as rich and worn as a flying carpet. For a moment, Leo found herself wondering what it might have been like to lie amidst those opulent reds and blues, speaking the dreams the room invoked to the old man with the gaunt face who was Freud in his last years.

'There's a definite magic about it,' a voice beside her said softly. 'Almost as if you could feel a geography of the mind being mapped through all those stories of pain and desire.'

Leo turned to see a tiny, dapper man with a moon-shaped face and the round, melancholy eyes of a circus clown. The face beamed at her. Beneath it sat

317

a polka-dotted bow-tie, brashly at odds with the sober three-piece suit.

'Leonora H. I expected you at the Savoy later, but hardly here. What a pleasant surprise.'

'Dr Field! How lovely.' Leo embraced him, happy at the coincidence. Aron Field was one of the few of her stepfather's friends she genuinely liked.

'I didn't know you mingled with the London confraternity.'

'I don't normally. But a friend passed on her invitation and I thought I'd take the opportunity . . .'

'To see the museum. I know. I try to come here once on every visit to London. So you don't know Paola Webster?'

Leo shook her head.

'I'll introduce you, if you like.' He hesitated. 'She's quite a woman.'

Leo couldn't altogether read the slightly comical expression that went with the statement.

'I would like,' she said emphatically.

'Shall we go and mingle with the fray, then?'

After the meditative hush of the study with its pale antique gods, it was the room in which the party unfurled that felt unreal. It took Leo a moment to adjust to the animated figures. Mouths and faces looked too large, hands were unnecessary protuberances, clothes were too bright. She blinked, took a proffered glass from a tray and followed Aron Field past a painted rustic wardrobe into the midst of the spacious room.

At its far end, beyond the gathered crowd, she noticed glazed doors opening onto an illuminated garden which she hoped was their destination. But progress was slow. Aron knew a number of the guests, and he stopped to chat, to catch up on gossip as well as to introduce Leo in effusive terms.

'If you're looking for Paola, she's over there.' A tall, thin woman with an austere face beneath an abundance of grey-streaked hair pointed them diagonally across the room. 'Near the books table.'

'Signing, I imagine.'

'That, too.' The woman gave Aron a wry smile. '*Scar Tissue* is poised to do very well.'

'Steamy, is it?'

'Hard-hitting and graphic. If I were you, I'd watch my—'

The din in the room wiped out her last words, but Leo thought she had heard '*cojones*'.

They wove their way towards the edge of the room, where a large woman in a flowing plum-coloured trousersuit stood amidst a circle of evident admirers. Her mouth was generous, her eyes as luminous as her black hair. A heavy African necklace hung from her neck, giving her the air of a hieratic priestess. She stopped in mid-sentence when she spied Aron.

'Dr Field. How exceedingly good of you to come all the way from New York. I am honoured.'

Leo saw a droll smile form on Aron's lips. 'Not quite all the way from New York, but bringing congratulations nevertheless. Let me introduce you to Leo Holland. Another New Yorker.'

'Hi.' Leo made the leap into a garrulous persona. 'I've heard so much about you.'

'Oh yes?' The woman radiated pleasure and hugged Leo against her capacious bosom without a moment's reticence.

'Yes, yes. From my step-father. He's an analyst, too. Dr Samuel Gould.'

Paola Webster's smile widened.

'Funny you should choose to have your party here,' a young woman on Paola's other side intervened. Like an Eighties pop star, her hair was close cropped enough to reveal scalp. Tiny studs bedecked her ears. 'I didn't think you were on speaking terms with Freud.'

Paola gave her a look freighted with machine-guns as well as daggers. 'I wanted to make the point that we are all one great family. In all families there are battles, but also great dollops of love. Isn't that right, Dr Field?'

Aron nodded sagely.

'Yet, it's quite clear that your position—' the young woman continued.

Sensing that Paola was about to be deflected into a long argument, Leo rushed in.

'My friend Isabel Morgan also spoke very highly of you.'

Conflicting emotions played over the woman's vivid face and settled into a bright, smiling mask. 'Dear Isabel, a glorious woman. Such a fine journalist.'

'I was hoping you could tell me how she was,' Leo heard herself saying. She had just understood something. 'I know she was seeing you. And now, well, she's disappeared.'

The mask cracked. For a fierce, fleeting moment the face breathed venom. 'That is not my responsibility.' The words were a low growl. And then the smile returned, not directed at Leo now, who had been banished into invisibility, but at a mountain of a man who looked as if he had parachuted in from a cyber-convention. Black, unstructured suit, wide brow merging into a white-gold tail, a gold chain, inordinately large teeth, bared now in a beam at Paola.

'Wonderful book!'

'You've read it. You're a true friend.' Paola stepped into his bear hug.

Realizing that she was about to lose her chance, Leo turned to Aron Field. 'You have to help me, Aron,' she whispered. 'Fix it so that I can see her privately. The sooner the better.'

'Are you sure?' Distaste flickered over his face.

'Please.' Leo gripped his arm. 'It's just for once. I'll explain later.'

He adjusted his bow-tie and tapped Paola on the shoulder.

The woman veered round, her smile fixing itself into a rictus as she met Leo's eyes. The large man at her side glanced at them for a moment, then moved away.

'I have a favour to ask of you, Paola,' Aron began smoothly. 'You can't refuse a colleague who has come from so far. My young friend here, who is such an admirer of yours, wants an interview with you. She's only here briefly and then she's back to Manhattan, where I should tell you she goes under the name of Leonora H. A household name in New York. Her cartoon strip is our best.'

'It is only that I am so busy at the moment, Dr Field.'

'Half an hour. Breakfast tomorrow. Why not? You remember that conference in LA you were talking to me about . . .'

The woman gave him a beady look. 'All right, Dr Field. You win. For you, I do it.' She turned to Leo. 'Half past eight. I will have exactly thirty minutes. Dr Field will give you the address.' She wound her arm through Aron's. 'Look, Dr Field, there's Daniel

321

Lukas. You know him, yes? It is good to see him here. Perhaps it means he has at last shed – how do you say? – his widower's weeds. Too much mourning is as unhealthy as too little.'

'Mourning?' Leo asked.

The woman charged past her, dragging Aron Field along. 'Let us go and make him feel welcome. I shall introduce him to Hilton. He has been wanting to meet Daniel properly, in order to make contact with the Institute and its grandees.' She winked at Aron.

'Mourning,' Leo repeated, not quite realizing she had spoken out loud until she heard a comment from her side.

'Yes. Lukas's wife died last year. Very sad. She was a fine painter. I knew her rather better than I know him.'

Leo turned to take in a man with a broad, friendly face.

'You don't remember?' He smiled with a hint of self-deprecation. 'The plane from New York. We sat next to each other. I'm Tim Hoffman. And don't tell me, I do remember. I'm cursed with memory. You're Leo Holland. Small world, as they say.'

'Tim Hoffman, of course. Hello. Very small.'

'Shall we go and join your friends?'

Leo hung back. 'No, no. Not right now.'

She needed a moment to feed this latest information into her portrait of Daniel Lukas. It skewed it severely. She converted the taste of guilt in her mouth to anger, as if he had presented himself to her under false pretences.

She saw him emerge now from the room's sea of faces. He looked thinly handsome and rather forbidding, the soot beneath his dark eyes lending a pale gravity to his face. There was a pocket of air around him, as if people were unwilling to approach. Leo watched as Paola Webster filled it.

She had a sudden rush of vertigo. All these people coming together and she couldn't make out the pattern.

'Yes. Lukas took it hard.' Tim Hoffman interrupted her thoughts. 'He cut down his practice. And Paola's right. He hasn't been coming out much. By the way, I couldn't help but overhear you mention the friend you asked me about on the plane. Isabel Morgan. Troubling that.'

'I used to work with Isabel.' The young woman who had challenged Paola Webster suddenly addressed Leo.

'Did you?' Leo looked at her with new interest.

'Yeah. Some years back.' The woman grinned. It gave her face an elfin aspect. 'Shall we go outside? I could use some air.'

A waiter refilled their glasses as they walked out. Past a small bookshop, some doors opened out onto a gracefully proportioned garden where more guests stood talking.

'That's better. I'm Lyn McAffrey, by the way.'

Tim Hoffman offered cigarettes. When they had lit up, Leo asked them both, 'What do you think of Paola Webster?'

'Well, she makes good copy.' Lyn grinned again. 'She's never afraid to be controversial. I'm a journalist, so that's always a plus. I'm curious to see whether Isabel includes her in her book.'

'Her book?' Tim asked.

'When we last bumped into each other she told me she was busy writing a book about therapies. She had her Isabel-mischievous air on.' Lyn giggled. 'Did Paola get her to give it up?' She addressed Leo. 'It wouldn't surprise me. Isabel was seeing her.'

'I don't know. No-one's seen or heard from Isabel for almost a month.'

'Which means she's holed up somewhere and tapping away. Isabel was ever like that.' She enunciated it with a touch of self-mocking drama. 'She'd seem to be doing nothing, and then she'd vanish and the work would appear at great speed. We'll have a book in no time.'

Leo weighed this statement against her fears and wished she could believe it. 'When did you last see her?'

'Well, now that you mention it, probably not since Christmas. Time goes at such a pace.'

'Maybe that's the solution,' Tim Hoffman said reflectively. 'Your friend has hidden herself away to write. I often long to do that.'

'Hey, there's going to be a speech.' Lyn pointed to a man who was waving people back into the main room. 'I wouldn't miss this for the world.'

'What surprises me', Tim said as they crossed the threshold, 'is that Daniel Lukas is here. I wouldn't have thought he'd have much time for Paola Webster. They have such fundamental disagreements.'

Pretending she knew what he was talking about, Leo nodded, then lagged behind. She didn't want to bump into Daniel. Not now. There was too much new material to digest. She recalled that Isabel's upstairs neighbour, Mike Newson, had originally alerted her to the fact that Isabel's therapist was a woman. Yet, driven by Isabel's e-mails, Leo had pursued her own blinkered course. It came to her now, in a confusing rush, that it was probably Paola who had said to Isabel that her friend only knew people by sleeping with them, which was what had occasioned that uncomfortable, yet somehow loaded, moment between them.

Leo put it out of her mind to concentrate on the speakers. From her position at the far end of the room she could hardly see, but she heard a man announce that the publishers took great pleasure in the appearance of *Scar Tissue*.

Paola Webster's voice was clearer. For some reason its booming tenor reminded her of her Wife of Wrath. She couldn't concentrate on the list of fulsome thank-yous, nor on the broad and ringing mission Paola outlined for psychotherapy. Nor, as she stood on tip-toe to get a better view, could she imagine what would have drawn Isabel to seek out this overbearing woman, unless it was indeed a question of research. Once more Leo had the sinking feeling that, with each step she took to bring her closer to Isabel, her friend became more alien and mysterious.

In the midst of the clapping that broke out when Paola Webster had finished, Leo felt a tap on her shoulder. 'Let me take you away, Leonora.' Aron Field was at her side. 'I've got a chariot waiting, and now there shall be two of us in it.'

Leo agreed without a second's hesitation. As they made their way through the room, she spied Daniel Lukas talking to the bullish man with big teeth. They made such an odd pair that she stared for a moment. Now that she saw him in profile, there was something uncannily familiar about the man's face. But as Daniel's eyes strayed in their direction, she averted her own and hastily followed Aron through the door.

One of the cardinal rules of psychoanalysis, as her stepfather often reiterated, was that one didn't meet patients in social situations.

Maybe bed didn't count, Leo told herself with bleak humour.

15

The black sedan drove them sedately through the evening quiet of Camden Town and past the university buildings and small terraced hotels of Gower Street. Aron Field plied her with questions about Becca and, as she talked about her daughter, Leo realized just how happy she was to see him. He brought with him a bounded world of the familiar. After these weeks of living on a teetering edge, she entered it with gratitude.

'So what brings you to London, Leonora?' he asked when they had moved into the bustle of the West End. 'I hope it's something exciting. A new friend?' He raised an eyebrow in a parody of innuendo. 'Or a British deal for your Merry Wives?'

'No, no. Nothing like that.' Leo sighed despite herself.

'You'll forgive me. I'm a meddling old man.'

'It's not that.'

Leo looked out at the passing crowds, at the pictures on the front of the Coliseum. Like their conversation, the traffic had ground to a standstill.

'Should we get out and walk the rest of the way? We're almost at the Savoy.'

'I've never been there, you know.'

'Nothing but the best for Leonora H.' Aron Field

put his arm through hers with old-fashioned politeness and guided her through the fray. 'We shall be four. I hope you'll like the company.'

Leo was no longer listening. Halfway down William IVth Street stretched a long billboard ranked with posters. Each of them bore the heading, MISSING PERSON. She stopped and gazed into the faces of young men and women. They were ordinary snapshots, but the descriptions beneath them had a heart-rending quality. There was Joel, five foot nine and sandy-haired, who had left home at the age of sixteen, four years ago, and whose mother begged for his return, underlining that all was forgiven. There was Angie, a delicate seventeen-year-old, who had disappeared only three months before on the way to her school in Bath. There was Alan White, an upright-looking forty-eight-year-old, whose wife and daughters wished for some sign. There was Jerome, a black youth with vast eyes and a mop of short dreads, who had vanished in Tower Hamlets over a year ago.

Tears leapt into Leo's eyes. So many missing. So many missed.

'What's wrong, Leonora?' Aron Field's voice reached her as if from a great distance. 'Is there someone you recognize here?'

Leo shook her head. 'I'm worrying about a friend of mine. That's why I wanted to see Paola Webster.'

'Is she missing? How old is she?'

Leo began to explain as they walked. 'How difficult for you,' Aron exclaimed when she had told him a little. 'The sense of betrayal, the breaking of a trust.'

'That's not what I feel,' Leo interrupted too sharply. 'Well, that's only a tiny part of it. I just know something has happened to her.'

'She's an adult, so let's hope it isn't something terrible. If it's an episode of some kind, she could be in a hospital. Have the police checked?'

Leo nodded.

'Put it out of your mind for now, Leo. This is such a grand place. It deserves to be enjoyed.' He waved his arm over the sweep of the Savoy lobby with a proprietorial gesture. 'Like stepping back into my youth. My parents used to bring me here.' He chuckled. 'And I think it's changed less than I have. So this is my hotel whenever I come to London.'

Leo could suddenly see him as a shy little boy, dreamy hooded eyes gazing out of that round face as he walked slowly down the stairs into the mirrored splendour of the lounge and half disappeared into a capacious chair.

'Frank Sinatra used to stay here,' he confided. 'Come, let's sit where we can see all the comings and goings, and we'll order drinks while we wait for our friends. But perhaps you'd like to powder your nose first . . . or whatever it is that ladies do these days.'

Leo smiled at his innocent excitement, asked him to order a whisky and soda for her and left him for a moment. When she returned, she saw him conferring with the maître d' at the entrance to the restaurant. He was back instantly.

'All arranged. And here are our drinks.' He raised his glass to her. 'To Leonora H. Let us hope your friend is soon returned to you.' He took a sip from his glass, then bent towards her across the low table. 'I had a patient once whose wife went missing, Leonora. She vanished, just like that.' He snapped his fingers. 'Between sessions, as they say.' His face took on an air of theatrical self-mockery. 'My patient was beside himself. He contacted the police, did all the necessary, and on the couch he started to talk, for the first time really, about his wife. I could see, as he spoke, all the hints she had given him about her leaving, but he hadn't heard them. He had closed himself off, been blind and deaf to her. I tried to jog him into awareness. About a month later he received a letter from his wife. She was in California with a lover, but the line he quoted to me asked whether he had noticed her absence. He was quite shocked at that.' Aron laughed. 'But I can see from your face that this example provides no solace. I'm in the wrong case.'

'I think you are,' Leo said gently, though guilt whisked through her. She, too, had not been alert enough to Isabel.

He gave her a rueful look, then broke into a wave. 'Here are our friends.'

Looking up, Leo wished the walls would swallow her. She froze into her chair.

Aron Field was oblivious. He walked forward to hug an elderly woman with a smooth cap of white hair and shook hands with the man at her side. 'So good of you to offer to pick Emily up on your way,' Leo heard him say. And then they were all in front of her.

'Leo, this is Emily Robson, my dearest friend in London and a grande dame of our profession, and Daniel Lukas, only recently met at a conference, but much admired, not only for his sterling work with adolescents, but for his writing. And this fine young woman here is Leo Holland, better known as Leonora H, who produces one of Manhattan's wittiest comic strips. I hope you'll all like each other.'

Aron's introductions seemed to go on for ever.

'Leo Holland.' Daniel Lukas's voice played over

Leo's name with only a hint of scepticism. 'I believe we've already met.'

Leo raised her eyes to his. His face was unsmiling, but his hand was stretched towards her and she shook it before she found her voice.

'Yes, I believe we have,' she echoed with a glimmer of bravado. 'Was it earlier this evening, at the party?'

'It could well have been.'

He played along with her charade, just as she had played along with his. But for a split-second, Leo had the sense that he suspected her of having connived to set up this meeting.

'Such a wonderful surprise to have Dr Field in London,' she said and then quickly turned her attention to Emily Robson. The woman had a remarkable delicacy of feature, like a porcelain doll whose hair had accidentally been dyed white. There was a quietness about her, too, which seemed to emit calming waves. As they moved into the restaurant, Leo tried to stay within their reach. She owed it to Aron not to ruin his dinner.

At the table, Aron placed her opposite Daniel so that every time she looked up, she was forced to confront him. She kept her eyes pinioned first to the tablecloth, then to the menu, which was so difficult to take in that, with a laugh that sounded false to her own ears, she girlishly asked Aron to order for her. Their conversation floated somewhere above her, as distant as the sparkling diners at other tables or the lights which played through the far windows.

When she tuned in, Aron seemed to be bemoaning the fact that in the United States, psychoanalysis was no longer the respected field it had once been, largely because the insurance companies wouldn't pay for its necessary extent, but for other reasons, too. People wanted quick fixes, wanted their symptoms removed, when that was, after all, only a beginning.

Leo couldn't tell if Daniel agreed with him. His tone was rather flat. What she heard was a statement about a burgeoning field for the talking cure, which had grown so broad and diverse that it was perhaps being killed off by its very success. Killed off, too, by a rush to medicalize any form of even marginally eccentric or annoying behaviour. Fidgety children now suffered from attention deficit hyperactivity disorder and were put in the care of doctors who prescribed Ritalin. Moody women who irritated a largely male cohort of psychiatrists were given a convenient malady, PMS or pre-menstrual syndrome. Teenagers rebelling against parents and at odds with themselves and the received world developed or were diagnosed with depression or anorexia.

Leo found herself interested. She wished she could shed the combination of nervousness, embarrassment and guilt that had tied her tongue in knots. The lobster bisque in front of her might as well have been rank sewage for all she could taste of it. She reprimanded herself. Whatever threat she had uttered to Daniel on leaving him on Friday, there was no need for her to feel like this. After all, it was Daniel and his colleagues who made up the rules, who forced this discomfort on her, not the other way around. If she had met her doctor on a similar occasion, there would have been no problem. But then, she didn't tell her doctor the things she had told Daniel.

Leo bolted her wine, noticed only with her second glass that it was a wine intended for savouring and tried to do so.

'The men are boring you with all their shop talk, aren't they, Leo?' Emily Robson's soft voice broke into her thoughts. 'They're terrible once they get started.' The older woman gave her a smile which had a hint of both complicity and mischief.

'No, no. Not at all.' Leo hesitated. 'It's fascinating, this notion that our culture promotes illness, relieves us of responsibility by naming a disorder and providing a cure. But aren't you all, as shrinks, colluding? You know, Aron, the friend I came to visit here, the one I was telling you about, she was in analysis with Dr Lukas. And I'm afraid it might have made her ill.'

In the long silence which met her statement, Leo watched the uncomfortable exchange of glances round the table. Daniel was tapping out an inaudible rhythm on the table with his fork.

'Though I think she left him for Paola Webster.' It was a question, but Daniel didn't respond. Instead, Aron Field stepped in to oil the wheels of conversation.

'Not a choice I would necessarily have recommended.'

In the way Daniel now met her eyes, Leo found her confirmation. But he wouldn't hold her gaze. Instead he listened to Aron, who was repeating to the others what Leo had told him about Isabel's disappearance.

'So she just vanished from one day to the next,' Emily said softly. 'Like those mad French travellers at the turn of the last century. They just had to take off and go. A veritable fugue which was both insanity and provided relief from the suffocating provincialism of their everyday lives.'

'Emily thinks', Aron offered a gloss, 'that there are fashions in psychic illness. That's not to deny their reality or suffering, but simply to say that the overt symptoms which signal disturbance change. We no longer have the grand hysterics of Charcot's

Salpêtrière. We have multiple personality disorders instead. Or war neurosis transmutes itself into Gulf War syndrome. The age combines with doctors and patients to produce a certain kind of disorder.'

'Yes, I can see that. But Isabel wasn't mad.'

'What picture do you have in your mind when you say that word?' Aron asked.

Leo saw a woman lying listlessly on a bed, only moving to tear her hair out in great clumps. Her face was a silent scream. She saw a man wielding an axe over a huddled figure.

'None,' she said, and added more confidently, 'Certainly not Isabel.'

'Well, since she's Australian, maybe she just went walkabout.' Aron's smile was well intentioned. 'And she'll come back when she's ready.'

Leo shook her head. 'There's a chance that she went out to investigate a story and met with trouble. A story about genetically modified substances. Foods, I think.'

'Yes.' Daniel met her on it. 'Isabel had been interested in all that for some time. Before it all became a media item. I suggested to her that her interest was a mask, a genetic cover-up. And that what she was masking was an interest in the other kinds of genes. Roots, you might say.'

They all stared at him. He went on, heedless. 'She countered me by accusing me of being a paid-up member of the Freudian temple, one built on the ills of the family. So, of course, I would have to say what I said.'

'An interesting patient,' Aron murmured.

'She was writing a book about being one. On being a patient. A story about all of you.' Leo threw down the gauntlet publicly. She studied Daniel's face for a reaction.

There was a controlled smile on it. 'I hope she finishes it. That, too, will be interesting. Though inevitably an embarrassment to the profession.'

Emily surveyed him. 'You're very sanguine about all this, Daniel.'

He shrugged. 'It isn't in my control.'

'Daniel is right,' Aron intervened. 'Whatever scandal people may want to draw from it, a book that contests our work only proves how adamantly secular the so-called Freudian temple is. We do not indoctrinate our patients. Not like those New Age therapists with their uniform beliefs. Monastic, that's what they are.' Aron was suddenly passionate. 'They create disciples. Create believers. A monastic community of believers instead of a simple, troubled family, whatever its internal warfare. Much harder to escape a cult. Especially when drugs are on hand to keep you placid and happy.'

Leo wanted to turn the conversation back to Isabel. 'I don't know whether Isabel explored that angle. All I know is that she's vanished. And another friend of hers is dead.'

Aron gasped. 'You didn't tell me that, Leonora.'

She nodded dismally. 'The added complication is that she was also using a false name: Iris Morgenstern.'

'Iris Morgenstern, did you say?' Daniel addressed her.

She looked at him. His eyes glimmered with some knowledge she didn't understand. 'Yes. Did she mention that name to you in her analysis?'

'Leonora,' Aron rebuked her. 'You know better than to pose a direct question like that. After all those years with Sam. Sam Gould is Leo's stepfather,' he explained to the others.

334

'It's all right, Dr Field. I don't mind,' Daniel intervened. 'In fact, Isabel did mention that name once. It's rather unusual, so I remembered it, though we did stop seeing each other early in the autumn.'

He seemed to be waiting for Leo to challenge him. Instead she said, 'Do you think Paola Webster would know something?'

Daniel grinned at her. It gave his face an open and engaging quality, as if shutters had been opened to sunlight. It struck Leo as the only spontaneous expression she had ever had from him. It made him attractive in a way she hadn't imagined, like a man who might enjoy football or mountain walks, instead of an endless teasing out of meanings in the privacy of darkened rooms.

'You could ask her. But don't say I sent you.'

'Why?'

The waiter arrived with their second course before she could press him, summoned perhaps by Aron's baleful glance. The large plates with their artful display of food and colour usurped everyone's attention. Surreptitiously, Leo watched Daniel. Was he to be trusted, she wondered? He hadn't, after all, betrayed her in any way to Aron or Emily.

As he caught her gaze, she felt warmth creeping up her cheeks. She made some excited comment about the food, the place, and felt increasingly like an awkward schoolgirl who couldn't strike quite the right note.

'Tell us about your cartoon strip, Leo. Have you put an analyst in it?' Emily Robson suddenly asked.

'I wouldn't dare. But a lot of therapists have walk-on parts – aromatherapists, hypnotherapists, reflexologists, yoga therapists, beauty therapists, chakra counsellors, take your pick.'

Aron laughed. He began to entertain them with a rendition of some of Leo's characters that was so theatrically apt that Leo found herself giggling. The wine helped. 'Maybe you can pose for a walk-on part as an analyst, Aron,' she heard herself saying.

'I'd be honoured. How would you caption me?'

'As an expert on love and hate, maybe.'

'Don't forget grief and hurt. And giving and taking.'

'Done.'

They had moved a long way from Leo's pre-occupations. Oddly, it was Daniel who brought them back.

'I was just thinking, Leo. Do you know whether the police thoroughly checked out the possibility that Isabel has left the country. Gone back to Australia, perhaps? I did suggest that to them.'

'I imagine so. Missing persons don't seem to be a priority, unless they're children.' After all these weeks of refusing her questions, Leo was a little taken aback by his sudden interest in Isabel. 'Do you think that's what she did? Because, if she did, she didn't contact her aunt there. I've spoken to her.'

He shrugged. 'It's possible. It's a big country. And she wouldn't have had to leave from London. It wouldn't be unlike Isabel to spend a weekend in Amsterdam, or wherever, and fly from there, on impulse.'

Amsterdam. Norfolk leapt into Leo's mind. Doubts attacked her so thick and fast that her voice sounded strangled. 'Why wouldn't she let me know?'

'That's something I really don't have an answer to.'

As he said it, Daniel wondered whether his words were quite true. When Emily had talked about the fugues of the so-called mad travellers, he had had a sudden acute sense of Isabel.

Paola's intense ministrations coupled with Leo's friendly concern, now so evidently an acute and perhaps justifiable anxiety, could well have pushed Isabel into flight. Isabel would have liked neither the dependence their care signalled nor the one it demanded from her in return. It was all too close to home – a childhood home.

But maybe he was just dreaming a flight for himself through her. A fugue. An escape while one's everyday self went into abeyance. Mute. Yet there was another channel he must force himself to pursue. That had become clear. Whatever name this Leo took, Gould or Holland, her worry was undeniably contagious.

He could feel her now, wanting to leave, but not knowing quite how to extricate herself. She would be ringing the police as soon as she reached home, ordering them to check all flights to Australia from a variety of European cities.

Aron Field's invitation had beguiled him into a bizarre predicament. He hadn't expected any guests tonight, apart from Emily, and certainly not a patient who had left him on hardly the best of terms.

Of course, he had bumped into patients outside their analytic hour before, but it had always been possible to move away after the first nod of recognition. It had its interest, yet he sensed that, had he been going to see Leo again as a patient, he couldn't have allowed it. He would have felt forced to leave on the grounds of any excuse he could contrive. Why? Was it simply that he felt he had to stick to certain rules since he broke so many others? An empty formulation passed down through time.

'How's your little boy, Daniel?' Emily's question jarred his reverie and also provided an instant answer to his internal query. It wasn't so much how he saw Leo that was the problem, but how the fantasies she might begin to have about him would play over and through her. Evidently Emily hadn't guessed that he had already met Leo under rather different circumstances. That was to the good.

'He's fine. Managing very well,' he replied and quickly deflected her by posing a professional question to Aron Field.

Watching him, Leo was aware that the shutters had abruptly come down again, closing off any access to the man within. Why wouldn't he tolerate questions about his son? Because they probably led to thoughts of his dead wife.

She pushed her chair away from the table. 'I know this is very rude, but I really must go. You'll excuse me. I just feel that I need to follow up what Daniel's said and ring the police.'

'If you wait, Emily and I can drop you.'

Startled, Leo met his eyes. 'No ... no, really. That's very kind. But I don't want to cut your evening short. I . . . Thank you, Dr Field.' Leo stumbled, feeling like an awkward girl again. 'It's been a terrific evening.' She kissed him quickly on the cheek and raced up the grand staircase, only catching her breath as she reached the door.

When her taxi turned off Finsbury Square into streets made desolate by night, Leo began to rue her hasty decision. She should have accepted Daniel's offer of a lift. She could have invited both him and Emily up to the loft, pressed Daniel further in his forthcoming mood. Far better embarrassment than the ghostly emptiness that awaited her.

The residents' parking bays were all occupied, but there were no lights visible anywhere in the building. The taxi pulled up short by the fenced car park. Reluctantly, Leo got out of the cab and dug into her bag for her purse.

It was then that she had the distinct feeling of eyes focused on her back, probing, penetrating. She veered round. Like some kidnapper waiting in ambush, a shadowy figure lurked on the outdoor steps of the building. At her gaze, he strode away quickly.

Leo shivered. She had an eerie feeling that the man knew her. Which meant that she had seen him some-where before. Where? The toad from Origen leapt into her mind. Yet the walk wasn't quite right. Or was it?

'It's eight fifty, miss.' The taxi driver urged her on.

'Yes, of course.' Leo took out a £10 note and had a desire to ask him in for a cup of tea.

'Keep the change,' she murmured.

He grunted a 'Ta'.

She watched him speed away, then raced along the street. She peered over her shoulder while she unlocked the door. She took the stairs two at a time, double-locking the flat as soon as she was inside and turning on all the lights. Her heart was pounding, but its sound was the only noise in the apartment.

As she surveyed the room, she had the uncanny sense that someone had been here, yet nothing seemed to have been disturbed. She walked around, deliberately allowing her heels to set up a comforting clatter, and checked each room in turn.

There was no red light signalling on the answering machine. No Beast, either, anywhere in sight. For the comfort of a presence, she pressed the all messages button and heard the woman from the South Bank, Paola Webster, Norfolk, Faraday and Isabel's aunt all over again. Then came a new message, one she was certain she hadn't heard before. Norfolk was checking in from Amsterdam, asking her how she was, but leaving no return number.

Leo stared at the machine. Something must have gone wrong with its mechanism, a failure in its new-messages system. Either that or ... Leo shivered again. Either that or someone had been in here and listened to the messages. For whatever reason, Isabel's flat was being watched by someone who had the keys.

She rushed to the door and barricaded a chair against it, then quickly rang Faraday. She told him what Daniel Lukas had said about Amsterdam, adding, incoherently, that Isabel could have chosen any other city to leave from. Keeping her voice even, she also said that she thought someone had been in the flat. Then, having wedged another chair in front of her bedroom door, she went to bed and drew the covers over her head, like a child terrified of the bogeyman.

She tried not to let the violent images which cascaded through her mind augment her fear.

Paola Webster's office was a minimalist duet in black and white. A vast black sofa faced a white one across the expanse of a geometric table. Beneath it, on the pale beech floor, lay a black-and-white rug. An ample desk with co-ordinated leather chairs stood at the far end of the room. Etchings decked the walls. The only splash of colour was a vase filled with blood-red tulips. And Paola herself, vivid in green, her lips carmine.

The room made a bold statement and Leo had to admit she was impressed.

The woman wasted no time. 'I speak to you as a favour to Dr Field, but also because I, too, am concerned for Isabel. She is a strong woman, but I am concerned.'

'When did you last see her?'

The woman threw her a censorious look. 'In January, I believe it was. She was fine then, doing well—'

Leo interrupted again. For some reason she didn't altogether understand, she felt she had to keep the advantage. 'What did you talk about?'

Paola laughed. 'You are a little naïve, perhaps. We talked about what patients always talk about: family, love, pain. Is there anything else? Here, Mariella. Put it here nicely.' She gestured towards a thin young woman who had just come into the room. The girl meekly followed her gesture and placed a tray on the table. 'Now you pour the coffee. Nicely, nicely. Yes, that's good.'

The girl pushed the cafetière filter down and shakily poured two cups of coffee, passing one to Leo without meeting her eyes.

'Thank you, Mariella. You can go now. Help yourself to a croissant, Ms Holland. They are fresh.' Paola bit into one with relish, wiped a crumb from her top and rushed on. 'Where were we? Yes. I do not have much to tell you. My idea is that Isabel is in Australia.'

'Could she have had . . . some kind of nervous collapse?'

Paola stared her down. 'If you keep interrupting me, Ms Holland, our time will be gone and you will have discovered nothing with which I can help you.

Yes. It is possible. Just possible. Though I do not think altogether likely. Isabel had discovered in the course of our work together that her mother had helped to do her father in, as you say.'

Leo lurched forward, spilling a little coffee on her lap.

Paola scowled, then carried on in a bland tone. 'She was learning to be a woman, despite all that. Learning to hate herself less. She was going to go to Australia to find proof, to confront, to question her mother. Then, as you undoubtedly know, her mother died. This must have been difficult for Isabel. And she didn't return for my help. We still had some way to go. There was still much self-hatred and confusion. She should not have cut so soon.' Paola made an abrupt slicing gesture. 'The healing takes time.'

'Killed?' Leo managed to bring the word out at last. 'Her father was killed . . .'

A scornful look met her stumbling query.

'Yes. Many terrible things happen in families, Ms Holland. Do not appear so surprised. You should read my book.' She pointed to a copy of *Scar Tissue*, which was prominently displayed on the coffee table. 'Your background is perhaps one of a certain financial and emotional privilege. You have been spared. You are among the lucky few.'

'Isabel . . . ?'

'My idea is that Isabel is in Australia finding things out. Otherwise she would be here with me. Deep down, she is a sensible person. It is only unfortunate that her mother died just then. Most unfortunate. Do you have children, Ms Holland?'

'Yes. A daughter.'

The woman scrutinized Leo with an anatomist's

342

coldness. 'Just the one. No more. The experience wasn't good enough?'

Leo was about to protest, but Paola carried on. 'Are you kind to her, not too cold, too distant, too nervous?'

'I don't think so.' Leo was amazed at the woman's gall. 'And you?'

'No, I cannot. But that is an old story.' She wiped her mouth primly. 'Do you sleep with Isabel?'

Leo put her cup down with a clatter. 'What makes you ask?'

'Do not look at me like that. It is not a crime. When Isabel came to me all her antipathy was towards men. I thought that, maybe, as we worked that through, she might have experimented. She is a sensual woman. You have had therapy? No. I do not really need to ask. It might do you good, Ms Holland. Meanwhile, do not try to control Isabel with your nervousness.'

Paola looked at her watch and tapped it. Her time was up.

Leo took a moment to get up. She felt as if she had been flattened by a steamroller. No wonder Isabel hadn't been herself at Christmas.

She rose slowly and met the woman's eyes. 'I think, Ms Webster, that if there is any controlling going on here, it's being done by you. Thank Mariella for the coffee.'

She turned on her heel and walked towards the door. On the desk, she noticed a squat fertility figure, all giant belly and inchoate fleshy stone. She had an odd desire to fling it to the floor and watch it shatter. But it wouldn't shatter, she reminded herself. It would lie there, eternally composed, however hard she flung it. She threw a question she had forgotten instead.

'Does the name Morgenstern mean anything to you, Ms Webster?'

'Even if that is not a trick question, Ms Holland, I have no answer for you. Now go, please.'

Leo half ran down the street of stately white houses into Fitzjohn's Avenue. After last night's episode with the prowler, she had assumed the interview with Paola would be a waste of time. She had veered again to thinking that Norfolk was right, that Isabel's disappearance was due to her investigation into the work of the biotech multinationals who were still looking for something in the loft. But she had come anyway.

Now the frail rubber dinghy of her suppositions lay in ruins, shredded by the hard rock of Paola Webster's shattering certainties.

The full terror of what Paola had communicated burnt into Leo's mind as she made a pretence of tidying the flat in anticipation of Isabel's aunt's arrival. Murder, the woman had suggested matter-of-factly. Without so much as a tremor. The flatness of the announcement seemed to render its content less significant than the fact that Isabel hadn't continued her therapy with Paola.

Yet the impact on Isabel of unearthing and confronting such a momentous family secret must have been devastating. Was it this savage fact of her early history that had propelled Isabel over the edge and made her shun everything and everyone in order to undertake a mission so dangerous that it had already resulted in the death of a colleague? Could it also be what had prompted her to accept money from one multinational – as Faraday suspected – in order to spy on another?

Somehow, Leo reflected, she would have to broach the whole hideous tangle of Isabel's early history with her aunt. It was quite possible that Isabel's row with Martha had been about precisely this.

The sound of the doorbell gave her a start and put an end to her musing. She wasn't expecting anyone, unless Faraday had taken it upon himself to arrive unannounced to check things out.

She tiptoed to the videophone and saw no-one. Thrusting her shoulders back, she peered through the eyehole. For a moment she didn't recognize the distorted face. When it came into focus, she quickly opened the door.

Mike Newson stood there, a crooked half smile on his narrow face. He was holding a suitcase in his hand.

'Hi. Everything OK?' He walked past her without waiting for an answer and deposited the case in the middle of the living-room floor.

'Someone came to deliver this earlier. You weren't here so he left it with me. It's Isabel's.'

Leo stared at the case, unable to take in its material reality.

'Courtesy of Qantas. Lost in transit.'

'Where?' She stooped to read the passenger label. The name Iris Morgenstern was printed on it, together with the loft's address. But there was no destination marked. 'Lost where?' she repeated.

Mike Newson shrugged. 'He didn't say. He was just a delivery bloke.'

Leo threw him a sour look, but he carried on, undeflected, his smile growing bigger. 'Guess she had to buy new gear in Perth or Alice Springs or Melbourne or Brisbane or Sydney. Or maybe Singapore or Hong Kong. But we can all stop worrying. She's somewhere down under and she'll be back soon.'

With a shaky hand, Leo unzipped the case. It wasn't locked. Inside the clothes were neatly folded.

'Yup, this is Isabel's.' Unhindered by modesty, Mike Newson shunted aside some lingerie and pulled out a linen jacket. 'I remember it distinctly. She wore it for the pilot.'

Leo took the jacket jealously from his hand and placed it on the sofa. The cat appeared from nowhere and curled himself into its folds.

'By the way, whatever happened to your joint project?'

Mike ran his fingers through his hair and bent abstractedly towards the case again. 'Nothing.' He lifted a pair of trousers from the case and flung them towards the sofa. His face had a belligerent edge. 'It went down the plughole. The commissioning editor thought Isabel was too old to front it. My mistake. Don't tell her.'

Leo wished he would go. He didn't. He shuffled his feet instead and cleared his throat. 'Rosie tells me you do this fabulous cartoon strip about Manhattan. I'd love to see it.'

So that was it. Leo restrained a wild laugh. She had come up in his estimation. She was someone in the world, that dreamt-of world that he had splashed onto his walls and windows.

'I'll send you both a book when I go back.'

'OK, thanks. Great.'

No sooner had he left than Leo slowly emptied the case, one item at a time, searching for she didn't know what. Why wasn't she feeling elated? Was it simply that she sensed Faraday would now give her a

346

peeved look and stop his investigations? Isabel's disappearance was either a matter for the Australian police or it was no matter at all. Emotional temperature, her friend's or her own, was of no interest to him.

Yes, Isabel was in Australia. She must have gone there right after she had left the hotel in Lynton. Her business was too intimate and shaming to communicate, even to Leo. Or perhaps she had still hoped to arrive in New York on the appointed day.

From under a pair of trousers, Leo pulled out a glossy brochure announcing the marvel that was Bioworld and sat down with a bump. So the biotech investigation was part of the Australian trip, too. Isabel had the presence of mind for that, if not for ringing Leo.

For reasons she couldn't altogether place, Leo felt as if her face had been slapped. Betrayal. That's what it was. It left a flush of humiliation in its wake. She needed Isabel, needed her openness, her vibrant sense of life, far more than Isabel had ever needed her.

Yet her anxiety wouldn't disperse. It hovered like a black cloud over her head, despite the brightness of the day and the tangible relief that the suitcase should have brought with it. Maybe Daniel Lukas was right. Maybe she was simply loath to recognize that Isabel's life was not an integral part of her own.

PART FOUR

NOTES TOWARDS A CASE HISTORY (III)

After she had broached the matter of her father and his death, I didn't expect Anna to turn up for her next session.

I guessed that, if I had become even a little important to her, even a little real, she would play out abandoning me to ward off the inevitability of my abandoning her – as her father had done and with such utter finality. It was the pattern of her life, a cycle of repetition in which she was trapped – leaving as soon as anyone became too real, averting being left. Leaving if she felt needed or sniffed the signs of her own growing dependence.

I was wrong. She came punctually. But she wouldn't talk about death or her father. She started to give me dreams. The next weeks were filled with dreams and with accounts of her mother's cold harshness. Her mother, it became clear, had never forgiven her father for being who he was, or for dying on her and leaving her to cope independently. Her relationship with Anna was a series of incessant, invasive plaints interspersed by absence. She would never talk about the father or his death, nor was Anna, when she could speak again, permitted to. It was as if the man had never existed.

In her dreams, Anna was often underground in a

dark, oozing labyrinth, almost like the interstices of a body, but with no visible exits. Or she was paralysed, unable to move. I took this, at first, as an identification with her father, a residue of the period of his illness, her greatest dread. But it was also the paralysis of the repetition she was caught in. Never having been allowed, or able, to confront her feelings about her father's dying and death, these feelings had gone underground, leaving her to replay again and again a pattern of seduction and betrayal she could cope with. Eroticizing the damage. Mastering early trauma by transforming it into excitement. Part of her had learnt to enjoy the paralysis of repetition. Seduction and abandonment also freed her from a certain kind of emotional responsibility. Better not to have any responsibility if that primary one – keeping her father alive – had been so impossibly great and inevitably doomed.

And now she was trying to break out of the magic circle. Why else would she be coming to see me?

I knew I had to tread carefully, but I felt we had at last found a path. Our work together would consist of unlinking the emotions attached to her father's death from the charge of her failure to keep him alive. We would need to cut the connection between loving and failure, loving and death, and also, perhaps, to redescribe men as something other than a passive absence, a disgusting absence at that, in need of pleasuring.

For the length of a month, maybe two, I was as buoyant, regarding Anna, as a practitioner can hope to be. Then things took a retrograde turn. At first I didn't realize what was happening. Anna had grown utterly silent. She would lie on the couch, her eyes wide open, and stare at the ceiling. She was numb. I thought she might, in some sense, be reliving or re-invoking the period of her childhood muteness. Once, towards the end of a session, I quoted Winnicott at her: 'What a joy it is to hide, but a disaster not to be found.' I also signalled to her that I would fall in with who and what she wanted for as long as she wanted, but that I was also there to resist her projections, to remain an analyst. She didn't respond.

And then, one day she came in and started to attack me. She told me I was useless, a waste of her time and money, a charlatan. She accused me of never giving anything of myself, of hiding, of creating a twosome of utter inequality. She railed. It was a magnificent performance in which she threw the entire book of psychoanalytic failings at me. I steered her towards the possibility that she might be fuming not only at me, but, through a screen, at her father.

She gave me her old booming laugh and told me that that was a pitiful attempt at self-exoneration. Next I would sink so low as to bring up Oedipus.

'Never that.' I laughed with her and, after a moment, she changed her tone and asked me in a small, hesitant voice why I couldn't tell her about myself, just a little, to equalize things.

I was so pleased to have her emerge from her long silence that I broke a rule and told her a few things she probably already knew: that I had always been a North Londoner, that I had a wife and a child.

'In fact, a rather staid, boring man,' she offered with a touch of avidity as she pulled her watch out of her pocket and got up to leave. She seemed lighter and my spirits lifted in tandem.

'I've always meant to ask you,' I said. 'Why do you carry your watch in your pocket?'

She looked at me askance. 'I don't like it round my wrist. I don't like bracelets, either. For that matter, I'm none too fond of necklaces.' And off she marched without a goodbye.

Since I was alert to the manner of exits and entrances now, that puzzled me. The following week puzzled me even more. Anna reverted to her own first principles. The stories began again. They were back with a vengeance. She was in full dramatic flow, the dinner-party raconteuse par excellence, telling me now about the totemic practices of the New Guineans, then of the sexual mores of the Inuit, or narrating the complicated plot of a recent film or an office imbroglio. I tried to find common threads, or to bring her back to more germane matter, but I couldn't budge her. Her language poured over me, an unstoppable torrent. I had the feeling its intention was to drown.

One dark late afternoon, it did. I fell into a doze. There was no excuse for it, not even the difficult night I had had at home. I don't know quite how long the sleep lasted, but I woke in some confusion. There was a hand on my thigh, stroking, creeping upward. I was aware that my penis was hard, though not quite where I was, not until the fingers curled round it.

I grabbed her wrists, held them hard and shook her. 'We don't do that kind of thing here,' I said in a punishing voice, though the punishment was directed at myself. 'Never.'

Her look was wild, panic-stricken, but she didn't meet my eyes. She was staring at my fingers tight round her arm. I let her go. Before I could think of an appropriate phrase, she was out the door.

That evening, I seriously considered ringing her to

apologize. But on reflection, I decided it would be best for things to go no further outside the bounds of convention than they already had. Perhaps it was cowardice. Nonetheless, I decided that since she was due the following day, it would be best to discuss the matter in the appropriate space. If she didn't turn up, I would think again.

She arrived punctually and lay down with a laugh that was slightly shrill. She was wearing the red dress she had worn for her first session and she launched right into an account of a play she had apparently seen the previous evening, a play in which the heroine works as a part-time prostitute in a chic club. I tried to use this as a way into the matter left over from our previous encounter. And then I noticed that, as she spoke, she was rubbing her wrist, rubbing it not with easy, soothing gestures, but gouging, prodding.

'I'm sorry if I hurt you, yesterday,' I said.

'Hurt?'

'Your wrist.'

'My wrist?'

'Yes, your wrist. The one you don't like bracelets on,' I heard myself saying.

She started to cry. She had never done that before. Vast, silent tears streaked her cheeks. And then, as if it surprised her, she said, 'I've remembered something.'

She told me then, told me hesitantly, that during the period her father was ill and lay perpetually in his bed, she would sometimes lie next to him. The bed was very high and she would scramble up from the chair next to it and stretch out beside him, beneath the sheets if it was cool, or on top of them when it was hot. They would lie together in the dark or the half-light as she talked. Her father's breathing was loud. She could hear it, like air whistling out of a balloon. She didn't like the sound of it, but she loved her father and knew that she had to stay with him. While she stayed with him, her mother stayed away, and her mother was cruel to her father. She knew that. Little Anna was his protector.

Sometimes, while she was telling him the bedtime stories he so liked, or when she paused, he would put his hand round her wrist and guide her fingers to stroke his body – down there, too, where the knob grew between his legs. She had to stop talking then, because the knob always made a lump come to her throat, like a block of wood you couldn't speak over. She didn't mind, though, not even when the knob fizzed, like a bottle of soda pop, and made her hand sticky. Her father's cheeks would grow pink then and he'd look healthy and would place dry lips on her forehead and call her angel, his story angel.

One night, when it was very hot, her mother burst in on them. In the gloom her face was savage. She smacked Anna across the face and screamed something, then pulled her by the wrist. Her father screamed, too, and pulled her by the other, and between their screaming and tugging she felt she was being pulled apart, until her mother won and dragged her, screaming and sobbing now, back to her own room, and told her she was a bad, evil child and had been warned to stay away from her father. And now to keep her away, she would be punished. Severely punished. She was tied to her bed, tied by her wrist and left in the dark. Left for she didn't know how long, because it must have been then that she got ill. And when she was better her father was dead.

Later, in one of the schools she was sent to, during

the period of her muteness, she remembered cutting at her wrists, not deeply enough for heavy bleeding, but enough to cause herself pain. Inflicting pain on herself was a way of controlling it and thereby reducing her vulnerability to the pain the external world could produce in her.

And so, in these memories, what had seemed to be Anna's mere taste for not wearing any item of jewellery round her wrists revealed its deep history – a history of being pulled apart by warring parents and punished for something which, in itself, might have left little residue were it not for the chain of events it was part of. That chain created the trauma which was written on the text of her body, though debarred from her thoughts. Now that words had been given to it, the talking cure could begin to do its work.

The memories also gave me another clue to Anna's perpetual seductiveness. To move beyond it to a deeper self would be to allow the other person to see the foulness that lay beneath. She had internalized her mother's judgement of her and had to keep moving.

Over the next weeks, Anna and I turned these scenes inside out and upside down, viewing them from all perspectives, weighing them for what the world likes to call goodness and badness, finding their residues in her subsequent behaviour.

Other memories came, too, including one of her father in an earlier guise, a giant of a man who carried her everywhere on his shoulders, who told her stories of fantastic voyages – of how they would travel together, go to an exotic India, ride elephants, climb mountains, visit Shangri-La. It was an exhilarating time.

And then, abruptly, with no forewarning and to my utter surprise, Anna left, never to return. The moment she picked coincided with a phase when she had chosen to cast me in the role of the punishing mother. Perhaps in my eagerness to see her through, I was a little too punishing in my interventions. But there were other forces at play, on my side as well. I wasn't as alert to her as I might have been. And on her side, there may have been an unconscious decision that whatever else might change, she preferred herself in the role of Scheherazade. The period of seduction was over. It was time to kill me off, as far as her own life was concerned, to reproduce the electric charge of the grand finale, rather than slop around in the messy indeterminacy of everyday half measures.

She gave me the finale in a message on my answering machine. In her most pleasant voice, she told me she was seeing someone else, had been for some time. A woman. She should perhaps have told me sooner. And then her voice altered, grew ugly, menacing. It wasn't a voice I recognized. In it she threatened to report me to higher bodies for breaking the rules, for getting my dirty paws all over her.

I wondered whether this was the voice of her new therapist. Or perhaps her latest version of her mother.

I worried about Anna. We had unfinished business.

Analysis, unlike stories, rarely has a climactic end.

16

Leo lopped the large branches of lilac here and there and plunged the flowers into the bowl. They tipped and bent, refusing her arrangement, so that she had to start all over again. Nothing was right today. Nothing would be right. She had known it as soon as she'd woken from a dream in which the dead girl, Jill, danced and swayed, only to fall naked onto a cold slab. It was far too early to be awake. But the throb in her head, a residue of too much wine consumed alone, prevented a return to sleep. She had got up and drunk two glasses of cold water, showered and made coffee and told herself that, if nothing else, it was a good time to phone Becca.

Becca, miraculously, had picked up the receiver. But it was clear from her artificially cheerful hello that the last person she wanted to speak to was her mother. Her answers to questions were uncharacteristically terse. There was impatience in her tone. Leo had sensed a kind of shuttered secrecy which could only spell 'man'.

She hadn't pressed. Daniel's words had come back to her again, as a low ironizing command. It was time to live in herself, not through her daughter, let alone Isabel. She relished the sound of his voice even less than the new one her daughter used. But she had kept her own tone light, and sent a kiss before hanging up to return to an empty stretch of day.

An early walk to the market hadn't helped. Daniel's voice had insinuated itself into her ear again. Not the pleasant-enough voice of the man at dinner, but that darker, edgy voice which walked a tightrope between fantasy and the real and could topple you over into either. 'Is this sleeping with me something you would wish for yourself?' it reiterated.

Leo had pushed it away only to find Norfolk's equally discomfiting notes taking over her inner ear. He had rung last night. With droll seductiveness, he had told her that, despite the fact that he missed certain parts of her, he had to stay on in Amsterdam for another few days. And he was full of news she could barely follow. He had taken a sample of the soil he had collected in Devon to Amsterdam with him and had had it tested. There was something distinctly irregular going on. Unidentifiable bacteria had been found in the sample. This was one of the techniques used for genetic modification, but he had only ever seen it under lab conditions. He had grown excited, and told her Isabel was on to something big. More tests were being run. He would have news soon.

Leo had begun to confide the qualms Faraday had planted about him, but he had cut her off, said he had to go, even before she had been able to tell him about the returned suitcase and that Isabel was almost certainly somewhere in Australia.

Maybe, Leo thought as she jabbed the last lilac into the bowl, she should just pick herself up and go back to Manhattan tomorrow morning to take up the fraying strings of her own life. She needed to, as

Daniel Lukas had made so graphically clear. The first thing she would do when she walked in the door was throw out Jeff's perverse clock. No more time for moving backwards. Time for the new instead, for painting walls and rearranging the furniture of home and mind. Or she could go to San Francisco. No, no, not that.

What was clear was that she was of no more use here. All her searching for Isabel had only made her friend more elusive and had cast doubts on the very existence of their friendship.

The cat leapt onto the table and prodded the bowl of lilacs with his pink snout. Beast looked thin, a little haggard, not the proudly contemptuous bulk of a bristling tom she was used to. Whatever the lore about the independence of cats, this one was evidently pining for his mistress. Leo stroked the heavy fur. The cat shied away from her touch without so much as a single purr.

She looked out the window. The cars beneath sparkled in the sunlight. In the distance, a woman lay on a small stretch of flat roof and basked as voluptuously as if she could hear the rumble of the Mediterranean beside her. Leo wished the sun could lift her spirits, but they felt as flat as a failed soufflé.

No, there was nothing for her to do here now but wait for Isabel's aunt, and that only out of simple courtesy.

The woman she opened the door to was not at all the person Leo had envisioned. Instead of a statuesque older version of Isabel, a small woman with a face of sweet gentleness stood before her. She had apple-round cheeks as burnished and crinkly as a russet and softly curling grey-flecked hair. She wore neatly

361

tailored trousers with a matching tan jacket that seemed a little big for her. She smiled with the easy warmth of habit, but her dark eyes, despite the absence of visible tears, were ravaged. In them Leo read the fears she herself had conjured over the last weeks.

'Leo Holland?' She stretched out her hand to grasp Leo's like a life-raft. 'I'm Martha. Martha Morgan. I'm so pleased to meet you. Isabel told me you were her nearest and dearest. Thank you. Thank you so much for returning my telephone call and alerting me. I've been frantic with worry.'

Leo took her bag and led her in, offered tea or coffee.

'The first. I'm as parched as the desert on a summer's day.' She looked around with an air of wonder. 'So this is what Isabel has made of herself. Grand. Grand. I knew it. I've never visited her in England before. Never could allow myself to leave Elinor. If only I hadn't—' She stopped herself and followed Leo into the kitchen.

'Tell me what you know.' Her voice changed. Any hint of fluffiness fell away from it. 'I don't want to waste any time. Don't omit details. Tell me from the beginning, please.'

Leo poured tea and began to speak. She had intended to start with the arrival of Isabel's lost suit-case. But now, with the woman's sorrowful eyes intent on her, it seemed heartless instantly to convey that her long journey was pointless, that Isabel had failed to alert her aunt to her arrival in Australia, just as she had failed to inform Leo that she would not be coming to the US. So, leaving out only Jill Reid's death, she told her briefly about the investigation Isabel had been engaged on in the West Country, and about the last time anyone had definitely seen her, at the Lynton Arms Hotel. She was about to tell her about the suitcase when Martha interrupted.

'You told me she was calling herself Morgenstern?'

'Yes. Iris Morgenstern. So that the initials stayed the same. I imagine because she wanted to carry on using her e-mail address.' Leo looked at her curiously. 'Your name is Morgan, too? So . . .'

'Yes, Morgan is our family name, my sister's and mine. I never married.' Martha's smile floundered. 'Elinor reverted to the family name, when . . . Morgenstern was Isabel's father's name. Iris is her middle name. She hated it, never used it, though, when she was tiny, he used to call her that.'

Leo sat back in the sofa and gasped audibly. Paola Webster's disquisition rang in her mind, and with it came a bleak image of Isabel. Isabel wearing a crying child's face. Isabel in thrall to a hideous past, impelled to travel to Australia to exhume decomposing remains, family poisons too shameful to pour into a friend's ear. Leo wouldn't have known how to communicate that narrative to a friend, either.

'I think we need something stronger to drink,' she murmured and fled into the kitchen, in part to prevent Martha from reading her face.

But the woman followed her.

Her eyes fixed on the wine bottle, Leo said, 'I'm sorry, Martha. I suspect your trip here was unnecessary.' She busied herself with the finding of nuts and olives while she explained about Isabel's returned suitcase.

The woman's face when she finally dared to meet it wore a puzzled expression. 'No, no. Unless I completely misunderstood what Isabel last told me, that

couldn't be right. Maybe the case was lost on her last
trip and finally made its way home. I don't see . . .'

'What did she tell you?'

'That she'd traced him.'

'Traced whom?'

'Morgenstern.'

'You mean his grave?' A picture of dank jungle
undergrowth leapt into Leo's mind. Black and white
and grey. Murky shapes in a crumpled newspaper
photograph. She had never traced her own father's
grave. But Isabel had.

'Brave Isabel,' she said softly.

Martha was shaking her head and saying yes,
simultaneously. 'Isabel never told you. You don't
understand. It isn't easy to understand. I don't really
understand, either. I don't know why I did it.' Her
eyes had filled with tears. She rubbed them away
with clumsy fingers, but they kept coming. 'Be
patient with me. I didn't realize. I thought it would be
for the best. Truth is always for the best, isn't it?'

There was no need for an answer. Martha had
turned away from her. She was addressing some
higher authority.

Leo had the impression she had stumbled in on a
stranger's internal monologue. It was filled with pain
and guilt, the origins of which were mysterious to
her. She waited until Martha had composed herself.

'I should start from the beginning. Yes. I've been
thinking about it all so much. And then you'll understand. You'll know whether Isabel said something to
you which may help us find her.' The woman
appealed to her as she wrung her hands. The fingers
were gnarled, bitten at the nails. She got up and
gazed out the window.

When she started to speak, her voice was so soft

that Leo found herself holding her breath in order to hear. The beginning, it seemed, was as long ago as it was far away. She was thrust into a time before Isabel's birth and a place which ached with heat and remoteness. In her mind's eye, because she had never been to Australia, she found herself conjuring up images of the deep American South, in which Martha's beautiful sister, Elinor, strode through a large ramshackle farmhouse with all the high-spirited nervousness of a Katharine Hepburn left alone after a father's death and intent on managing a declining estate.

The sisters quarrel. Martha, the younger one, wants to sell up and move to the city, to Melbourne, or further still, to Sydney, in order to study. Elinor tells her to go and not to bother coming back. Loath to abandon a sister whom she knows is hardly practical, Martha nonetheless goes. For some eight months there is no contact between them. Then Martha writes and Elinor writes back. She writes back effusively, ardently. She is in love. A young man has come to the farm in search of work. A young man with the bluest eyes and the most charming disposition. He has a dream. He wants to turn part of the property over to vines. They are to be married. Martha must come to the wedding. There are, after all, only the two of them, bar an aunt in Melbourne and some far-flung cousins.

Martha comes home. Her sister is at her most radiant and the young man is indeed young. He is twenty-two to Elinor's twenty-seven. And he is handsome, all golden limbs, broad shoulders and dreaming eyes. Martha is pleased for her sister, though, as the reasonable sibling, she is a little put out when the young man deflects any questions she puts to him about his past. She is more put out by the visible bump that protrudes from Elinor's middle, even in the flowing white linen of her chemise-like wedding dress. Since Elinor makes no mention of it, she doesn't, either. Nor does it take long for her to fall under the young man's sway. Everything else apart, he speaks so fluently. He is intelligent. He has a stack of books on viniculture, which he has ordered from far and wide, amongst other books on anthropology, on oriental religion, on Nietzsche. They talk and talk, and when the time comes for Martha to leave, she is more than a little sorry to do so.

Though she writes to her sister with some regularity, Elinor now doesn't respond. Martha is not particularly surprised. Elinor has more important things to think about. The first contact she has with the newly-weds is some six months later. Alexander Morgenstern phones her. He asks her to come. He doesn't say why, and she assumes that the baby is due and Elinor has asked for her. She goes, despite the fact that it means taking time off both from work and the university courses she juggles part-time.

When she arrives, she knows instantly that something is wrong. The flowers and shrubs that are Elinor's pride have been allowed to shrivel and die. Elinor is not unlike them. She sits in a rocking chair in the kitchen and rocks. Her hair is matted and frizzled. Her eyes have grown huge in her thin face, but they do not focus. She barely acknowledges Martha's presence. When Martha looks down, expecting to see the vaster bump that is baby, there is nothing there. She thinks miscarriage and rushes to hug her sister. But then a frumpy girl walks in holding a lump of greying blanket. Inside it there is a baby. The child is beautiful, rosy-skinned, with blue eyes which cling to her face like a softness.

Martha takes the baby and learns from the girl that she is called Isabel and is about three months old. Martha holds her and holds her and, as she holds her, she knows that she has never felt or seen anything as lovely. When at last she looks around her, she also sees that nothing else in her old home is lovely. The place reeks. Dishes are piled high in the sink. There is dust everywhere. The floors might as well be outdoors.

She sets to work, talking to Elinor as she scrubs. Her sister doesn't respond. Nor does she acknowledge Alexander's presence when he comes into the house with another man. He pretends not to notice. Maybe he really doesn't. He hugs Martha, gestures round the place vaguely and says she can see why he called her. He kisses the baby and cradles her, then sets about making dinner with the other man. Elinor doesn't get up. She only gets up when the other man walks her towards the table.

Martha realizes her sister is ill, but she doesn't know what to do about it. Nor does the doctor she calls in, who merely tells her what he has said to Alexander before. It will pass. What Martha can do, she does. In the three weeks that she ends up staying, she turns the house over and finds a slightly older, more responsible girl to help care for Isabel. In the evenings, Alexander no longer talks about vines. None have appeared. He now talks about India and China and Buddhism and about a dream of studying medicine. Once again Martha is captivated. She cannot understand why her sister is so unhappy.

The only thing that changes in Elinor during the course of Martha's stay is that she cannot bear to see Martha holding Isabel. When she catches her at it, she snaps and calls for the baby to be brought to her. Isabel rarely cries. But she cries when she finds herself in her mother's lap. Cries unstoppably, her little face contorted.

As if the ache of memory was too strong for words, Martha had stopped speaking.

Leo refilled her glass. 'Post-natal depression,' she murmured.

Martha nodded. 'But we didn't have the term then, or any way of dealing with the condition.' She paused again, lost in recollection.

Leo prompted her. 'What happened?'

The woman took a deep breath and met her eyes briefly. 'The depression lifted eventually, but in a way that only made things worse.' She lowered her voice. 'Something had happened to Elinor. Something irreparable. It was as if she hated him now. Hated Isabel, too, by turns. She would row with him, scream, even when I was there. Tell him he was a no-good, a bum, loathsome, contemptible, useless in all ways. I have to say, I felt sorry for him. He was a young man, with his whole life to lead, and there was my sister behaving like the very worst of shrews. Bed problems on top of all the others, I think. She was rigid with distaste whenever he was in the room. She wouldn't sleep with him. It had all got mixed up with the horror of having babies.'

Leo gazed at the kind, worn face. A look she could only interpret as longing had come over the woman's features. Her eyes were misty.

Martha shifted in her seat. 'Things went from bad to worse. I think I realized, even then, that Elinor was a little mad, but doctors in the area didn't diagnose that way. You were supposed to grin and bear it. I was frightened for Isabel, too. But she grew strong and sturdy, and more delectable each time I came to visit. I suggested to Elinor on one visit that she let me take the child away for a while. It would give her a break, a chance to rest, a chance for her and Alexander to patch things up between them. But she more or less spat in my face. She would move, with no signal in those days, from impassivity to venomous rage. She was beautiful again, though a little thin, dramatic. Not at all like plain old me.

'Then Alexander took ill. Maybe he'd been working too hard. A terrible unshakeable bronchitis, compounded by despair and I don't know what. I came to see them at the time, and we talked a little. He told me that, if he got better, he was going to go away. I understood that he had to, that it was probably for the best. And he went. Slipped away quietly one day. Just didn't come back when he was meant to. I wasn't there at the time, but Elinor called for me straight after.

'She was livid, angrier than I had ever seen her. When I tried to suggest that maybe it was for the best, since they hadn't got on, she raged, said I understood nothing, didn't know the utter brute he was. She showed me bruises . . .'

Martha paused, put fingers to her forehead, as if to rub out a migraine or memory.

'She screamed, said terrible things. Said that if I came off my intellectual cloud and stopped to look at the family accounts, I would see just how much he had stolen over the years. That was it, she claimed. He was dead. DEAD. Wiped out. Had never existed. His name was never to pass our lips again. She had announced it to Isabel, too. The child had been ill with a fever. Maybe she caught it from him. When she came out of her delirium and Alexander was gone, Elinor told her that her father was dead. Already buried. They were going to move. But in the time it took to sell up the place, she would go to boarding school.

'Elinor told me that if I gainsaid her, she would never allow me to see Isabel again. She made me swear. I did. I begged her once again to allow Isabel to come with me. But she wouldn't. She didn't altogether trust me. Perhaps with good reason.'

Martha covered her face with her hands.

'So Isabel grew up thinking her father was dead. But he wasn't.'

Martha nodded, her face bleak. 'He wrote to me a few times. Postcards. One from India, another from Nepal, then one from the United States. He wanted me to know he was doing well. Thriving, in fact. Far from the mad, bad sisters.'

'You loved him?' Leo heard herself saying. She flushed.

The woman nodded once, abruptly, then rose. She started to pace, her sturdy legs beating out an erratic rhythm on the parquet.

'I even went to bed with him,' she said softly. 'During one of my stays, when Elinor was at her beastliest. I thought he had married the wrong sister. I was the one who appreciated him, who understood him. I'd learnt that he had grown up in an orphanage. He'd had a sister there who'd died, far too young. Don't ask me how I found out. But I wanted to make up for all that. And for my sister. Another form of madness. I don't think Elinor knew, but maybe she sensed it. And then I spent my life making it up to her.' She shook her head sadly. 'But none of that matters. What matters is what I said

370

to Isabel. Fool that I am. Stupid, romantic old fool.'

She dropped onto the sofa, as if she didn't intend to rise again. Her face was ashen.

Leo stirred herself. 'I should make you some food. Or take you out. There's a nice—'

'No, no. You're too kind. And I'm really not hungry. But you must eat.'

'A little something. For you, too.' She helped her out of the sofa. 'It'll do us both good. We'll need our wits.'

'Yes, of course. I'm wandering. We have to face essentials.' She squared her shoulders and started to talk again, tersely now, to get the matter out quickly.

'After Elinor's funeral, Isabel stayed with me for a few days. She wasn't . . . I don't know quite how to describe it, but she wasn't herself. I understood that. Elinor and she had never had an easy time of their relations, and now it was too late to make it up. But Isabel was wild. She told me that Elinor deserved to die, should have died much sooner. She had killed Isabel's father, after all. Hadn't she. Hadn't she? And I had colluded in the cover-up. I was dirt.

'I don't know where she got the idea, but she wouldn't let it go, and finally I told her. I had always wanted to tell her, but she had never been very interested in her family history, had never asked questions about her father. So it seemed best to let sleeping dogs lie. Then, too, I had my promise to Elinor to keep. She had somehow constructed her life on this fiction of hard-done-by widowhood, and had ended up believing it was true. I was afraid, as well. You see, part of Elinor hated Isabel. Maybe because she was so like her father – visibly, I mean. So Elinor hated him in her, the constant reminder of him. It can happen, you know. I've seen it. In divorce cases . . .

371

So it seemed best never to bring the matter of Morgenstern up.

'I'm wandering again. The point is that, when Isabel started to accuse her mother of murder in those days just after Elinor's death, I leapt to Elinor's defence. I explained a little of what had happened, but mostly I stressed that her father might still very well be alive. She hadn't killed him. I told her he had been a good man, and that he had loved her. I thought that might help her cope with the fact that he had left, never to return, and had never manifested any interest in her after his departure.

'I explained to her that, in the way things can, something had simply gone terribly wrong between him and Elinor.'

She paused and looked at Leo with a plea in her face. 'At first she wouldn't believe me, wouldn't believe that Alexander was really alive, that Elinor hadn't somehow murdered him. So I showed her the picture.'

She rushed off, leaving Leo in the kitchen to drain the pasta and toss a salad. When she came back, she was carrying a sheet of much-folded paper. She smoothed it out and showed it to Leo.

'This is it. You see the picture, that's Alexander Morgenstern.' She jabbed towards the centre of a small workaday photo showing four suited men and two women, amidst columns of print. 'The tall one, in the middle. He's a good twenty years older than when I last set eyes on him. But that's him. I couldn't mistake that face.'

Leo looked at the black-and-white photo. The man had a bony face and a high forehead, but seemed otherwise unremarkable in the indistinctness of the group photo. The caption beneath it, however, allayed any doubts she may have had. It read, 'The team at the Morgenstern Foundation.'

Martha was hurrying on. 'I happened on the picture ten years ago, maybe more, at the clinic I was attached to at the time. I tore it out of some American medical mag. The Morgenstern Foundation apparently ran a drug-addiction recovery programme which had met with some success. Anyhow, for some murky reason, I kept it. And then I showed it to Isabel.

'She looked at it briefly and threw it back at me. She said she didn't want to know anything about a man who had molested his child and then abandoned his sick wife and daughter. She raged. She said that if I thought she was about to seek him out, I was crazier than my sister. She, Isabel, had never chased after men of any kind in her life, so why begin now? A father was no different. We had all conspired to turn her childhood into a tissue of lies. Even me. Even the good sister. She wanted nothing more to do with any of us. And she was glad the mother who had invented such a scheming evil lie was dead. She left the next day.'

Leo met Martha's eyes. 'And that was the last you saw of her?'

The woman raked an unsteady hand through her hair. 'The last I saw, but not the last I heard.' Her voice trailed off.

'Let's take this to the table.' Leo busied herself with setting places and heaping pasta onto plates. She was trying to imagine how she would feel if someone announced to her that her father had never, in fact, died; that he had spent the last twenty-five years living in the depths of Malaysia; that the death that had so affected her, that affected her fears still, was a ploy of her mother's.

373

Martha broke into the snarl of her thoughts. 'I phoned Isabel to apologize. I left countless messages. She didn't return my calls for weeks. I wrote letters. I really thought I had lost her.' The tears leapt into her eyes again. 'Then she rang me, just like that, out of the blue. She told me curiosity had got the better of her. She was going to check this Morgenstern out – if he was still around. The foundation in Seattle wasn't. She had done her usual round of thorough investigations – rung and e-mailed, checked the archives of the magazine.'

Martha fluttered the worn sheet of paper in the air. 'The foundation closed down several years ago. There had been some fishy business, but no-one would tell her quite what. Embezzlement of funds, maybe, or threats of a malpractice suit against a doctor. Anyhow, the odd thing was that no-one by the name of Alexander Morgenstern seemed ever to have worked there. Nor could two of the members of staff she managed to track down tell her why it was called the Morgenstern Foundation. One of them thought it was from a quotation by some poet, another thought it had originally been funded by a bequest from a Chicago millionaire, long dead. So Isabel told me to get my best glasses out and make sure the picture I so wanted to be of Morgenstern really was. I confirmed it.

'The next time I heard from her, it was a message. I could kick myself for not being there. She sounded gleeful. She had found him, she said. She had called in favours and tracked him down. He was obviously a character. Maybe he even deserved her. She giggled in a way that distressed me. Excitement and dread, all mixed up. Apparently Alexander had changed his name. He was no longer Morgenstern. He had remarried and divorced, though she was sure I wouldn't want to know that. And she was on his trail. He was closer than either of us could have imagined.'

'Did she tell you his new name?'

Martha shook her head miserably. 'And when I tried to ring back there was no-one. If only I was on the net, then maybe . . . But I'm too old.'

'So when I told you Isabel was using the name Morgenstern, you assumed it was because she had found him.'

'Yes. And I'm sure that when Isabel said he was close by, she meant he was in England. Maybe even in London. I . . .' She averted her eyes. 'When I didn't hear from her again, I assumed it was because she was raging at me. Somehow, this Morgenstern I had presented to her as a good father hadn't lived up to the mark. And she hated me for it. Then, when you rang, that theory didn't make sense any more. She was using his name, after all. But then why be angry at you, or at any of her friends, because of all this, and not contact you?'

Martha paused. She pulled nervously at a button thread. 'What worries me as much as anything else is that Alexander had a cold side. He could cut off, wilfully blind himself to what he didn't want to see. It could feel brutal. Elinor was right about that. And Isabel . . . well, there was a fragility about her when I last saw her, which I hadn't noticed before.'

Her voice trailed off. Leo had a sudden sense that the woman was thinking of her sister. She was glad of the silence. Her mind was reeling. Isabel had taken on a teetering depth in time. She couldn't assimilate everything that Martha had told her, not all at once.

One thing, however, was clear. What they had to do was get Faraday to run a search on a name change. If she'd had her computer there, she might even have been able to do it herself – contact the public record office in Seattle, then do a run on telephone directories throughout England.

But Faraday would have gone home long ago and all this was too complicated for a message. She would ring him early tomorrow morning.

Meanwhile, she had to lie down and think. Ever since Martha had mentioned that Isabel's father was alive, she had been assailed by images of her own father. With them came confusion.

As she settled Martha into Isabel's bedroom, the force of the revelation her friend had experienced took her over. The shock of finding life and possibility where there had been only the void of death. She could feel her friend's vertigo, a dizzying sense that one's entire life had been constructed on false premises. She would feel cheated, betrayed, in the first instance by her mother. The mother she had begun to think was a murderer. There would be rage at both of them over all that needless pain and the realization that the longed-for father had been complicit in a masquerade, had lived a double life somewhere without her, hadn't loved her enough.

Yet there would be curiosity, too – hungry, rampant, a child's desire to know, to discover. And hope. A dream of recovered joy. He would explain away his actions, embrace her, take her on his knee. No, not that. Leo wasn't a little girl any more. Isabel wasn't a little girl. Her father wouldn't know the woman she had become.

A lump rose in Leo's throat. A lump of disappointment, a kind of visceral bewilderment, as if she had set out ardently on a quest, only to have the grail turn to dust in her hands.

She chased away the images.

The thing to focus on, she told herself as she stared at a white expanse of ceiling, the important thing, was that if Isabel was with her father, whatever her emotional state, she was alive. Whether here, as her aunt thought, or in Australia, as Leo still half believed, Isabel was alive. Not trapped or bruised or beaten or confined in some muddy ditch or wrecked car, nor in any of the other hideous sites Leo's imagination of disaster had cast her in.

Isabel was alive and safe and soon they would meet, even if it was on the other side of the world.

17

'Ms Holland, Faraday here.'

Brisk tones chased away the mists of troubled
sleep. Leo held the phone closer to her ear.

'Sorry to wake you. I didn't want to miss you. Can
you get yourself to Lynton today?'

'I don't understand.'

'You will when you get here. I'll be waiting for you
at the police station. You can't miss it. Follow the
signs to the town centre. Two o'clock should give you
plenty of time.'

'Isabel's aunt, Martha Morgan, is here from
Australia. Should I . . . ?'

'Bring her along.'

'But Inspector Faraday—'

A click signalled the end of the conversation.

Leo shrugged away confusion and woke Martha.
Barely two hours later they were sitting on a high-
speed train bound for Bristol. Leo described in more
detail how Isabel's trail had led her to the seaside
town, how Isabel had been picked up from there by
a man who was probably a chauffeur for some
biotech multinational.

It came to her as she said it that the man could just
as easily have been someone linked to Isabel's father,
or even Morgenstern himself. A Morgenstern who

had been forced into a workaday job after the collapse of his foundation. But she didn't say this aloud. Martha wouldn't have wanted to hear it. She didn't look well this morning. She looked frail. And she was stiffly restrained, as if she had given far too much away the preceding evening and now, out of self-respect, had to hold herself in check.

From Bristol, they hired a car. Leo wanted the activity. She drove with the fixed focus of a Grand Prix racer, vigilantly denying any stray thought. The stark beauties of Exmoor might as well have been a series of car graveyards or derelict badlands.

They arrived in Lynton in good time, and found the house that bore the police sign they were searching for, though it looked as unlikely a candidate for a police station as the next homey brick structure.

Faraday appeared even before Leo had fully opened the door. His thin face gave away little. It wore a blandly reassuring smile as he greeted them. He commented on the weather, which seemed to be clearing after morning rain, then guided them back down the external staircase and along a damp street.

'It's not far to go,' he said.

'Where are we going?' Leo asked, so softly that she realized she didn't want an answer.

Faraday cleared his throat. 'I think we may have found Isabel Morgan. I'm sorry. Sorry, too, to make you come here. But we need a definite identification.'

A hammer pounded at Leo's temples, blurring her vision. She put one foot carefully in front of another. Somehow, despite everything, she had already known.

'An identification?' Martha stopped mid-street.

Faraday nodded and put his arm through hers. 'She's not a pretty sight. I'm sorry,' he repeated. 'Sorry we couldn't prevent it.'

'Prevent what?' Leo's voice was a scream. Passers-by turned. She wanted him to say it.

'Two youths found her. Yesterday morning. They were fishing. The body had got stuck between boulders at the farthest end of the beach. We don't know how long it had been there.'

'The body . . . ? It . . . ?' Leo spat.

'This way.' He tugged on Martha's arm, led them through a lane and down some steps. Abruptly, they were in a room that might have been any other, except that it had a bone-numbing coldness and that smell was in the air. That lingering antiseptic reek. A high, sheeted slab of a table stood at the room's centre. A young woman in nurse's white hovered to one side of it. At a nod from Faraday, the sheet was lifted.

A face appeared. Not a face, a bloated, mottled parody of a face which looked as if it had been bruised and picked at by a hundred sharp teeth. Dry, tufted hair of a green-gold tinge floated and frizzled round the decaying mask. One eye lay open to stare in blind shock at a distant horror.

Leo turned away, as if the seeing would blind her, too. She was vaguely aware that Martha had collapsed into a chair. Her hands obliterated her face.

'Is it her?' Faraday asked softly. 'Is this Isabel Morgan?'

Leo met his encouraging gaze. She shook her head savagely. 'No. No. No. No.' She was whimpering. This wasn't Isabel. Isabel was beautiful, alive, animated. Isabel brought beauty into a room as certainly as an old master gave it life with oils. Her kind of beauty was a gift. It wasn't beauty that could be created artificially on page or screen by cameras and make-up and light, and extinguished just as quickly. Extinguished like this. It was the beauty of a personality through time. The kind of beauty that was life itself. Isabel would always be beautiful. This wasn't Isabel.

'Are you sure?' Faraday directed her attention to the corpse that wasn't Isabel once more. 'I was certain it was, from the photographs and from your description. I know. The sea, the mackerel, the rocks have done their damage, but do have another look. Maybe the clothes, such as they remain, may help.'

With a single swift gesture he whipped the sheet off the body, and Leo saw the muddy white of a long-sleeved T-shirt, the rise of a bosom, the flap of discoloured trousers. The fingers of the hand were bitten and gnarled. On the third, a ring marked the bulge of the flesh. A thick silver band with an oval aquamarine at its centre. She stared at it, wishing it away. Why was it there? Still there when everything else had been so utterly transformed. She had bought the ring for Isabel as a birthday present. They were in Paris together and, on the rue St Andre des Arts, they had passed a tiny boutique stuffed to the brim with rings and necklaces, earrings and pins, old and new, artfully crafted and stark in their simplicity. Isabel had chosen the silver band with the aquamarine. Because she loved the sea.

Leo averted her eyes. 'It is her,' she murmured. 'I don't want it to be her. But it is.'

Through the blur of tears, she was suddenly aware of Martha. She had hurled herself onto the corpse, covering it with her arms. A piercing wail filled the room.

Faraday lifted her away gently.

She was moaning now. 'My baby. My baby. Poor baby.'

She wouldn't leave her.

Faraday urged, tugged and, at last, guided her to the door, gesturing to Leo to follow.

She took one long, last look at that distorted figure who wasn't Isabel and then they were out of that chamber of death into a world of high skies and cold wind which clawed at her cheeks.

'I'm sorry,' Faraday said again. He led them into a pub, put brandy in front of them and insisted they drink.

Martha's eyes were glazed. She was pulling at her hair, muttering beneath her breath. 'My fault.'

Leo squeezed her hand and held it.

Faraday's voice reached her ears over a pounding which could only be her blood. 'You were right to be worried, Ms Holland. I always trust the nearest one's worry. But we were too late to save her. For whatever reason, she must have wanted to put an end to things. It looks like she jumped. Her neck's broken. I'm sorry we didn't find her in time.'

Leo looked at him in incomprehension. 'You . . . you think Isabel did this to herself? Never. No, no. She wouldn't.'

Martha stared up at her, bewilderment in her face. 'But Leo,' her voice croaked, 'she . . . she loved the sea.'

'So you think, Miss Morgan, that Isabel had reason?'

Martha nodded once, brusquely. 'My fault.' She began to tell him, erratically, what she had told Leo the night before.

'I need a breath of air,' Leo said and slipped away before they could stop her.

She didn't know which way she was going, but she had to be alone to let the mounting frenzy of thought

382

and emotion play through her. She walked quickly through zigzagging streets, up a lane, and suddenly she was on a beach and there was nowhere else to go except the length of a small, pebbled bay, along which the sea heaved its mocking strength.

She gazed at it. The eternal return of the waves had brought Isabel to rest here. She clutched her arms around herself, as if to feel the unfairness of the continued existence of her own flesh.

Why was she now so perversely certain that Isabel hadn't done away with herself? It was one of the thoughts that had haunted her, perhaps the core of the reason she had pursued Daniel Lukas and Paola Webster. An Isabel broken down, picked apart, her will to live destroyed. Yet now, now that Isabel's fractured body was too clearly in her mind, she refused the possibility of suicide. Was it simply that she couldn't allow in the stinking slew of self-recrimination which would follow from the reality of her friend's suicide? She should have been able to prevent it; she should have reached her friend in time; she should have noticed the signs. If she were truly a friend.

Leo walked, kicked a pebble into flight, hurled another into the sea so that the spray landed in her face, mingled with what she hadn't known were tears.

Or was it that once the reality of suicide took hold, it grew too seductive? A temptation which couldn't be resisted. She stared at the waves and blotted out their siren song. The Isabel she knew and loved wasn't like that. There was too much fierceness in her. Too much sheer love of life, whatever her distress. If she knew anything at all about Isabel, it was that. It was that part of Isabel which wasn't like

383

Leo, who faltered over the boundless variety of experience.

Leo turned. High above her in the distance graceful buildings curved and stretched. She must be standing beneath the road which she had walked to reach the Lynton Arms. Isabel had left there. She hadn't left alone. Where had she gone?

'Ms Holland.' Faraday's voice reached her above the incessant mewl of the gulls. 'Ms Holland, here you are.' He gripped her arm, as if he were afraid she was about to replicate Isabel's dying. 'I've left Miss Morgan. It is miss, isn't it? I've left her at the police station. Did you come here to see where we found your friend? I'll show you.' He was deliberately matter-of-fact.

He walked her towards the far end of the strand. Leo started to talk. A tangled tumult of talk, trying to convey her conviction that Isabel would never have killed herself, that somehow her death had to be linked to the investigation she was carrying out. Like Jill Reid's death. Yes. Had they found out any more? About Plantagen or one of the other companies on the list which had been sent to her. Yes. Why had that list been sent to her? No accidents here. No suicide. But purpose – evil, greedy, covert intent. Norfolk had told her about strange contents in the soil. Faraday must speak to him. And where had Isabel gone when she'd left the Lynton Arms? Had they determined the day of her death yet? There was more to uncover. More about the father she had been seeking out, too. Faraday had to carry on, had to be thorough. What was the man's name, if he wasn't Morgenstern?

She talked and talked as she gazed at the rivulet between the boulders where the corpse that wasn't Isabel had been found, and when she had talked herself out, Faraday said softly, 'A thorough post-mortem is being done, Ms Holland. At the moment, we only know that Ms Morgan died between five and fifteen days ago. And that there was a fall. As soon as we have anything more definite, I'll let you know. By the way, those plantlings you gave me turned out to be ipomoea. Ordinary morning glory.' He made a noise which wasn't quite a laugh. 'That rather scuppered one of my theories.' He met her eyes.

'That nice Mrs Donald,' Leo heard herself say.

'What?'

'She must have given them to her. Isabel had asked about her husband.'

Faraday looked as if he was going to question her further, but changed his mind. 'Try to take it easy, Ms Holland. Do you think you can drive? Only I feel Miss Morgan should be taken home. Given some sedation, perhaps.'

Leo stared at him blindly. She shook her head. 'I'm not going back to London. You can drive her. I'm staying here. Up there.' She pointed to the cliff. 'Up there where Isabel stayed. The Lynton Arms Hotel.'

When they returned to the police station, Martha was equally firm.

'I'm staying, too. I'm staying with Isa— With Leo.' She squared her shoulders so that she seemed to grow several inches to meet Faraday's gaze.

Faraday shrugged. 'That's fine, then. If you're certain. I have the hotel number if I need to reach you.' He turned to Leo. 'You won't do anything silly, will you, Ms Holland?'

'Call me Leo, Inspector. You'll follow up those leads?'

'We'll do our best.'

385

This time, Leo took the track and drove straight up the narrow incline to the Lynton Arms. Pippa emerged from the hotel's depths to welcome her like a long-lost friend. After Leo had introduced Martha, Pippa drew her aside.

'Was it her?' she whispered, her face at once solemn and eager.

For a moment, Leo didn't know what she was referring to. Then she realized that news must travel more quickly than lightning in this small, out-of-season resort. She nodded once, too abruptly.

'I'm so very sorry. If there's anything we can do, just say. You'll be staying tonight, won't you? I can give you two rooms with sea views.' She winced. 'If that's . . . that's what you'd like.'

Leo conferred with Martha, then followed Pippa up the miniature grand staircase. Once they had placed their bags in identical chintzy rooms, where the wallpaper swirled with roses, Leo asked if tea was possible. And maps. She needed some Ordnance Survey maps.

'No lack of those. I'll bring them with tea. In the dining room. A full tea. You both look as if you need it. By the way . . .' she glanced towards Martha then drew Leo into the hall and lowered her voice, 'I heard something. It made me very sad.' Her tongue seemed to stumble. 'One of the guests . . . She told me that the chauffeur, that big black car, it belongs to a clinic, somewhere west of here. She didn't know the name. I guess your poor friend couldn't take any more—' She stopped abruptly as Martha appeared at the door. 'I'll get that tea, shall I? And those maps.' She raced off with a forced smile.

'You're plotting something, Leo. I know it, and

I'm coming with you.' Martha's voice was determined. 'I won't weep or babble. That's a pledge.'

Leo met her eyes, read the plea in them and nodded.

Beneath the arc of the trees, the narrow road was as dusky as if night were poised to fall. Better than fog, Leo consoled herself, her attention glued to the terrain. She was looking for the place where Jill Reid's car had gone down the incline. If the police tape had been removed from the spot, she might not recognize it.

She had pushed the mileage button on the dashboard when they'd set off. She wanted to determine the distance that separated the two deaths. Isabel might have died in Lynton. But equally, her body could have been carried by the sea and lain there, hidden by boulders, for any number of days.

Noticing a narrow break between the gnarled trees, Leo brought the car to a halt. The place looked familiar. She switched off the engine; 3.2 miles, the gauge read.

'Why are we stopping, Leo?'

She hadn't explained to Martha and she did so tersely now.

'A friend of hers, you say. Died here?' Martha's eyes filled with tears.

Leo was already out of the car. She trod carefully over the crackle of broken branches. There was no tape to stop her from moving across the scene today, though she spotted a piece of it, bright against mud. Where the incline grew steeper, she slipped a little and clung to the trunk of a tree. She wedged her feet carefully now, taking one step at a time. Beneath her she could hear the sea slashing against rock. When she reached the precipice, she shunted away dizziness and stared straight down, clinging to a gnarled oak as she did so. A stone ridge met her gaze, peaks of shale, and only beyond them the sea.

'Leo. Don't.' A scream reached her, distorted by wind.

She turned and saw Martha clambering towards her. She waved to reassure her and scrambled hastily back up the hill. The poor woman had thought she was about to mimic Isabel. But this was not the spot for mimicry. If Isabel had gone down here, flung by her own or another's will, her fall would have been stopped by rock well above sea level. It was a hunch disproved. An unwanted vision disproved, too. It had come to her in a flash of perverse jealousy and out of a searing sense of abandonment that Isabel might have played out the Thelma and Louise fantasy they had nurtured over Christmas with Jill Reid, rather than with her – and taken the fantasy to its fatal conclusion. The lay of the land proved otherwise.

'Don't worry.' Leo put her arm around Martha's shoulder. 'I was only checking something out.'

They drove on. Leo was still intent on the road, as if some sign might leap out at her and shout, 'Here.' Twice she stopped to climb out of the car and get a good look at the contours of the coastline. Twice Martha came out after her. On the second occasion, when the sea suddenly appeared unobstructed by rock at a sharp drop beneath them, the older woman clasped her arms round her shoulders and started to sway slowly. She broke into a loud keen.

'Isabel.' She wailed pain into the elements. 'Isabel, Isabel, Isabel,' and then she crumpled, her legs giving way as her voice rose.

Leo caught her, held her up and planted a kiss on

her cheek, as if she were a child. There were no words to use. She helped her back into the car.

A little further along, they came upon a tiny clifftop hamlet, complete with a coastguard's cottage and a squat church which looked as ancient as the hills. Behind it, the horizon had lifted high enough to illuminate an endless stretch of blue-tinged charcoal that was the sea.

'I'd like to stop here, Leo, if we could.' Martha spoke for the first time since they had got back into the car. 'I'd like to go into the church for a moment.'

Leo pulled up on a verge where the road widened a little. She took Martha's arm and led her through the wooden gate which gave on to the churchyard, then hastened their pace past the ranked graves, their inscriptions half obliterated by time and weather. The wind whipped at their jackets, made talk impossible, emphasized the silence within the granite walls of the church once they had shut its heavy door behind them.

Martha sat in a pew by the altar and bowed her head as if she would never lift it again. Leo waited, huddled in her own thoughts, until a burst of indignation propelled her outdoors. She sheltered from the gusting wind for a moment in the small porch, then wandered restlessly amidst the tombstones.

The slabs were flint thin and looked as if they would bend in the wind. But many of them had stood here for centuries, mutely outliving their dead in the bleak wildness of the landscape. She paused by a stone and wiped a fragment of moss from its inscription. Edward Bagshaw. Edward. Her father's name. Her father who had no stone under which to rest to speak his presence to strangers. But he lived on in her memory, nonetheless, perhaps even a little less restlessly now that she had confronted something of the muddle of pain, anger and longing which his abrupt passage had left. This Edward, she noted, had not had the luxury of even her father's lifetime. He had died at the mere age of twenty-three, much mourned by his mother, Mary, father, Edward, and three sisters.

With a quick look over her shoulder, Leo placed a covert kiss on the cold stone and thought of Isabel. The odd thing was that the thick cloud of anxiety that had hampered her movements over the last weeks, perhaps longer, had lifted. A slew of other emotions had come in its place, but that was gone. The worst had already happened.

She walked hurriedly back to the porch. Martha came out as she reached it. The woman's eyes were moist, but she nodded at Leo. 'Thank you for allowing me to stop,' she said softly. 'It helps a little.'

Leo drove on with no exact sense of destination, though Pippa's words hovered in her mind. On this side of the hamlet, the road was slightly wider and offered an occasional passing place as it plunged into a valley only to climb remorselessly to a new height. For a brief stretch, they had dazzling views of the sun setting pink over headlands of yellow gorse and purple-red heather.

On a whim, she veered onto a narrower track which seemed to dip inland. A mixture of trees and hedges obstructed the eye line. It was darker here in the shadow of the precipice, inhospitable. As they followed the road, something about the lay of the land gave her an uncanny feeling of déjà vu. She pulled up short and looked out the rear window. There were lights on the crest of the hill behind them. A house. She turned the engine on again, something nudging at the corners of her mind. A bend and another twist in the track and it suddenly came back to her. This must be the road on which she and Norfolk had met that road hog who had knocked off their wing mirror. The fog had rubbed out contours, distorted distances. She had seen the house then, emerging from the mist and disappearing again, like a ghostly presence.

She drove at a snail's pace, willing the huge car to manifest itself once more. And then she remembered. The man at the wheel. He had been wearing a cap. A chauffeur's cap? She wasn't sure. She rolled down the window and let the wind play over her face, breathed deeply.

The road forked now and she paused, slowly taking the turn which she thought might lead her back towards the sea. Suddenly she felt Martha shaking.

'What is it?' Leo asked softly.

The woman pointed upwards. 'They're horrible.'

Beneath the rose-tipped grey of threatening clouds, two buzzards circled, their wings blacker than coal. As she followed their downward passage, a discreet sign came into view, a blue oval with a single gold star, glistening slightly in the setting sun. She drove past it, then braked abruptly.

'Did you see that?'

'What? You mean the birds?'

'No, no. The sign.' She screeched the gears as she moved into reverse. 'Look.'

'The Morning Star Foundation,' Martha read. 'Sanctuary. F. F. Hilton, Director.' She gave Leo a quizzical look.

'Morning Star.' Leo's voice rose. 'That's the English for Morgenstern.'

'So it is. I should have known that.' Panic flashed

across Martha's face. 'Do you think he . . . ? I couldn't . . . '

'I don't know. But we're going to check it out.'

The road narrowed after a stretch and seemed to curve back on itself. A dense, towering hedge of blue-green cypress now stalked their passage to the left. Cut into its midst, a grand ironwork gate appeared. Through it, Leo glimpsed the roll of grounds, an eccentric play of trees, boulders and pebbled paths, at the far end of which stood a massive stone structure, lavishly gabled, as if its architecture had been conceived by an austere Kubla Khan lost in infernal dreams, or perhaps by some medieval abbot intent on the most stringent of monastic strongholds.

'Are we going to go in?' Martha turned from the gate to Leo and back again. Her voice was a quivering whisper. The location seemed to demand it.

'It doesn't look altogether welcoming, does it?'

Martha shook her head. 'But there's a smaller door on the side and a buzzer.' Her features were trapped between desire and fear.

'And a car park.' Leo pointed to a small arrow on a placard wedged in front of a cypress.

She followed its direction, and the car park emerged a good distance down the slope, on the other side of the road. It, too, was shrouded by imposing firs. But the smattering of cars reassured Leo.

'At least we know it's inhabited. Why don't you wait here? I won't be long. I'll just ask a few questions.'

Martha released a pent-up sigh. 'If you're sure I wouldn't be of some use. If he's there, how will you know?'

She shrugged. 'I just want to find out what kind of place it is.'

The air in the enclosure was very still, as if the wind didn't reach it. When she emerged from the seclusion of the car park, she noticed that the single-track road didn't stop here but wound downhill and merged into a panorama of distant farmland. She walked quickly, and had almost reached the top of the incline where the road curved left when she heard a motor behind her. She turned to see a black Mercedes climbing the hill with stately dignity. She squeezed into the bank of the road to let it pass. A capped man was in the driver's seat. He didn't acknowledge her presence. Nor did the woman who dozed on the back seat.

A vision of Isabel came to her with sudden hallucinatory force. Her friend had been here. She was certain of it. Isabel had been in that car. And this must be the place Pippa had mentioned.

Leo watched the Mercedes stop at the lavish iron gate, which opened with inching remote control. She slipped in behind it just before the gates swung shut again, then tracked its passage.

From inside the grounds, the landscape lost some of its bleakness. The sky was high. Rock flowers dotted the crevices of the scattered boulders. Within a circle of small trees, she heard the sound of a fountain. A bald-headed man in a flowing saffron robe emerged from around the far corner of the house. Perhaps it was indeed some kind of monastery.

As she came closer, she noticed that the house curved round on itself to form an inner courtyard. At the utmost limit of the grounds, in the shadow of the cypresses, stood two secondary structures built out of the same pale stone, tinged with a honey glow in the late afternoon light. A large beech arched generously to her other side.

The doors of the house had just opened. A figure in what looked like karate whites was bringing a wheelchair to the Mercedes. The woman was placed into it. Leo ran, so as not to miss the opportunity of another open door and a good look at the chauffeur.

She found herself at the threshold of a large, square hall, wainscoted as far as the dado and then painted white. What looked like ancestral portraits decorated its expanse, though none of the faces resembled each other. A wide staircase curved gracefully up to the second floor. To its side stood a chest-high wooden counter, with an assortment of leaflets on top of it. Behind, she could see the flicker of a PC. The reception area, she presumed, and walked softly towards it.

Randomly, she picked up one of the leaflets, only half looking at it.

All the activity in the room was by the doorway on the far right. The capped chauffeur was holding the door open. He was smaller than she had presumed, given the size of his head and torso and the ruddy pugnacity of his face.

A bigger man in karate pyjamas pushed the dark-haired woman in the wheelchair through. She was protesting about something Leo couldn't make out to a tall, slender woman who was also clad in white. The uniformed woman shushed her with the manner of a stern nurse.

'We don't raise our voices here, Helena,' she said in a hushed tone that carried the authority of its irrefutable command all the way to Leo. 'You'll be settled in just a few minutes, and then the Director will come and talk to you.'

As she spoke, the woman's pale eyes landed on Leo and an eyebrow arched in unhappy query. She ushered the woman in the wheelchair through, together with the two men, and closed the hallway door.

Leo looked away and pretended to read the leaflet in her hand. She started. She had seen this leaflet before. 'Evolution', its cover announced. Where had she seen it?

'Yes, how can I help you?'

Leo focused on a face of icy prettiness, pale hair swept back in a knot, yellow-flecked eyes with tiny, glistening pupils, a perfect Grecian nose, raised now to look down on her.

Leo's mind raced. 'I hope you can, Miss . . .' She waited for the woman to fill in a name.

'Heather.'

'Heather?' Leo repeated.

'Yes, Heather. It's our policy only to use first names here. I'm sure you understand why.' Cold eyes scrutinized her and seemed to evaluate the cash value of her clothes, her bag.

'Of course,' Leo murmured, though she hadn't the vaguest idea.

'Our guests also normally arrive pre-announced. No-one else was expected this evening.' Heather was polite, correct in her bearing. Leo couldn't place exactly what it was that made her so forbidding. Maybe it had something to do with her slow, careful enunciation.

'I guess I'm not exactly a guest. You're from California, aren't you?'

Heather's nod was brief. 'I go back to my first question. How can I help you?'

Leo noticed that, in the course of this conversation, she had been gently but firmly negotiated towards the door.

'A friend told me about your place and asked me to meet her here. She sent me your brochure. I've just arrived from New York,' Leo improvised.

'And who is your friend?

'Oh, haven't I said yet? Isabel. Isabel Iris, if you've got two Isabels.'

Heather's forehead creased in a parody of concentration.

'Why not check it out on your PC? That way you can tell me her room number as well.' Leo gave her an innocent smile.

'My memory is rather well trained, thank you. I recall your friend Iris exactly. A handsome blonde woman with a murky aura. Troubled, I mean. A little like you.' The woman said it with controlled disdain. 'It's a shame she didn't contact you in time to tell you that she had left us. The Sunday before last, I believe it was. The reason I don't remember precisely is that I was away that weekend.'

'Are you certain of that? Did she leave a message for me? Please check it out. It's a long way to come.'

'No message. No need.'

A red light had begun to flicker from the ceiling just above the reception counter. Before she could ask what it signalled, Heather continued, 'I have to ask you to go now.'

'But . . .'

The door was already open. 'If you want to book into our retreat, a reservation is required. Places are at a premium. The brochure will tell you that reception is on Friday evening or Saturday morning. And, of course, for a first-time guest we need a professional referral.'

'A professional referral?'

'Yes. A professional referral.'

Without quite realizing she had been ejected, Leo found herself on the exterior stairs.

'There are hotels scattered all over the region.' Heather gave her a sliver of a smile now. 'Fifteen or twenty minutes should get you to the first one. But hurry, if you don't know these roads, it's best to drive before dark. We look forward to your visit.' The door closed with a soft thud.

Expelled as deftly as a field mouse by a stiff broom, Leo nursed a rebellious inclination to bang on the door. But it would serve no purpose.

Instead, she walked slowly down the pebbled path and examined the well-tended terrain. Isabel, or rather Iris, had been here until ten days ago, according to Heather's memory. If that was to be trusted, it meant she had stayed for around two weeks. On the Thursday of the first week she should have flown to New York. What had prevented her from doing so, or at least from alerting Leo? And what had happened afterwards?

Leo unfurled the leaflet she had inadvertently twisted into a narrow tube and stared at it. Of course. She knew now where she had seen it before: on the bedside table in the loft. The guest bedroom. She had glanced at it on her first night in London and wondered whether it was Isabel or a visitor who had left it there.

The tinkling of chimes diverted her attention. A group of people emerged in single file from a hedged enclave at the far corner of the grounds. Each and every one of them wore the white karate garb. Maybe the guests, too, had to shed their usual clothes once they entered the Morning Star Sanctuary.

She stopped to watch the procession for a moment. All of them had their eyes focused on some middle distance that excluded her presence, even as they came close to her. She wondered if any of them had once borne the name Morgenstern. She almost shouted it out at the top of her lungs in a perverse desire to see which one looked up.

No, far better to play things by stealth. Tomorrow she would follow in Isabel's footsteps and book herself in.

On impulse, she turned off the main path. A man in white was digging the earth in a flower bed. He glanced up and gave her a vague smile. His face was familiar. It came to her that she had seen it on some poster. Yes. It might even have been in Becca's room some years back. They only used first names here, Heather had said. Celebrities, of course.

Leo walked towards the outlying houses. They formed a wall of stone, partly covered by ivy and punctuated by windows. The doors were perhaps on the other side, from which she was cut off by the impenetrable hedge of thick cypress. She glanced up, and her eyes fell on a second-storey window. A woman was standing there looking down at her. She stood with utter stillness, her eyes two holes in a face that looked spectral beneath its tangled mass of hair. The sadness in her face was so great that, without thinking, Leo raised her hand in a wave.

The woman didn't respond. For a fugitive moment, Leo had the odd feeling that she had walked into a nineteenth-century novel to confront the original madwoman in the attic. Yet there was no caged-animal-like panting here, or scurrying or raving. The woman still hadn't moved. She still stared.

Feeling a chill settle on her which had little to do with wind or weather, Leo walked away quickly. If only she had come here ten days earlier, she would have found Isabel. Isabel, who needed her. Isabel, who had eluded her like some will-o'-the-wisp and now lay dead on a cold slab, her life purloined.

Leo gazed blindly into the distance, refusing the silky fingers of depression which threatened to numb her with their seductive force.

18

The bar at the Lynton Arms had all the attributes of a gentleman's club scaled down to lilliputian proportions. There were a few richly worn armchairs, their leather eroded into comfort by a century of capacious bottoms. There were two card tables, one of them currently in use by a bridge party. Green-shaded lamps cast a quiet glow, put to shame by the leaping flames of the log fire. Framed ducks and deer nestled on burgundy-papered walls, oblivious to the threat of the antique rifle above them.

A crisp-shirted young man with perfect aquiline features presided, filling glasses with whisky or brandy at the briefest of signals.

Leo nursed a drink and watched Martha. Her eyes were red-rimmed and heavy, kept open by sheer will-power, as if to close them even for a second meant to be pursued by nightmare images. Leo leant over and squeezed her hand, watched the older woman focus with difficulty and force a smile which evaporated as quickly as it had come.

'If only I hadn't said anything to her, she'd still be here.'

'You don't know that.' Leo was stern. 'We don't know anything. But we will. I promise you, we will.'

'It won't bring her back.'

'No. It won't do that.' Leo emptied her glass and put it down on the table with a clatter.

Pippa's appearance provided a welcome distraction. Leo had been waiting to speak to the woman, but the opportunity hadn't yet presented itself. She gestured her towards them. The trim Bea was right behind her, cat-like in pearly angora.

'Let us get you both a drink.'

'It's on the house, dear.' Pippa beckoned to the young waiter while Bea flashed her an admonishing look.

'I wanted to ask you,' Leo began, 'have you heard anything about the Morning Star Foundation. It runs a place that calls itself a sanctuary. It's the clinic Iris went to.'

'Morning Star? Pretty,' Pippa reflected, 'but I don't think I've heard the name before.'

'I know the place you mean.' The waiter interrupted as he placed drinks before them. His accent, Leo now noticed, was distinctly French. 'To the west of here. It's for addicts. Rich addicts. Maybe famous. For recovering quietly. Very, how do you say, hush, hush.' He grinned.

'Was your friend . . . ?' Pippa began.

'Definitely not.' Martha suddenly roused herself and answered for Leo. 'Most definitely not.' She threw Leo a pleading look. 'I know. I work with them. Kids.'

'No-one's suggesting that, Martha.' Leo calmed her and turned back to the waiter. 'Is it only for addicts? And what kind?'

The youth shrugged. 'I'm not certain. I met another Frenchman last summer. He worked in the kitchen there for a few weeks. He said they were *fous*. Crazy people. He didn't stay long.'

'Just as well you came back to us, eh, Robert?' Pippa beamed at him. 'Robert is from St Malo.'

'Mr Seale wants a drink, Robert.' Bea was crisp. She turned to Martha. 'Your niece was a fine woman, Miss Morgan. We wish she had stayed with us longer.'

Tears filled Martha's eyes. Pippa placed a mottled hand on her arm. In a crooning voice, she began to sing Isabel's praises.

Leo stole away from the sympathy which diluted rage. As it was, the burden that had been pressing down on her shoulders all day had taken on an unbearable heaviness. Beneath it, she was being crushed into paralysis. A numbing of anger. An acceptance. An easy nullity. No, she mustn't let herself succumb to that. Otherwise Isabel's ghost would rumble underground and never be put to rest. Like her father's. She wasn't a child any longer. She needed to act. She needed to explore the path which had led Isabel to death, even if, at the end, she was forced to come to terms with the possibility that her friend had abandoned her without a second thought.

She lay down, and the Morning Star site came back to her in all its slightly ominous tranquillity. She saw the tall row of impenetrable cypresses, the white-clad men processing through the grounds in hermetic self-absorption, the painfully thin woman gazing through the window of the subsidiary house, the bulk of the hill at the back of the property.

She only realized that she had been asleep when a dream made her start in terror. Tears were pouring down her cheeks. The pillow was wet with them. She let the sobs rack through her. She had been under-ground again in that oozing labyrinthine city. She had lost something and had to find it amidst those deserted buildings and paths and pipes. The ooze had turned into rain, and then into a deluge. The ground beneath her feet swirled and heaved. A rushing current carried her, propelling her through streets, and as the water level grew higher and higher, a body floated towards her. She clutched at it. Isabel. She had found her. Found her too late.

Loneliness washed over her like a flood. She was alone. A small child alone in the night watching shadows play over the walls, a storm of trees metamorphosing into terrible shapes. There was no-one to call for.

Leo forced herself to sit up and switch on the light. She took a few deep, ragged breaths. Some baleful sandman had thrown grit and ash in her mouth. She reached for the bottle of mineral water on the bedside table. Her head was pounding.

Somewhere she must have some pills. She stumbled into the bathroom and brushed against the sink. Its cold clamminess brought with it an image of Isabel on that slab. Isabel and, before that, Jill Reid. Her mind seemed determined to partner them.

She popped two tablets into her mouth. Something niggled at her again, like termites gnawing at the edge of her vision. She swallowed.

Drugs, the waiter had said. A recovery programme at the sanctuary. There had been drugs in Jill Reid, too. The pathologist had remarked on that. What would the post-mortem on Isabel reveal? And Norfolk, he had talked of the floating borders in the biotech sector, drugs and food. Then there was the company brochure she had found amongst Isabel's clothes: Bioworld. And her medicine cabinet, ransacked by the burglar.

Her mind whirled. Why had Isabel's case been

returned by Qantas if her body was here in the Devon sea?

She turned off the light and quickly switched it back on again. No. She didn't want the darkness. She fumbled in her bag and brought out the leaflet with the enigmatic title. Evolution. She read it through several times. It described an idyllic setting in the countryside, which offered retreats, meditation, counselling, yoga, massage and a variety of therapies, which would bring one to a higher plane of being. The language reverberated with New Age terminology. There was no mention of a drug-rehabilitation centre.

The last page gave practical details. A plan began to take shape in Leo's mind.

The door within the elaborate gate opened smoothly to Leo's ring. She took a deep breath and, straightening her shoulders, prepared to enter the sanctuary.

The raked gravel crunched beneath her feet. A crow descended onto the lawn and gazed at her with its bleak eyes. The air was unnaturally still, as if the ranked cypresses refused the common wind. But for a solitary figure, meditating beneath a tree, there was no-one visible in the front grounds today. Her eyes strayed towards the distant annexe in search of the spectral woman at the window. But the far buildings were in shadow, their interiors an impenetrable façade.

Leo walked slowly, conjuring Isabel to her side, willing her to reveal her state of mind as she'd moved along the same path.

Last night she had talked to Norfolk, at last back from Amsterdam and in the London loft. She had conveyed the terrible news, heard the catch in his breath and that single 'no' of disbelief. She had told him that Faraday assumed suicide, but that she couldn't quite believe that – not of Isabel.

'Yet she liked grand exits,' Norfolk had mumbled.

'She liked life more,' Leo had insisted.

She had sketched in what Martha had told her, then explained that Isabel had stayed in a place run by the Morning Star Foundation until a week ago, Sunday.

Norfolk had said that he would drive down in the morning, but she had urged him instead to follow Jill Reid's trail from Plantagen and the biotech line, as well as checking in with the local Greens once more. Isabel's trajectory after she had left the sanctuary was unaccounted for.

Norfolk was more than prepared to do that, and to do some digging about the Morning Star Foundation. The name rang a faint bell.

Leo repeated that he needed to communicate with Faraday, or he might suddenly find himself hauled into a police station. Leo would ring him as soon as she had any news. She told him, too, that he might check out Qantas and the returned suitcase with its Bioworld brochure, and keep an eye on Martha, who was staying at the Lynton Arms.

After she had spoken to Norfolk, she had left a message for Daniel Lukas, telling him that she needed his referral since she was going to check in to the Morning Star Foundation's sanctuary. They would undoubtedly ring him rather than write, since she had insisted on early access.

A white-clad man appeared at the door before Leo could find the bell. He was young, straight-backed, with light brown hair and a dimple in his smooth chin. His eyes were very blue and slightly averted.

405

'Welcome, Leonora.' He bowed fractionally and smiled. 'I am William. I will look after you.'

Leo detected a hint of German in his hard 'W's.

'Call me, Leo,' she said, a little thrown by the fact that she had already been identified.

'Leo.' He took her case politely. 'Come. This way.'

There was a kind of formal informality to him, as if he had learnt casualness in a precise school.

She followed him into the wainscoted hall and glanced towards the far corner where the counter stood. No icy Heather to contend with, only a pretty young woman who smiled and nodded her through. Leo walked with more alacrity.

They didn't head for the door through which the woman in the wheelchair had gone. They went up the staircase, instead, and along a dusky corridor. But for their presence, the place was so quiet it could be uninhabited. It passed through Leo's mind that there had been no need for the fuss which had attended her insistence that they must make room for her this week. The woman she had spoken to on the telephone wasn't Heather. This woman had a throaty, educated English voice, and she had made her hold on for a good ten minutes before coming back to her to say that, yes, they could just squeeze her in, given her particular needs.

Leo had sensed that it was neither her needs, nor the pressure of her dates, that had done the trick. It was the name Dr Daniel Lukas that had seen her through. Between the lines of the Evolution publicity material, she had read a desire for legitimation from some kind of establishment. With the Dr in front of his name, and the reputation Aron Field had made her aware of, let alone the gathered crowd at Paola Webster's launch party, Daniel could certainly serve as 'establishment' for any organization which listed an assortment of counselling and therapeutic functions as part of its brief.

Maybe, too, entry had to be made difficult if it was to prove worthwhile.

They had just turned a second corner when William opened a door on their left.

'This will be your room,' he said in his soft voice. 'You will find instructions on the table. We wear whites here. They are on the bed. If you wish us to store your usual clothes, that is possible, too.' He bowed slightly again and was gone.

Leo stood in a spare, white room that might have been a monk's cell. The floor was pale beech, the bed a pallet covered in a white rug-like blanket. Two towels lay on it and two white suits, all neatly folded. There was a sink in the corner and a bare wooden table by the window, together with a hardbacked chair. A door gave on to a cupboard, with three built-in shelves and a rail with five hangers. The walls were bare.

She could suddenly hear her mother's voice: 'You'd think, for the price, they could throw in a mirror and a shower.'

There was a scent in the air which she couldn't place. It attacked the nostrils with a cloying mixture of sweetness and fern. Leo looked out the window. It opened on to an unexpected world of twisted gorse and bracken. Beyond, a steep incline loomed, rocky and bare, higher than any prison wall. The wild beauty of the view both astonished and dismayed her. She must be at the back of the house. She would see little of its activity from this vantage point.

On the table lay two sheets of printed paper. Both had the word 'sanctuary' at the top, in a bold, seriffed typeface followed by the tag line, 'Clear your mind. Cleanse your body. Centre your spirit.'

The one on the left contained a list of house rules. As she read, Leo had the odd feeling she had landed back in boarding school. She should be pleased, but she sensed that this was a rigorous boarding school where laughter would be a disciplinary offence, like the ones Isabel had once described to her. There were no chattering girls' excited voices here. A flurry of prohibitions was in force. The sanctuary did not permit the use of mobile phones or computers. There was a ban on alcohol, smoking and all non-prescribed drugs. Prescribed drugs were to be noted at the first interview.

Guests were asked to wear the provided whites indoors and out, weather permitting.

Doors had no locks. Any valuables could be stored.

This was a refuge. Guests were asked to obey the rules of silence at the appointed hours. Conversation was to be kept to a minimum during meals.

Though guests were encouraged to take solitary, meditational walks and partake of the sanctuary's exceptional natural beauty, certain areas were restricted. These were detailed on the accompanying map.

There followed a schedule which would be personally adapted for a stay of one, two or more weeks.

It included yoga, meditation, t'ai chi, group therapy of various kinds, individual counselling, shiatsu and Thai massage, as well as lectures. Each guest would be called for a meeting to adapt the schedule to their particular needs on the first full day of their stay. Everyone was asked to attend the orientation lecture on the first evening and as many of the subsequent lectures as possible.

Leo pulled up the window, annoyed that it bumped to a stop two inches up. But the air rushed through, fresh and with a tang of the sea. She breathed deeply and returned to the map.

Her own room was marked with a red dot. She was indeed in a rectangular block of a building constructed around a courtyard. The courtyard showed a canopied shape, which the code at the side designated as a lecture hall and meeting room. The rooms facing the courtyard all seemed to be workspaces of one kind or another. There was a refectory to the left of the entrance hall and a storeroom in the cellar.

This, together with the entire right-hand side of the building, was clearly marked out of bounds. So were the two annexes and the area around them. From the general plan of the grounds, she realized they were far more ample than she had originally surmised.

What went on in the areas marked out of bounds? She guessed they must house the addiction centre. She would have to make her way in there, somehow. Given what Martha had told her, it was more than likely that it was there she would find the one-time Morgenstern.

She unpacked her bag, put her clothes in the small cupboard and washed quickly. The woman with the educated voice had specified only one necessity on the telephone: soft-soled shoes. Leo had dutifully packed a pair of trainers. She put these on now, together with the rough white-cotton T-shirt which had been provided as a kind of vest to wear under what she still thought of as a karate uniform. Maybe different levels of staff wore different-coloured belts, Leo joked to herself to allay her rising apprehension. She didn't know quite where it came from. Maybe it was simply the strong sense she had of Isabel at her side.

Leo turned up the trousers and sleeves, both of which were too long, and left the room to embark on an initial exploration. She had done no more than walk a few metres along the corridor when a soft voice called to her.

'Leo.'

Leo jumped. William had appeared from nowhere, as quiet as a cat on padded feet. Had he been designated as her minder? Would he always and ever be with her? She stilled herself.

'Yes, William,' she replied softly.

'If you have anything to store, I can do it for you now.'

'Oh, I hadn't thought. Maybe later. I'd like to go for a stroll now.'

William looked worried. 'There isn't really time before dinner.'

'A quick one. Come with me, William. Work up an appetite. And you can show me round.' Leo gave him a wide smile.

As they reached the staircase, they met a woman wearing a dramatically broad-brimmed hat and the sweeping sunglasses of bygone glamour. She nodded vaguely in their direction and hurried down the corridor. Leo noted that she wasn't preceded or followed by a figure in white.

'Who's that?' she asked William chattily.

'Candice,' he murmured, with visible reluctance.

'A frequent guest?'

He nodded and opened the front door a little brusquely.

There were more people in the grounds now, some carrying small cases. The Mercedes was drawn up at

410

the side. Leo reflected that, in her anticipation, she had arrived early for the Friday evening turnaround.

William led her briskly away from the main drive and along one of the side paths.

'How long have you been here, William?' Leo queried.

'Oh, eight months. Maybe more.'

'And did you plan, when you came, to stay that long?'

He stumbled, then righted himself quickly. 'I . . . When I came I was a little lost. I had no plans. I was over there.' He waved obscurely behind them. It took Leo a moment to realize he was pointing towards the out-of-bounds area. The addiction centre.

'I see.'

'I was seeking.'

'What were you seeking?'

They had reached a row of tall shrubs and William led her to a break in them. The waters of a small rectangular reservoir gleamed in the setting sun. William's eyes glowed, too.

'A way. A path,' he said firmly.

'And you found it here?'

He nodded.

'The therapists helped you.'

He stiffened a little. 'The Director.'

'Oh, I see. What's he like?'

'You'll see him later.' He was gazing into the distance, walking more quickly now.

Leo didn't want him to subside into silence. 'So you were in a state of crisis when you arrived and the Director put you right.'

'He showed me the way, yes,' he corrected her, his lips curling with just a trace of contempt. 'The path to wisdom.'

'Evolution. The path to wisdom,' she mused.

'Yes. A life free of craving. Peace. To feel at one with the world.'

Leo met his eyes with what she hoped was a soulful expression. 'My Australian friend Iris told me about the sanctuary. That's what she was looking for, too.'

'Iris? The Australian. No, no,' he blurted out. 'She was underhand. She was secretly writing an exposé. That's why—' He stopped himself. In the distance a gong had sounded. 'Come, Leonora.' He set up a pace too brisk for conversation.

Leo followed and wondered whether Isabel had perhaps let slip that she was writing a book on therapies. That wasn't like her.

It was too late to question William directly any further. They had arrived at the dining hall, an austere high-ceilinged room where, despite the rows of people already seated at the long pine tables, a resonant hush prevailed. William directed Leo to a gap and made to hurry off.

She had the distinct sense that the extra speed in his step meant that he was scurrying off to report their conversation to some higher authority. Good, she thought to herself. She wanted everyone to know that she was interested in Iris Morgenstern.

She slipped into her place, smiled at the man next to her and said hello. He was about thirty-five and his narrow head was bullet-smooth above lowered eyes and a hawk nose. He nodded at her, then brusquely returned his attention to the heaped greens and carrots, tomatoes, celery and fruit which made up the evening meal. These he chewed with studied slowness, as if each mouthful were a rosary bead. The woman on her right, whom she addressed next, was no more forthcoming, though she, by contrast, ate with furtive haste, and then sat with her face fixed to her plate.

From behind her, Leo thought she heard an explosion of laughter, but, when she turned, there was no-one there, though the gong had sounded again, loud in here. Isabel, she suddenly thought. Isabel watching the theatre of the place and giving her a little nudge of fellow feeling, urging her to rise with the others.

Leo trailed behind the bullet-headed man. They were outside for a moment in the still air of a courtyard. Then the file brought her inside the canopied area at its centre. The rows of chairs were already largely filled – enough of them for some sixty to eighty people, she estimated. She sat down quickly.

On the platform at the front stood a large raw-boned man. His receding white-gold hair gave him a wealth of brow and flowed down to his shoulders where it blended with a white-gold beard. The ever-present uniform was smoothed over a generous paunch. His eyes were a dazzling blue and his smile beamed beneficence. Softly illuminated by spotlights, he had the look of a biblical sage or an ancient Viking bound on a seafaring mission. He stretched out his arms dramatically and began to speak in a resonant voice.

'Welcome. A special welcome to all our new friends at the Morning Star sanctuary.' His eyes landed on various members of the audience, including the woman with the swooping sunglasses, and seemed to pause overlong on Leo. She looked down at her feet as his voice boomed above her.

'Sanctuary – an asylum, a refuge, a safe place where you can shed the dross and conflict of everyday life and focus on essentials, on the cosmic journey. A place where everything combines to re-invigorate the body, balance the psyche, awaken the spirit. All of us, with our various skills, are here to help you attain those ends, to help you evolve, to help you heal, to open new frontiers, to set you on the right path – the path of truth, of success.'

'Who's that?' Leo whispered to her neighbour.

The woman replied with a look that suggested she must be a Martian not to know. 'The Director. F. F. Hilton.'

Leo was about to pose another question, but the woman put a finger to her lips.

The Director's voice was soft now, so that the room itself seemed to strain to hear him.

'Many of you are here because you are in some kind of crisis and in search of health, an equilibrium. Life can be difficult. It is often hard to bear. In the midst of it we are too often like children; our desires are great burning passions which demand instant satisfaction. But desires change. That is the first point to take in on your evolutionary journey. What made us happy yesterday no longer does today. Cravings are impermanent.'

Leo leant forward as the giant of a man strode across the dais, addressing them now from its far corner.

'Poisons are at the source of unhappiness. They need to be expunged. The poison of ignorance that leads us blindly to believe that the next purchase, the next lover, the next job will bring us satisfaction or peace. Too often, it doesn't.'

He moved back to the centre of the platform and his voice rose theatrically. 'The poison of attachment. Attachment to a person, to status, to money, to a way of seeing, a pattern of behaviour which is repetitive, a compulsive habit. Such attachments trap us. We become possessed by our possessions.

'Now let me tell you why you are really here. You are here to learn to let go. To learn to relinquish your psychological habits – that armour of conditioning that has kept you trapped in blindness and misery.' He stretched out his arms as if to embrace them. His eyes rose to the light. 'Everything you do here will contribute to the evolution of this new, stronger you. Let me feel your gathered energy.'

Leo had stopped listening. It had hit her with a visceral blow, like a punch in the stomach. All the air had been knocked out of her. This man, this F. F. Hilton, was Isabel's father. She was certain of it. The eyes, the stature. Something about the set of the jaw as he walked down the steps of the dais now and along the far aisle of the lecture hall.

Watching him closer to, a second realization struck her. She had seen this man before in a different guise. He was not the white-garbed leader then.

His eyes landed on her and she averted her own, not too soon to see him nod with that inclination of the head that turned the gesture into a slight bow.

Did he know his daughter was dead? Leo wondered.

She looked back towards him. His gaze was elsewhere. It fell on a figure with a cap of short, wavy black hair some three rows in front of her. The figure turned suddenly to reveal a young face of wildly passionate beauty, high cheekbones, deep-set eyes, a generously curved mouth and the palest of matt skins. A flush crept up the girl's neck and suffused her face, as if she were a child who had been found out in some secretly sinful activity. A second later, she

415

pushed her chair back and bolted, intent on fleeing the Director's eyes. After a moment, he, too, was gone.

Heather, Leo suddenly noticed, had been standing beside him, and as she stared after him, her lips curled in an expression Leo couldn't read.

Meanwhile, the bullet-headed man she had sat next to at dinner was addressing them from the platform. Leo half listened to his words as she tried to stem her mounting confusion. F. F. Hilton was also the man she had seen talking to Paola Webster, and again to Daniel, at the Freud Museum. He had been black-suited then, his hair tied back in a ponytail, like some ageing Microsoft executive. Were they all in cahoots together?

'Take water,' the man on the platform was saying. 'We can say of water that it is a colourless liquid essential to life or a chemical substance made up of two parts hydrogen to one part oxygen. But is this really, and only, what water is? Splash it on your face, drink it, take a bath in it. Experience it through all your senses – sight, touch and taste. Feel the wetness. Then remember that you, too, are what water is, a mobile column of water. Water is your tissues and your blood; your heart, your lungs, your brain, your skin. It is not just something out there, but in here.' He pounded his heart, his stomach and his hips with abrupt force. 'There is no distinction between inner and outer.'

Leo gripped the edge of her chair. There had been no distinction between inner and outer for Isabel, either, but it had hardly been a happy lack. The water had been inside her, bloating her skin, stopping the action of her lungs, covering her in its force, killing her.

'You are earth, too – iron, copper, phosphorous, magnesium. Without these minerals you would die. Each of them is identical to the minerals in the earth. There is no real difference between the copper in your body and the copper in a pot. And all of these minerals come from the stars. We are stardust, star children. Not only the lights that twinkle in the heavens, the stars are also our flesh and bone.'

Leo scraped her chair back so loudly that her neighbours turned around. Without meeting their eyes, she brushed past knees and padded from the room.

Stardust, star children. Morning Star. Morgenstern.

It came to her that she needed to speak to Faraday urgently to find out what the autopsy had revealed. What was inside Isabel, apart from water, that had once been outside? Did it bear any resemblance to what had been inside Jill Reid?

In the chill air of the courtyard, she paused to roll up her trouser bottoms, which flapped around her feet and slowed her down. It was as she bent to reach their thick cotton that it flashed through her with the force of an epiphany. Hadn't that bloated corpse which wasn't Isabel worn the discoloured remnants of flapping trousers? A white shirt, too?

Disquiet flooded through her. Blood rang in her ears.

'Is there anything wrong?' William was suddenly in front of her.

'I need to telephone,' Leo said bluntly.

Disapproval glimmered in his eyes. 'We have no telephones here for guest use. Here we let go of such things. It is better that way.'

'But I need to,' Leo insisted.

'You will have to speak to Heather, then. Or

Olga. After the lecture.' His sigh was audible.

Leo made for her room. William's soft tread was right behind her. He reminded her about putting her things in store. It would do her good to shed unnecessary possessions.

Leo gave him the suit she had arrived in and her small store of jewellery just to get rid of him, then she sat down wearily on the bed.

No telephones for guest use. The words echoed in her ears, and with them came the sound of Isabel's voice, pitched in wryness now and tinged with a heart-rending weariness.

'Not easy to ring you and explain, Leo,' she murmured. 'Not easy.'

19

Leo dreamt. She dreamt she was in a steep tropical clime of lush vegetation and terraced rice paddies. Her father was with her, holding her hand as he urged her forward across a swaying footbridge. Beneath them the valley plunged into a winding river. She didn't want to cross over. She took tiny steps. Her feet were small, too, white in new trainers edged with red earth. Look straight ahead, her father advised. She did. On the far side of the gorge, she saw a brightly robed woman balancing a load on her head, one arm raised in a graceful curve. In the blink of an eye, the basket slipped. It fell to the ground with a clang. Like bells. Bells everywhere. And then the woman fell after it, tumbling, tumbling towards the swift flow of the river. She wanted to race after her, but her father held her back.

She woke with a start, dry-mouthed, the imprint of her father's hand still warm on hers and the bells echoing. At the edge of the window, against a flat grey expanse of sky, she made out the curve of a slope. It brought her back to where she was and alerted her to the gong's morning call.

She lay there, putting the pieces of her present self together again, assembling her thoughts for the day that awaited her. A knock at the door jarred her into complete wakefulness.

'Leonora. Your meeting with Heather is at nine, straight after breakfast. She will arrange your schedule. I shall wait for you in the dining hall.'

'I'll be there, William.' She forced brightness into her voice. 'Don't you worry.'

But Leo worried. Ever since she'd noticed last night that her whites bore a resemblance to the tattered trousers on Isabel's corpse, a host of suspicions had taken hold of her. She needed to talk to the Director immediately. Depending on what he said, she would share her fears with him. Or not. Someone in this establishment could well be implicated in Isabel's death. She was certain of it. She also needed to telephone Faraday.

'Leonora. So pleased we could find a place for you at such short notice.' Heather's cool blondness confronted her almost before William's knock had sounded.

Leo looked at her. There was no irony in the woman's voice or face.

'I guess I am, too,' Leo replied.

They were in an airy rectangular room on the top floor of the building. A single branch of gorse stood in a glass vase on the corner of a desk. On the floor there was a mat. From somewhere she heard the tinkle of chimes.

'I need to get some details since you're a first-time guest.' Heather sat down at the desk and motioned Leo to sit in the other chair. With brisk efficiency she grilled her on her medical history, her smoking and drinking habits, charted it on a neat form. She asked her to walk up and down, breathe deeply, touch her knees and her toes. Every now and again she placed a hand on her spine as she did so.

'Good. Now lie down, please.' She gestured to the mat.

'Why?'

'Please.'

Heather worked her hands up from Leo's ankle to knee, pressing hard as she went.

'Ouch,' Leo exclaimed.

'Good. I'm doubly glad you're here.'

'Why, is there something wrong?'

'A little less suspicion, Leonora, and all will go well.' Heather was busily filling in a schedule sheet. 'You're toxic. Lay off the coffee and tea. Drink a lot of water, at least a litre a day. I'm booking you in for deep massage, yoga, t'ai chi and, of course, daily meditation. That's first thing in the morning. You need it, believe me.'

'What did Iris do while she was here?' Leo asked abruptly.

A shadow passed over the woman's face. It was gone as quickly as it had come and she answered evenly, 'That's something you'll have to ask her.'

For a split-second Leo was about to blurt out that she couldn't ask her. Couldn't ask her because she was dead. She pulled the zipper on her mouth. Not yet. It wasn't time. 'What's F. F. Hilton's background?' she asked instead.

Heather's formidable eyebrow arched. Leo noticed that it was thick and matt, like mouse fur. 'That's a question to put to him. You'll be seeing him in a moment.' She handed Leo the schedule sheet. 'You fill in the rest of this with the Director. You're a privileged woman, Leonora. He doesn't always see first-time guests personally.'

An image of Hilton talking to Paola and then to Daniel at the launch party leapt into Leo's mind. 'My referral obviously had an effect on the murkiness of my aura,' she said with a touch of spite.

Heather refused the bait. She was looking just beyond her. 'The Director's office is on the other side of the stairs.'

Leo didn't move. 'I need to use a telephone, Heather. There's some business I left unfinished.'

'You're here to get away from business, Leonora. And Frederick Hilton is not a man to be kept waiting.'

The woman was already urging her through the door, where William lurked, her very own stalker.

'Please, I—'

'If it still feels so urgent after you've seen the Director, come back at . . . let's see' – Heather glanced down her schedule – 'four fifty.' She gave Leo her crisp, businesslike smile and turned to the woman who was coming up the stairs. 'Welcome back, Maxine.'

A few moments later Leo found herself in a lofty room with breathtaking views on three sides. She was in one of the building's eccentric gables, she realized. The entire extent of the grounds and the countryside beyond were spread before her. Below, the couple coming up the drive looked like children. In the middle distance, beyond the razor-straight divide of cypresses, she could see a small lake. White-clad figures moved slowly in its vicinity. That had to be the addiction clinic, she noted, and there, too, everyone wore the regulation uniform.

The room had all the makings of a panopticon. A panopticon with an interior designed by a West Coast minimalist. Vast sofas in thick linen of varying creamy stripes decked the large space. An off-white carpet straddled the glistening beech floor. The stretches of wall between the windows held geo-metrical abstracts in pastel shades which she determined, after a moment, might equally well be meditational symbols. One angle of the room was given over to a straight-edged desk of thick beech.

The Director emerged from a door behind it. Close to, he looked even bigger, a mountain of a man. The beneficent face beamed at her, like a child's drawing of the sun, as he stretched out his hand.

'Leonora. Welcome to sanctuary.'

Leo offered him a tentative smile. He took her hand and grasped it warmly.

'I wanted to see you personally to ascertain that we offer you the best possible week here. I haven't yet had the opportunity to speak to Dr Lukas.'

Leo had an image of Daniel refusing to pick up his telephone or return calls.

'Am I correct in assuming that he referred you here principally because of the trauma group I run? That meets in the hour before lunchtime.'

Leo swallowed the protest she had been about to make and nodded. She wasn't here to protest, but to investigate.

He walked back to his desk and, as he did so, she took in his profile – the distance between eye and brow, the slight flare of the nose, the smooth expanse of cheek before it edged into the white-gold beard. Yes, if she whittled away the flesh, the resemblance was definitely there.

She was working herself up to posing the question when she noticed his feet. They were oddly small for his bulk, and dapper in soft leather. They brushed the floor with a distinctively flat-footed amble. She stared at them with a sudden frown.

His polished voice called her back. 'Tell me a little about yourself, Leonora. What troubles you?'

He was sitting behind his desk now, gazing at her with that bountiful smile.

'Morning Star,' Leo heard herself say. 'Morgenstern in German. Such a good name for a foundation. Was it yours?'

He hid his visible consternation with a sage's stroking of the beard. 'No, no. A friend.'

'The bright morning star, day's harbinger,' Leo quoted from some store of memory, cloaking the apprehension which had come over her with his denial. 'A good name for a sanctuary. Milton, I think.'

'I'm not terribly familiar with his work, Leonora. I'll take your word for it.'

'I think it's Lucifer's star, too.'

'Let's get back to you, shall we?' The smile was wearing thin. 'Tell me about yourself. Your troubles, I imagine, aren't in the stars.'

'The trouble is anxiety, really.' Leo giggled. 'Maybe that is in the stars these days. I need to get a better grip on myself. I have these visions. Fear. Panic. It takes me over. Dr Lukas thought . . .'

'Have you ever been raped?'

Leo shook her head fiercely.

'No. Then burgled, perhaps. Assaulted?'

He was staring at her, examining her closely. It made her avert her eyes. Beneath the desk she spied those neatly shod feet again. Something gnawed at the edge of her consciousness and with the sensation came that laugh again. Isabel. Isabel who was everywhere here. Present, despite her death. More present than in those weeks when Leo had been oppressed by the mystery of her absence. As if she had come home to her in death.

424

Leo blinked away the clutch of tears.

'I think I'd like you to dream for me, Leonora.' Frederick Hilton glanced at his watch. 'Yes, there's time now. It'll help me to help you. There are techniques, you know. Ways.'

Before she could say anything, he had ushered her through the door and shut it behind them. The room they were in now was small and dim, like a cave or a womb, with one rounded wall. There were no windows. The only light came from two high rectangular slits, like crossbow recesses. It fell on his desk, illuminating a row of stones, honey-white, pale grey, striated and granite-dark. They lay there like so many ancient presences.

He gestured her towards a cream-clad divan in the shadow of the wall and sat down opposite her, half lolling in a throne-like chair. His hands were clasped behind his large head.

'Since you're interested in names, let's think about yours. You like to be called Leo, don't you?' He smiled at her again, his lips pinkly moist above the white of his beard. 'Is that the kind of Leo who roars mightily or the kind who protects her cubs against all comers?'

Leo tried to still her jangled nerves. How had he guessed she preferred to be called Leo?

From somewhere in the air, Isabel's musky perfume invaded her nostrils, together with a heavy scent of perspiration, a clogged odour of fear which seemed to rise from the recesses of the divan. She prodded a strand of hair away from her eyes and met his. They were wide now, the pupils pebble bright. Isabel's eyes. Or was she imagining things? She tried to force the face into the remembered magazine photograph. It was too fleshy to fit, yet she didn't think she was wrong. Had he denied Isabel, too?

'Leo?'

'A little of both, perhaps,' she rushed to answer him, unable to leave his eyes.

'Good. Yin and yang.' He leant towards her and she giggled again.

'And yours is Hilton. Like James. The inventor of Shangri-La.'

She had said it off the top of her head, but his abrupt guffaw made her think she had struck some dissonant chord.

'Most people think of hotels. But let's go back to you, Leo. You suffer from excessive anxiety, you tell me. It impedes your roar and hampers your ability to protect. In my long experience, I have found that this kind of debilitating anxiety grows not only out of sexual fears, but out of a fear of death, of dying. I think we need to travel to the source of your anxiety and uncover it. Travel inwards to your internal family, the people and forces who inhabit you.' His voice had taken on a lulling quality. 'Travel back, too, perhaps, to the origin of your problems in a past life, to some forgotten trauma, some sin or crime or violent act for which you are still unconsciously atoning. So that it controls your life by stealth. The long perspective helps the healing. As, of course, does the eradication. Forgetting is important.' That disturbing gaze was fixed on her face.

'Travel back to a past life . . .' Leo murmured. 'I don't think . . .'

'Don't resist, Leo.' His eyes flickered. 'I don't like working the resistance. I'm not a Freudian. Co-operation will be far more useful. Did you dream last night, Leo?'

'Yes,' she began uneasily. 'I dreamt of my father

426

leading me by the hand across a swaying bridge.'

'Excellent. A wise older man guiding you. We all need a father to guide us.'

She would ask him now, she thought. Ask him directly. Isabel's father.

Something stopped her. Maybe it was Isabel, hovering protectively at her side. Or the stone he was holding in the palm of his hand, turning it over and over, like some mysterious weapon. She shivered. His fingers were small, like his feet, his nails neatly manicured, the half-moons perfectly outlined.

'Look at this rock, Leo. It's so beautiful. See how its history is etched in its markings.' His voice was soft now, almost inaudible, a gentle chant. 'Layers and layers of recorded history to be recovered at will. Look, look at this shape here, the imprint of a fossil, a past life . . .'

It came to Leo with a clang louder than any hourly gong that she was being hypnotized. She jumped up. 'I . . . This isn't what I've come for. No hypnosis. I'm not a good subject.' She managed to say it without a note of panic, but her hands were clammy.

His face darkened. A muscle played in his cheek. The stone felt the grip of his fingers. A controlled ferocity. He really didn't like resistance.

'But Leo,' he said in his genial way. 'Hypnosis is the way to truth. If Dr Lukas has sent you to me, it is precisely for that. That is what I am known for.'

'No, no. It wasn't for that. It was for the place itself, an asylum, a rest cure, the calm,' Leo invented.

'You are a recalcitrant young woman. Lie down again, please.'

She had a feeling that, if she didn't, he might push her. She stretched out again slowly. Her head had just reached the cushion, when a beep sounded insistently.

With a scowl, he reached beneath his white shirt and brought out a pager. 'You rest here, Leo. Relax. I'll be back soon. Dream another dream for me. Rich, evocative.'

His hand rested for a moment on her forehead, shrouding her eyes, and then light dazzled her as he walked into his bright outer office. She saw him reach for the telephone before he shut the door again. A few moments later she heard the undeniable thud of the solid door of the outer office.

Silence followed.

She waited for a full, long minute, then rose quickly. This was her chance. The desk drawers. She tried them one by one. The top one slid open to reveal nothing of more significance than an assortment of fantastic fish lures ranged in a box. She wondered if these, too, were used for inducing hypnosis. Hardly necessary, she imagined, but maybe patients liked the external ploys. Another drawer contained an assortment of mandalas. The last and largest drawer was locked.

She had no idea what she was looking for, but she knew that it was necessary. Isabel was urging her on, forcing her into bravery.

Behind the divan she noticed a sliding door. She slid it open. This was more like it. She was in a store-room of some kind. There were no windows. Boxes lined part of a wall. Two filing cabinets, too ugly and official for his perfectly arranged rooms, stood next to them. She tried the drawers. All were securely locked. She swore beneath her breath, then paused to listen again.

Everything was quiet, though the soft-soled shoes

everyone wore produced an occasional squeal against the floorboards. She had to be vigilant.

She prodded open the lid of one of the narrow boxes and saw a host of small bottles ranged in neat rows. Medication. With a glance over her shoulder, she put one of the bottles in her pocket, then quickly replaced the lid of the box. On the other side of the small room, packets of what looked like stationery were stacked. One was open. Without bothering to peer, she folded a sheet into her pocket, then moved to the far corner.

The light here was so dim that she stumbled, her feet tangling in what appeared to be rags or old sheets. She pushed these aside and suddenly a luminous face peered up at her from the floor. One of those happy-face stickers that Becca liked to place here and there.

Leo scrabbled around to find what it adhered to. A second tiny face jumped out at her and, simultaneously, she felt a smooth synthetic surface, a square object. She tugged it towards her. A computer. Her heart was making too much noise. A Mac, and next to it was a second machine. A notebook. Her own. Certainty coursed through her, riding roughshod over her confusion. Those small feet, she remembered them now. For a split-second her eyes had been level with them on the floor of the loft.

She lifted Isabel's computer. That was the one she had to get out of here.

She was already at the sliding door when voices stopped her progress. They were coming from the large outer office. She stilled her thumping heart. She had time to stretch out on the couch, but then she would have to leave the computer behind. No.

No. And she couldn't face him. Why had he broken into the loft? What had he been looking for?

She lurched back behind the door. Her pulse louder than the voices, she inched it to, leaving only the tiniest crevice for her fingers. She held her breath.

The voices were moving closer.

'Not now, Heather. I have a patient in there.' The Director's voice.

'Still that Gould woman? You know she came here earlier in the week asking about Iris Morgenstern?'

Leo heard a door opening. The voices grew clearer. They were in the den-like room. She forced herself into utter immobility.

'Damn it, she's gone. I'll have to catch up with her later.'

'Good. Then we can talk. You've been very elusive these last weeks, Fred. What are you up to?' Heather's voice was heavy with accusation.

She sounded, Leo suddenly thought, like a jealous mistress.

'Nothing to worry your sweet self over.' Hilton oozed charm. Leo could imagine the seductive set of his heavy face.

'You said you'd be back early on Monday. You didn't get back until Wednesday. I don't like that. Where were you?'

'You know better than to ask.'

A hint of menace had come into his tone. Heather stood her ground.

'I'm asking.'

'Meetings. Drumming up business. This and that.'

'They weren't in your diary.'

'Heather, if you get up to your old tricks, I'll have to punish you.' A harsh laugh. 'In fact, I went to Paola Webster's party. Good for clientele, as you can see. An instant referral from Daniel Lukas. His first. Important that.'

'I wouldn't have found a space for her.'

'You leave those decisions to me.'

'That Morgenstern woman was nothing but trouble. She stomped about the place as if she owned it. And she'll publish something vitriolic, you wait and see. Nor did she pay her bill.'

'She will. It was a sudden departure.'

'And why was that? Exactly what methods did you use on her, Fred? I don't like it. And I don't know why you asked me to have that diskette sent to her. If she left it behind, too bad.'

Leo stopped her sudden rush of breath. The diskette with the map sites had come from here. Why? Nothing made any sense.

'Now, Heather, spite is unnecessary.'

'Azleck found her prowling around next door, you know.'

'Drop it, Heather. I told you not to worry your pretty little head about her.' It was an order. Silence followed. Leo tried to shift her tense posture without making a sound.

'There's something else, Fred,' Heather continued stubbornly. Leo could visualize the determined set of her shoulders.

'I think it was too early to bring April over from the other side. She's totally unstable. These multiple personalities—'

'It's an experiment.'

'We don't need any more experiments, Fred. I don't know what kind of deals you've been doing with your drug companies, but I don't want a repetition of what happened last time.' Heather's lowered voice carried the threat now.

431

'You never learn, Heather. You never learn that people are stupid. And that there's excitement in science. Adventure. Put something in and see what comes out. Presto.'

His laugh had a manic tinge and Heather's voice was shrill in return.

'I don't want to know about that.'

'We're partners now, Heather. You know how much I depend on you.'

'Too much for what you give. You're fucking her, aren't you?'

'Now, now. Come here, my jealous little vixen, and Daddy will make it all better. Come. Come. The old lap still has room for you.'

Leo heard the slight shudder of springs.

'Yes, you know what Daddy likes. No lessons needed for little pussycat Heather. Tell me a dirty story, Heather, while I scratch those furry little ears of yours.'

A sound like a mewl reached Leo, and then a tiny child's voice and a rhythmic creak. The air around her seemed to grow tepid, close. It cloyed at her nostrils. Breathing was difficult. She inched away from her place at the door towards the far corner of the storeroom. Her eyes had grown used to the dark. The glint of light through the crack played off the filing cabinets. Behind her the creaking grew more insistent. And then, just when she thought she could bear no more, she saw it, as if Isabel were standing there and pointing the way. A latch. A small door, like those leading to servants' quarters.

With sudden swift decision, she picked up the computer she was certain was Isabel's and wedged it against her chest, beneath the loosened belt of the uniform. Trying to keep pace with the sounds behind her, she unhooked the latch, eased the door open and squeezed through.

She was at the top of a narrow staircase. Light poured in from a small, barred window. She adjusted her eyes to it and crept down, her arms firmly crossed over her chest.

The stairs came to an end after one floor and gave on to a door at the side. Her pulse jagged, she turned the knob. There was no way back.

A rank, feral odour attacked her, though the room she was in glistened white and chrome, too bright. Counters topped with vats and instruments stretched everywhere. At one of them a woman, syringe in hand, was bent over what looked like a rat. Leo gasped, despite herself, and the woman turned round. She frowned.

'Sorry, sorry to disturb,' Leo stammered, her eyes wide at the scuttle of creatures in a cage at her side. 'The Director sent . . . Azleck . . .'

The woman examined her for what felt like too long. Then, at a squeal from the trapped animal, she shrugged and gestured her towards the far door. Her attention was back on her work even before Leo had reached it.

Leo walked down a long corridor, punctuated by the slatted internal windows of a hospital. She was, she realized, in the prohibited section of the building. The addiction clinic. It was too tricky to try and explore now. She had to get the computer back to her room. She kept her eyes straight ahead.

A man in a doctor's coat emerged from one of the rooms. She tilted her head in a quick nod and continued on her course. Not too quickly, that would attract suspicion. An even pace, a look of purpose, one arm propped casually against her chest. She turned a corner.

She could feel Isabel smiling at her, winking once in joyous complicity.

At the far end of the corridor, beyond a staircase, she saw what looked like an external door. She would try that. She suddenly longed for the outdoors as avidly as a prisoner in solitary confinement.

The bar wouldn't give. The door was locked. A tremor went through her. She turned away, and was halfway down the corridor again when she heard the unmistakable squeak of a heavy door behind her. She rushed back.

A painfully thin woman with strands of lank hair falling over her face stared at her with glazed, frightened eyes. 'Hey, we're not supposed to . . .'

Leo was already slipping through the door. She rushed down a short flight of stairs. Clean, crisp air. The sky. Blue now. High. She breathed deeply, then paused to look around her. She was uncertain of her whereabouts. She seemed to be at the back of the far wing of the building. She guessed that she would have to walk right round it to get to the front door. But no path led to her left along the back. The only lane led to her right, and that, she guessed, would take her into the central part of the addiction clinic grounds. From there, she would somehow have to cut through the thickly ranked cypresses. The grounds were bound to be peopled.

Her only alternative was to head straight up the cliff. What looked like a narrow trail, flanked by gorse, climbed in front of her. Where would it abut? No matter. Better that lonely track than the hundred eyes she would otherwise meet. She shifted the computer into a more comfortable position, took the risk of winding the black strap round her neck and began to make her way up.

The path was steep. Each step dislodged loose earth and a tumble of stone. She slipped and clung to a shrub, recognizing too late the prick of gorse. She sucked her fingers and steadied herself, wishing she had four feet rather than two. The bulk of the computer in her middle distorted her balance. Like a crab, she moved sideways as the trail grew almost vertical. Another dozen feet and she caught her breath.

She was on top of a jagged headland. The wind gusted fiercely, whipping at her hair and clothes. Before her, the sea snapped and roared and foamed against rocky outcrops. Her mind whirled with the water's frenzy. She peered down the vertiginous incline. Dizziness overtook her. The sea's lash, the shriek of the gulls, the whistling wind, all conspired to create the sound of the name. Is-a-bel. It raged and moaned around her. Here. It had happened here.

Leo stared and stared, then veered away from the hallucinatory power of the call. Her senses were playing tricks on her. She had no evidence. She forced herself to turn left, to keep her eyes away from the sea's turbulence, to follow the twisting contours of the precipice, but the sensation of certainty wouldn't leave her.

In the distance, a lone figure appeared, marching in her direction. She tucked the strap of the computer beneath her shirt. But the man disappeared from view before she had taken ten steps. There must be another path leading downhill. Good. She kept her eyes firmly on the ground, trying to blot out the clamour of wind and sea and mind.

And then Isabel was suddenly beside her, a whimsical smile on her face, her hair blowing tendrils

435

20

A white-clad group were performing t'ai chi under the spread of a beech. Water lilies floated on the surface of a small pond. Leo paused to get her bearings, then fixed her eyes determinedly on the middle distance and prayed that she would meet neither Hilton, Heather, or William before she reached the refuge of her room.

A young woman was sitting behind the counter in the entrance hall.

Leo nodded briefly in response to her quizzical look, then, keeping her pace even, made her way up the stairs.

At last she was at her door. She closed it quickly behind her and, for good measure, wedged the single chair firmly under the knob.

Perspiration had gathered in her armpits. She could sniff the sharp smell of her own fear. Unsteadily, she placed the computer on the small windowside table and unzipped the bag. Had it been whipped from Isabel because it contained the material for her exposé? Whipped away with her life? Or had she left it behind, impelled to flee the sanctuary in whatever turmoil of emotion?

Had Frederick Hilton, the intruder in the loft, taken her own computer thinking it was a second one of Isabel's? He would have found out differently once he had switched it on. He would also, undoubtedly, have learnt her name – Leo, signed at the end of letters – though not the name Gould, under which she had registered. Had he recognized her from the loft? Was that why he had questioned her about being burgled and assaulted, wanting to know, too, whether she recognized him? Hence the hypnosis.

Leo forced away cascading thoughts that left only dread in their wake and plugged the computer into the socket. The screen showed the basic icons, but when she tried to access documents and files, one after another, they were empty.

Wiped. Everything had been wiped. She slammed her fist on the table and stared at the screen in bleak incomprehension. All this, and now nothing.

But files could be retrieved. How? She swore in frustration, wishing Norfolk to her side. Or Becca, who had painstakingly tried to explain the ins and outs of programs to her. Becca. She needed to ring Becca. She hadn't spoken or written to her in too many days. But there was no phone on her desk here.

Desolately, Leo clicked on each of the icons in turn. Tools came up, and with it a list. Norton Utilities. That rang a bell. Norton. Almost as good as Norfolk. Leo chivvied herself, remembering how Becca had told her something complicated about a retrieval system for lost and binned files. She clicked on it. Not wiped. Painstakingly, she read the instructions.

The knock on the door burst in on her more fiercely than a gale.

'Yes,' she said breathlessly.

'You are there, Leo. Good.'

Leo rushed to grasp the doorknob just as it

began to turn. 'I'm just changing, William.'

'I need to take you down to the kitchen.'

'What?'

'Didn't Heather explain? Everyone does—'

Leo cut him off. She couldn't afford an argument now. 'Give me five minutes, William. I'll meet you by the stairs.'

She listened carefully to make sure she heard the slight squeak of his step, then she swiftly wrapped the computer in a shirt and placed it in her case. She was already in the corridor when she remembered the contents of her pockets. She turned back to empty them, and paused for a second to look at the sheet of stationery she had nicked. Ritter Pharmaceuticals. The name meant nothing to her. She tossed the sheet into her bag, together with the small bottle. Her pulse was racing again. She would have to find some excuse to spend time in her room later.

'Where have you been, Leonora? I came to find you for your t'ai chi hour and you weren't here.'

'The Director kept me.' Leo gave him what she hoped was a bright smile.

'I see.' William accepted it. 'Heather probably explained to you about how we like everyone to participate in the running of the place. It helps to forge bonds. You've been assigned to the kitchen.'

'Oh.' Leo was vague. 'I think I left my schedule sheet in the Director's office.'

William sighed, as if he expected no different from her. 'I'll see what I can do.'

The kitchen was a large, long room adjacent to the dining hall. A low and welcome buzz of conversation played amidst its occupants, punctuated by the clatter of pots and the whirr of blenders. Near her, some ten people stood on opposite sides of two long steel-topped counters, which reminded Leo uncannily of the lab she had seen. The people were chopping vegetables and arranging them in bowls and platters.

Another glistening counter heaved with plates and cutlery. On the far side of the room there was more activity. Trays were being loaded onto trolleys. Near the windows, a team in chefs' hats bent over cookers. A lingering smell of boiling cauliflower and cabbage pervaded the air.

Introduced by William, Leo took her place at the first counter beside a willowy woman with a sophisticated sweep of auburn hair and pale, unseeing eyes. She was peeling carrots with a sleepwalker's automatic motion. A second pile lay in front of Leo.

'My least-favourite activity,' Leo grumbled, picking up the peeler.

The woman turned to her. A grin animated her face. 'Can't say I like it much, either, in everyday life. But my platter arrangements didn't make the grade, so I got moved over here.'

'Oh?'

'Kathy just doesn't have an eye for symmetry,' the woman opposite them said. She was plump, with vivid pink cheeks her hair pulled back in a girlish Alice band, even though she must have been in her mid-thirties. 'Beauty is important.'

'Sarah thinks that if her dishes are beautifully enough presented, darling Alister, he of the muscled cranium, will pop into her room at night to display more naked beauty.'

'Kathy! Stop it!' Sarah dropped the radish she had been shaping into a flower.

'True, isn't it? So when did he last visit?'

Sarah stalked away, only to come back a moment

440

later with a boxful of cucumbers, which she dumped in front of Kathy. 'Jealousy is a poison,' she intoned. 'Toxic. A compulsive habit to be shed.'

'How long have you both been here?' Leo asked.

'Two weeks for me, three for her,' Kathy responded. 'But it's my third visit. Don't know why I keep coming back. Not really. But I do. Guess it beats Prozac. And Frederick Hilton is magic.'

Leo peeled and nodded. 'My friend Iris told me it was quite a place. Did you bump into her?'

'Iris? The Australian woman?' Sarah looked up at her.

Leo nodded.

'She caused a real stir. The t'ai chi master had a pash for her. But Iris, it turned out, preferred women.'

'You don't know that, Sarah.'

'Don't I?' Sarah's cheeks turned even pinker. 'Well, that short-term woman, the one who treated the place like a health farm and kept trying to sunbathe during meditation, spent a whole night in her room and constantly turned up there. I know. I was next door. That's why they sent them both away.'

'What was the woman's name?' Leo jabbed her thumb with the peeler as she remembered Paola Webster's insinuations.

'Iris wasn't a particular friend of yours, was she?' Kathy asked, emphasizing the word particular. 'I only ask 'cause they're quite liberal here, but homosexuality's a definite no-no.' She eyed Leo with visible concern.

Leo shook her head.

'How are we doing here, ladies?' One of the men in a chef's hat admonished them. 'A little more concentration, please.'

441

They worked silently for a few minutes. A tray-laden trolley creaked past them.

'Where do the trays go?' Leo asked.

'The other side. They get special food. It smells ghastly.' Kathy wrinkled her tiny nose. 'But they get to arrive by helicopter sometimes. Very grand. Everything has its advantages.'

Leo looked at her aghast. Daniel Lukas leapt into her mind. She wished she could speak to him, query him about Hilton. But there was something else to be gleaned here. After a few moments she began again, 'Can you remember the name of Iris's friend?'

Sarah gave her a searing look and returned to the arrangement of her platters. 'Something ordinary,' she said abruptly. 'Something like Ann or Mary or Jill. That was it. Jill.'

Leo gouged the soft part of her thumb again. She watched the blood rise and trickle. It trickled onto her sleeve, bright red against a landscape of white.

Behind her she heard a sob. She turned. There was no-one. Maybe it had been the sound of her own grief.

Leo swallowed a few forkfuls of food, then stole to the door of the dining hall as inconspicuously as possible.

At the threshold, William's lanky form blocked her passage.

'I'll show you to the group-therapy room, Leo, if you've finished.'

'I'm too tired for therapy,' she groaned. 'I need to rest. I didn't sleep well last night.'

He waved a sheet of lined paper in front of her. 'I fetched this for you from the Director's office. He made a point of it. He said I was definitely to bring you there.'

Leo froze. She was in no state to face Frederick Hilton. Had he already noticed that Isabel's computer was gone? No, she mustn't panic. She had covered her tracks and left the blanket more or less as she had found it.

'And you're scheduled for a massage later. That will relax you.'

'I desperately need a breath of air.'

'I'll come with you. We have the time. After today, you know,' he said as if he had read her mind, 'when you're familiar with things, I won't be looking after you any more.'

'Thank you, William. You've been assiduous in your duty.'

He bowed slightly, immune to her irony.

The group met on the other side of the large dining hall in what might once have been a breakfast room, but was now denuded of all features. The linen blinds were drawn. There were no pictures on the white-washed wall. The three people who had already gathered when Leo arrived sat in silence. Five more soon trooped in to find a place round the circle, each of them eschewing the large armchair which patently awaited Frederick Hilton's bulk. He didn't smile when he came in. The group was serious business.

His voice fell into the expectant hush like a stone into a pond, sending off palpable ripples of disquiet.

'I want you to introduce yourselves and tell us the secret or thought that has most preoccupied you over the last months.' He paused.

Leo caught his glance for a moment, then quickly averted her eyes.

'Leonora. We'll begin with you.'

Leo stifled a gulp and sat mutely. She gazed at the

floor. It was covered with a hairy straw matting.

'We're waiting, Leonora.'

'I'm American. I come from New York.' She hesitated. Then, with a sense that Isabel was willing her on, she threw down the gauntlet. 'My best friend just died. Her body turned up not all that far from here, a bloated, mottled corpse.'

There was a collective gasp in the room. Leo was staring at Frederick Hilton. Consternation ruffled his sanguine features. It was rapidly mastered. Only his hands betrayed any fugitive emotion. They were tight on the arms of the oak chair, the short fingers white against the wood. Was he surprised by the fact of Isabel's death, Leo wondered, or at the fact that her body had now been discovered? She watched him closely.

'Poor Leonora,' Kathy, the willowy woman she had met in the kitchen, murmured. She leant forward, as if she wanted to put her arm round her.

'A friend of mine died last year,' a man opposite offered, raising elbows from knees and the head he had until now kept determinedly bowed. 'I felt like hell. My turn next, I thought. Still think.'

'And you are?' Hilton prompted.

'James. From London. I'm here 'cause I'm stressed out.'

'Her real secret is that she's bent,' Sarah, the plump woman with the Alice band, interjected before he could go on.

'And your secret, Sarah?' Kathy came back. Her eyes flashed. Her posture was rigid. 'Don't tell me. Your secret is that you're a first-class bitch who wants to fuck everything in sight. Or maybe that's not a secret.'

Silence fell on the room. From somewhere a breeze ruffled a blind. A fly set up a buzz.

Frederick Hilton cleared his throat. 'Sarah, I want you to consider for a moment why you feel the need to attack Leo. Is it because she's uncomfortably new to the group? Is it because she's attractive?' He threw Leo a sudden complicit smile. 'Or is it because her words held all of our attention? Don't answer me now. I want to return to Leo for a moment.'

The silence fell again as all eyes focused on Leo.

'Where do you feel the loss of your friend, Leo?'

'Where?' Leo baulked. She looked around the room as if she might spy Isabel appearing from the corner of a blind. Her friend had been in here, of that she was certain.

'Yes, where?'

'Her shoulders. They're all hunched up.' A spectacled man to Leo's side, who hadn't spoken before, answered for her. He had the thin, intent face of a chess player. He took off his glasses and wiped them with an obsessive motion, concentrating on his fingers as he went on, as if by rote. 'She's carrying a heavy burden. The dead are weighing on her. She needs to shield her body from their weight, their blows. We can help her exorcize them.'

'Thank you, Simon. Thank you for your flow of expertise.' Frederick Hilton's face bore no gratitude. He rose from his chair with the alacrity of a far lighter man and positioned himself behind Leo.

She cringed as his hands touched her shoulders and pushed down on them.

'She doesn't want you to touch her. Can't you see that?' Sarah blurted out.

He paid no attention. His fingers dug into Leo's shoulders with the force of a blunt instrument. 'What blows do you fear most, Leonora?' he asked in his low, chanting voice. 'Blows from your parents? Your partner? Or yourself? Self-punishing blows. The blows of guilt. For not having been good enough to your friend, understanding enough. Before she died. Before she became a bloated, mottled corpse.'

Leo felt a wave of nausea attack her stomach. She scraped back her chair and, without a backward glance, fled the room.

She didn't stop to return Heather's greeting on the stairs. She didn't stop until the chair was barricaded against her door. She threw herself on the bed and tried to contain her panic.

She couldn't leave now, she told herself, although her legs ached for motion. If she were stopped at the gates with Isabel's computer, all would be lost. She would have discovered nothing. And she would have doubly betrayed her friend.

No. Before she could leave she had to read those missing files, or somehow, at least, find out why they had been erased.

After several false starts, Leo at last managed to get Norton to perform its work of retrieval. She scrolled down the long list of files and noted that the last large bulk of deletions had all taken place on a single date: 3 May. That must have been a Sunday, Leo calculated. The day before the loft had been broken into. The day before her first session with Daniel. The day on which Heather had insisted Isabel had left the sanctuary.

Leo entered the first file and scrolled down, stopping erratically to read snippets here and there as they leapt before her eyes. She didn't know quite what she was looking for. All she knew was that there was an urgency to the task. At any moment someone could break in on her.

It was a large file and seemed to contain a portion of Isabel's notes on GM foods and related experimentation into pesticides and fertilizers, as well as covert action plans. On a hunch, Leo ran a search on Jill Reid, but the name didn't come up, though Plantagen did on numerous occasions, as did Bioworld International. Norfolk would want to see this. He could go through it more carefully.

Leo clicked back into Norton and quickly retrieved the first of two files labelled MS, which she rightly assumed referred to Morgenstern. The writing here was sketchy and contained what seemed to be quotations from newspapers and records of conversations. They detailed a legal case, quashed on grounds of insufficient evidence, against the addiction centre in Seattle, brought by a certain Tom Rushton on behalf of his son, and alleging that the centre was carrying out illicit drug trials without the informed consent of patients. A death had occurred.

Leo sped on until she found a brief paragraph in bold. 'F. F. Hilton, Frank Frederick Hilton aka Alexander Morgenstern. Name change registered in Washington State, October 1975. Married Ida MacInnes, 1982 (bigamy?), sister to multimillionaire J. P. MacInnes.'

The knot in her stomach tightened. She moved quickly on to the second MS file.

'Gotcha!' it began. 'Carla has come through. The Morgenstern Foundation was set up in 1974 in Chicago with a bequest stipulated in the will of Dr Adam Morgenstern. The sum of $3.5 million was left to one Alexander Morgenstern for the purposes of establishing it. He set it up, was listed as a trustee, then moved and changed his name. Why?'

Leo scrolled through a list of questions and

follow-ups, then stopped to read a paragraph twice.

'Have been ringing the list of Morgensterns in the Chicago phone directory. Came up trumps with an old lady, a cousin by marriage of Dr Adam Morgenstern. Told her I was researching the foundation. Had to seduce her into chat. She told me there had been consternation in the family after Adam Morgenstern's death. A nephew no-one had ever heard of had turned up a few years before Adam's death. He claimed to be the son of A. Morgenstern's brother, lost and presumed dead in the Second World War, a death Adam had escaped. Adam left the purported nephew the largest part of his fortune to set up a foundation in his lost brother's name. Bingo! What no-one knows, and I haven't been able to find out yet, is whether the relationship was genuine or invented. The old lady was pretty sure it was a con.'

Towards the end of the file there was another note in bold.

'In 1986, Progene Pharmaceuticals (mentioned in the trial proceedings) made a large charitable donation to the Morgenstern Foundation. One of their directors is named as J. P. MacInnes. In 1992, Ritter Pharmaceuticals, a subsidiary, made a hefty donation to the Morning Star Foundation. Ritter also works out of Australia. Worth a check. (Contact Norfolk.)'

Leo paused to let this sink in, then moved into another file, this one labelled 'PW Diary'. Only after she had browsed through a few pages did it come to her that these were Isabel's notes on her sessions with Paola Webster.

There were graphic accounts here of Isabel's unhappy life as a small girl in Australia. It made Leo think of Isabel's book on childhood and gave her another sense of the impetus that may have lain behind it.

The file also contained commentary, much of which, as Leo scrolled towards the bottom, had an acerbic edge.

'Paola has helped me to so many vivid memories. The details are truly miraculous, as if I were evoking them for the page. Imagining them in my best prose, perhaps, for her enthusiastic ears. Doesn't she find it as odd as I do that in these memories I can see myself from behind and above, as if I were a cameraman on a crane working for an astute director? Yes, I can see my blond curls, the dimples at the backs of my knees. Can see myself from above, lying down on the bed, a poor little prostrate beast. Truth in 360 degrees. I don't think so. I really don't think so. That little girl is no more or less me than Alice in Wonderland. Mustn't allow myself to be taken over by the voyage through the looking glass.'

A later paragraph read, 'I know that I am colluding with Paola, yet while I am doing it, it feels real, and the reality has an effect on me. Half of me emphatically believes that Elinor really did kill him. Why not? It's as possible as anything else in the past. The result is that I've secretly started to think he was wonderful. My lost father invades my dreams, grows ever larger and more appealing. This isn't what Paola wants at all. She wants me to hate my parents equally. For all her enthusiasm, her universe is based on hatred. And it's taking its toll on me. I've become afraid of all those dreadful forces impinging on me, tearing me apart. Men tearing me apart. Women. Strangers in the street. Keep them out. Keep everything out.'

Tears plucked at Leo's eyes. She wiped them away.

No time now. No time. She had to see if there was anything here about her friend's last days.

'Tell me, Isabel. Tell me,' she murmured as if her friend were in the room with her. She moved into the next file. DL – Daniel Lukas. A diary again, sparser this time. She jumped to its end.

'The goodbye was over the telephone. I timed it for my birthday: 10 September.'

So Daniel hadn't lied about that. Leo's mind reeled with too many thoughts. No time.

She studied the list of files again, still unsure what she was looking for. The words 'Journal – Winter Spring' appeared before her, and she clicked on it. As she read, tears filled her eyes again, half blinding her to Isabel's words, but not to the terrible play of her emotions.

What leapt out from the text with a grim clarity was her friend's internal state. Since her mother's death and her aunt's revelations, Isabel had been walking dangerously close to the edge. She was in the grip of an obsession which translated itself into the jerky prose of entries that detailed her search for her father and her arrival at the sanctuary.

Predictably, Isabel had broken the rules. She had used her computer here to make hurried notes on the workings of not only the sanctuary, but the addiction centre. It seemed that she had intended to come here for only a few days to check F. F. Hilton out and then join Leo in New York.

What had kept her at the sanctuary was less clear – her attempt to penetrate the secret life of the addiction clinic, her mounting fixation on Frederick Hilton, or the savage tearing apart of defences which had gone on in the trauma group and counselling sessions. Whichever it was, Isabel had felt unable to leave.

One of the entries read, 'I thought I'd be safe when I found him, free of the buffeting ghosts. Alexander Morgenstern. F. F. Hilton. Mr Kurtz. Me. The bad me. Evil. Sunny surface. Worms inside. A viper's nest. Wriggling. A rancid stench. Malign. Kill them off. This time for real. For good. Yes.'

Two entries invoked Leo's name, almost with a kind of sorrow, though never with less than friendship. Leo, Isabel felt, couldn't understand the precipice on which Isabel hovered, the flailing ghosts, the painful whirl of fragments which had become her mind, the hatred which oozed from her every pore.

'I can, Isabel,' Leo murmured into the void, then shivered as she read, 'I've told him. He denied it. He denies me. I don't know why. Maybe my unexpected arrival activates his own spectres. Maybe he thinks I'm after his money – in order to set up the F. F. Hilton Foundation. Hah! Whatever the case, he won't acknowledge me. He refuses to admit who he is. Who I am. The man is a fiend. A raver. He wants to murder and create. He'd like to kill me off. For a second time. As he did in memory. He won't. I won't let him. I'm going to win this one.'

A trembling took Leo over. She had to force herself to read on.

Then there was a letter.

Dearest Auntie,

After Mother's death, when you pulled the curtains back to reveal the family secrets, you know I was angry at you. Why tell me at all, if your promise to her of silence meant that you had to wait so long? I understand that you didn't want to die with the lies clutching at your throat. I understand, too, that, in your

451

wonderfully optimistic way, you foresaw happy reunions with long-lost fathers, chased from the familial home by the only thing that never died in Mother: her rage. I suspect, too, that you were always a little in love with him. Why else keep tabs on his trajectory from Sydney to Nepal and eventually to the United States? It couldn't have been easy, even with your formidable skills. Or did he, at least in the early days, write to you, if not to his wife and daughter, to boast of his pilgrim's progress?

I'm sorry to sound like such an old cat, but the episode has me walking the tiles and screeching at the moon. When you first told me I really thought I would do nothing. Why bother? He abandoned us so many years ago. And, as I said to you, I've never chased after men of any kind, so why should a father be different? But it got to me, you know. Grew under my skin like an insidious fungus, until I couldn't look at myself for blotches. So I thought I'd track him down, have a look at him, unravel the fabric of lies that was my childhood and see if he was worth daughtering. My memories of him, such as they are, hardly made that apparent.

And, as I said to you on the phone, I did track him. Must have inherited your investigative talents. Though through one of those coincidences which attack you when you least want them, I had a little inadvertent help from my therapist. The entire world really is at only six degrees' remove. Serendipity.

As I write this, I'm sitting in what is certainly one of the stranger places I've been to. Spooky.

He runs it. F. Frederick Hilton is his new name. Good name, though it hardly bodes well that he felt the need for a new one.

You will not be pleased to know that he's a loathsome worm of the first order. I realized that even before I told him who I was and he denied all knowledge of Australia, of us, and of me, as if I were the worm – though a look in the mirror would probably obliterate the need for DNA tests. I never thought I was particularly ugly, but now I see I am. Hideous, in fact. It's as if he's brought home to me the malign side of myself. The man who leaves everything behind. The great abandoner. Makes me quite want to do away with myself. (Don't worry, I won't – if only for your sake.)

And I'm sorry, Auntie. I'm going to have to do something about him. Not only because he won't accept his unloving daughter, but because, as I suggested in my message, he really is involved in all kinds of murky business, has been from way back, from what I can make out, with some mean old megarich guys who feather his nest for a substantial return. I haven't the energy to detail it to you now, but you'll see it all in the papers soon.

Needless to say, conscience is not one of his strong points. Power, on the other hand, is. He revels in it like a demented god. I almost wish that my fantasy of Mother having done him in were true. It would have been one of her nobler acts.

Maybe, one day, we'll have a chance to muse on all this and laugh. At the moment, it doesn't feel good.

There's no printer here, so I won't be able to post this straight away. A mate of mine arrives tomorrow. Jill Reid. She's become a true friend. Her spirit is the guardian of my sanity. She'll see me through this. She will. I'll either leave with her or give this letter to her to post. I know you've probably been fretting over my silence. There's been cause.

Love you,
I.

Chill fingers encircled Leo's throat. She kept their clutch at bay and leapt up. Isabel hadn't committed suicide, of that she was now certain. And whatever had happened to her had happened here and had implicated Jill Reid, too. But what? She had to speak to Faraday. She had to get out of here and get Isabel's computer to Faraday.

No, no. She wasn't thinking clearly. If anyone saw her with the machine it could be whisked away. And there was more at the sanctuary she needed to learn. For now, all she wanted were her car keys and purse. She couldn't phone Faraday from Heather's office and risk being overheard. She would have to go to the nearest village. Perhaps Isabel had done that, too, in order to contact Jill Reid.

She wrapped the machine back in her shirt and stashed it in her case in the closet. Glancing at her watch, she noted that she had missed not one, but two sessions. Even the sound of the gong hadn't penetrated her concentration. They must now be in the midst of their hour of silence.

She stole from her room. Nothing stirred, either in the corridor or along the stairs. The front hall was empty, too. Leo saw a sudden chance. She made for the telephone behind the counter. Faraday's number was etched in her mind. But the dialling tone didn't respond to her fingers. She looked around furtively and pressed nine, then tried zero. Still nothing. Not even for an emergency triple nine. There must be some switchboard which immobilized the phone from a central location.

Damn them. She cursed inwardly and ran towards the door. Skirting a number of solitary walkers, she made for the front gate.

It was solidly locked. In frustration, she pushed and pulled at it so that it set up a clatter. The thought came to her with a sudden lash of terror that she was locked in. Like Isabel had been locked in. And Jill Reid.

'Can I help you, Leonora?' Frederick Hilton suddenly appeared from the edge of the gate. He was dark-suited, his hair tied neatly back, not the guru now, but the businessman. The smile he gave her was so charming, the eyes so caring, that for a moment her mind whirled with the thought that Isabel had fantasized everything and infected her with delirium.

With a blip of a beeper he let himself in. Before she could make a move, the gate clanged shut.

She kept her hand on it. 'I wanted to go down to the village and telephone.' She met his smile. 'It seems to be so difficult here. And I need to speak to my daughter. In California,' she added, as if that would make the difference.

He tut-tutted her. 'Attachments. We try to discourage them. At least while you're here. In the sanctuary.'

'I know. But it's her birthday. An important one. And it's about the only time I can phone. You know, with the time shift.'

'Of course. I'll tell you what, Leo, you can come up to my office and use the phone there.'

Leo's heart sank. 'May I?'

He nodded slowly, holding her gaze. 'And then, since you're not being silent,' he winked at her, his tone confiding, 'we can finish our session. I'm sorry we were interrupted. It happens rarely. And now I know how much you have on your mind. A terrible loss. I understand why Dr Lukas sent you here.'

He put his arm loosely round her shoulder, the good doctor, guiding his patient along the gravel path. Leo felt a rising bewilderment. She couldn't put the two parts of him together. Like his bulk, oddly reassuring now, but out of kilter with the smallness of his feet in their polished black shoes. And the fiend Isabel had evoked in contrast to this beneficent presence. She threw him a sideways glance. In this light she couldn't see the resemblance Isabel had been so aware of. The eyes perhaps, that deep, bright blue. Would Daniel's aegis see her through questions about Isabel?

She was breathless by the time they reached the top floor.

'A drink, Leonora?' He was treating her as an honoured guest. 'Nothing alcoholic, of course, but fruit juice or mineral water.'

'Water would be wonderful.'

He pulled open what looked like a cabinet to reveal a small fridge and simultaneously pointed her to the telephone. 'Nine for an external line.'

Trapped in her own lie, Leo decided she had to ring California. There was no way she could get to Faraday with Hilton standing over her. And Martha, though closer, would be too tricky. She would have to ask for her by her full name, one he would surely recognize.

A shot of pure joy coursed through her as she heard her daughter's voice. It had been too long since she had spoken to her. She hadn't wanted to tell her about Isabel. Not yet, with everything so terrifyingly unclear.

'Becca, darling, it's me. How are you?'

'Fine, Mom. I tried to ring you, but a man answered.'

'That was Norfolk, darling.'

'You OK?'

'So so.' Leo remembered herself as she felt Hilton's gaze. 'Happy birthday, precious.'

'What?'

'Yes, and many, many happy returns.'

'You gone nuts, Mom?'

'Maybe I have. Yes. I'm at the Morning Star Foundation. It's a refuge. In Devon.'

'Really.'

'Can you ring Auntie's number in London? They'll want to hear from you. Especially today. Such an important birthday. Please. And don't forget to speak to Faraday, too, while you're at it. Yes. Faraday. He's to pick me up here. I love you, darling. It's so good to hear you. But I have to go now. Not my phone. A special big kiss for the eighteenth. Bye.'

She heard Becca spluttering, 'Auntie? Faraday?' But she hung up. She only hoped that Becca would repeat something of what she had said and that Norfolk would see the sense in it.

Frederick Hilton handed her a drink.

'Thank you. And for the phone. Do you have any children, Mr Hilton?'

'I think of you all as my children, Leo.' He was gazing out on the grounds, like a seigneur examining the extent and variety of his property. The proud sweep of his arm seemed about to land on her and she edged away.

'Every single one of you.'

'Yes,' she met him on that. 'I can see that. But it's not quite the same thing.'

'Shall we go through?'

'It's so lovely here. A beautiful space. I'd almost rather . . .'

'Chat,' he finished for her. 'But that's not why we're here, is it now?'

Leo faltered. 'I guess not.'

He stretched out a hand to her. Reluctantly, she let herself be led into the dimness of the back room.

She perched on the divan, unwilling to lie down. 'I . . .'

'Let's not waste time, Leonora. Leo.' He eased himself into the chair at the side of the desk just in front of her. He was so close she could hear the rise and fall of his breath.

'In the group session you were talking about a friend of yours who'd died. Tell me more about her.'

The statement took her by surprise. She watched him. He had reached for one of his stones and he played with it, letting it fall from hand to hand.

'Tell me everything. It will help the distress. The shock of seeing that bloated, mottled corpse, I think you called it.' His eyes held hers, two crystal-bright points of light, exuding power, expecting acquiescence.

'Two bodies,' Leo said. It came to her with a sudden prickling of the skin that he was a strategist. He wanted to find out what she knew. That was why he had tempted her up here. She had to tread carefully. Very carefully.

'Do lie down, Leo. Try to relax. Two bodies.

458

Trauma indeed.' There was a soothing note in his voice, like oil on rough skin. His thumb circled the surface of the rock in a rhythmic motion, as if to smooth it of any marks. 'Describe them.'

'You knew them both,' Leo heard herself say. 'One of them was your daughter.'

Isabel's laugh bounded into the room, wild as a Maenad's. It met the curve of his lips, a fleshy pink against the white beard.

'You know, in my line of work people are always imagining me as a parent. A wise guide. A leader.' His voice lulled. 'Do rest your head, Leo. That's better. Yes. We all need fathers. We search for them here and there. We find them where we can.'

'She looked like you.'

That laugh again, as if Isabel was urging her on, applauding.

'Do close your eyes, Leo. Tell me about your friend.'

She let her lids flutter shut to avoid his hypnotic stare. 'She used the name Morgenstern. That was your name, wasn't it, before you changed it? In 1975. Morgenstern. Martha said it was you. The Morgenstern Foundation. Morgenstern; Morning Star.' She was chanting it, like a refrain she might have learnt as a child. She felt very calm. 'Why wouldn't you recognize her?'

'You're interested in names, aren't you, Leo?'

Something jabbed at her arm. Her eyes flew open. He was bent over her, a syringe in his hand. She bounded up, struggling against him, and managed to get to her feet.

'What do you think you're doing?'

'My work, Leo. What else would I be doing?'

A cold malevolence sharpened his features. His

459

eyes glinted. His nose flared. His lips curled in a malign grin as he flung the syringe into the bin.

Suddenly, with a surging sense of horror, she saw it all.

'What did you do to her? What did you do to her?' She was screaming, flailing out at him. 'You killed her. Isabel. Isabel.'

'Lie down, Leo.' His voice was like a mallet. A slap descended on her face. 'Lie down.'

Her head felt woozy. Her legs trembled, too fragile for her weight. Her eyes were moving in and out of focus, so that his flesh and his voice seemed to fill the room. She lurched onto the divan.

'Now tell me everything you know about this Iris Morgenstern.'

She tried to get up again. She wanted to leave. But his icy voice cut through her movement.

'Lie down, Leonora, or you'll fall over. Fall over just like the friend you love so much.'

'Fall over.' The words reverberated through her. Her tongue felt thick. Blood swirled round it, pounding through her head. She lay back, despite herself, as docile as a performing poodle.

'Tell me.'

The command crumbled a barrier in her mind. Words poured out of her of their own accord. She couldn't catch hold of them, couldn't get a grip on what she was saying. But the words tumbled. And with them, hatred. Hatred of him, his power, the poison he had poured into her.

'A ripe bitch,' she heard him mutter. 'Talked too much. An orgy of accusations. Just like her mother.'

'What did you do to her?' She was shouting. 'What did you do to her?'

'You want to know what I did to her?' A

low-pitched, devilish rumble came from his throat. 'Little Leo wants to know.' His hand was on her thigh. He squeezed. 'I'll tell you. Why not?' That sneer again. Contempt. 'You won't remember a thing, after all. Not a single thing.'

He laughed and prodded at her stomach. Jabbed. 'I did that. Just that.' He prodded again, his fist hard, like one of his stones. 'And she fell. Fell like a leaf. Bye, bye, blackmailing bitch. So easy. So very easy.'

Vertigo gripped her. She saw the precipice. Isabel was falling. Leo was falling. Coming apart. Coming apart together.

'You killed your daughter.' Water washed over her ears, drowning her breath.

The ragged head towered above her. Too big. Huge. She could no longer make out its outlines, only the pinkness of his tongue, like a lapping dog, over jagged white teeth and yellow-gold frazzle where a chin should be. His lips were pursed. He blew through them, a low moan like the wind.

'She fell like a leaf in a sudden gust. A sacrifice for the sanctuary. Like Iphigenia. Agamemnon and Iphigenia. But hardly as innocent.'

It was a whisper and she craned her head to hear. She could see his hand on her breast. No, not her breast. There was no sensation. A crab scuttling on a field of white.

His voice was a long way away. 'Now tell me, does Lukas do this for you?'

Lukas, she thought. Daniel. Where was he? She lay back and whimpered. Then she remembered something. A scratched, ashen face. 'And Jill Reid. What happened to her?'

A sound like a hiss. From a long way away she felt

461

another jab in her arm. Words like gibberish. The room was swirling.

'Isabel and Jill went up the hill. Another spying bitch. Watching. Blabbing. Had to be stopped. Couldn't be helped.'

Malign laughter boomed around her. It came from the ceiling, a great distance away, as if they were in a church and everything was amplified and resonant. A roar interrupted it, an unbreachable edict uttered by some infernal god.

'You won't remember a thing. The beauty is, you won't remember a thing.'

Hands were holding her down. Large hands. Too big. Too strong. She fought against them. She was at a dentist's, in some foreign country where the air was heavy and thick. There were hands pressing on her. She clawed at them. A mask came towards her face. Big and black, obliterating her breath. Obliterating her. Black. Everything was black.

Leo woke to the sensation of blood. Blood thick and too sweet in her mouth. She could feel it streaming through her lips onto the white towel. She tried to spit, but her head was too heavy to lift. She opened her eyes and looked around for the dentist's cup, which should have been sitting there on the white porcelain ledge next to the chair. But there was no ledge, no cup, no chair. Perspiration gathered on her brow. With it came a cold, clammy fear. She wasn't at the dentist's. She wasn't a child. Who was she?

Her head swirled with the effort of orientation. It was heavier than a cement mixer's load of concrete. She sank back onto the pillow in despair. A pillow. She was in bed. Everything grey as sludge. Dim, with red pinpricks of light flashing at the corners.

She closed her eyes and breathed deeply. Her chest felt constricted. Sleep pressed against her eyelids. She fought it.

Slowly the room acquired a shape. It was a small room. The bed was too high up. At her side, she made out the shape of a table. There was something on it. She reached and fumbled. A lamp. She managed to pull the cord and faint light filled the room. Not her room. Not any room she recognized. The objects refused to mirror her. Panic clutched and churned her stomach.

There was a sink. Water. Her dry mouth ached for it. Carefully, she lifted alien feet off the bed and felt them at last reach a distant floor. Dizziness swooned through her.

She sat very still for she didn't know how long and then, with enormous effort, walked towards the sink, grasping at it to steady herself. She reached for the plastic cup with trembling hands, filled it with water and drank, the water dribbling down her chin. She drank and drank, splashed water on her face.

Not her room. Not her room. The words set up a refrain in her head. A refrain amidst a delirium of voices, shouting now. In her head. Battling. Too loud. Drowning out her own.

How had she come here?

There was a hole where her mind should be.

She forced herself to the window. Small, short steps. Better now. She took a larger one and she was there. A white curtain. She pushed it aside and pressed her face to the glass. Bars. Bars and a charcoal expanse of nothing except her face come back to her, its outlines wavering. She shuddered.

She made herself walk towards the door. One step at a time. One step at a time. Maybe she was still

463

asleep. She turned the knob. Nothing. Locked. A scream rose to her throat. She made it real. She screamed and screamed, pounding against the wood of the door.

It opened so abruptly that she fell backwards. A woman stood above her.

'None of that now. Quite unnecessary.' The woman half carried her back into bed. A big woman with steel-grey hair and an unmoving face.

'Where am I?' Leo's voice was a croak.

'Hush.' The blankets came round her, tighter than swaddling clothes. Her arm lay against them, too white. Something jabbed at it. A spot of red appeared and then disappeared with the lights.

If only there wasn't this dizzy thudding in her head. And the voices, scrambled. If only she could think straight. How long had she been here?

Her mind refused sequence and order. Somebody had rolled all the cells flat, taken a large pair of scissors and begun to snip randomly. The cut-outs were scattered on the floor, but she couldn't make out their shapes.

No shapes. She was ill. Alone. She burrowed under the blanket and hugged herself.

Utterly alone.

A dying animal.

21

Daniel Lukas shifted gears and veered round what he hoped would be the last bend in this desolate road. He had anticipated neither the wild beauty of the surroundings, nor the remoteness, nor the length of time it would take him to get here. He had set out early, well before Robbie had left for school, and he had rashly hoped he would make it back before bedtime. If he were lucky, and there was nothing amiss, that might still be the case. But it was precisely because everything told him that something was amiss that he had made the journey. As it was, he felt he had prevaricated for too long.

It was only as he had mulled things over after that evening at the Savoy, when Leonora had mentioned that Isabel had been using the name Morgenstern, that it had come home to him just how remiss he had been. If Isabel was now masquerading under the name he remembered she had told him was her father's, if she was suddenly so enmeshed with him that she had abandoned her everyday life, then serious trouble was indeed brewing.

He was also all too aware that if that single night with Isabel had never taken place, he would certainly have reacted differently to the last telephone message she had left him. When had it been? In February some time. He could still hear her voice, overwrought, pursued by ghosts, talking a mile a minute, telling him that she had recently discovered that her father was alive and had been alive all along. What did it mean for the story she told herself about her past? Should she seek him out? She needed to see Daniel. Needed to see him badly.

Daniel's response had been considered. He had told her he would make an hour to see her first thing the following morning, if she really needed him. But given that she was now Paola Webster's patient, surely it was Paola she should be consulting.

It was the kind of judicious approach he half knew Isabel would baulk at. And, of course, she didn't take up the hour. Nor did she phone again. He had acted correctly, appropriately, yet he had also failed her. He might as well have said to her in a moment of pique or wounded male, as well as analytic, vanity, 'You made your bed, now lie in it.'

And now, to top it all off, there had been that message on his machine just a few days back from Leonora. Her voice, too, had been strained, her thoughts jumbled. She had alerted him to the fact that she was checking into the Morgenstern Foundation. No, no, she corrected herself. She meant the Morning Star Foundation. In Devon. She needed his referral. They would ring him. Isabel had gone there.

The alarm bells had gone off in his mind. So Paola had lied. Or she hadn't followed Isabel's actions closely enough. He had paused to think through the coincidence of the Morgenstern/ Morning Star names, and his memory had thrown up an odd fact, garnered years back at some conference in New York. It was when he was working mostly with adolescents and had something to do with a scandal on the West Coast, some clinic that had closed down. The Morgenstern Foundation.

Even before he could assimilate all this, Frederick Hilton's insinuating voice had oozed off his answering machine, thanking him for his referral. The speed of it. He was so pleased that they had made proper contact at last. He hoped the referral would be the first of many.

He had only met the man two or three times, but he knew he didn't like him, didn't trust him. He didn't like Paola's link to Hilton, either, though she considered him her great friend and collaborator. At its best, he felt that Hilton's whole enterprise was a suspect mixture of doubtful therapies, bogus mysticism and New Age crystals. At its worst, he didn't like to think.

And now he had two patients in thrall to the man.

He would have left London immediately had arrangements not had to be made.

At last a sign announced the place. He parked in the designated space and strode towards the front gates. Locked. He hadn't expected that. It gave him pause. He looked through the bars at the large gloomy structure and assortment of outbuildings, then, with a sinking heart, he searched out a bell.

'Dr Daniel Lukas for Mr Frederick Hilton,' he said authoritatively.

'Do you have an appointment?' a bland voice asked.

'Just tell him I'm here. And I'm in a hurry.'

Moments later the gate opened. Daniel strode down the drive. From the steps of the rather grand front door he saw a figure coming towards him. Hilton.

'Daniel. Welcome. A surprise visit. A pleasure, a great pleasure.' Hilton was puffing as he stretched out his hand. 'Let me show you around. It's quiet now. Everyone's inside at lunch. Have you eaten?'

'No need. I haven't much time. I just wanted to see Leonora Gould-Holland. And to talk to you about a little problem.'

'Leonora, yes.' The man rubbed his hands together. 'A difficult woman.' Hilton walked with reflective slowness, so that Daniel had to moderate his own pace. 'I'm afraid it's not altogether a convenient time. She's resting. She had something of a turn.'

'Oh? How's that? She was fine when I last—'

Hilton cut him off. 'Yes. We had to sedate her. She was surprisingly violent.'

'Sedation?' Daniel stopped in his tracks and stared at him. 'Are you qualified to . . . ? Are you permitted to prescribe here?'

Hilton laughed softly. 'Not myself, of course. But we have a doctor – two, in fact, on call for the addiction clinic. Plus a trained staff. Perhaps you don't know. For the heroin addicts, we use the newest Naltrexone programme. Rapid opiate detoxification under anaesthetic, followed by Naltrexone induction, with counselling, of course. Three months can do it. Six months is—'

His words disappeared beneath the stark sound of shattering glass, as loud in the tranquillity of the grounds as a gunshot. In the distance, to his left, Daniel made out his name being shouted, over and over again in a rising pitch.

He headed off across the lawn in the direction of the sound, sprinting as he heard the fear in the voice.

Poised at a second-floor window of a far building,

he saw a ghostly apparition, a gaunt woman he didn't recognize. She was perfectly still. For a moment he was bewildered, then his gaze shifted to another window. Leonora. Her hair was dishevelled, as if she had been pulling at it, her eyes so vast in terror that they seemed to obliterate her face.

Hilton caught up with him, panting. 'Violent. I warned you. We'll have to give her another injection.'

'Dr Lukas. Take me out of here. Please.' The urgency in Leo's voice overrode Hilton's.

Daniel threw him a scathing look. 'I'd like to see my patient now. Alone.'

A stocky young man had emerged from the side of the building to check out the commotion.

'Take Dr Lukas up to see Leonora, David. Don't leave them alone. She can be dangerous.'

'I beg your pardon.' Daniel stood to his full height and gave the man an icy glare. 'You're out of line, Hilton. Seriously out of line. I'll talk to you again in a few minutes.'

He raced up the stairs without waiting for an answer.

Leo's state sent a tremor through him. She was trembling, her face ghostly pale, the pupils of her eyes too bright. She clutched at his arm as if he were a life-raft. There was blood on her hands where the glass had cut her.

'What have you been giving her?' He addressed the young man, who shrugged in response.

'Not my department.'

'No, of course not. Leonora,' he said softly, looking into her eyes. 'Let's wash those cuts. And then do you think you can get dressed? I'm going to take you away from here.'

'I . . .' Her tongue stumbled, as if it were too thick

for speech. 'My things. I need my things. Room thirty-seven.' She pointed through the window to the main building.

'I want you to go and fetch Leonora's things, David. Everything. Every scrap of paper. Every piece of jewellery.'

'I'll go. I want to go.'

Daniel studied her. There was determination in her glazed eyes. 'All right. We'll all go. Anything in here that's yours?'

She shook her head and then held it in her hands, covering her face.

'Are you dizzy, Leo?'

She smiled at him gratefully. 'A little. Not so bad now. The effort . . .'

The cuts washed and patched, he walked her slowly along the narrow corridor.

'Who was that man you were talking to outside?' she asked.

'That man?' He paused for a moment. 'You mean Frederick Hilton? Don't you know him?' He hid his surprise.

'I . . . I'm not sure.' Tears gathered in her eyes. 'I don't know.'

'Don't think about it now, Leo.' He veiled his anger in soothing tones. 'It'll be fine. We'll take care of you now.'

Frederick Hilton had disappeared by the time they reached the front door. Running across the lawn towards them was another young man in white. He inclined his head. 'Dr Lukas. The Director has sent me to see to you. He was needed elsewhere.'

'William,' Leo burst out. 'Oh good. William, I need to get my things. I'm leaving.'

470

An unreadable expression played over his face. 'I'm glad you're feeling better, Leonora. I'll go down to the store after I've seen you to your room.'

'My room, yes. Thirty-seven.' Leo was mumbling to herself. 'I need to go to my room.'

When they reached it, she made straight for the small cupboard and heaved out her case. It made her stumble. Daniel rushed to help.

There was a rapt smile on her face. 'Go on, William. Get the rest of my things while I pack.'

No sooner had he left them than she whispered, 'It's all right. It's here. I knew it. I knew that. I remembered that.' She threw things every which way and took out a computer. Before he could stop her, she was plugging it in, accessing files.

'What's here, Leonora?'

She didn't answer. She was searching, reading. Reading with her finger on the screen, as if the individual letters refused to stay still and shape themselves into words. She gestured to him and he bent to the screen.

'It's Isabel. Her journal,' she murmured, the tears gathering in her eyes again. 'I'm not making it out properly.'

Daniel read quickly, his anxiety mounting with each new page. He wanted to ask Leo a host of questions. A knock at the door prevented him.

At its sound, Leo started to tremble again. Clumsily, she switched off the machine, placed it in her case and began to toss her belongings over it, tucking them round the computer, hiding it.

Alert to her fear, Daniel called out a loud 'one moment, please', and helped. His foot crunched a small bottle which had fallen to the floor. He stared at its label. 'Sodium Amytal'. His hand clenched into

471

a fist. How much had that blasted man pumped into her? It would account for some of her disorientation and her febrile state.

'How many injections were you given, Leonora?' he asked softly.

She stared at him, her face blank.

'No, of course, you don't remember. Why don't you get changed now and then we'll go and talk to Frederick Hilton.'

Her eyes grew wide in panic. Her features blurred. 'Fre . . . ?' The name wouldn't shape itself on her lips. She rubbed her temples. 'Holes in my mind. Black holes. They suck everything up. I can't find anything.'

Daniel took her hand and stroked it softly. 'It'll come back, Leonora. You were hypnotized. You were also, I imagine, given repeated doses of a hypno-sedative, and God knows what else. Just take it easy. Take it step by step.' He opened the door to William, took the bundle from his arms and told him to communicate to the Director that they would be with him in some ten minutes.

A woman with a voice as smooth as her sleek blond hair stopped them at the end of the corridor.

'I'm sorry, the Director can't make time for you now.' She addressed Daniel. 'He sends his apologies. I should also personally say that I'm very sorry Leonora suffered an episode. It happens sometimes. You know, the silence, the meditation, it doesn't suit everybody all of the time.'

'That's noble of you, Miss . . . ?'

'Heather.'

'Well, Heather, unless you want to see this place closed down by the end of the week, I think you had better take us to the Director right now.'

Heather stared. 'I don't think—'

'I'm not asking you to think, Heather. Just lead the way.'

Something sparkled in Heather's eyes. 'Whatever he's done, I had no part in it. Leonora can testify to that.'

'At the moment, Leonora can barely see straight.' Daniel's tone was acid. 'This way, is it?'

'No, up here.'

Leo took the steps slowly, as if a great weight had been tied to her feet.

'Perhaps it would be better if you waited, Leo. Heather will get you a cup of tea or coffee.'

'No.' She clutched at his arm and shook her head adamantly. The fear was there again in her eyes. 'No, I'm coming with you.'

When Hilton didn't open the door to Heather's second knock, Daniel moved angrily in front of her and turned the knob. A small, oddly triumphant smile shaped itself on her face. He didn't pause to interpret it.

'Hilton, we need to talk and I haven't all day,' he called loudly into the large room even before he had spied the man.

Hilton was sitting at his desk, his back to them, swivelling in his chair and looking out at the expansive terrain before him like some general poised to marshal his troops. The telephone was held to his ear.

'Pick me up in twenty-five minutes. No more.' He put the receiver down without a hiatus and turned round to face them.

'I'm busy, Daniel. There's an emergency on. Didn't Heather explain?' The smile sat uneasily on his broad face, but it sat there nonetheless. Daniel wanted to rip it off.

'This is the emergency, Hilton. One emergency at a time.'

'I'm opening a big new centre in Australia and . . .' He stopped himself, as if the boast had taken him too far. 'But, if you insist.' He gestured companionably towards some chairs.

'Australia?' Daniel recalled the frenzied content of Isabel's journal. She must have threatened him, accused him in some way. Frederick Hilton wasn't, he guessed, a man who would take to threats kindly.

Hilton waved the query away. 'Have a seat. Though I'm not in the habit of conducting case conferences in the presence of a patient.'

Leo was staring at him with that blind look, as if she needed to touch his face feature by feature to make sense of it. She moved cautiously to the chair furthest from the desk and perched on its edge.

'Did I mention that we were discussing Leonora? I don't think so. No. I want a word with you about a former patient of mine. A patient of our colleague Paola Webster, too. You know who I mean. Isabel Morgan. Latterly, she sometimes went by the name of Morgenstern.'

Daniel caught the flare in the man's face, then saw it settle.

'Yes, another delusional. You seem to specialize in them, Daniel. She left here a few weeks ago. I didn't see her in personal sessions. Or perhaps only once.'

'No, no, more than that,' Heather intervened. 'You remember.' She was staring at a small suitcase, which stood by the side of the desk.

Hilton cut her off, his voice razor sharp. 'I believe you're needed elsewhere, Heather. You can leave us now.'

'It would be better if—'

'Go, Heather. Now.'

With a nod at Daniel, Heather strode from the room. Her head was high.

'Impertinent woman,' Hilton muttered.

'But not delusional.'

Hilton met Daniel's eyes. 'No, perhaps not. It comes back to me now. I may have seen this Morgan or Morgenstern woman more than once. So many patients come through here. Sometimes I think you're lucky, Daniel, working on your own. All those one-to-ones. Nothing as complicated as this to run.' He swept a lazy arm around the vista.

Daniel grunted. 'So, your diagnosis after two, three or four meetings is that Ms Morgenstern was delusional because she recognized you as her father. Because her aunt – her aunt in Australia – identified you as the father she had long believed dead.'

Hilton rose abruptly from his chair. He walked towards the window and looked out at the grounds. 'Is that what she told you?' he murmured. 'You know better than to trust your patients' fantasies.'

'I know better, but her aunt is not my patient. We can always go for the hard proof. Run a DNA test. You and Isabel – or Iris as she chose to call herself for her research.'

Leo's voice cracked into the sudden silence. 'Isabel's dead.' The words came out as a moan.

'Dead?' Daniel stared at her.

Leo nodded.

'Didn't you know?' Hilton was suddenly back in his chair. 'Daniel, Daniel.' He shook his head, grief etched in his features. 'A tragedy. Suicide, it was. Terrible. I remember now that Paola warned me she had tendencies in that direction.'

'Dead,' Daniel repeated, as if he couldn't take in

the reality the word signified. 'Suicide? When? Just after she left this place?'

'Now, now, Daniel, we're not going to run a competition between our respective therapies to see which one is responsible.'

'What did you pump into her? In this country, you know, it's illegal for a non-medical practitioner to prescribe, let alone inject, drugs.'

Hilton's eyes landed on Leo. She stirred nervously beneath his gaze. Something was there, floating just at the edge of her eyelids. If only she could see it. She closed her eyes.

'Leave it alone, Daniel. I told you before. We have doctors here. And the woman's dead. Finished. It's over. It's the past. She couldn't make the grade. Couldn't reinvent herself. All over. Finished. Let me get you a drink.'

'And that's what you think, isn't it? That's what your work is about. Reinvention. Killing off the past. A little injection, a little hypnosis, another injection. Wipe it all out. Wipe out the problems. Wipe out family, lovers, attachments. Eradicate the past. Rewrite it any old which way, so long as it helps you grab on to the next thing. Forget the trail of bodies left behind.' Daniel heard his voice rising, and he suddenly had a distinct image of Isabel. Isabel trying to come to terms with the pain of abandonment. Isabel remembering the years of her muteness.

'Is that what you did? Reinvent *yourself*. Australia.' He clapped his hands together as if he were squashing a fly. 'Gone. India. Gone. Seattle. Gone. How many other selves were there in between on the rise to these heights of power? How many women and children left behind? Buried. Denied.'

Daniel hadn't realized he was standing until

476

Hilton was fixed in front of him, his feet spread on the ground, like a boxer's, his cold blue eyes at the same height as his own, the threat in them manifest.

'Careful, Daniel, careful. Let's not quarrel over a deluded hysteric. All right, if you want to caricature me like that, I can do one of you, too. All those years of careful probing, wallowing one might call it, just to find and accept the poor weak-kneed creature that you are. All those old-fangled Oedipal universals. Blighted families. Jealousy. Unattainable desire. Guilt. Shame. Conflict. Pah.' He slammed his fist on the desk. 'Power. That's what counts. Power over the world. Shaping things. Making things. Shaping people.'

'As long as you do the shaping. And quickly. An instant refashioning. You're even worse than Paola. She wants to find victims so that she can induce them to take revenge on the masters. And you, you want to create a bunch of white-clad history-free sheep, who follow you passively along the path to the brilliant New Age. And Isabel wasn't a follower.'

Daniel held the man's eyes forcibly, as if they were engaged in a duel. Frederick Hilton lowered his first.

'She was your daughter, wasn't she? I can see it. What did you do to her?'

In the distance Leo heard a whirring. A helicopter. It was coming. Coming towards them. She put her hands over her ears.

Hilton rushed towards the windows. 'There's my ambulance service. Bringing in a very important patient. I'm going to have to ask you to leave, Dr Lukas.' He smiled cynically as he emphasized the doctor.

The noise of the helicopter had grown deafening. The machine was now directly above them, casting its shadow through the window. There must be a landing pad on the roof of the building. Daniel looked at Leo. She was huddled over, gazing at the rotors' shadows which whirled across the floor. He put a hand on her shoulder. She didn't stir.

Leo was watching the furious patterns the blades made, splintering over her feet, slicing across the desk, slashing across that man. That man. Isabel's father. Isabel dead. She clutched at Daniel's arm.

'He killed her.' The words lacerated her throat, cutting through the fog in her mind like blades. 'Isabel. Killed Jill Reid, too. He told me. Yes. Jill Reid. Take a blood sample from me, Daniel.'

Daniel clasped her hand and looked towards Hilton. The man had vanished. Against the noise of the helicopter he hadn't heard him move. He raced from the room. Leo was right behind him. On the right of the hall a door stood slightly ajar, wavering in a gust of wind. They ran towards it. At the top of a steep, ironwork staircase they saw Hilton, case in hand, a coat thrown over his arm.

'He's going to get away,' Leo mumbled.

'No, he won't.' Daniel was already halfway up the stairs.

'Be careful,' Leo shouted after him, forcing herself towards the noise. One step at a time.

By the time she reached the rooftop the whirring had slowed. Two men were leaping out of the 'copter, followed by a third.

'Norfolk,' Leo shouted. 'Norfolk. Inspector Faraday. Hold on to him. Don't let him go. It's him. Stop him. Morgenstern.'

Hilton was already back at the door, running down the stairs. Norfolk and Faraday caught up with him at the landing. Leo saw Norfolk frisk him with

478

surprising expertise. Faraday had a grip on his arm and was showing his ID, as was a second man. She suddenly recognized the ruddy-faced officer from Barnstaple. Rawlence, she remembered. The holes in her mind were filling up.

It was Rawlence who spoke. 'F. F. Hilton, we're taking you in for questioning in the case of the murder of Jill Reid, an employee at Plantagen.'

'Really, Inspector!' Hilton brushed the hand from his arm as if it were a niggling speck and adjusted the lapel of his suit.

Rawlence continued bullishy. 'John Stapleton, the head of Jill Reid's lab, has now returned from the US and tells us that she spent her last days here at your foundation. The car she was found in belonged to one of your former employees and had been left here in his absence. A sample of Jill Reid's blood shows traces of the same compound we found in the body of one Isabel Morgan. We want to question you about that death as well. You do not have to say anything, but it may harm your defence if you do not mention when questioned something which you later rely on in court. Anything you do say may be given in evidence.'

Rawlence took a deep breath. 'You'll go quietly?'

The scowl on Frederick Hilton's face settled itself into an oily smile. 'Of course I'll go quietly, Officer. I'll help you all I can. But you're barking up the wrong tree. I'll just make the requisite call to my solicitor.'

'Go right ahead.' Faraday drew a folded document from his jacket pocket and flashed it in front of him. 'Search warrant. All in order. The boys from the squad should be here soon.'

Hilton glared. 'And just what do you think you'll

find here, Inspector, as you upset our patients?'

'I imagine we'll find quite a few things of interest, Hilton,' Norfolk growled with marked insolence. 'There are a few little additional matters we need to look into as well. If I were you, I'd ring your charitable benefactors. By which I mean Newman in Australia. I don't think Ritter Pharmaceuticals will be altogether pleased at our presence here.'

Frederick Hilton took a threatening step towards Norfolk. 'And who are you?'

'Christopher Norfolk at your service.'

'Christopher Norfolk?' Hilton spluttered. 'You're that warped journalist who sent me that black-mailing letter. I'll have you done for libel if you print a single word.'

'What letter?' Norfolk was all innocence.

'I was sure that accusing bitch had written it,' he muttered, then broke off abruptly and reached for the phone.

Norfolk stopped his hand. 'Exactly which Sheila are you talking about, Hilton?'

'Get your grimy paws off me.' Hilton shook him off.

'He means Isabel,' Leo said softly. 'I think you'll probably find it all on her computer.'

Hilton stared at her. He made a sudden menacing move in her direction. 'Where did you get—?'

'That's enough, Hilton.' Faraday stepped in front of him. 'Get on with your call.' He gestured towards Rawlence, then turned to look at Leo, as if for the first time. 'Are you all right, Ms Holland?'

'I am now.' She smiled at him.

'You've got one clever daughter there, Holland.' Norfolk put a proprietary arm across her shoulder and gave her a squeeze. 'I sure am glad to see you in one piece. I was finally getting the full grisly low-down on the Morgenstern Foundation and its little alias here when she rang. Luckily, Faraday decided to believe my story.' He winked at her. 'But then he had some new evidence to go on.'

'You omitted to tell me, Ms Holland, that Mr Norfolk had a double—' Norfolk coughed. Faraday stumbled through his sentence. 'That Mr Norfolk also worked for the Australian government.'

Norfolk grinned at Leo's visible astonishment. 'It's OK, Holland. Just a little part-time job. Couldn't tell it all. Heh, who's the bloke? Part of the establishment?'

Leo introduced Daniel, who had been standing by with a bemused expression on his face. He took Faraday aside for a moment. 'There's something else you should look into, Inspector. I found sodium amytal in Leo's room. It's hardly an unusual hypno-sedative, but I strongly suspect this establishment may be administering it, and I don't know what else, in undue doses. Probably, too, with insufficient medical supervision and without the patient's consent.'

'That's only the beginning of what's going on here, I imagine,' Norfolk grumbled. 'In Seattle there was a trial and a rumour storm – both somehow quashed – that they were carrying out trials on a new morphine compound, something in that grey area where legit pharmaceuticals meet street drugs. Trying out varying doses on their patients – without their knowledge, needless to say – to see how they responded. To see what levels proved toxic. I imagine they're trying out some other bits of experimentation here. Captive guinea pigs, with rich clients as a front. Or maybe just a little diversification.'

481

Leo stared at him. She was feeling dizzy again. There was too much to take in.

'Experiment. Diversification. That's the name of the future,' Hilton stated, his head high, his voice cold.

'Inspector, Leonora needs to rest. With your permission, I'll take her home,' Daniel intervened.

Faraday nodded. 'Of course.'

'Not so fast.' Frederick Hilton stepped in front of Leo, towering over her. 'Not so fast.' His face was glistening. He was gazing into her eyes. He spoke very slowly. 'You've taken something of mine, Leonora.'

Leo backed away, her knees trembling, but she couldn't avert her gaze from the dazzle of his eyes. Words tumbled into her mind, a lost quotation: 'His count'nance as the Morning Star that guides/The starry flock, allur'd them, and with lies.' Lucifer. She didn't know whether she said it aloud. He was speaking.

'You will give it to William before you leave.'

'That's enough, Hilton.' Daniel snapped and placed himself between them. 'Quite enough. And it's too late. I've been into Isabel's computer, too. Your daughter's computer. Though you're hardly worthy of her. It's going to be placed firmly in Inspector Faraday's care, together with a sample of Leo's blood. The past's catching up with you. I don't think you're going to be able to deny this bit of your life with quite your usual alacrity. Hold on to him, Officer.'

Rawlence's fingers bit into Hilton's shoulder.

The man veered round and shook him off. For a moment his gaze, like that of a cornered animal, passed to each of them in turn. And then a piercing laugh burst from him. 'We'll see about that, Dr Lukas.' He spat out the name. 'We'll see about that.'

22

Four evenings later, Leo waited impatiently for the bell at the loft to ring.

Bar the occasional walk, she had spent much of the last few days here, recuperating and talking to Martha, whose tears flowed more uncontrollably than her own.

The woman's misery was compounded by guilt and the sense of a double loss, not only of Isabel, but of the nostalgic core of her youthful dream of Morgenstern. She had wanted to see him, but Faraday had prevaricated. Maybe he had sensed, as Leo did, that the confrontation and the ensuing rage would destroy her with its ferocity.

Leo had tried to help her find solace in the fact that, however devastating the circumstances that had cut Isabel's life short, she had at least lived it to the full. She had told herself that as well, over and over again. It didn't fill the abyss of loss, but it helped a little.

Norfolk had driven Martha back from Devon. He had hugged Leo tightly on his arrival and brought news. Hilton, aka Morgenstern, was in custody. The staff of the sanctuary, together with the guests who had been there during Isabel's and Jill Reid's stay, were being questioned.

'Some of our little white-clad birds are singing very happily.' He had laughed. 'His assistant, or administrator, that Heather woman, had a lot of grudges. Only too happy to get them off her chest. And we found a letter locked in his desk. It was signed with my name, though in Isabel's handwriting. It threatened to expose his illicit activities, as well as his alleged bigamy, not to mention child abuse. Since he assumed she had written it, he had motive for his heinous acts. Plenty of motive, given that he was planning to open a sanctuary in Australia.'

'Odd that she signed it in your name.'

'Probably thought she needed back-up. A double Aussie threat. Here. You'll want these.'

He had presented Leo with a pile of diskettes copied from Isabel's computer, as well as her own laptop. 'Now we know who our burglar was, Holland. I imagine he was trying to keep us off his trail, laying false clues so that we'd have reason to pursue Isabel along the Green path, which he knew about from her files or hypnosis or whatever. More crucially, he was sniffing out any other evidence there was here of his paternal links to Isabel, so that he could destroy them.'

'But why?'

'I guess he didn't want his empire rattled. He'd whitewashed his credentials and couldn't face another attack of smut, one that might actually scupper the whole enterprise this time round.'

Leo had nodded. 'I've been thinking and thinking about it. He must have decided to send the diskette with the Ordnance Survey map co-ordinates and the lists here after the burglary alerted him to my presence. To deflect us. I suspect he organized for Isabel's suitcase to be delivered, too. To muddy the scent. Send us veering off in all directions. Hence the Bioworld brochure inside it.'

'A good break for me, though, Holland. That and your phone call. It sent me looking back through my e-mails from Isabel. There was a slightly cryptic one in early April, asking me if I knew anything about Progene and Ritter Pharmaceuticals, telling me to look into any charitable donations they may have made, in particular to the Morning Star Foundation. It was all amidst other stuff. I never pursued it, since my main brief is GM and agriculture.'

'All this time we'd been following the wrong bogey. We got caught up in the press hysteria.'

'That's not quite fair, Holland. Isabel had been investigating the GM sector and she came up with some valuable stuff. Though I grant you, it wasn't what led to her death.'

'And if fate and the tides hadn't deposited her body at Lynton, he might have got away with it. Isabel would have become another missing-person statistic.'

Saying it, Leo had wondered again if that wouldn't have been preferable. Some kind of hope of Isabel's return would have been kept alive. Yet, even as the thought played through her, she knew that would have been utterly to contradict Isabel's spirit. The person she was. The woman who had to *know* at all costs.

'You wouldn't have allowed that, Holland,' Norfolk surprised her by grumbling. 'You're as stubborn as a mule. No, no, I've got my creatures wrong. A veritable bloodhound. Just like our friend.'

He had ruffled her hair then and kissed her gently. 'I don't know how many of Isabel's files you managed to get through, but I think you'll find she was very fond of you.'

486

Leo had sat down to read and reread the diskettes deep into the night.

Once again she felt Isabel's vertigo, not unlike her own over these last weeks, but more devastating. Her friend had been buffeted by the ghosts which had surfaced in her analysis with Daniel, and then more savagely in her therapy with Paola Webster. Each one of these flailing presences murmured different accounts of a buried history whose truth was probably not single. The sudden materialization of one of them in the person of Morgenstern, or Hilton, with his charming surface and deeply amoral malevolence, had filled her with the sense that she wanted to eradicate everything that had made her. She wanted to destroy the incarnation of the past which was also embedded in her. Half hoping for salvation, for sanctuary, she had found its opposite.

When she read the latest entries invoking her own name, Leo was overcome by sorrow. It was clear that Isabel had felt Leo couldn't understand the extremities of emotion she was prey to, the painful obsessive swirl that had become her mind. It was easier to confide in relative strangers. Like Jill Reid.

More than ever, Leo wished that she could embrace her friend and tell her that she did understand. Now she did. Understood viscerally. They all carried their own quota of ghosts which occasionally surfaced to give them a taste of madness, to unravel the cloak of sanity and place them at the mercy of the elements. Some of them were lucky enough to escape merely with the bitter memory. Though no escape was necessarily permanent. Except, perhaps, death.

She also wished that she could tell Isabel that Morgenstern had been apprehended, that Leo's blood test had shown a sizeable quantity of the same compound they had found in Jill Reid's and Isabel's blood, though Isabel's also carried traces of some as-yet-undesignated drug. Too late, Leo had been able to help her friend.

In the journal of Isabel's last months, Daniel made a sporadic and not always happy appearance. Isabel's anger at his know-it-all state replicated what Leo had felt. But there was more. One note read, 'I had to leave him. My feelings about men are always so extreme. Love. Hate. Longing. Fear. We began to untangle that together, but I still had to go. *Basta.*'

Towards the end of the file, Isabel referred to him again, almost whimsically, as if it was she who had failed him and not the other way round. She quoted him, too, a little enigmatically, saying that some boundaries, after all, were worth preserving.

Of analysis or therapy as a whole, Isabel's notes seemed to have no general view to offer, except to say, with a touch of acid, that it was probably as good or bad or sound or treacherous an edifice as the practitioners who lived in it.

Leo thought all this through once more as she waited for her guest. Martha had located an old friend and, on Leo's urging, had gone out for the evening. Beast purred round her legs, and she picked him up and went to stand by the windows which gave on to the now desolate car park. Rain splattered across the panes, bursting into rivulets. Like tears. Tears for Isabel. She let out a sigh and stroked the cat's fur. 'Do you want to come and live in Manhattan, Beast?'

The cat leapt out of her arms and bounded across the room. She smiled after him. A Beast as wilfully independent as his mistress.

That first evening, on their return to London and after the hospital visit, Daniel had insisted that Leo spend the night at his place. Martha was still in Lynton and Leo couldn't stay on her own. There might be flashbacks, hallucinations, fear. He couldn't, in good conscience, leave her.

Leo had taken it for the medical injunction that it was, though she had sensed there was another note underlying his insistence, one she couldn't altogether make out. She'd thought it had something to do with making amends to Isabel.

They had spent what she could only describe, despite the circumstances, as a cosy evening. Robbie had entertained her with chit-chat and had insisted that they draw together. Their joint creations had made them both smile. Afterwards, she had joked with Daniel that his son was a far better therapist than he was. And Daniel had looked at her a little oddly, then laughed and said that his wife used to say that, too.

Only when the lights went out and she was dropping off to sleep in another strange bed did the full horror of the last days attack her – bounding, dizzying images playing on her eyelids, so that she had to open them to chase them away. A huge, salivating doglike face coming too close, a constricting mask being forced down on her, needles jabbing at her arm. Most of the holes had been filled by conjecture, if not yet by memory. She didn't think Morgenstern had penetrated her with more than a needle. That was more his style. And maybe there were some things it was better not to know. She had escaped, after all. And she didn't feel she was in flight. Sex was hardly the worst thing. She would say that to Daniel.

*   *   *

The doorbell rang at last and she rushed to answer it. He was up the stairs quickly, and she remembered that he had that other side to him, the ball player.

'Not late, am I?' Daniel smiled.

'Don't think so. I still haven't got my watch back. It's the one thing that's missing.'

'If that's all, you're in luck.'

She returned his smile and ushered him in. She suddenly felt shy, as if this were her own house and he might judge her by it. A bizarre thought, Leo reflected, given everything she had already spewed out on his couch, let alone since.

He was looking round curiously, pacing the large room, taking in its various perspectives. 'Yes, I see,' he said at last.

'What do you see?'

He grinned. 'Sometimes I think analysts should be like old-fashioned GPs and make home visits. To get a look at the stage on which some of the internal landscape plays itself out.'

'And what do you make of this?'

'It's new. It's bare. It's waiting to be written on. How are you, Leo?' He surveyed her with critical appraisal.

'All right, everything considered.'

'Yes, everything considered.' His voice turned grim. 'Are you managing to sleep?'

She nodded. 'And to dream.' A shrill laugh came out of her. 'Sometimes I'm surprised he didn't kill me, too. I imagine it was the magic aura your name provided.'

'I wouldn't put too much value in that. I suspect he simply overestimated his not-inconsiderable powers, and underestimated yours. He assumed you wouldn't remember your conversations. He didn't know you'd

490

found Isabel's computer. Then, too—' He stopped abruptly.

'What?'

'Nothing.'

'Tell me.'

'Another few weeks . . .' He stumbled for words. 'Another little while on the drugs and your hold would have become precarious.'

She nodded sagely, as if he were talking about someone else. She handed him a glass of wine. 'I still don't really understand why he wouldn't acknowledge her as his daughter. I can't think of a better one.'

'Luckily you're not him.' Daniel raised his glass to her. 'Too much denial, I imagine,' he continued. 'Hilton had to believe fully in who he was at any given time in order to keep the balloon inflated. Maybe, too, he could only conceive of her overture in his own image. Could only think, if she was a relation, that she was out to get him in some way. The way you told me he had got at that uncle in Chicago. I suspect that, for him, any return of the past constitutes a danger to his present identity.'

Leo reflected for a moment. 'I don't think he set out to . . . to murder Isabel, you know. It just turned into an expedient and fortunate accident, from his point of view. He would have preferred to win her over by charm, or change her intent to expose him by administering drugs, hypnotism, threats, whatever. But the opportunity presented itself and he was having trouble mastering her. Isabel was never particularly good at saying yes to authority. And she hated him. Had plunged from idealizing him from a distance to loathing him for what he really was.'

'An entire childhood trajectory compressed into a

few weeks. Too much to bear,' Daniel murmured.

Leo caught the culpable note. All of them were floundering in guilt, except Hilton himself. Because they knew the past mattered, whereas he had the capacity to stamp it out. Until Isabel came along . . .

She rushed on. 'What puzzles me is Jill Reid. Why concoct an accident for her? I've worked out what he did, you know. Pictured it, anyhow. He drove her over to that spot. She was sedated up to the gills. Oversedated. He pushed the car over the verge and smashed the windows for good measure to make it look right. Then he walked back. But why not just do what he tried to do to me? Obliterate the memory.'

'Maybe there wasn't time. She was due to leave, remember, and his assistant, that blonde woman, would have suspected if she'd haphazardly been converted into a long-stay patient after Isabel had left, so to speak. Others would have wondered, too. He couldn't allow that.'

Leo shivered as Frederick Hilton's bulk seemed suddenly to fill the room. 'His own daughter. Two women. They shouldn't have died.'

Daniel put his arm round her shoulder.

'No. They shouldn't have.' His voice cracked. 'Power run amok. It was brave of you, you know. Very brave. To put yourself at risk in that way. To care so much.'

Leo shrugged. 'I couldn't have done it if I'd thought. And without Isabel guiding me, taking me over. A little like possession.'

'And now?'

'Now, I'm just my small, mourning self.'

'Not small. And with a life in front of you.'

'Hope so.' She met his eyes.

They were silent for a moment and then he handed

492

her a sheaf of paper. 'I've brought you something.'

Leo glanced at the typed sheets. 'Notes Towards a Case History', the title stated.

'Not me?' she said apprehensively.

'Read it. Tell me what you think.'

'Now?'

'Not now. Now I'm taking you out to dinner.'

'I don't think I could eat with it hanging over me.'

'You may not want to eat after. With me.'

'We'll both have to take our chances.'

Daniel laughed softly. 'Yes. That's right. We'll both have to take our chances.'

THE END